TETHERED TO SHADOWS:
The Healing Journey of Six

Judy Hudson

Cover designed by CreateImaginations.co.UK.
Author Photo by Tia Runia

~~~

The Baby Girl's Lullaby is recorded in <u>Songs of the Totem</u> by Carol Beery Davis, published in 1939, and located in the Open Library funded in part by the Internet Archive. Corrections to the translation were graciously provided by Xh'unei – Lance A. Twitchell, Assistant Professor of Alaska Native Languages, University of Alaska Southeast.

*Dedicated to
the courageous people
who taught me about
perseverance*

Acknowledgements

Many thanks to the loving support and critical input from those who helped this novel become a reality. Friends Myrna and Willie Allen hosted and loved me for weeks, revisiting the parts of beautiful Juneau that is the setting for Tethered to Shadows. They engaged me, as well as the fictional characters of the novel, to create realistic settings and events.

Readers, who very graciously gave critique and edits include: Myrna Allen, Carolyn Cronk, Michelle Meeker, Charlotte Hudson, Carol Collins, and Evonne. My 208Wildwriters Critique group, Chris Holloway, Colleen Skaggs, Carol Huffman, and Jeremy Jones, have been fun, insightful collaborators. Myra Gilliam with the U.S. Forest Service enlightened me about what natural resource activities might occupy a local archeologist.

Kenneth E. Rodgers' content edits were invaluable. My creative daughter, Holly Lyons, gave great perspective.

And many thanks to my family and friends, whose unfailing support and encouragement, sustained me when I doubted myself.

Table of Contents

Chapter One
An Expanse of Water

THE BALD EAGLE STOOD watch as the incoming tide pushed the skiff gently toward shore. In the distance, two rowdy seagulls vied for position as the colony settled on the water. The small tree-covered islands stood in shadows as the retreating sun cast its final glow on the glassy water.

The eagle's hooded eyes studied the woman's movements as the skiff drifted parallel to the shore, scraping against the rocks. She used an oar to secure the skiff against a piling, the only reminder that a boat dock once existed there. With slow movements, she locked the motor in tilt position. As she reached for the box, the eagle flexed its wings, lifting up from the branch of the Sitka spruce yet holding on to its perch. The eagle watched every movement in the boat, anticipating a reward.

Dana reached in to the cooler and grabbed a small cod, tossing it on a sandy wash twenty feet from the boat. She sat motionless as she watched the eagle swoop down to retrieve its prize. The eagle pranced on the fish as it searched the beach for any threat before it tore into the flesh with its fierce beak.

Moments passed as Dana watched the majestic bird. She knew its trust of her presence was a gift and each encounter could be the last. She had watched bald eagles all her life, but never this close. This one studied her.

Dana's breath was imperceptible. Any wrong move would destroy the moment. It was a covenant between them — the eagle anticipated her gift each time she returned from fishing, yet asked for nothing more. She reserved one fish for the eagle in exchange for a few sacred moments of mutual observation.

Finished with its reward, the eagle lifted off the beach with one powerful thrust of its wings, launching into an upward spiral over the trees before settling back on its branch.

The spell was broken. Dana stood up, lifting one long leg out of the skiff and straddled the boat while she unloaded the heavy cooler and gear. Stepping to the front of the skiff, she dug her heels in the rocks for leverage and pulled it a few feet further above the high tide line. An anchor hitch secured the boat to a blackened square boulder on the shore.

Dana's eyes scanned the shoreline, settling on the modest log home above her. Dusk had shrouded the windows in black. Its large wraparound deck overlooked the vast Lynn Canal, a ninety-mile fjord that separated Juneau and a string of discontinuous communities from open waters of the Pacific Ocean.

She lugged the ice chest and gear over to the steel mesh stairs that climbed from the shore to the deck, pausing to fill her lungs with the salty crisp air. Adroitly, she loaded the gear into an open cabinet attached to a pulley system set in tightly between the stairs and house pilings, snapped her fishing pole on to the cabinet face, then reached arm over arm, pulling on the rope to lift the cabinet to the deck. After securing the rope, Dana began the steep climb to her home.

Pausing mid-way on the landing, she turned to embrace one last view of the scenery before her. Aware of how much her mood had changed in the last three hours, she lifted her arms toward the sky to express her gratitude. She had needed this alone time on the water desperately. She smiled at the irony — *the one place I feel truly grounded is when an expanse of water is beneath my feet.*

The recurring nightmare had intruded again last night. It haunted her most of the day, fueling a sense of foreboding. But now, after a few hours on the water, she could see clearly that it had been just a bad dream, stuff from the past — not the present.

The ocean had that effect on her. It put everything in perspective. On these waters, interspersed with islands and surrounded by mountains of old growth forests that bordered the Juneau Icefield, she was confident again. She could allow God to take care of her worries, and she could simply enjoy being His child. It was only then that the ever-present apprehension would subside.

This evening she was again certain of who she was: Dana Jordan, Clinical Professional Counselor; resilient woman rooted in the Alaskan way of life; blessed to be living in this time, this place, with the man she loved.

Dana turned and skipped up the remaining steps to the deck. Nicki and Mica raced around the corner to meet her, their tails seeming to wag their big furry bodies. She paused to love on both dogs, then her focus shifted to Hub, who had just appeared from the shop, still wiping his hands with a grease rag. His grin and intense blue-grey eyes that studied her every nuance made her quiver inside. Her contentment turned to anticipation as she melded into his encircling arms. She inhaled the scent of his latent aftershave that competed with the smell of his work.

"How was it?"

Dana knew he meant her time alone. Even though he didn't like her to go in the boat by herself, he understood her need for solitude and respected her maritime skills. "Wonderful. Especially with you here to welcome me home." She fit perfectly in Hub's arms, and could have stayed there longer, but he shifted his hands to her shoulders and pulled away to look in her face.

"Catch any?"

"Three Coho and a Humpback. I'll smoke them up this weekend. And the eagle came down again. About twenty feet from the skiff. It was incredible."

He nodded, then waggled her shoulders affectionately. "I'll finish up here and join you in a few minutes."

Dana reluctantly released him, and headed for the mudroom. She slipped out of her rubber boots, hung her wool jacket on the hook, and released her dark wavy hair from her cap. Lionel encircled his huge feline body around her leg, prancing on her toes until she picked him up and nuzzled him. Dana carried him to her cozy living room where she lingered over the view of the islands across the water. "Thank you, Lord. Your magnificence fills my soul."

***

Dana unlocked the front door to Jordon Counseling. The building was nestled between two look-alike houses built in the 1920s. The house uphill hosted Juneau Book Nook, enticing seekers to browse among the organized chaos of thousands of books stacked on every conceivable surface and shelf. Its slight musty smell hinted of old stories that begged retelling, and book bargains if the browser would take the time to discover them among the nooks, crannies and unsorted boxes.

The house downhill had been Gastineau Tailor for many years, but now stood vacant since Mr. Orr moved south to be near his adult children. Dana grimaced at the orange For Sale sign taped inside the front window that declared its current state of friendlessness. *Oh, I hope whoever buys it will retain the historic feel of this block.*

All three houses had shingled siding, boxed dimensions, and peaked roof lines that spoke of an earlier century when Juneau was a thriving gold mining community in the Alaskan Territory. Jordon Counseling was now a quaint twenty-first century office painted vintage colors of dark sea green and taupe, with updated windows framed by burgundy shutters and awnings.

As Dana opened the drapes, she thought about how she and Hub had worked nights and weekends to remodel this building. It had stood vacant for several years, weathered, deteriorating, and threatened by encroaching moss. The little house had called to Dana the first time she walked past it with her nascent idea for a private counseling practice. Not only did this neglected part of Juneau's history need rescuing, she needed a cozy office close to the business district. It was a perfect spot—a short steep climb from downtown Juneau, just above the heavy foot traffic in the summer months. A spectacular view of the Gastineau Channel beckoned from the waiting room.

Dana set out ceramic cups, a variety of tea bags, and sweeteners on the counter. She wondered if the *sourdoughs* who had settled here a century before drank tea. Who were they? Who had constructed such sturdy buildings to withstand more than a century of Juneau's harsh winters? What life stories had they witnessed out these windows? What hardships had the wives and daughters endured when

Alaska was an inhospitable territory?

The history and ambiance of this little block was important to Dana and Hub, even while they transformed the house into a professional office. The frame-and-panel fir door of one bedroom now opened to Dana's private office. The lathe and plaster walls were refurbished when a bedroom and the living room were joined to create a multi-purpose room. The tiny kitchen and antiquated bathroom, although updated, still featured the original plank wood floors.

The months she and Hub had spent remodeling this house held some of their most treasured memories. They worked side-by-side, replacing plumbing, wiring, and roofing to meet code, yet still honored the history of Juneau and these little homes. They had been exhausting weeks with a lot of sacrifice and uncertainty, yet they were so contented. *When did we lose that closeness?*

They had been so young then — married seven years, and still hopeful of starting a family. Dana walked over to the oval mirror by the front window. She looked frankly at the forty-two year old looking back. *You really should try some makeup to cover those shadows under your eyes, Girl. Something more than brows and a quick smear of lip gloss?* She lifted her slim hand to touch the crow's feet starting to show at the corner of her eyes, and noticed how rough her hand was from fishing. *Nope. It's just not me.*

She and Hub would be celebrating seventeen years of marriage, and a friendship that spanned more than half their lives. They were good partners, filling each other's gaps. His humor balanced her serious nature. Her inquisitiveness challenged his comfort with the routine. When she doubted herself, his steadfastness quieted her fears. They enjoyed each other's company, yet respected each other's need for separateness. If only they could put to rest the *Lost Year* — the year that had changed everything, and had taken away so much of their future.

Chapter Two
Hannah's Fearful First Step

HANNAH SOBA HAD BEEN sitting in her red Isuzu pickup outside the Jordon Counseling office for ten minutes. Her hand shook as she pulled out her third cigarette since leaving home. *I can't do this. I don't know what to say – where to begin. I can't do this.* She started the engine and backed up to the gold sedan behind her, turning the wheels to pull out onto the street. Then she paused, closed her eyes and sighed heavily. *I've got to. I can't lie to Sheila again.*

Hannah re-parked, and opened the door before she could change her mind, crushing her cigarette with her shoe as she stepped on to the pavement. As she climbed the three concrete steps to Jordan Counseling, she could see through the window that a woman was moving around inside. Her instinct was to retreat before she was noticed, but the woman had spotted her and nodded. Hannah took a deep breath, straightened the shirt that had crept up to her waist, and opened the door.

"Good morning. You must be Hannah. I'm Dana Jordan."

Hannah cringed, fearing the woman would shake her clammy hand, but was relieved when she just gestured a welcome to her, inviting her to sit down.

"Could you use a cup of coffee? Tea? I've got some brewing."

"No, thank you."

"Okay. If you change your mind, just let me know. I need a little paper work before we get started." The woman smiled as she handed Hannah the clipboard and pen. As Hannah settled into her chair, she thought how attractive the counselor was—natural and fresh; long dark hair with strands of silver too perfect to be dyed. She was tall and slim, narrower at the shoulders than hips. Graceful. *She could never relate to my kind of life.*

Fifteen minutes later, Hannah followed the lady into her office. Dana took the clipboard and motioned Hannah to a small couch placed at an angle from her chair. While the lady scanned the papers she just completed, Hannah looked around and tried to stop the trembling in her body. There was a pleasant fragrance in the office—citrus. She tried to study the décor, thinking it would help her to look normal while the woman reviewed what she had written. Several pictures on the wall depicted the ocean and people fishing. One photo featured a Tlingit woman standing with her back to the photographer, spreading out her elbows to display the button blanket she wore. *The Killer Whale Clan,* Hannah thought. She couldn't see the woman's face close enough to know if she might recognize her.

"Hannah, thank you for coming today. I know it is often hard to take that first step. I promise I won't pressure you. This is your hour, and we'll go at a pace that you're comfortable with. Feel free to ask me questions at any time."

"Uh, I can't think of anything right now. My friend, Sheila…my boss, really, said you were a good lady, and I should see you."

"Well, thank you. I hope I can help. Let me cover some of the basic information, then could I ask you a little bit more about some of the symptoms you've checked here?"

The lady's face was kind, and her questions so gentle, that Hannah began to feel more at ease as she tried to concentrate on what she was saying about confidentiality. She knew all about those laws from her job. They too had to protect patients' medical information and double check their identities to make sure the patient was who they said they were. It seemed like overkill to Hannah, since she generally knew the patients or their families from somewhere in Juneau. Hannah's thoughts were so busy, she almost missed the question directed at her.

"Can you tell me a little bit about yourself and why you decided to seek counseling?"

Hannah began to fidget, aware that her hands were still clammy and trembling. "I've got a good job. I'm a Personal Care Attendant…I think I mentioned that…with SEARHC—

the Regional Health Consortium. I take care of adult people who need some extra help. In their homes. People count on me. I...I need to be there. It's really important that I be there for them. But sometimes I get so down, I can't make myself get going. Sometimes I call in sick, or I'm late. My boss said I would get fired if I miss any more work."

"I understand. Tell me more about when you get down, Hannah. What is your behavior like when it's really tough?"

Hannah talked about how hard it was to get to sleep at times, and that she tossed and turned all night. When she finally did fall asleep, the alarm would go off. Other times she woke up with horrible dreams that caused her heart to beat wildly. "Then I can't get back to sleep again. The dreams stay with me all day. I can't shake them."

"Is there a recurring theme to the dreams?"

"Yeah. Generally I'm trying to get away from someone. I'm running and running, but I can't move very fast. And someone grabs me. I can't see his face, but his hands are huge, and I can't escape. Sometimes I scream, and my boyfriend wakes me up. Then it keeps him up."

"Uh huh. That must be distressing. Can you tell me a little about your growing up years? Your family situation and siblings?"

"I was born in Petersburg. We lived with my grandmother mostly — me and my little brother. I raised him, really. From the time I was six. Grandmother worked in the cannery, and it was all she could do to keep us going, but that was the happiest time of my life."

Hannah's face showed little emotion as she told her story, her thick black hair spreading across her shoulder as she leaned forward and seemed to focus on the space between her and Dana. Her alcoholic mother was seldom present and brought a lot of tension when she did show up to sleep on Grandmother's couch for a few days or weeks. "She and Grandmother argued a lot. Then she would just disappear, never saying goodbye. I learned to not expect anything — not get my hopes up."

Her voice faltered. "My father took us when I was nine, and we moved to Juneau. He was mean when he drank. He hit us a lot, especially my little brother."

"What is your relationship like now with your family?"

"My mom died. I don't see Dad much—mostly when he wants something. My brother is around. I try to help him when I can."

Hannah described a chaotic life, yet she was articulate and graceful, sad but not bitter. She avoided references to her Native heritage, almost as if she was trying to deny that part of her identity. Her boyfriend, Richard, was thirteen years older than she. "He gets nervous when I'm not around, so I have to make sure he knows what I'm doing."

Hannah felt embarrassed to tell this lady about Richard's problems, but admitted that he drank heavily. She looked out the window to distract from the topic. Dana made some notes on her tablet, then asked more specifically about Hannah's personal history.

She revealed that she had used alcohol and drugs extensively since she was about ten, but quit the drugs two years ago. "I slip up with the alcohol once in a while, but the drugs aren't a problem anymore. I'm court ordered to do a twelve step program, and it helps me to think about stuff differently. I have to give urine samples to my Probation Officer too, so that keeps me from doing anything stupid."

"Well, the good news, Hannah, is that you're only twenty-five years old, and you have overcome some big obstacles already. You've got a good job that takes very special skills and training, and you obviously have a lot of tenacity. Many people don't confront their demons until they're much older and perhaps have a long trail of broken relationships and heartaches."

Dana scrunched her eyebrows, tilting her head as if she was unsure of what to say next. "Hannah, I'm planning to start a therapy group in a few weeks—a group for women who have experienced hard times similar to yours, and struggle with some of the same things you do. It's a closed group, unlike the twelve-step meetings, so you would meet with the same five or six women for about nine months."

Hannah's eyes widened and her chest expanded with a subtle intake of breath, her face clearly expressing fear.

"It is totally your choice to work with me individually or in group, but I'd like you to think about it. I know it's scary to think about opening up in front of other people—the other women often have the same fear, but what I find is that they quickly bond with each other, and learn this can be a safe place to examine some of the things that can haunt us. There's something about hearing someone else's story, and realizing you have those similar feelings or responses that help with the recovery process.

"I'll never put you on the spot or expect you to say more than you want to — it will be a small group and a safe place to do some healing at your own pace. We start out slow, exploring topics such as, 'How we got our ideas about being women; what we expect out of relationships; how do we set boundaries, or limits, with other people; how to take better care of ourselves; how to forgive ourselves and others who have hurt us.'"

Hannah let go of some of the tension in her shoulders as Dana spoke, realizing she wouldn't be forced to make a decision now. "I'll think about it."

"Okay. Let's meet next week and we can discuss it further. Is that okay?"

Hannah left the counseling office with her head spinning. Her hands were shaking as she lit a cigarette and pulled away from the curb, grabbing her cell phone to let Richard know where she was. *She's nice enough, but I don't know about a group — nine months! They're not like me — I couldn't talk about my stuff. I don't think so. I'll just go until things get better at work and Sheila gets off my back.*

Chapter Three
Ellen's Private Angst

ELLEN PATTON STUDIED THE cruise ships out her kitchen window as she finished her daily routine of bleaching the white porcelain sink and polishing the spotless faucet. Her rubber gloves snapped as she methodically loosened each finger to remove them. She then folded the gloves neatly and placed them in the tray under the sink. The smell of bleach and latex lingered in the kitchen.

There were only four ships this morning — three at dock and one anchored in the bay. It looked like the Sea Princess. She watched as one shuttle boat pulled away from the great ship to deliver its load of tourists at the Juneau city dock. Another shuttle boat waited its turn to load the next group. Ellen could imagine the visitors' anticipation — trying to cram all the Juneau highlights in to one eight-hour stop over. The shuttle boats reminded her of Army ants — synchronized, purposeful, repetitive, efficient. It was a routine she often watched out her window overlooking Gastineau Channel.

Just a few more weeks, she thought, and the tourist trade will dry up as the ships head for warmer sea ports. The crowds will disappear and Juneauites can reclaim their sidewalks. *And I will be able to put the shop back in perfect order!*

Ellen was calmer when things were manageable. Orderly. Predictable. She could keep the displays sparkling and straightened — angled for the best lighting. She could attend to each customer without interruptions from impatient browsers. She could close the store precisely at six o'clock.

Even though the end of tourist season meant a significant drop in revenue, Ellen didn't dread the change. The slower pace allowed her to reorganize and plan her time more thoroughly. Then after Christmas, when the long dark days became dreary, she would close the shop for a few weeks to get recharged in a sunny clime. Mark might take a vacation with her this year—perhaps to Hawaii. Maybe he would propose again, and maybe she would say yes this time. *Yes, that would be good.*

Damn it! Just the thought of making that decision brought The Dread on, and she headed for the bathroom. *Why does it always affect me this way? Every time it comes to an important decision in my life, my anxiety skyrockets and my stomach cramps up.* She spoke out loud, "Oh...I can't think about that right now."

Ellen's anxiety had been a part of her life for as long as she could remember, but with medication for her stomach, and strictly controlling her activities, she could live with it. That is until this last year. *If I could just get my life back in control—make some decisions and stick to them! What's wrong with me? Mark says he loves me. I know he loves me. Why can't he just get on a budget and get his bills paid?* Her resolve set her jaw as she spoke aloud through her teeth, "I-will-not-bail-him-out!"

Ellen was still an attractive blond at fifty-two, although it was harder to style her thinning hair in a way that complemented her narrow face. Mark liked her hair long, so she kept it at shoulder length, even though the wind and rain created a disaster for her. When Mark wasn't around, she used a plastic scarf outdoors to keep the dampness from ruining her style.

Ellen's stomach began to settle as she banished the question of a future with Mark. Finishing up in the bathroom, she considered her hair in the mirror. *I look like the little ole ladies who get off those ships with their bubble hair and plastic caps. I'm not that old!* With a moment of resolve, she thought, *maybe I'll just cut it.* But that thought was quickly chased by, *but then Mark would have a fit. He says he likes it long. But it's almost stringy. Maybe Suzanne's can come up with an easier style that will keep Mark happy.*

Ellen had been widowed for six years. Her twenty-three year marriage to Steven hadn't been horrible, as she looked back on it now, but at the time, she thought it was unbearable. She had even made an appointment with a divorce lawyer, lamenting that Steven wasn't there for her. She had been so lonely.

In retrospect, she could admit that he had been a good provider and a good man. She had felt secure with him for the most part. Their marriage was good in the early years when she was busy making a showcase home for him—catering to his every desire and supporting his corporate climb. Then they got Rachel, and raising her became an all-consuming job, one that Ellen embraced whole heartedly. She loved being a mom and doting on her beautiful daughter. But as Rachel grew into her teen years and was more independent, Ellen realized how empty her marriage was. *I don't know if I ever did love him. I don't think I know what love is.*

For awhile, she worked part time at an exclusive home interiors store while they lived in Central California. Then later in Washington State, she helped a few friends redecorate their homes, earning the moniker, Personal Consultant. *If only I could organize my life like their homes. Why can't I just accept the people in my life for who they are — not expecting perfection? Why can't my daughter accept me the way I am? I wish she could see that Steven was not perfect. He was so indifferent much of time, even to her.*

Ellen's shoulders slumped as she recognized the parallel between her late husband and her daughter. *She's taking over where Steven left off!* Rachel hadn't called for six weeks and two days. Ellen had left seven voice mails on Rachel's phone, each revealing increased irritation about not hearing back from her. Finally she called the dorm monitor and learned that Rachel was all right—she just wasn't speaking to her mother for whatever reason. *Well, so be it.*

Ellen stood in her neat living room, her arms crossed and elbows clamped close to her body. *I've got to stop letting this get to me! But darn it, I was the one who took her to every dance recital, every soccer practice, every basketball tournament. I was there after school with the fresh baked cookies. I was the one to arrange the elaborate parties for her and her little friends.* It didn't seem to matter what Ellen did though—she couldn't get Rachel's approval. *I wish Steven hadn't been killed. Maybe I will talk to someone about it.*

Chapter Four
Annette – Again Forsaken

ANNETTE SHIPLEY HUNG UP the phone so hard it knocked the cradle off the stand. "Well, Mother, once again you've confirmed that you really don't care about me or my family." Annette's voice reflected the firmness she wished she could have mustered while her mother was still on the line. "Just once, why couldn't you think of me and what I need? Just once, why couldn't you be there for me?"

Annette's thoughts flashed back to the little girl she was in Salem, Oregon, so often left to fend for herself, running throughout the neighborhood finding ways to stay out of trouble with the grownups. She wanted her mother's attention so desperately, yet it seemed that when she finally got it, it always turned sour.

Mom had been so busy trying to impress her assortment of boyfriends, there was seldom time for the quiet child with big brown eyes who seemed to know too much about the ways of the adults in her small world. She had a dimple in her left cheek that showed itself only when a smile was coaxed from her little round face. Her thick unruly hair wanted to stretch out every which way, defying her mother's occasional attempts to tame it with a curling iron.

Annette thrived on her mother's attention in those rare moments, hoping she would finally make her mother happy. If only she could be pretty like her mom, or funny like her brother—maybe then Mom would love her. But more often than not, her mother's attention would turn to Annette's scruffiness or choice of baggy tee shirts and cutoffs, and then the cutting words would begin to erupt, sending Annette running outside. Those biting words still haunted: *I don't know whose child you are — you certainly can't be mine with that kinky hair. How will you ever get a boyfriend if you look like you fell off the turnip truck? They'll call you scar face if you keep bunging yourself up and climbing in those trees!*

No matter how Annette tried, she couldn't seem to avoid the scratches and bruises that came with playing in the field across from the apartment complex. It was the only time she could think about other things, and not be so worried about pleasing her mom. There had been a big old poplar tree near the center of the lot, which offered her sanctuary. She could climb higher than any of the neighborhood kids—to the highest branch before it got too wobbly. She felt like no one could see her there, but she could still watch the stairs leading to their apartment, and the front door that would reveal who was coming to see her mom. And when they would finally leave.

She could watch her older brother and sisters, as they disappeared down the street with their friends, or climbed into the back seat of the noisy car when their friend Juan came by. She longed to go with them, but they always yelled at her, and said she was too little.

Sometimes though, her oldest sister, Fannie, would bring Annette a candy bar, and would paint her fingernails. Fannie would say, *Don't be sad Little One…someday you'll grow up to be beautiful. Then everything will be okay.* Annette could almost believe it because Fannie was beautiful, and they had the same big brown eyes and hidden dimple. Maybe she would grow up to be like Fannie.

Annette remembered little else from her childhood. There must have been more, but she just drew a blank, except for the memories that haunted her—random images or odors that came out of the blue. The memories were fuzzy at best— disturbing. But when they escaped from the locked doors of her mind, she noticed how her chest squeezed inside and she could hardly breathe.

Like now. Annette's body was rigid, her fists pushing against the counter as she fought tears that threatened to escape. *I just need a break — a few days, or a week.*

Annette was certain she could get her house in order if she could just get some rest—get caught up. Get her motivation back. Her kids demanded so much from her, and

Jackson needed more of everything—more quiet; more errands; more attention; more sex. She was so tired.

Making the disastrous call to her mother had taken every ounce of resolve Annette had, but she had been desperate. Now she remembered why she never asked for anything—it cost too dearly. The guilt trip. The rejection. Her mother's biting response echoed in Annette's mind now—*you expect too much, Annette! I never had any help when you little bastards were ruining my life. Just get over it!*

Annette slumped into the chair at the kitchen table and let the tears fall. *I don't know how much longer I can take this.* She found herself eating from the family-sized bag of tortilla chips before she even realized she had taken it and a jar of cheese sauce from the pantry. She hated herself for going off her diet again, yet she couldn't stop. She ate quickly, as if the urgency would soothe the gnawing in her torso and heaviness in her arms. After a few moments, the churning inside her gut began to quiet and she closed her eyes to indulge the perfect balance of saltiness, cheese, and heat from the chilies. The chips crumbled slowly as she savored the taste. *Perfect.*

As the squeezing inside her chest began to release, she realized the bag was nearly empty, and most of the dip was gone. She sat there staring across the room, the numbness reminiscent of the pot highs she experienced in her youth. Then came that familiar sickening feeling that followed an eating binge. The indulgence sat just above her stomach, threatening to eject. She wished she could purge—just be rid of the twenty minute bender, but she knew she would have to wait for her body to absorb the onslaught.

Annette sat for several minutes looking at the wall, unseeing. The clock chimed at the half-hour, breaking into her trance, reminding her she had to pick up Joshua from school.

Wearily, she stood up, forcing herself to move. Her steps faltered as her feet objected to the sudden demand. The fatigue pulled at her entire body. She sighed. *I wish Jackson would help me. Doesn't he understand I can't do this by myself? Maybe I should try antidepressants again. No, I'd just gain more weight.*

Maybe I should talk to someone. I can't keep going on like this.

Chapter Five
Jodi –Darkness Approaches

THE BOEING 737 ARRIVED an hour late, disgorging a load of weary passengers at the Juneau airport. The flight from Seattle was known as the *milk run* because it stopped at several small communities before arriving at Juneau. This evening, a black bear had wandered onto the runway at Sitka and delayed the flight from taking off.

It was past ten o'clock when Jodi Johnson walked through the waiting room in her field uniform, carrying her bulging backpack and a Gore-Tex jacket. Her shirt displayed the green and yellow U.S. Forest Service patch on the upper sleeve, suggesting a person of authority. She wore the uniform well: She was taller than most women—slim, yet with hips that clearly distinguished her from the typical male variety of *Smokey Bear* people. Her easy walk and eye contact with fellow travelers suggested approachability.

No one would be there to meet her, yet her eyes followed other passengers as they found their loved ones in the foyer. Admittedly, she was a people-watcher, and airports were perfect for unobserved speculation about the travelers and what might have brought them here.

She walked through the lobby and out the front door toward the parking lot before remembering she left her pickup at home this trip. She backtracked to the sidewalk, and picked up her pace.

It was an easy walk to her downstairs apartment off Glacier Highway. The stretch felt good after two hours in the airplane. The midnight sun promised to accompany her these several blocks, and the clear cool evening was ideal. She checked the angle of the sun and briefly considered a run with

Bounder, her golden Labrador and best friend, before it got too dark, but decided that would be pushing it. She needed to unpack and get resettled. And then there was the appointment tomorrow.

Jodi unconsciously slowed her pace, her serene expression turning to a grimace. *My new shrink – Dana Jordan. Ten o'clock. You'll need to gear up for this one, Kiddo.*

Jodi's countenance slumped as she thought about her disastrous encounter with a counselor in grad school. A professor had suggested she might get some help for her stress headaches and learn to sleep better, so she gave it a try. The therapist, a grad student herself, tried to psychoanalyze Jodi, probing into her personal life that had nothing to do with her headaches. Jodi decided quickly this wasn't the right venue for her, and left abruptly. But she remembered a physical discomfort afterwards that lingered for several days. It caused her even more stress than she had going in to the appointment.

As she walked, Jodi began to unconsciously massage her left shoulder. *Well, Dana isn't a grad student, Jodi. And you're not a naïve student. You've gotta get some help with this depression before winter sets in!* She picked up her pace as she recalled the high school play where she was introduced to Dana during intermission. *She's probably close to my age. Seemed mature. Confident. Easy to talk to about the play.*

***

In spite of the pep talk she gave herself, Jodi did not sleep that night. After tossing and turning for several hours, she gave up and pulled out a Louis L'Amour novel to quiet her mind until daylight. After a short walk with Bounder and a double shot espresso, she felt somewhat revived and ready to face a shrink.

Dana's quaint office was serene—a couch, indirect lighting, comfortable chairs. *Quite the contrast to our typical government-issue.* Jodi studied a deer hide drum on the wall with the Tlingit painting of the bear.

"Jodi, come on in. My apologies for the delay—I had a call that lasted longer than anticipated."

Jodi followed Dana to her private office, taking the plush chair angled sixty degrees from what was obviously Dana's chair. Jodi was aware of the caffeine finally kicking in — either that or her adrenaline. She was surprisingly alert, considering how little sleep she'd had, and somewhat hopeful. She liked this woman's professional demeanor wrapped in a welcoming smile.

"It's good to see you again, Jodi. Thanks for emailing the paper work to me in advance. I'm intrigued by your occupation...an archeologist? However did you get into that field?"

Jodi chuckled, a distinctive throaty sound that bubbled into a grin. "Well, I musta been destined to be an Archeologist. I've always been drawn to science, but as a ten-year old, I discovered the Anthropology section of the library, and learned that people actually got paid to investigate ancient ruins. I couldn't dream of a more fascinating career. It still feels like I should return a portion of my salary to Uncle Sam because I enjoy the work so much." Jodi's chuckle made it to the surface as she and Dana considered the irony.

Dana asked, "And so, why Alaska? I always think of Archeologists in hot dry deserts with little picks and safari hats to shield the sun."

Jodi's laugh was forthright. "Well, that's part of it. Actually, I initially worked in South America on some digs, then it got to be a seasonal thing, so I taught at Stanford during the school year. But Alaska has always called to me. I have an affinity for the Tlingit and Haida cultures, and wanted to learn more firsthand. So, when I saw an opening for an Archeologist for the Tongass National Forest, I thought I'd give it a try. That was two years ago. And it's been truly gratifying."

"What is the best part?" Dana appeared mesmerized.

Jodi scrunched her lips as she considered. "I guess working with the Native people. Administering the Antiquities Act. I work with village elders and communities to return Native artifacts and remains to the villages. Sometimes it gets pretty challenging because of different perspectives of how it should be done. But it's...it's almost a sacred responsibility to me — to protect these national treasures and honor the Tlingit and Haida cultures.

"But most of the time I tromp around in the woods testing for antiquity prior to any ground disturbing activity —

like a proposed road or campground. I love that too."

"Fascinating. What a gift to be able to work at something you enjoy so much."

Dana asked other questions about Jodi's hobbies, general health and prior counseling, then said, "So Jodi, tell me about the depression. You indicated trouble with sleep and the *winter blues*. I see you're taking medication now for it."

Jodi inhaled deeply, nodding her head before she launched into the dreaded subject. "I uh, I've probably had it all my life. Especially in the winter...with the long nights. I use a SAD light and it helps some, but it's pretty tough. My doc says I should move south to a more sunny clime, but I hate to do that. I love my work here...and I'm just not ready to throw in the towel. I thought maybe you could help me...you know...without getting me on your couch and digging into my gray matter."

Dana laughed at Jodi's humor, but recognized the clear signal to use caution with deeper issues. She deftly changed the topic to Jodi's familial history.

Jodi shared that her roots were in Illinois, growing up on a small farm with a younger sister and both parents. While her mother doted on her sister's musical talents, Jodi got lost in her science books. "I guess I was the odd duck in the family. My folks didn't emphasize education necessarily, yet I had a thirst to learn. Luckily, I had a science teacher who took an interest in me and encouraged my academics. I graduated at seventeen — valedictorian of my class — thanks to her, and had a full ride scholarship to Stanford. The rest is history. Here I am."

Dana asked tentatively, "So Jodi, what instigated seeing a counselor now? What has changed in your life?"

"The fall. Winter is coming on — the days shorter; nights longer. I get more restless. It's harder to sleep, and I don't sleep well anyway. I feel a dread inside."

"Have you ever thought about hurting yourself?"

"If you mean suicide, not really. I wouldn't do that. But I think about it at times — like it would be easier if I weren't here."

Jodi answered more of Dana's questions, and participated in a breathing technique to reduce tension. After they made an appointment for the week following, Dana asked, "Jodi, you might also want to consider participating in a small therapy group I'm starting in a few weeks. It's an excellent venue to explore what makes us who we are, and how unresolved emotional wounds can hold us captive. We can talk about more details next appointment, but it's a very empowering process when women come together in a safe environment to explore sensitive issues. Will you consider it?"

"Sure. I'll think about it."

Chapter Six
Raydine – A Change in Venue

DANA'S WORK WEEK WAS almost over—just a session with Raydine, then one with her newest client at five o'clock. Hopefully she could get out of the office early—maybe even slip out on the water for a quick check on how the silver salmon were running.

She pulled Raydine's bulging file. Her mouth contorted as she considered the bulk of medical notes provided by the psychiatrist. *I still question his diagnosis. If she can work through the trauma of her upbringing, I bet those Bi-Polar symptoms will disappear; or at least be very manageable.*

The front door opened, signaling Raydine's arrival, Dana decided it might be a good time to review progress with her today.

As Raydine settled in to her favorite chair, Dana assessed her demeanor. *Fleeting eye contact. Moderate energy. A little disheveled. Some agitation.* Raydine's thick brown hair had become such an indicator of how well she was functioning. Today it hung straight—combed but no attention to the style she sometimes wore. Her mouth puckered as she gave Dana a cock-eyed look over the top of her glasses, as if to say, *I'm here; now tell me what's next.*

Dana chuckled at the familiar dynamic between them. In the past, Raydine would try to remain passive, allowing Dana to do all the therapeutic work , but Dana had learned to keep Raydine aware of this tendency and to be deliberate about her choices. "Raydine, you are too cute! What's going on?"

Raydine acknowledged the deflection, fluttering her eyes. "I don't know if I've got anything to say today. I'm just...I don't know. Funky. Things are okay. Cyndi's mad at me.

"What's that all about?"

"I made her go to the grocery store with me. She wanted to stay home and play on the Internet, but I wouldn't let her. She got huffy and rude. I lost my temper and yelled at her. Then she said some mean things."

Raydine's eyes wondered as she sighed. "She's a good girl. I hate to depend on her, but I have to sometimes."

She rubbed her forehead, as if to push her thoughts around. "It seems like when I get better, she gets grouchier. Then we fight. It's almost easier if I'm...holed away in my room."

"Is there a role reversal there, Raydine—when you're down, she takes care of things? She's the grownup. Then when you're better, she's...the child again?"

Raydine was thoughtful for a moment, her big brown eyes searching the evidence. "You're probably right. She likes to be the boss...in control. And when I'm strong enough to be *mom*, there's a tug-of-war between us. What's wrong with me? Why can't I just forget about all the junk from the past after all this time...at least pretend to be normal? Other people get on with their lives...why can't I?"

"I don't know what *normal* is, Raydine. I've felt abnormal a lot myself. But let's take a look at where you're at today compared to where you were six months ago. Six months ago, you were suicidal, and most people in that state of mind would have been hospitalized. But you pushed through. Do you have self destructive thoughts now?"

"No. No, I really don't. I need to be here for my little girl. And I guess I do have some hope. Maybe it won't always be this hard."

"What else is different?"

"I haven't had a drink in thirteen months."

"Wow. Good for you!

"How's your sleep?"

"Well, thanks to the meds, I sleep hard. Probably too much. But I am taking my meds regularly now. And most days, I get out of bed. I'm up when Cyndi gets home from school. We talk, and watch our favorite TV programs."

"How about relationships, Raydine. How are your interactions with Doug; with others?"

"He's still staying out with Joe, working on that lodge. I

told him he'd better decide if he wants to have a family or not, because I'm getting tired of him not being home. But it really does seem easier with him not around." Raydine grimaced as she mumbled. "I guess it's easier because I don't have to try as hard."

"Good insight. That's tough to acknowledge. What about your family?"

Raydine sighed. "I avoid them, and that's probably the best thing I've done in the last six months. I haven't asked them for anything. I know what they think, and I'm not going to pretend like everything is okay. My sister called last week and gave me a rash of crap. She thinks I should just get over it. *It's in the past. He said he was sorry. Can't you just move on?"* Raydine's anger seemed to renew her determination.

"I will never forgive him. Or let him around my daughter. My mother stays with him knowing he's a child molester—I can't just get over that. He ruined my life! And there he sits in the big house, making good money, doted on by my mother, seeing my sister and her kids, and acting like he's Mr. Good Guy. I hope he burns in hell!" Raydine's chin trembled as she slumped back in her chair. "It's not fair."

Dana's kind voice was soft. "No, it's not."

After a few moments, Dana added. "And it seems to me that there's some progress there even in your angst. You're claiming your power to be a part of the family—or not. To forgive—or not. To speak of the truth, even though they're uncomfortable with it. Six months ago, you were still pretty dependent on them, weren't you? Stuffing your feelings…holding your tongue…letting them dictate the terms of your relationship?"

Raydine nodded. "I guess that is progress, huh? It's sure hard to believe it. I'm so tired of this."

"Things look black and white right now, but you're a courageous woman, Raydine—confronting very difficult issues. You are making progress, and I'm confident you'll discover options that are right for you. I'm honored to walk along side you."

Dana shifted in her chair. "Raydine, there's something I've been wanting to ask you. Would you consider being part of a small therapy group—of just women? I'm planning to start a new group in a few weeks, and I think you would benefit by being with other women. As a group, we'll explore topics like identity, relationships, struggles with moods and life; how the past influences the present. It could be very empowering to join together with other women and talk about things of the heart. It helps to be affirmed by others in a safe environment, and to understand how alike we are in some ways."

Raydine responded quickly, "Yeah—I'd like to do that. I think that would be good."

"It's a nine-month commitment, so I'd like you to think about it. We have two weeks before we start, so we can talk about it next session."

"Okay. Could I keep seeing you like this...alone?"

"Yes, we could do that. Or you might come every two weeks. We can just see what your needs are as we go along."

"Okay. I think so. Yes, I'd like to interact with some other girls. I trust you, Dana, so if you think that's what I need, well, I'll do it."

As Raydine was leaving, she noticed a tall blond woman in a sage green uniform of sorts. She smiled briefly when their eyes met, and stepped out of the office with a little more confidence than she had before.

***

As Dana drove out the road toward home, she thought about the five women who would likely make up her new therapy group. Jodi was intriguing; quick witted; clearly very bright, but not the least bit nerdy. Dialogue with her could easily slip into intellectual interests, like preservation of the rain forests. *I'll need to check myself with her — make sure I keep the focus on the therapeutic issues.*

She is one brave woman! I know that I wouldn't be comfortable tromping around with the bears. Solitude on the water — yes. But brown bears on land are a little more intimidating than my skiff in a squall.

Dana thought about how the women might mesh in a group. They were each so unique in their lifestyles, personalities and their ways of coping with life. Yet each was fighting her own inner demon. Jodi had accomplished a lot academically, and worked in an exciting occupation, yet seemed bereft of close relationships. Sweet Annette's days

Judy Hudson

were filled with managing a busy family, yet she was filled with self-loathing. Prim and proper Ellen was a little intimidating at first with her intensity and elegant persona, but beneath the surface, she was a worrier stymied by indecision in her personal life even though she was a successful business woman. *I sure hope it's not a mistake to include her in the group. She really is vulnerable...but in a different way.*

Hannah – what a lovely young woman! Her eyes carry such pain. She has no idea of her strength and beauty. Raydine. Raydine could easily become 'the Child of the Group' if I don't watch the dynamics. She could become so involved with their stories that she leaves herself behind.

Dana pulled into the drive, seeing the welcoming committee of dogs, but no Hub. She checked her disappointment, knowing that the end of season would soon allow more time together. *Maybe we'll reconnect then. I need him. I need his strength and certainty. Why can't I just let him know that?*

Chapter Seven
Group Beginnings

DANA TOOK SOME DEEP breaths, trying to settle her jitters about starting this new group. She could never predict how the women would interact with each other — who would align with whom; what personalities might clash; who would readily invest in the process, and who might be recalcitrant.

Sometimes there were surprising associations made, crossing life styles, age groups, educational and economic backgrounds. That was part of the adventure for Dana — learning what each client needed; her thought process; what individual strengths could be reinforced; what memories kept her tethered to a past that interfered with her present. Dana loved to draw each person out in a group setting to help her discover her own truth and vision while being affirmed by other women.

When group dynamics went well, it was exhilarating. Yet so much could go wrong, especially in the first few weeks before the women became invested in the process and each other. Too much disclosure too early could be overwhelming for everyone.

Remembering Lisa now caused Dana to grimace. Lisa was a woman in her thirties who joined a therapy group when Dana was fresh out of grad school. In the third week of the group, Lisa divulged way too much information, bragging about sexual exploitations that stunned Dana and likely the group members as well. Although Dana recovered her surprise and tried to affirm her client's courage, Lisa never returned to group. Dana called and left messages, encouraging her to return, but she never saw Lisa again. It still felt like a failure to her.

That group struggled after losing Lisa, never finding its identity as a haven for healing. The group stayed together, but it lacked the synergy that could make it such a powerful process. Dana felt she had failed everyone. It was this kind of pitfall that created the edge now as she reviewed her notes in preparation for the evening. It was nearly five o'clock — *show time.*

Dana peeked into the waiting room, which would serve as the group room for the next ninety minutes. She saw that Jodi, Ellen and Raydine were seated, each finding a way to avoid eye contact with the others. Ellen was intently reading a slip of paper — her posture almost rigid. Raydine dug in her sizeable hand bag as if something critical needed to be found. Jodi appeared to be relaxed, as if patiently waiting for an event to start.

Awkward as usual for beginnings, but hopefully it will be very different for you gals soon, Dana thought. She worried that Hannah and Annette hadn't arrived. Without them, the group was too small to be effective. She prayed for wisdom and guidance...and for them to all arrive.

After closing the door of her private office, Dana put on her most welcoming smile as she joined the others in the group room. Annette was just arriving, looking apologetic. "I hope I'm not holding you up. I couldn't leave my kids until my husband got home. He was a little late."

"We're just getting started. In fact, we have one more person to arrive." Dana motioned to the whole gathering. "There's bottled water and tea over there, and some treats on the table. I'm pretty informal, so help yourself."

Jodi unfolded her long legs and moved toward the table. "Well, I'm gonna take you up on that offer. I could use something to wet my whistle." Ellen followed suit, looking relieved to have a task.

The awkwardness in the room diminished some as the women offered each other drinks, or declined biscotti. *The power of food as an icebreaker,* Dana thought.

After the women settled in their seats, Dana made small talk, hoping the last person would arrive before she began to talk about the plan for the next nine months. She was relieved when the door finally opened, and Hannah stepped in hesitantly. She clung momentarily to the door as if she might bolt.

"I'm sorry to be late. I…I couldn't get my pickup started, and I had to jump it."

"No problem, Hannah. I'm so glad you made it. Please come in…we won't be a whole group without you," Dana turned to include the other women. "And that is true of each of you. When one of you misses group, which I hope will happen rarely, it's like having a birthday party without the guest of honor. You're each so important, there will be a big hole if you're not here."

Dana began to talk about the group process after Hannah settled in. "It's a closed group, meaning it will be just the five of you from start to finish so that you can really get to know each other and learn to trust the confidentiality of the group.

"The idea behind group work is to create a safe and supportive environment where each of you can explore how things of the past continue to get *hung up* with things of the present—things that cause you grief."

"I will generally have topics to stimulate your thinking and discussion, although we'll be flexible and able to meet your needs at the moment."

She spoke about how they would be organized, what topics they might expect, and some ground rules that would make it a safe place to share what needs to be shared. "We'll explore how trauma and painful memories can encroach on the present, impacting our self confidence. And how relationships can be complicated by *old stuff* that's still unresolved."

The women listened intently as Dana continued to describe what they might expect. Although there were no questions and little facial expression, she noticed some fidgeting and eyes that seemed to be tracking internal dialogue.

"We'll also look at ways of coping—things we do to survive crazy-making situations, like addictions, avoidance, or staying in unhealthy relationships. And how we can choose more effective ways of coping, or dealing with people and situations."

Dana had a way of making a point by saying the same thing in a couple different ways…making it understandable from different perspectives. She described her role in the group as more of a facilitator than a teacher or participant. "I want this group to be about you...not me. You have the best answers for yourself — my job is to help you discover them."

She spoke of the need to respect the confidentiality of each other and what is said in group. "There are some exceptions to that rule, of course. If one of you were to disclose that a child has been abused and it hasn't been reported, I am obligated by law to report that — if the victim is still under the age of eighteen. Or if I thought one of you might harm yourself or someone else, I would break confidentiality in order to get you help...or the other party if you're planning to take someone out!"

The humorous spin on the required disclosures seemed to ease the gravity of the topic, yet the message remained clear.

After answering a few questions that surfaced, Dana silently made eye contact with each woman, signaling a shift in direction. "What I'd like to do now is for each of you to create a name tag that says something about you as an individual. Share just your first name, and use any materials you'd like. This isn't an art class, and I'm not a teacher, so don't worry about skill. Then we'll introduce ourselves, using our name tags. Also, I'd like you each to say at least one thing you hope to get out of participating in this group. So...a little about yourself, and something you hope to get from this group experience."

Quietly the women moved to the side table, looking over the assembly of colored card stock, markers, buttons, glitter, glue, feathers, and beads. Dana encouraged them along and began making her own name tag by cutting out the shape of a boat. After ten minutes, all the women appeared to have completed their assignment and had settled back in their chairs.

"I'll start," said Dana, "to break the ice ...and allow you some time to think. I'm Dana, of course, and I've lived in Alaska all my life, except for graduate school. I've been married to my high school sweetheart, Hub, for seventeen years. He's my best friend, and he tolerates a lot of my idiosyncrasies. We don't have children, which has been a big disappointment to us, but I guess it wasn't meant to be. Our two dogs, Mica and Nikki, command all the attention around the house, and Lionel, our orange cat, allows us to share his abode." The humor generated chuckles, cutting through some of the apprehension in the room.

"I'm a fisher woman—I essentially lived on the water since I was an infant. I was first mate on my dad's commercial fishing boat from the time I was about ten—hence the shape of my name tag." Dana pointed to the red card stock she had cut in the shape of a boat.

"My dad is my hero. My mom disappeared when I was quite young." Dana's voice softened, her eyes diverting to the space in the center of the group. "She's not been a part of my life.

"I can't remember a time when I didn't want to be a counselor...or a *people helper* of some kind. I guess I had enough of my own wounds that I had to spend a lot of time and energy figuring out how to navigate through life...how to not be consumed by loss. So, as I learned about myself, I learned how I might help others. I've been doing this now for about seventeen years.

"When I'm not fishing, I like to pick blueberries or knit, or read—I read a ton of books. I like to hike. And go to local plays and concerts. I'm pretty casual.

"And what I hope to get from this group—umm...I look forward to getting to know each of you better." Dana touched her heart as she spoke, an effect that seemed intimate. "I am honored that you have agreed to work with me in such a personal way—to trust me to walk with you down this path of self discovery and healing."

Her eyes constantly moved to make contact with each woman as she spoke. "I hope I can provide a comfortable setting, bring up the right topics, and ask the right questions that will help *you* discover the wisdom and answers that you have within *you*."

Dana's head tilted, her eyes squinting as if checking for anything further. "That's about it for me. Now, who would like to go next?"

Hannah and Raydine diverted their eyes; Ellen and Annette looked at each other as if to say, *please go first.* Finally, Jodi said, "I'll go next. I'm Jodi. I've only been here about two years—I came to Juneau to work for the Forest Service."

She leaned forward, resting her forearms on her knees.

"Let's see, umm, I've got a dog — Bounder. I'm single — never been married. I like to read. I...umm...spend a lot of time in the woods. I look for archeological evidence in the forest so it can be protected if there's any logging activity — road building, bridges, campgrounds and such. Sometimes I work with villages to reclaim their ancestral artifacts."

She straightened her long body back in the chair, crossing her legs. "And sometimes I sit in lengthy bureaucratic meetings and hope my eyeballs don't roll back in my head!" Jodi's chuckle percolated in her throat.

After a brief hesitation, she blew out her breath, and said haltingly, "I'm not totally sure what I want to get from this group. It's kind of hard to talk about it." She squinted one eye and looked to her left as if there was an invisible person just beyond the group giving her counsel. "But I get pretty depressed, especially with the winter coming on. Otherwise, I really like Southeast Alaska, and I love my work. I just thought it would help for me to talk to someone about things...the depression.

"So, I finally worked up the nerve to go see Dana, and she got me involved in this group before I could think twice!" Jodi's humor broke the ice a little more. "Not really. I'm glad I'm here. And I'm looking forward to it, although it's a little scary to think about where she might take us."

After joining the others in laughing at Jodi's humor, Dana asked, "And what does your name tag say about you, Jodi?"

"Oh, I forgot." Jodi held up a narrow brown card where she had drawn three faces stacked upon each other with a heavy black marker. "This is a totem...sort of. As you can see, I have no artistic ability whatsoever. I meet a lot with Tlingit and Haida people in the villages around Southeast, and I enjoy learning about their culture and figuring out how I can help preserve it. That's what I do as an Archeologist."

"Interesting, Jodi. Thank you. I hope your arm is healing up where I twisted it." Jodi just smiled.

"Who will go next?"

"I will. I'm Annette Shipley." Annette's soft voice was steady, her dimple pronounced by her tentative smile. Her hands seemed to be held captive between her knees. "I've got three boys — Jason is ten. Jeremy is eight; and Joshua is almost six and a handful. I've been with my husband for almost eleven years—married for nine. And...umm...we do pretty good, I guess."

She looked at Jodi. "I battle with depression too. I tried antidepressants years ago, and maybe I'll try them again if I don't get on top of it soon. I don't know. I don't like taking them, but I might need to. I just can't seem to make myself get moving. It's overwhelming at times...my husband works a lot and isn't much help, and with three boys, it's...constant. Sometimes it's hard to be around people. I guess that's it."

"What do you like to do, Annette? Do you have hobbies or interests that engage you?"

"Oh, I forgot." Releasing her hands, she held up her card that had several layers of colorful squares and lopsided circles glued to it, Annette said, "I used to scrapbook. But I haven't done it for awhile. I used to paint, but it's been a long time. Actually, I used to do a lot of different crafts, but with rambunctious boys..." She shook her head and looked at the others as if she didn't need to finish the sentence.

"And what do you hope to get from this group, Annette?"

"Oh, yeah." Annette licked her lips, her voice dropping when she spoke hesitantly at first. "My growing up wasn't the best. My mom can be pretty hard to handle, and sometimes I'm afraid I'll be just like her. That's depressing in and of itself. I don't know—I guess I just want to feel better about myself."

"That sounds like a pretty good goal, Annette. Thank you."

Ellen's eyes darted between Raydine and Hannah, her head not moving with her eyes, her lips pursed. She said, "I guess it's my turn. I'm Ellen."

Ellen's sharp voice was startling at first compared to Annette's gentleness. Dana wondered again about how she would fit in with the more vulnerable younger women.

"I'm not sure I belong here. I have a good life—I don't get depressed so much, but I do get...anxious." Ellen's face showed her distaste for the word, although her straight posture in the center of her chair did not shift. She continued, her words erupting in spurts. "I get so caught up in what my boyfriend might think, or what my daughter says, or whether I should stay here or not—*any* decision about my personal life seems to make me physically ill. I worry about everything, even things I know don't matter. I want to get more confident of my choices and not second-guess them all the time.

"Oh, I guess I'm supposed to talk about my family. I was married for twenty-three years to Steven. He died in a car accident six years ago, and I'm still worrying about it."

The others smiled at her apparent humor. "We have one child—a daughter who is twenty. In college."

Ellen's thumb counted off three fingers, as if double-checking her assignment. She held up her rectangular card showing a carefully outlined white sow and black bear cub centered on a colorful pattern. "Oh, I guess this is my attempt at drawing the symbol for Alaskan-made handcrafts, and the colors represent my enjoyment of art and decorating. I have a little boutique downtown...Arts and Treasures."

Hannah gushed, "Oh, I've been to that place...your store. I love it!"

Ellen smiled at the complement before she continued. "And I like to decorate houses and to organize things. I'm real persnickety about how things should be. I have a good eye for design.

"And, Dana, I like how you've done this office. It's very welcoming. If you want advice on any changes, I'll be glad to help you."

Deciding how to take the backhanded compliment, Dana nodded and hoped her smile portrayed warmth. "Thank you, Ellen. I'll keep that in mind."

Dana made a mental note of how the tension in the room had diminished in spite of Ellen's stiffness. There was more eye contact among the women. Although they were hesitant to make comments or ask questions of each other, their body language was more relaxed and attentive to whoever was speaking. "Now, how about...Raydine. Would you like to go next?"

"Sure." Raydine's instant smile was beguiling, although her hands fidgeted. "I'm Raydine. I live with my daughter, Cyndi. She's fourteen. She's a good girl...I'm real proud of her. I'm married—sort of. Doug and I seem to get along better when we don't live in the same house. So we're not living together right now.

"I, uh, just want to figure out what's wrong with me. I mean, I know I'm bi-polar, and I'm taking medication, but sometimes I just can't handle things. I used to have a great job, but I haven't been able to work for a year. Now, I sort of hide away in my room." Raydine grimaced, revealing white even teeth, and looked at Dana through the top corner of her glasses.

"I like to fish too. Sometimes I go in the boat with Doug, but a lot of the time I just fish from shore. Cyndi and I have a place off Douglas Island we like to go to. We have pretty good luck. And I guess that's it.

"Oh...my name tag. I like flowers. This is supposed to be fireweed. I love how wildflowers decorate the landscape."

All eyes moved to Hannah as the last one to speak. She fingered her long black hair as her eyes darted to Dana, then Annette, who sat next to her. "My name is Hannah Soba. I'm twenty-five. I don't have any kids. I've never been married. I live with my boyfriend — we've been together for two years. I work for SEARHC — that's Southeast Alaska Regional Health Consortium. I'm a personal care assistant — a nurse's aide, essentially. I help people with bathing and things they can't do for themselves...in their homes. It's a good job...I really like it.

"I don't have any hobbies. I used to dance, but I can't go to bars any more. I can't be around alcohol because I'm an alcoholic. And I want to be more confident.

"Coming here is totally scary — I still can't believe I did it. But I'm hoping to learn to trust myself more."

"You're very brave, Hannah. I'm so glad you're here...even though it wasn't easy. And what does your name tag say about you?"

Hannah looked askew at her name printed on a plain white card followed by *RN*. She flicked it while looking boldly at Dana. "Someday, I think I want to become a nurse. I like what I do now...but maybe I could help people more if I went to school. Someday."

Dana's encouraging smile made her eyes squint. "My guess is you're very good at what you do, Hannah, and will make a wonderful nurse when that time comes."

She looked around the room, making eye contact with each woman around the circle. She spoke slowly, emphasizing words that she hoped to impress upon each person. "It takes a lot of *courage* to open yourself up to questions; to *know* yourself in a deeper way; to *confront* that which is painful.

"It is an *honor* for me to be part of your journey, and my prayer is that, working together in this group, each of you will discover wonderful strengths within yourself. And that you will be able to heal the wounds that still control you today.

"*Change* is often subtle…it happens without our awareness sometimes. And that's something good about meeting weekly—to increase our awareness and make changes thoughtfully.

"We'll take it a step at a time. I'm excited about working with you."

She took a deep breath before she continued. "What I'd like to do before we wrap it up for the evening is to ask each of you how you're *feeling* right now." Dana tapped her chest to emphasize the focus on her heart. "Take a moment to check in with yourself…what are you feeling right now? What is your body telling you? Anything you notice."

She paused as she watched for reactions. Hannah, Annette and Raydine's eyes were moving but unfocused, apparently searching inwardly. Ellen's mouth set hard; her eyes held steady to the side of Dana's shoulder. Jodi's eyebrows scrunched briefly.

"And then, what are you *thinking*—do you have any questions or comments? Will you be back next week?"

Jodi offered, "I'm feelin' pretty good. Real good, in fact. I like the structure you put in place—our commitment to be here for the duration, and your caution to keep it in-house—what we say. That's good. I'm in."

Annette inhaled deeply, "I don't have any choice. I can't continue living like a slug. I feel like I'm at the bottom of a pit, and tonight I have just a little bit of hope…just a tiny bit of light *waaay up* there at the top. So…that's what I'm feeling—hopeful."

Hannah glanced at Dana and Jodi, nodding her head, "I plan to be here. It's still a little scary, but it's okay."

Raydine smiled as she tipped her head at Dana and shrugged one shoulder. "I'm excited about it. I think this is going to be really good. I was nervous about opening up in front of others, but I think this is going to be all right. Good…it'll be good."

Ellen's posture was only slightly less rigid. "I'm

committed. I don't agree to things unless I'm sure I'll follow through, so when I told you I'd come tonight, I was committed to be here the whole time. I just wonder — what if I decide to go on a vacation during the holidays, will I be able to come back?"

Dana's answer was swift, "Oh, yes. I'm sure all of us at some time will have a need to be gone, but we'll work around it.

Ellen nodded and looked away as if to indicate that settled the question.

"Anything else?" Dana looked around again, making eye contact with each person. "Okay, then, I'll see you all next week — same time, same place."

Chapter Eight
The Therapist's Secret

"WE'VE ONLY JUST BEGUN," Dana sang into the darkness, the windshield wipers competing with her beat. She had a good feel about this group of women. *I think they're going to connect. And what an interesting mix of personalities!*

There wasn't any predicting who would bond with whom, or *how* their stories would unfold, but she was certain this was the right time, and they were the right people to come to this particular group. *Trust the process — bring people together in a safe setting, point them in the right direction, then get out of their way as they learn to trust each other and be guided by their own wisdom and values.*

As the light rain became more earnest, Dana's thoughts turned to each woman in the group, going around the circle mentally, noting their body language and testing for congruence with their comments. Ellen was stiff and watchful, brief with her introduction, yet Dana could see some thawing around her edges as she laughed at her personal struggle with decision-making. *She's insightful about how it's affecting her life.*

Beautiful Annette hiding her size behind a superfluous jacket. So sweet; so attentive to the other women; compassion exuding from every pore. She is the big sister every girl would love to have — the mom who was born to be one. She is going to be a great asset to these women.

Raydine. I've worked with that girl for nearly a year, and have never seen her so...so engaged. She's quite social! She wasn't afraid to open up to these new women...she almost welcomed it. This just might be the forum she needs to regain her confidence...maybe she'll see her own strength through their eyes.

Jodi. What an interesting woman. She's so intelligent and so accomplished. She could easily set herself apart from the group, yet she is engaging and humble. I hope she'll let the others meet her needs too. It might be a big step for her to let them be close.

When Dana's focus turned to Hannah, she thought about the tension Hannah held in her body—her narrow shoulders rounded; her dark eyes avoiding direct contact with anyone. Even though she was more relaxed toward the end of the session, Dana knew this whole process was a big step for her. If it weren't for her supervisor's admonishment, she probably wouldn't be here.

Precious Hannah is so young...and vulnerable. Lost. She needs a mom.

Unexpectedly, Dana got that sickening feeling in her stomach. *She isn't much older than my daughter—wherever she is. I wonder what path her life has taken—if she's in need of a mother's protective love and guidance, like Hannah. Is she out there somewhere, Lord, needing what I could offer?*

Dana's foot had backed off the accelerator, and she had slowed to thirty miles per hour before she noticed the headlights beginning to crowd behind her. She signaled to turn at the Chapel by the Lake, then slowed even more as she followed the winding road to the hidden refuge. She parked in front of the old chapel where she could overlook the quiet lake.

This familiar spot was so picturesque—especially nearing post-season when she didn't have to compete with the infernal tour buses. Dana had often brought visitors to this place for a *Kodak moment* when she gave them the quick *Juneau Overview,* but it was also a good place to stop on the way home. It was public yet secluded; she could make that mental shift, leaving her counselor role behind, and embracing her wife and homemaker role. Tonight she needed that transition time.

She wasn't sure what had triggered the sudden melancholy about Alex, the name she used for the daughter she gave up at birth. Most of the time, Dana was confident that she had made the right decision. She envisioned Alex with an active loving mother and father, somewhere in California, hiking, biking, reading, learning; engaged in playful banter; affectionate, and *normal*. Most of all—normal.

She often day-dreamed about their way of life and closeness, and how confident Alex was because of her parent's love and protection. But tonight she felt the emptiness in her womb—a coldness in her breasts. Her arms ached to hold her daughter. Not knowing was the hardest thing to accept. All she knew was that her daughter would go to a mature, stable, Christian family who desperately wanted a baby girl.

Dana had prayed for the ensuing twenty years that Alex was happy and safe. She just wished she could know for sure. She told herself she didn't even need to meet Alex—she would be content just knowing that it had been the right decision, and Alex had grown up in a loving family, pursuing her own interests and gifts, growing into the person God designed her to be. And somehow she could understand that her birth mother loved her.

That's it—her birthday is coming up. September twenty-seventh. And Hannah's vulnerability. That must be what triggered the sadness. Or maybe the maternal instincts that Hannah brings out in me. That must be it.

The wrenching in her chest began to subside as Dana thought about these associations for several moments. As she tuned in to the quiet lake before her, she could feel the tension leave her neck and shoulders. *Thank you, God. I give her back to you. I pray you will quiet this longing I have to know her. About her. To know that she forgives me.*

***

Hub Cordell was headed home from the shop early, grateful that he was beginning to see the end of fourteen-hour work days. Most of the boats on the landing were scheduled for winter maintenance or overhaul, so he could finally cut back on his shop hours. Going home this early was like a holiday. I think *I'll surprise Dana with a little candlelight ambiance, cuddle in front of the fire, and take it from there.*

His steps became more deliberate as he dropped his coat and boots in the mudroom, rubbed on the dogs, and mentally organized how he would start dinner and pickup the clutter before his shower.

As the hot water washed over his muscular body, Hub turned his thoughts to the few times he and Dana had been able to carve out *together time* during the summer months. Brief morning dialogues as he left for the shop had become the norm, with quiet late evenings, both too tired to make love.

How has it gotten so routine? We used to be hungry for each other, even when fertility tests were dictating the timetable.

As he dried off and absently reached for a chamois shirt, the reflection in the mirror showed a broad-shouldered man of average height, a pronounced jaw line and big blue-grey eyes accented by thick black eyelashes. His damp light brown hair fell forward, just meeting the heavy black eyebrows that almost joined in the center.

It started to change when she opened up her own business. Hub thought back to that winter ten years earlier. After their regular jobs, they had put in long nights for months, taking the inside of the old house on Third Street down to the studs. They rewired the electrical system, installed new plumbing, refinished the floors and made a lot of cosmetic changes. It had been a labor of love, helping her step out on her own.

In retrospect, he realized what a turning point it had been for them both. He had purchased the shop from Mr. Shipley; she launched her private practice; and they began to face the fact that Dana would never get pregnant. Little by little, the priority of having a family succumbed to the priorities with their new business ventures.

She was adamant that she didn't want to pursue adoption—she would devote her attention to helping others instead. Although Hub would have liked to raise children, he knew the greatest burden would fall to Dana, and if she wasn't zealous about the idea, it was a bad one.

It was such a big decision, and has so dramatically changed the direction of our lives, yet we seldom talk about it. Maybe someday Dana will be able to...what? Just talk? Hub looked in the mirror, rubbed his scratchy jaw, and reached for the razor.

***

It was nearly eight o'clock by the time Dana come through the back door. Tim McGraw's *It's Your Love* played on the stereo; candles were lit. The living room window featured a promising sunset spreading color across the charcoal green water.

"Yum, smells good. What have you been up to?" she asked as she set her tote down next to the counter. As Hub brought a glass of wine and folded her in his arms, she said, "Wow, this is a treat to have you home so early. And all this.

What have you done with my husband?"

"There's baked halibut, baked potatoes, green beans, and me." Hub punctuated each menu item with kisses that tiptoed around her face.

As she leaned into the curvature of his arms, she said, "I so needed this — especially you. Thank you, Hub."

Dana mentally put a wrap around her grief as she returned his slow seductive kiss. She knew she could unwrap it later and remind him of Alex's birthday, and tell him how Hannah had triggered her mothering instincts. She was determined to take her own counsel — *stay in the moment, and just appreciate what Hub is trying to do for you.*

Chapter Nine
Hannah's Tender Loving Care

JUNEAU'S RAIN AT TIMES seems to have a paranormal quality to it—wet beyond wet. And today the rain was incessant. The sky was so dark, it was hard to tell the time of day. Fewer cars were out as Hannah drove out the road to check on her third client. Dear Mr. Owen was still recovering from a hip fracture and needed some help changing his bed and picking up his apartment so that he wouldn't fall. It was important that he get up and walk about often, but he needed to avoid bending over or carrying anything over five pounds.

Hannah considered Mr. Owen as one of the elders of the community—a kind and respectful man with the wisdom of age behind his twinkling eyes. She didn't remember a grandfather of her own, but if she had had one, she would have wanted him to be just like Mr. Owen. He was always so considerate of her, not wanting to impose on her energy or time for other clients. Sometimes she had to snoop around to determine what might make his life and recovery a little easier, because she knew he would not ask for help if he thought it was less than crucial.

"How are you today, Mr. Owen? Did you sleep well?" Hannah took some time to be present with him, to look him in the eyes, and really listen to him. It often made her late getting to the next client, but she couldn't be disrespectful to him or any of her other patients for that matter. They all seemed to understand it if she was late, knowing that she would give them her best also. If she could only get her boss to understand the importance of that part of her job, it would be perfect.

"I'm just fine, Hannah, and how are you doing? It must

be awful wet out there. The TV said we got three inches yesterday."

"I am grateful for slickers today, that's for sure. How is that hip doing?"

"Oh, it's telling me I can't play basketball this afternoon." His eyes crinkled as he chuckled at his own humor. "I finally took one of them pain pills the nurse left for me—them others made me too drunk, so I give 'em back to her. But I'm getting along purdy good."

Hannah continued to talk with Mr. Owen as she organized his sitting area, picking up the newspapers and leavings from his meals in front of the TV. As she moved to his bedroom to change his linens, she kept up the dialogue by speaking louder and peeking through the door as she traversed the bed. She worked efficiently, and had the small apartment cleared of tripping hazards, the bed changed, the bathroom cleaned, and the kitchen organized in less than an hour. She checked the refrigerator to see that he had the basic necessities.

Before she left, she sat with Mr. Owen again for ten minutes. Hannah worried about him feeling lonely, and she wanted him to know that she cared about him. He seemed to love her in return, and that's why she loved her work—she was important to Mr. Owen. What she did for him mattered.

As she left for her next client in Lemon Creek, Hannah lit a cigarette and called Richard. "What are you up to?"

"Why, are you worried about who I'm doing it with?"

Richard's comment was couched in humor, but it instantly filled Hannah with dread. She knew Richard could easily get another girlfriend, and he seemed to be more irritated with her lately. It still stung when she thought about his being with Rena, her second cousin, a few months back. He said he was drunk and didn't know what he was doing, but it still hurt to know he would get it on with another woman. He got mad every time she tried to tell him how she felt, or even ask him his whereabouts, but she just couldn't let it go. She kept thinking about how Rena and other women down at the bar would like to have him.

Her voice was higher pitched. "No, I'm not worried. I'm just in between clients, so thought I'd touch base. See what you'd like to do after I get off work."

Richard sounded like he already had a good start on a drunken evening. "I don't know. I ain't committing to nothin.' I might go shoot some pool."

"Richard, it's awful out here. Why don't you stay there just a few more hours, and I'll fix us a traditional dinner...maybe watch a movie together. Maybe I'll give you a special treat." She didn't want to sound pleading, but her fear came out in her voice.

"Yeah, maybe. Call me after you're done. We'll see."

Hannah knew that *yeah maybe* meant he was headed out for a night on the town, and her gut churning turned up a notch. After a few beers, she could predict there would be drama. She thought about cutting out on the last two clients and seeing if she could intercept him at the bar — perhaps convince him to come home before he got belligerent. Or maybe she could have a few with him.

"I can't!" she said out loud as she slammed her hand on the steering wheel, and began biting her lip, a habit she had struggled with since childhood. *That's all I need is to get one more write up for cutting out and I'll be toast. Or if I get caught in a bar by my PO. I'll call him after Ms. Perl — maybe he'll be in a better mood.* Her hand shook as she stubbed out her cigarette in the ashtray.

Chapter Ten
Reluctant Response

ELLEN HAD BEEN THINKING about the therapy group all afternoon, and was glad to escort the last customer out of the shop and set the closed sign in the window. She wanted to call her friend in Minneapolis and tell her how the group was going.

I'm so much older than those girls – I shouldn't have to be hashing over old stuff at my age. They've got real problems. Mine are minor compared to theirs. They wouldn't understand if I tried to explain. Of course, it might help me understand Rachel better – that would be worth a lot. Or to make a decision about my personal life – now that would be monumental.

Ellen gathered her slicker, purse, and keys. At the door, she covered her hair with the ugly rain bonnet, straightened the closed sign, and moved the new window ornament to the left a half inch, standing back to see if that was closer to perfectly centered. She stepped out in the rain, heading for the stairs that led to her apartment up on Gastineau Avenue.

Forty-seven, forty-eight, forty-nine. Her cell phone rang, interrupting her silent count of the steps to the last landing before her street above the city. It was tempting to let it ring until she got out of this retched rain, *but it might be Rachel. Or Mark. Or Vi*, her friend and sister-in-law. She reached under her slicker to her sweater pocket to retrieve the phone. *It's Rachel!*

She spoke sternly. "Well finally – it's only been eight weeks since I've heard from you. Rachel, what have you been doing?" *Damn it! I didn't want to do that – I didn't want to put her on the defensive right off. Why can't I just hear her out first?*

"Well, hello to you too, Mother. Maybe this is why I don't

call often—I get chewed on before the first hello."

"I'm sorry, Rachel. I'm just…it's pouring down rain, and it's dark and dreary, and I'm out in it—eighty-four steps from my door. And I've been worried sick about you. How are you?"

After a brief silence, "I'm okay. Term papers up the wazoo, but it's okay. Not much fun, although I've got a good study group, and that's helping. And Parker's a nerd, so he sets our homework priorities a lot."

"Have you got classes with him? Are you studying the same things?"

"No, Mom…we just hang at his place a lot more; or at the SUB—Student Union Building."

"Is that really such a good idea, Rachel? I mean, hanging at his place?"

"Mother, would you please remember I'm an adult? I get to decide what I do and where."

Ellen sighed in resignation. "I'm sorry, Rachel, I've just been so worried about you. I keep wondering how you're doing—and whether you might come up for Christmas. It's not the best time of year with the winter weather and darkness, but I would love for you to come. Of course, I don't have an extra bedroom—you'd need to sleep on the couch, if that's okay. Or I could get one of those inflatable mattresses we could put on the floor. Just a minute while I unlock the door."

Ellen put her slicker in the closet before resuming the conversation with her daughter. "So, maybe you'll come up?"

"I don't know, Mom. It's not the Juneau weather—it doesn't sound like it's much different from Seattle. But Parker is going to his parents for the break, and I'm thinking about going with him. They live in Utah. We want to do some skiing."

"Well…how serious are you with Parker? It seems to me that I should rank up there somewhere?"

The conversation continued with Rachel releasing limited information about her life, and Ellen apologizing for her expectations and misunderstanding as Rachel's attitude deteriorated.

Ellen's head began to throb, and she could feel The Dread coming on. "Rachel, I'm going to have to run. Can I call you back later?"

"No, I'm about done, Mom. I just want you to release some extra funds for the holidays. If I go to Utah, I want to pay my own way. And I've had extra expenses with books this semester, and it's just gotten a little tight."

Ellen's voice became more clipped. "Rachel, I can't talk about this now. I will call you back later this evening...or tomorrow morning, all right?"

Rachel's impatience came through loudly. "Whatever, Mother."

Ellen knew Rachel had hung up without saying goodbye, but she was desperate to get to the bathroom.

Chapter Eleven
A Mother's Terror

"COME ON, MOM, YOU'VE got to sign up for unemployment today." Cyndi sounded impatient as she spoke through her mother's bedroom door.

"I'll be out in a little while, Baby—I'm just not feeling very good today."

"Mom, it's three-thirty. If you don't do it today, we'll miss out on another check."

Raydine yelled, "All right. I'm coming."

Raydine sat up on the side of the bed, trying to garner the oomph to get moving. The shorter days and weather was effecting her depression. *Maybe Doug will get off early and take me down there. But then he'll get on me about stuff. No, that won't do. Maybe I can go in just before they close. Oh that's right, Cyndi is going to the library this afternoon, so then I'd have to go alone. I don't think I can do that — not today.*

Raydine tried to think through any other way to avoid going out of the apartment today, but she knew she had to get her unemployment going. Doug might not pay the rent again. Raydine's jaws were clenched as she spoke into the gloomy bedroom, "I will not ask for one thing more from my parents."

Cyndi's demanding voice came loud and clear through the door again. "I'm going to the library at five o'clock, Mom. You have to go right now if you want me to go to the unemployment office with you. You can drop me off afterward."

"Oh, Honey, I don't know that I can make it that fast, and I know I can't do it without you. You'll just have to change your plans."

Cyndi's reaction was immediate as she yelled, "I can't

change my plans! You gotta get ready!" She stomped back to the kitchen, slamming a cup on the counter to emphasize her irritation.

Raydine moved toward the bathroom to make herself presentable. *I don't think I can manage a shower today.* She pulled on her sweats and counted out her medications, avoiding the mirror that reflected her disarray. She thought about the group her therapist had started a few weeks ago, and the other women she was getting to know. It was good to know that she wasn't the only one who struggles with Bi-polar; and to know the others can relate to not feeling normal. *Gee, Jodi's got a big important job, and the darkness gets her down. And Hannah had an awful family too. Maybe we've got something in common.*

Raydine attempted to chitchat with Cyndi while she put the coffee on and poured a bowl of cereal. Cyndi was sullen today, so it was harder to handle her mood.

The tension between mother and daughter this last week was high—as Raydine became more clingy, Cyndi became more belligerent. Then Raydine's fear of being rejected immobilized her even more. Cyndi had threatened to go live with her grandmother. Raydine knew she couldn't survive that—the thought of her daughter being under the spell of her step father was horrifying. She couldn't let that happen to Cyndi.

"All right!" Raydine yelled. "We go right now, and I'll drop you off at the library afterwards, but after pizza, you meet me at the front entrance at nine o'clock. And you have to stay at the Mendenhall Mall—no running around with anyone. I don't like it when I don't know what you're doing."

Their trip to the Employment Security Office was strained as Cyndi avoided conversation with her mother, and Raydine tried to make her daughter understand how hard it was for her to deal with strangers alone, especially when she didn't feel good. "If it wasn't so dark and rainy, Cyndi, I wouldn't have to rely on you, but I just can't help it right now."

Cyndi helped her sign up for unemployment on the computer, yet her tight jaw and body language let her mother know that she was out of patience.

After dropping Cyndi off, Raydine returned to the quiet

apartment unsettled. She longed for a few beers to make the shaking inside her core quiet down, but her doctor's words were almost audible in her mind: *You can't! You cannot drink any alcohol with these medications, Raydine! It could be life threatening. You cannot do it!*

Her image of being paralyzed by a stroke, unable to speak, abandoned in a care unit, was enough to keep her from going to the corner convenience store for a half-case. Her internal battle shifted to a sleeping pill and the escape into nothingness she would experience with her warm bed, but her mind replayed the argument with Cyndi. She had to pick her daughter up at nine o'clock, and she couldn't drive if she took the sleeping pill. *I have to stay up!*

Standing in the hallway, Raydine was torn between the comfort of her bed and the obligation she couldn't shirk. She slumped on to the office chair, making a promise to herself that she would play a few games of hearts, then pick up the living room. Then it would be time to pick up Cyndi.

An hour passed before Raydine thought again about her commitment. She looked around at the cluttered living room. It seemed overwhelming...the trash can was overflowing; the counters were covered with dirty dishes; magazines and unopened mail spilled over from the coffee table. She turned back to the computer, staring at the screen while she tried to find the motivation to get moving.

She remembered the need to check on Cyndi's internet activities—*I could handle that.* That would appease the warring factions in her mind.

Doug had shown her how to track Cyndi's internet history. She knew in principle that it was important to monitor teenagers' activity, but Cyndi was a good girl. They talked about everything. Now, as Raydine's pointer moved across the screen, she realized how little they had talked during this latest stretch of depression.

Using Cyndi's password, she opened up Facebook and soon found that Cyndi was involved in a new chat room. She felt the blood drain from her head, leaving her dizzy, as she scanned a long list of messages between Cyndi and one individual—Buddy. She gasped as she read the latest missive, holding her stomach, as if it would keep the cereal from coming up. The most recent messages from Buddy proclaimed his love for Cyndi and his desire for pictures that show more of her. He longed to hold her in his arms and couldn't wait to show her around.

Raydine cried out loud, "My baby—she doesn't know what she's doing. Who is this guy? I don't know who he is. He's a pervert. What is he doing with my little girl?"

Raydine grabbed the cell phone and slumped to the floor, praying Doug would answer his phone. She yelled into the phone with each ring, "Doug, pick it up! Pick it up!"

Finally when he did answer, Raydine blubbered about his need to come home right away—Cyndi might be kidnapped!

Doug promised he was on his way and tried to calm Raydine down as he drove out from Lemon Creek. He coaxed bits and pieces of the story from her, while reassuring her they would find her. "Hang on—I'll be there in a few minutes. She can't be far away. We'll find her."

Raydine's fear threatened to overwhelm her, but the rage she felt at *Buddy* was even bigger. She imagined all the possible scheming lies he could use to manipulate her innocent daughter, and how Cyndi was surely duped into something dangerous...like she had been as a child.

Doug arrived within ten minutes and took over the computer. He expertly navigated throughout Cyndi's profile and confirmed Raydine's fears. It was clear that Cyndi had been meeting *Buddy* on-line for two months. They had plans to meet today at the mall and drive around in his car. Buddy had promised he would let Cyndi drive.

Chapter Twelve
The Need to Run

HER HANDS WERE TIED behind her back, and attached to a tie ring in a barn—his barn. It was hot and dry inside, smelling of hay and horse manure. Her arms were numb except at the shoulder, where it felt as if her joints would separate if she relaxed her tension. She was beyond tired, but she didn't dare fall asleep. She had to watch for him and be ready. She had to make a plan, but she couldn't think of what to do. *He's coming.* The thud of his boots on the dry ground was getting closer to the door, and she could hear the clicking. When she heard him clicking his tongue, she knew he was going to do something horrible to her.

Jodi gasped for air as she bolted upright in her bed. Her heart beat wildly, and she was dripping with sweat. She took in great gulps of air for a full two minutes before she could get her bearings about her. *This is not real. It was the dream. I'm okay. I'm okay. It's not real. Did I cry out?* She listened for Mrs. Barrett upstairs in case she woke her up.

She got out of bed quickly and turned on the rest of the lights, checked the dead bolt on her front door, and grabbed the pepper spray out of her backpack. She wrapped herself in a blanket and sat up straight in the recliner, eyes wide and fully alert for possible danger.

She knew she would never get back to sleep at this hour, but felt immobilized. After several minutes, she felt her heart begin to slow down and her breathing become less ragged. She started to rock back and forth, and to cry. It was the sound of a wounded animal, high and keening. She held her pillow to her face to muffle the sound. Bounder leaned his head deeper into her lap and whimpered.

Long before the sun was up, Jodi took off for the Airport Trail. Bounder pulled at his lead, ready to get past the fencing so he could run free.

Jodi was grateful for his energy, because she wanted to outrun the nightmare. It was a dream she'd had for many years, and it always stopped in the same place, leaving her shaky and off balance. *Oh, God, please take it away. Give me freedom from such horror.*

Jodi began a slow run, feeling a little bit steadier as her body warmed with the exertion. Her pace was erratic as she sought footing in the shadows and unevenness of the path. It was muddy and sloppy. She could feel the wetness seeping up her pant legs as she pushed on. Eventually the airport lights illuminated the path better and her gait was steadier as her long legs took her further beyond the runway. Even though Jodi had unsnapped Bounder's leash, he stayed just ahead of her, as if knowing she needed his protection.

As the silent scream gave way to steady deep breaths, she pressed on. She was comforted by the rhythm of her feet slapping the ground — left, right, left, right. Her mind slipped into that familiar zone — she didn't have to think. Just push on.

After two miles, she slackened her pace. She could feel the beginnings of the headache that always accompanied the nightmare. As she became aware of her tense jaw, she took in great gulps of air and stopped to stretch her neck and jaws, hoping she could keep the headache at bay.

As much as she hated the long dark nights of Alaska, she loved the equilibrium she gained when she could be outside, especially in the forest. *God's majestic handiwork.* She was confident out here — she could escape. Escape what, she wasn't real clear about, but her whole body was freed. Indoors, it was as if her body was encased in an invisible shroud that bound her more tightly as the day wore on. The pressure released when she could escape to the outdoors. Although that binding was always there, it was less noticeable.

Jodi turned back toward her apartment, taking an easier pace to allow her body temperature to adjust. She became more aware of the cold and wetness, knowing she would be chilled by the time she reached the other end of the runway. Hopefully Mrs. Barrett would still be asleep so Jodi wouldn't have to explain her early morning traipsing.

Dear Mrs. Barrett—so thoughtful and concerned about Jodi's well-being, but at times it felt intrusive. Jodi hated to lie, but she had no explanation for her seemingly bizarre behavior. At times she holed up in her apartment, rocking for hours and blocking out the world. She couldn't understand why, but at times she simply could not cope with people, so she hid. Other times, the pressure to escape was overwhelming, and she had to be outdoors, like this morning. It used to be enough to just get outdoors, but it was getting harder. And soon the weather and snow would prohibit, and the depression would claim her.

Maybe…maybe I can talk to Dana about it. Maybe I should try some medication again. I can't take this to group, but maybe I could meet with Dana separately. I've got to do something.

Chapter Thirteen
Mothers and Daughters

"HOW'S EVERYONE DOING? Let's do a check-in and see how each of you are feeling right now; what things are on your mind. And as always, just share what you're comfortable with. It's a good place to...let *stuff* out."

After three weeks, Dana could sense that the group was starting to settle in—to feel a bit safer with each other and the boundaries they had agreed to in the beginning. She noticed they were starting to interact before group started, their conversations appearing more personal and encouraging. They were beginning to see they were not alone—that others experienced similar fears and shame.

Raydine was tense—her hands in constant motion, rubbing the sides of her thighs and knees; her shoulders scrunched; her hair in disarray. Dana gave her an inviting nod, recognizing her need to speak.

"I guess I'd like to say something.

"It's been a pretty rough week for me.

"My little girl..." Raydine paused, struggling to keep her gravelly voice in control as her eyes darted from Dana to Annette, her shoulders curling in protectively.

"My little girl...she umm...she went with a guy—in a car." Raydine's tears slipped down the sides of her cheek unchecked as she recounted the terror she experienced the Friday before, not knowing where her daughter was, or if she'd been kidnapped by a guy she'd met on the internet.

Raydine said she had called Doug, and together they drove every road in Juneau, looking for an unknown man in an unknown car who might have taken Cyndi. The police said they would be on the alert, but there wasn't much they could do until she was missing for twenty-four hours, or there was evidence of a crime.

After hours of driving, and making a few stops where Doug surprised a few couples by pointing his flashlight into their parked cars, they returned to the mall.

It was nearly nine o'clock when they made yet another search of the parking lot. As they were going inside for another check, they saw Cyndi coming from the far side of the parking lot toward the front entrance. She was alone.

"I lost it. I screamed at her right there in front of other people. I wish I could have been calmer, but I was so scared — I thought I'd lost my little girl."

"Was she Okay?" asked Hannah.

Raydine nodded. "I guess. She won't tell us anything about what happened. She said she just went riding with some friends, and we're over reacting. But she wouldn't tell us what friends she was with.

"The police couldn't get much from her either, but I think it scared her that we called them."

"Did they find the guy?" asked Ellen.

"No...we don't even know who he is, except that he goes by *Buddy* in his e-mails. The police said they couldn't do anything about it unless he harmed her—and she would have to testify, which she won't."

Ellen asked sternly, "What did you do to her?"

"She's grounded. She can't use the internet unless I'm there to watch her. Or Doug. Doug moved back home—he was staying with a friend 'cuz we've been fighting, but he's home now—to help me with her."

Dana said, "Raydine, that must have been terrifying. I think any mother would lose her cool in such a situation. Yet you didn't fall apart. You got help. You searched for her — alerted the police. You're disciplining her. You're here today...and sharing it with this group." Then she said more slowly, emphasizing Raydine's actions. "How did you get through it? What is it within you that helped you do what you had to do?"

Raydine's eyebrows furrowed as she looked for internal answers. "I don't know...I don't know. Doug was with me. I don't know how I did it. I guess she's my little girl, and I love her. I don't want her to have...I don't want her to be hurt. Like

I was."

Dana let Raydine's words hang in the silence for a moment before she looked intently into her eyes. "There's a strength within you, Raydine, that allowed you to do what you had to do in the moment. Don't under estimate the power of that part of you."

Raydine dropped eye contact—it seemed too much for her to accept Dana's praise. She then nodded and acknowledged the words of encouragement and comfort the other women gave her, appearing relieved when the attention was shifted to Ellen.

"Well, my problems are small compared to what you went through," Ellen nodded toward Raydine. "My daughter is older—in college and on her own, really. But she's so selfish. She only calls when she wants something. And when she finally calls, I go ballistic. I can't get to a real conversation with her, because when she finally does call, I'm so mad that I yell at her, and she gets defensive and shuts down on me."

Ellen began to share with the group, haltingly at first, that after her husband's death, the relationship with her daughter had gone downhill.

"She was always a Daddy's girl, and I never could do anything right in her mind. Since he died, though, she finds even more wrong with me."

Ellen looked up at Dana, pursing her lips and stiffening her posture. "I think she blames his death on me. He died alone in a car accident."

"Blame. Do you blame someone, Ellen?" asked Dana.

Ellen looked away, eyes downcast. "It wasn't my fault.. I wasn't even there—there was nothing I could have done."

Ellen spoke slowly as she was taken back to an earlier time, a time before she was widowed. "His work was very demanding—lots of social obligations. I hated it when he went without me, but in those last years, I hated to go with him. I always felt so...inadequate. He was involved with everyone. They all spoke the same language—investments, margins, holdings. He was interested in everyone but me—he was the main attraction, and I was just a...an appendage."

"Is there something about your not going with him that night that troubles you, Ellen?"

Ellen's eyes teared up, and she softened slightly. When

she spoke, her voice was steady, but softer, as if she didn't have enough breath to speak louder. "I could have gone with him. I could have not fought with him. I could have been kinder. Maybe he wouldn't have…maybe it would have been different."

"But how could you know?" Hannah's voice was surprisingly strong. "Shit happens!" She recoiled as she briefly looked around at the others. "Excuse my language, but it does. You may have been killed too—then where would your daughter be? You can't blame yourself."

Hannah's declaration established certainty, supplanting the question that had stood an instant before.

Ellen seemed to taste that thought a moment before she spoke. "Thank you…all of you. For understanding." Ellen dabbed her nose with a tissue. "It helps. Really. I guess that's why I'm here." She took a deep breath. "To think about things differently."

Chapter Fourteen
Sometimes It's Too Close

DANA THOUGHT ABOUT THE group process as she drove out the road toward home. She was pleased that the ladies were beginning to open up, supporting each other. *Hannah was so quick to defend Ellen!* Dana smiled into the darkness of her car, feeling something like pride for precious sweet Hannah. *She's got grit! She is such a delight!*

And that was a victory for Raydine. She didn't end up in the hospital with her anxiety, or relapse with alcohol when things got scary for her. Hopefully Doug's move home is a good thing. There are going to be more challenges for them if Cyndi keeps going down that road. Lord, please give them wisdom, and protect that little girl.

Her mind turned to Annette. *Annette's too quiet.* Dana unconsciously bit the side of her lip and tilted her head as she assessed Annette's comments and body language. *She's engaged with the group...very attentive to each person as they speak, but she's holding back.* Dana spoke out loud as she shifted her internal conversation to admonishment, "Give her time, Dana." *But don't let her get lost in rescuing others at the expense of herself.*

The group dynamics are good. They're settling in and learning to trust each other and the process. Dana's eyebrows scrunched as she pulled into her driveway. *So why do I feel restless?*

When she walked in the door, she could tell that Hub had dinner on. *Mmm...smells like sourdough bread.*

The rambunctious dogs met Dana in the mudroom, their coats still drying from being outdoors. She rubbed their ears and cooed what good puppies they were, slipped out of her boots, then dropped her tote by her desk. *What a sweetie – Hub started a fire for me. Maybe I'll finish up my bookwork before he comes in.*

As Dana slipped out of her wool socks and cardigan, she thought about how comfortable she and Hub were together. *Comfortable or familiar?* They handed off domestic chores almost seamlessly, whether it was cooking, canning, stacking firewood, or giving the animals their rightful attention. They were busy people, each involved in gratifying careers. *We're both good at what we do — blessed by being able to do what we love. We support each other. So why do I feel so antsy?* Dana's shoulders gave an involuntary shrug, as if shedding something objectionable off her back.

She had just settled at her little desk when Hub came in for dinner. "Do you mind if I work in the shop awhile tonight—after supper? I'd like to finish up on a project or two."

"What are you working on?"

"Oh, just some winter maintenance—thought I'd service your motor before I get the wood tools out for my winter projects." Giving Dana a quick hug, Hub said, "Gotta make sure you can make your getaways when the fish are biting."

"You're so thoughtful, Hub. Thank you! Yeah, that would be great. In fact, it would give me a chance to finish up some paperwork."

"How's your new group going?"

Dana dished up the chowder as she answered. "Good. Really good, actually. We've just finished week four, and all but one of the gals have opened up a bit; some more than others, of course. There's one little gal who tugs at my heart." Without realizing it, Dana's movements slowed; her voice softened. "She's in her early twenties—beautiful Native girl. So vulnerable. I want to wrap her in my arms and make her pain go away."

She glanced briefly at Hub. "Sometimes it hurts so much to think about what they've gone through."

"Is it too much, Dana? Are you getting too close?" Hub's large blue-grey eyes seemed to penetrate to her soul. He knew her so well and what might trigger her doubts, or discourage her.

Dana's eyes watered at his caring. For the briefest moment, she drew toward his tenderness, but the intimacy was too much—he came too close to the raw place. She glanced away, and when she answered Hub, it was her firm competent voice that responded. "Thanks, Hub…but it's just a hazard of the business. Really, I'm okay. What's going on in your world?"

Hub hesitated before he spoke, ignoring her question. "Could you just get some down time, Dana? Get out on the water? Have a massage? Talk about it—if not to me, then someone else?"

"Good idea. And I do meet with my peer group on Friday. I always feel better when we process some of our clients and concerns there."

The group Dana met with once a month involved three other psychotherapists and a Psychiatric Nurse Practitioner who processed difficult cases with each other. They had been together for seven years, ever since Dana launched her private practice. Not only had they become good friends and confidants, they offered accountability and support to each other as professionals. They could speak openly about their feelings of inadequacy, frustration, or internal conflicts and doubts. Dana found she could even speak a little bit about the pain she hid from Hub.

"Damn it, Dana, I don't need the details of your clients. I just want to know *your* details—what's going on with you." His crossed arms and posture revealed the frustration he held at bay. After releasing his breath, his voice was much calmer. "I've been sensing an undercurrent for several days now, but you won't let me in. Is it Alex?"

"No. Maybe. I don't know. Uh…I don't want to dig into it."

Hub's jaws worked up a grimace before his cryptic reply, "All right." He turned toward the sink and washed his hands, stepping into their routine of setting supper on the table.

After a few moments of stiff silence, he asked, "Well…is your dad coming for Thanksgiving? I need to plan a day in Haines—the McCaulley brothers brought their boat in from Yakutat, and want me to take a look at it—to see if they can avoid getting a new engine. I thought I might time the trip to ride the ferry back with your dad if he's coming down."

Dana responded with forced lightness. "That would be good. He would love four uninterrupted hours with his favorite son-in-law. Why don't you call and confirm—I'm sure he'll join us, but we haven't talked specifically about it."

"I'll do that."

They made small talk while they ate, avoiding conversation that might touch on Dana's tension.

After Hub returned to the shop, Dana curled up by the window with Lionel wrapped snuggly around her hip; Nikki and Mica on the floor. There was enough of a moon this evening to see the shadows of trees, and the silvery ripples on the black water.

The wood stove crackled as a log burned through. The quiet intensified Dana's thoughts about the earlier conversation with Hub. *I hate it when I put up The Wall with him. Who knows better than I how that hurts a relationship. He's so solid — so forgiving.*

She thought about calling her dad, longing to hear his reassuring voice. *No, he would sense my funk, and how would I explain it without getting into the truth.*

Dana's eyes watered as her thoughts were drawn to her deepest pain — the secret she still kept from her father. Even though it wasn't a secret with Hub, it was too painful to talk about her shame. They had no children. The one child Dana had, she had given away.

She set her jaw, but the tears defied her resolve. *She's been of legal age for two years — why hasn't she contacted me? Why didn't I keep her? I could have been a mom. Hub would have been such a good dad.*

In the early years, Dana was certain she had made the right choice to give her child up for adoption. She was confident then that an active, mature Christian couple with financial stability and loving wisdom would give her child a *normal* upbringing. That was Dana's greatest concern in those years — normalcy. She wanted her baby to grow up in a normal family with two parents who would nurture her child's dreams and provide her with stability.

Dana absently stroked Lionel as she pictured the little ragamuffin she had been growing up, raised by a young father who drank a lot in the years after her mom disappeared. She learned to be invisible in the evenings, getting lost in books, especially stories about young girls who had whole families. She looked to *Little Women* and the Judy Blume series to provide clues on how to act.

When Dana was nine, her dad quit drinking and rented a house so she could stay in school the full year. Her life became more predictable, but she still felt she had to guess at what was normal.

As she looked at the deepening blackness over Lynn Canal, Dana admitted her greatest fear back then: How could she face Hub—the man she had loved so completely for over five years, then impulsively discarded? If she kept the baby, she couldn't go home. Her child would be a constant reminder of her betrayal and shame. But how could she not return to her beloved Southeast Alaska? It held her roots—her identity. Without it, she feared she would lose herself—simply fade away.

Dana whimpered. *Why couldn't I have just taken the chance? How could I not know that Hub would love me any way — that he would have loved Alex? That there would be no more children?*

Many times over the years since, Dana came close to telling her dad about Alex. It was the only secret she ever kept from him, and it was a twenty-year barrier to their closeness. Dana counted the years of her life as *before* Alex and *after* Alex. Yet she couldn't make herself share that pain with her dad— he lost enough when her mother disappeared. Dana was determined to protect him from further heartache.

As she looked out the window and reflected on the year that capsized her life, she saw clearly that all those reasons were illusory. *I could have kept Alex. I could have learned how to be a mother — other women do.*

As the grief threatened to overwhelm her, Dana contended—*I was so young, and so vulnerable. So confused about who I was. He was such an imposter.* Mario, the man who was the other part of Alex.

Chapter Fifteen
Secrets Begin To Surface

"I WANT TO THANK you girls for, uh, being so open about your lives." Annette's voice shook as she spoke, making eye contact with each of the women in the group. "I apologize for not being more of a part of the discussions. I just didn't think I could add anything to what you've said. But I'm realizing that my holding back is not right, and I'm sorry if I offended anyone."

Raydine was quick to defend Annette. "That's okay — you're just fine. You didn't offend us...well, me, anyway." The other women nodded in agreement. Raydine looked over at Dana, "It's okay if she just talks when she's ready to, isn't it? That's what you said at the beginning, wasn't it?"

Dana smiled at Raydine's fierce defense. "Absolutely. Annette, thank you for what you shared." Dana unconsciously tilted her head as she gently looked into Annette's eyes. "Is there something else you'd like to say, Annette?"

The room was still; all motion ceased. Encouraging faces looked toward Annette, as if to say, *You can do it. I'm here for you.*

The tears trickled down Annette's sweet face as she spoke softly, yet steadily. "I guess my antidepressants are kicking in...finally. I've been down for so long, I don't know where to start. I don't want to seem ungrateful — my husband is a good man. He works really hard and does the best for us that he can. I don't want to say anything bad about him.

"It's just that with three kids, I can never get caught up. If there ever is some free time, I'm so tired that all I can do is sleep. And Jackson is always so angry — we fight all the time when he is home. I understand his anger—I'm not there for him. And the holidays are hard—I used to love to cook and bake, and have people over. But our families aren't around…not that it would make a difference if they were. I'm just dreading another Thanksgiving and Christmas alone.

"I'm sorry—it sounds so minor compared to some of things you all have shared. I need to just *buck up*." Annette sat back in her chair, appearing more relaxed after letting some of her distress spill out.

Jodi's eyes focused on the center of the circle, her slow speech hinting of her Midwest origins. "It seems to me that whatever it is that gets you down is important—it doesn't matter how it compares to anyone else. My situation is nothing compared to women in China, but it's pretty hard for me to buck up at times. The winters get pretty long and dark for me, and the depression is hard to ignore."

Dana hesitated before she asked, "What is that all about…any of you—just *buck up*. We hear that a lot, don't we—just *buck up*! Or move on. Get over it. Or we tell ourselves that's what we need to do. What is the message in those words?"

Hannah spoke initially. "That we're wimps—our worries aren't important. That we should be stronger. Others have it worse than we do. We just have to ignore the stuff that's bothering us. But I don't think that's right for Annette. She…you have three children! You deserve some help."

"Are you wimps?" Dana spoke to the group in general, and looked around at each face. "It seems to me that it takes a lot of courage to do what you are doing—to open up old wounds; to survive in spite of the difficulties in your lives; to keep on doing what must be done even when you're exhausted. Or afraid. Or without protection from the people who should have protected you.

"It takes a lot of courage to come here and dig into some of the *stuff* that has been controlling your lives. I can't imagine what it would be like to have three kids relying on me even when I don't feel up to it. Or the worry of a teenager who is out *somewhere* with a stranger. Sometimes, it's hard to navigate life when stormy seas threaten. It takes courage to face into the storm."

There was no response initially, as the women seemed to

consider the concept of courage.

Hannah leaned into her shoulder with her arm across her front, as if it sheltered her as she spoke. "I tried to keep my little brother from being beaten...I guess that took courage. I thought I was protecting him, but he's messed up anyway. He got into drugs too. I didn't keep him from it."

"How old were you, Hannah?"

"It started when I was five. I changed his diapers, fed him, watched over him. Got him to school...I taught him to fight back when the bullies took his things. Until the State took us. I was thirteen then."

Hannah's initial fierceness turned to angst, her voice almost a whisper. "I tried to keep us together, but they wouldn't let us."

"Can you see what a vulnerable...little...girl you were, Hannah? How you were trying to fill the shoes of an adult, but you were just a little girl. You did what you could — very courageously...but you needed protection and help for yourself. For him and for you."

Hannah nodded, pulling into herself, slouching back into the chair, eyes downcast. "Yeah."

"Hannah, what are you feeling right now? What are you noticing in your body?"

"It's really heavy — here." Her fingers patted the center of her chest.

"Okay. Take some deep breaths as you notice what you're experiencing."

After a minute, Dana asked, "Is there a particular image, or memory, that comes to mind with that feeling, Hannah?"

Hannah continued to look down, breathing deeply. Finally, she responded in a monotone, "There were no diapers. Shane pooped on the couch and there were no diapers. It got on Grandmother's afghan. He kept squirming — he wouldn't hold still. He made it worse, and I couldn't hold him and clean up the mess. Poop was everywhere. I didn't want to get in trouble, but I didn't know how to fix it before Grandmother got home." Hannah's tears slipped out the corner of her eyes, even though her face showed no emotion.

"You were so little, Hannah — doing a big person's job. What helped you do that? How did Little Hannah get through such a mess?"

Hannah's head and downcast eyes snapped up, looking directly at Dana. Her face suggested astonishment as she seemed to ponder the answer to the question. It was a moment before she spoke. "I guess I just did what I could. I cleaned what I could. I put Shane in some pants without a diaper and stayed outside until Grandmother came home.

Hannah's face softened, her mouth revealing a slight grin. "She wasn't mad or anything. She just went about taking care of it—I don't even remember how. It was okay, though. I just felt...helpless. Because I didn't know how to handle it.

"But I was just a little girl, wasn't I?" Hannah's eyes brightened some as she glanced at the other women before setting firmly back in her chair.

Jodi cocked her head at Hannah, chuckling, "You deserved more than kudos for handling that one, Girl!"

Dana added, "Jodi's right. Hannah, that could have been overwhelming for an adult, much less a little girl."

The silence in the room returned momentarily. Then Raydine took a deep breath before she spoke quietly. "I wish I would have had the courage to tell." She peeked over the corner of her glasses at Dana. Her gravelly voice took on more volume. "I didn't tell. What my father was doing to me. I was too afraid I'd get in trouble. Even when the school counselor asked me if anything was wrong, I didn't say anything. I guess I was afraid no one would believe me.

"I tried to tell Mom once, but she got angry at me." Raydine's shoulder shrugged, as if to say so that's it.

Dana's kind face softened her penetrating look. "So what kept you from going under, Raydine? How did you survive in spite of what was happening to you?"

Raydine's eyes circled downward as if searching for an answer. Her shoulders twisted as she shrugged."I don't know. I don't know."

Dana nudged. "But you must have done something. You didn't disintegrate. You grew up. You finished school. You married. You held a job that required a lot of skill. You're managing a household. You're raising a little girl. In spite of some very rough spots, you're thriving."

"I did. I am." Raydine's voice was uncertain. She shifted in her chair. "Not very well most of the time, but you're right—I didn't give up. I couldn't do that. Most of the time, I believe that—it's not okay to give up." Raydine sat a bit straighter.

Dana nodded at Raydine with a faint smile. "That's a big part of who you are, isn't it? You're not a quitter. Somehow, you figure out how to keep going."

Raydine gave a ragged nod and sat back in her chair.

"Could I say something else?" Annette's hesitant voice drew all eyes to her, as well as an encouraging nod from Dana. "There was something else that helped me. My aunt Celia. She was my mom's oldest sister. She never married or had kids of her own, but she would come get me in the summer for a few weeks, or sometimes when my mom was...out of control. I got to go stay with her by myself sometimes—the bigger kids didn't come. She doted on me—read to me. She listened to me! She made me feel important. Loved."

Annette struggled to control her emotions. "I wanted to live with her, but my mom didn't like her. She was jealous, I think, because her sister was better off. She wasn't...chaotic...like my mom. Anyway, Auntie Celia would...I can still hear her words... *You're not like them, Chicky. You're precious; smart. God loves you just as you are. You need to leave them to the Lord, Annie—you just be the best you can be.*"

Her chin shook as she tried to continue. "It's hard for me to believe that, but somewhere in the back of my brain, I think I knew I could make different choices than my family. And I did graduate from high school—a first for my family." She chuckled as she looked up at Dana, then around to the other women. "I had no choice with that. I lived with my aunt the last two years of high school, and she wouldn't let me *not* graduate."

Dana's slight smile and thoughtful eyes held the silence as each woman seemed to be absorbed in her own thoughts. Finally, she said, "Empathy. What we're talking about is empathy for ourselves, aren't we?

"When we're children, or even vulnerable adults, we don't have the ability to think things through; nor the power to make things happen. And especially, we do not know how things will work out—we're making choices based on limited information, and limited ability, at the time.

"Don't we sometimes judge ourselves harshly when we look back on the situations — applying our more mature perspective and hindsight? You may have noticed the quote on the wall over there — it's a quote from Soren Kierkegaard — *Life can only be understood backwards; but it must be lived forwards.*

"How harshly are you judging yourself?

"What advice would you give to your daughter or niece or the neighbor girl who sought you out for advice?" Dana's rhythmic voice settled the question as a statement.

Dana gauged how the energy in the room seemed to be spent — the tension of approaching the edge of deeper wounds released. After a moment, she quietly suggested each woman write out what advice they would give to a little girl facing a big dilemma like they had, and then commit to reading that advice a few times during the week. "Think about that advice — coming from the Mature You to the Little One that you were."

She ended the session by leading a deep breathing exercise, guiding their awareness of any residual tension in their bodies, and releasing it with each out-breath.

***

Annette was sitting in her car waiting for her windshield to clear as Raydine came out the door of the counseling office. She watched as Raydine looked around for her ride. On the spur of the moment, Annette decided to invite her for Thanksgiving dinner. She leaned out the car door, "Do you want to wait in my car?" she called to Raydine.

"Oh, he'll be here any minute. Thanks, though."

"Well...I was just thinking..." Annette got out of the car and approached Raydine at the bottom of the steps. "I was just thinking...do you think you and your family might come join us for Thanksgiving dinner? It's just my boys...and Jackson. We're not real fancy, but I thought it might be nice...if you don't have other plans...we'd love to have you over. Our husbands might find something in common. But if you don't want to, I understand — you really don't know me very well."

"That's so nice of you. Thanks. I don't know — maybe. Doug's kind of funny about going places, but I'll talk to him.

There he is now. Can I let you know next week?"

"That would be fine. And no pressure, really. I understand if it doesn't work out, or you have other plans."

Raydine had mixed feelings as she slid in the seat next to Doug. She liked Annette and thought she would like to spend some time with her. *But what if I have a panic attack? What if I have to leave in the middle of dinner and make a big scene?*

"What's happening'?" Doug interrupted Raydine's internal dialogue.

"Oh, I was just thinking. That girl in that blue SUV? She asked us over to their house for Thanksgiving dinner. She's really nice — I like her."

"What's her man like?"

"I don't know. They've got three boys. I think they're all younger than Cyndi, but I don't think they have any family. It might be nice to go for a few hours. I could take my Xanax just before we go, and if we just stayed for a little while, it might be okay."

"Hmm, maybe. I don't wanta get stuck with no stuffed shirt trying to figure out what to say."

"I could bake some pies…like your favorite — sour cream huckleberry. It might be good to get Cyndi out of the apartment and away from the Internet for a while."

They drove in silence for awhile before Doug spoke quietly. "That's a pretty big step for you, ain't it? Might be good, though. I could probably do that."

Chapter Sixteen
Unbearable Truth

"AND I'LL NEED YOUR budget priorities in the new format by the end of the week. I know it's hard to project five years out, but that's the way they've got to have it. Thanks, Bert, for your early draft. Will you be able to estimate the costs on that last contract? Jodi...Jodi?"

Jodi jerked slightly as her eyes and attention returned to her boss. She realized she had zoned out again while in the budget meeting, and all eyes were on her. She could feel the heat in her face and neck as she flushed in embarrassment. *What was he saying? Oh God, help me cover.* "Um, I'm sorry, Cliff. My mind wandered a bit. Could you repeat that?"

Cliff hid his irritation from the group well, but Jodi could read the set of his jaw and knew he was getting tired of her inattention. He had mentioned recently that she seemed to be preoccupied, and asked if there was anything he could do to help. She had apologized, attributing it to her headaches and promised she would see a doctor.

But Jodi feared she was losing it. She was exhausted all the time, and it was getting harder to concentrate. The nightmares had increased again, and she seldom got to sleep more than an hour or two each night. Knowing that the nightmares would come, she dreaded going to sleep, but then the tiredness took over and soon she would tumble back into the hot barn, hearing the footsteps; remembering the unendurable pain.

Remembering. Surely it wasn't remembering. It was remembering the dream — not the reality. It didn't really happen. Did it? I must be losing my mind. I've got to get on top of this.

Jodi stumbled through an apology to Cliff and her peers

at the meeting, joking that her *game was off*. She joked that Magnum PI reruns kept her up at night, but she felt humiliated. *I've got to get some sleep. I can't even concentrate on a stupid budget process. I can't lose my job.*

Jodi did follow up with her doctor, who increased her antidepressant medication and prescribed a sleeping aid. She asked if Jodi was seeing a counselor, and thought it would probably help her if she would.

Probably, thought Jodi wryly. She knew she needed therapy — *or an insane asylum*. More and more, she wished she would get hit by a big truck, or die in her sleep.

She was exhausted all the time — losing confidence in herself. Increasingly, she couldn't tell if something had really happened or if she just imagined it. At work, she had learned to approach dialogue tentatively — look for clues from others about context and just hope that her responses made sense.

The therapy group was good, and she liked meeting with the other women, but she couldn't tell them about the nightmares. She didn't want to burden them with her dreams, for crying out loud. *It was just a nightmare — a recurring nightmare. Their problems were real.*

A few days later, she was able to see Dana for an individual therapy session. She told Dana about the recurring nightmare, her exhaustion, and how she feared losing her mind, not to mention her job if she didn't get her focus back.

Dana looked at Jodi with those dark eyes that said so much — *I'm here for you; I understand; I can hear it, Jodi; I care about you.*

Dana spoke cautiously. "Jodi, what if your nightmare is real. Or at least some aspect of it?"

Jodi couldn't speak for a moment. Her heart was beating wildly, and her mouth had gone cotton dry. When she answered, her words were halting and her voice was all but a whisper. "I don't know how that could be. I would know if it was true. How could I forget something so horrendous if it was…real?"

And yet Jodi knew she had often asked herself that very same question — *What if it was true? What if I'm a Sybil and have just blocked out some horrible terror…or terrors? What if I'm not really who I think I am; or I've got an identity exposing myself in ways that I don't recall? There are so many blanks in my memory.*

More and more, I can't tell what is real and what is imagined. It's too much. I…

"Jodi, what are you experiencing right now—in your body? Can you feel your feet?"

It took a minute for Jodi to shift her attention to her body, and become aware that, in fact, she could not feel her feet or legs. Her stomach was trembling and her shoulder muscles were seared with pain. Her wrists were so weak, she couldn't lift her hands. She didn't have the strength to sit up straight, and felt like her head had morphed into a huge heavy distorted ball. She simply looked at Dana, unable to respond.

Dana spoke firmly. "Jodi, I want you to take some slow deep breaths with me right now. Inhale. One-two-three-four; hold for two counts; and exhale one-two-three-four-five-six. Count in your mind with me, and concentrate on your breathing."

Dana's breathing was exaggerated, compelling Jodi to mimic her, drawing her attention back to the present. Dana's steady voice matched the intensity of her gaze into Jodi's eyes.

After several minutes of breathing, Jodi felt herself drawn back to the present, as if coming from a place outside her body. She began to feel the coolness in the room, the breath in her lungs, the tingling all over her skin. Finally, she said, "I can feel them now…my feet."

"Good. Just keep breathing, and let yourself be grounded. You might shuffle your feet a bit."

As Dana continued to talk soothingly, Jodi became more aware of her body and how terribly tired she was. She slumped back into the chair, staring at Dana. Her mind was foggy, her thoughts calmer, but disjointed, as if they were travelling blindly through a cloudy tunnel with no exit in sight.

Dana's voice was nurturing, as if reassuring a child. "Jodi, I think you've been through quite a lot just now. I'm not sure what all you're thinking, but it's apparent that it was pretty tough. I want you to relax for awhile, then we can talk some more. I want you to know that you are okay, and we'll figure this stuff out, a little bit at a time."

Dana reached for a bottle of water and gave it Jodi. "Will you be okay here if I step out for a minute to rearrange my schedule? I want to allow some more time with you for right now."

Jodi nodded. "I'm okay."

Dana could see that Jodi was not okay—her eyes held the look of a frightened wounded doe. Dana quickly cancelled her last appointment and locked the office front door so they would not be disturbed.

As Dana sat with Jodi, giving comfort and reassurance, Jodi considered the possibility that her recurring nightmare might be based in fact. Her memories were foggy, but images flashed in her mind of gatherings at her aunt's farm. Aunt Darlene was such a dear lady, always fussing over Jodi and her sister, making their favorite dishes, and showing her sister how to quilt or make craft projects.

Jodi was never drawn to the domestic routines, but preferred to be outside. And her aunt's farm held great allure for a little girl with all the animals to be fed and loved on. She was much more comfortable with a shovel in her hand than a sewing needle.

Aunt Darlene seldom worked outside, other than the small garden patch at the back door. It was Uncle Howard who took Jodi all around the farm, letting her feed the lambs and chickens, and hose out the pigs' pen.

Jodi spoke softly—brokenly—as her eyes studied the scenes of her mind. "I remember. He let me drive his tractor. I was scared that I would brake too hard and tumble him off the back of the trailer. He fed the cattle off the back of a flatbed, and would holler at me to move forward as he pitched the hay. I could barely reach the pedals."

"Jodi, what are you feeling as you recall those memories?" asked Dana. "What are you aware of in your body right now?"

"I liked to work on the farm. I liked the animals." Jodi's face contorted in anguish, as her shoulders folded inward, and she sobbed.

After several minutes, Jodi sighed deeply, feeling so weak, she didn't think she could move. She became aware of the quiet room and was so thankful for Dana's presence. "I remember so little of my childhood. I can't remember if there was a barn—there had to have been a barn. Or a shop, but I can't remember. Why can't I remember that?"

"If it's important, you will. You have a wonderful mind,

Jodi, that's allowed you to cope and be successful in many ways. But sometimes our minds protect us from hurtful memories by blocking them — when it's overwhelming for us at the time or a stage of development. But the memories are there in your brain, and when it's important, you will have clarity about them.

"But it doesn't have to be all at once. You can remember bits at a time. And I think you've been through a lot for today. Do you think you can put this *stuff* in a mental container for safe keeping so that you can get some sleep tonight? And when we meet again — hopefully tomorrow, we'll take a look at a small piece of it."

With Jodi's assent, Dana led her in a visual exercise, imagining a container that would hold all the distressing thoughts for safe keeping.

Dana spoke with Jodi for awhile, assessing her stability and exploring support options. They made contingency plans for the possibility that Jodi might be overwhelmed if new memories surfaced. Jodi agreed to take her sleeping aid and to call Dana when she got home and when she woke up. Jodi thought she could take the next day off from work. When she left Dana's office, the *professional, self-assured* side of Jodi convinced Dana that she could get home safely.

***

Dana's gut churned as she drove home, thinking about Jodi. She argued with herself about releasing Jodi to go home alone, versus having her admitted to the hospital for observation. *She denies thoughts of suicide, but what if there is a part of her that is suicidal? But she would be so humiliated to be pressured into the hospital. And what might that mean to her professionally — I know she would resist…Dana, stop it. She was coherent, logical; she made plans to love on her dog and call you. She's going to call her sister tomorrow.*

Dear God, please protect her. It was the right decision. Dana, you can't control everything.

Chapter Seventeen
Castaway

THE SNOW FELL SOFTLY as some of the group members fixed tea and hot chocolate. Jodi had mentioned that a chorale group would be singing Christmas carols in a few weeks at the State House. "I went to hear them last year, and it was pretty special. There's some surprising talent here in Juneau."

"Oh I'd like to go—if I'm here," said Ellen. "I always enjoy the arts. We might go to Hawaii for the holidays, though. How was your Thanksgiving, by the way?"

"Really nice. My church has a gathering for Thanksgiving, sort of a potluck, then we hang out and play games. They're like family to me—they are my family here."

Hannah arrived, letting in the cold and a few snow flurries, at the same time Dana entered the group room.

"Sorry I'm late," Hannah said quietly as she unwrapped her scarf and hung her coat on the rack.

"That's all right, Hannah," Dana said as refilled her ever-present giant mug of tea. After they settled in their accustomed chairs, she asked, "So. How is everybody doing?" Dana's smile welcomed the group as she looked at each person, seeming to assess who was eager to speak, who might be hurting, or who might need to be drawn out. She could see that Hannah was troubled—she avoided eye contact; her shoulders scrunched as she moved stiffly.

Raydine seemed like a little girl with a secret bursting to get out. "I'll start. I got to go to Annette and Jackson's for Thanksgiving. And meet their boys. I had such a good time—I mean, we did...my family. Cyndi didn't want to leave, she was having so much fun playing with the little kids."

Annette interjected, "They sure like her. She's like the

Pied Piper—my boys would follow her anywhere. Raydine, she would be a great teacher. We all had a good time, and hope we can do it again soon."

"Wouldn't that be something? My little girl a teacher!" Raydine's face glowed, clearly pleased at the connection with Annette, and thoughtful about the possibilities for Cyndi. "What if...what if Cyndi could work with kids and forget about that Buddy! Oh I do hope so."

As the group settled in, sharing a few events over the holiday, Hannah sat quietly, her eyes darting occasionally at whoever was speaking. "You look like you could use a friend, Hannah." Jodi, sitting next to Hannah, spoke softly, but all ears were attuned, as if every woman's radar had picked up on a sister in pain.

Hannah's chin trembled as she nodded, and tears began to spill out. The quiet seemed to count the heart beats as the group waited, willing Hannah to feel their caring. Ellen reached for the tissue box and passed it quietly.

Dana said, "Take your time, Hannah. We're here for you."

Finally, Hannah lifted her head and looked at Dana, her resolve showing with the intake of breath and set of her jaw. "Richard kicked me out on Thanksgiving day." Her voice quavered, but she continued. "He said he was tired of my moods—that I hold him back. He doesn't like to be around me." Hannah raised her hands to her face, a soft wail coming from deep inside.

"He's a piece of shit, Hannah...and a liar," Raydine exclaimed, her face showing outrage. She looked defiantly around the group, then back at Hannah. "I'm sorry, but he is. You're worth everything, Hannah. You're so beautiful. You can come live with me."

Hannah showed a fleeting smile as she acknowledged Raydine's kindness. "Thanks. I've got a place to stay for now. My old boyfriend's brother said I could sack out on his couch 'til things settle. Sometimes Richard apologizes once he's had time to think...but it's been five days, and he won't answer my calls."

Dana gently probed. "Hannah, what exactly happened?"

"Well, I was planning to fix Thanksgiving dinner—I just had to work four hours in the morning to make sure Mr. O was set up for the weekend, then make a few more stops. Richard was pissed because I had to leave. He wanted me to stay home with him, but I couldn't. I can't afford to miss any more hours. When I came back, I drove by the Drop Inn, and his truck was there, so I went in to join him. He was hanging on a chick at the bar.

"I told her to get her own man, and he got mad at me. I tried to get him to come home, but he said I was too controlling—he was going to find someone who would be good to him. So I went home and cleaned the house. Fixed a turkey breast. But when he didn't come home by six o'clock, I went after him. He was ready to pass out, but he wouldn't come with me. His friend and I tried to get him in my car, but he was too heavy...I lost my balance, and he hit his head on the door...the ledge above the window."

Hannah told the story as if reliving the anxious moments as she tried to handle the situation, her hands grasping and clenching. "He was bleeding from his head...a lot...so we got him into his truck and I drove him to the Emergency Room. By the time he got sewed up, he had sobered up some, and I thought I would take him home, but he wouldn't let me drive. Then we got to Egan Express, and he pushed me out of his truck...in the rain...and drove off." Hannah's tears increased; her words became staccato, "He said he didn't love me—that I interfere with his fun."

"He left you? In that rain? In the dark? What did you do?" Ellen expressed the astonishment the others surely felt.

"I walked down Egan Express until a car stopped. An older couple picked me up. They took me to my friend's house.

"I love him so much. I don't know what to do. He won't talk to me."

"Hannah, are you in a safe place now?"

"Yes. Bonner's a good guy—he's like a big gorilla. He won't even let his brother around me, cuz he knows he was mean to me—my ex. He—my ex—used to hit me, and one time Bonner saw it, and he beat his brother up. I stayed with him for several weeks after that. He's a good guy."

"Hannah, has Richard gotten physical with you? Violent?"

Hannah hesitated, looking away from Dana. Finally, she

looked back up and said, "A little. But only when he's drunk, or if I make him mad. I can generally handle him."

"Hannah, you know that violent behavior escalates, don't you? It doesn't get better on its own. Usually it stops only when the person is compelled to get help—like by the court system—usually because they've hurt someone badly. Someone like you. And Richard is an active alcoholic, so his judgment is impaired. I think it would be a very dangerous situation right now for you to be with him...if he does call.

"I'm wondering if you can take a time-out from him, and do some healing yourself before you get back with him or into any other relationship."

"I don't think he wants me anyway."

Annette squirmed in her chair, her eyebrows furrowed and scrunching mouth exposing her dimple. Finally she said, "I don't know if this is helpful at all, but I used to pick the boyfriends who would tell me those same things—that I wasn't good enough; that I made him mad; that the fighting was my fault. That they would be happy if only I would just be...nicer, smaller, sexier, smarter...just whatever. And I believed it. I kept trying to be what they wanted me to be so they would love me. But I was never good enough. There was always a reason to beat on me, or leave me.

"When I met Jackson, I didn't know how to take him at first. I thought he didn't care about me because he'd leave when we'd have an argument. He never hit me—he'd just get away for awhile and calm down. I found myself sort of goading him, I guess to see if he would hit me. I didn't realize it, but I was testing him...trying to prove that he was like all the others and would leave me. Or abuse me.

"Then when I got pregnant with our oldest, I decided I had to figure this thing out—I didn't want my child going through what I'd gone through. As I look back now, I kick myself for staying with guys who would treat me that way.

"You deserve better, Hannah. You're lovely; and sweet. Nobody deserves that kind of treatment. You deserve a good man."

"Thank you." Hannah's eyes flitted around the group. "All of you." Looking at Annette, she said quietly, "It's hard to believe you had that kind of a boyfriend. You're so *together*."

Annette gave an encouraging smile to Hannah as others reinforced Hannah's value, and her need to leave her boyfriend behind.

Dana took a few minutes to talk to the group in general about the cycle of violence, describing how the basis of the relationship is about control and power versus love and respect. She described the predictability of the relationship dynamics, going from the highs of the *honeymoon* period, to increasing tension because that false behavior can't be sustained over time. Then incidents of violence would begin, often starting with words, then shoving and hitting that often escalates to beatings, choking, and other violence. "Then he might experience shame and regret, make new promises for change, and a new honeymoon period begins with best behavior *for-a-while*.

"Typically, women stay in the relationship because the honeymoon period is such a *high*—it temporarily fulfills a deep need in her. She holds out the hope that if *she* can just get things right, *she'll* be able to maintain that honeymoon period. The reality is, we just don't have that kind of power. We can't fix their moods; their choices; their addictions; their reactions; their self-esteem; their distorted thinking.

"And women very often will stay in an abusive relationship until there is no longer a honeymoon period—it's all tension and violence. Often by then, there are added dependency issues that make her feel trapped, such as children to protect, isolation from friends and family, or economic dependency. And when you're beaten down emotionally, spiritually, physically, it's hard to see your worth or your options.

"Statistics show that of all the women in this country who are murdered, one third are killed by their partners or exes. One third!"

The room was quiet as the women appeared to be thinking about what Dana described. It wasn't breaking news, but she had highlighted how hard it is sometimes to leave a love relationship—even when it's a bad relationship—to face being alone and to have no one.

"Hannah, does this cycle describe part of your relationship?"

Hannah nodded. "A lot, I guess. I mean, he usually calls;

tells me he's sorry; that things will be different. And they are—for awhile. But it seems to go back to where I can't do anything right, or he flirts with other girls."

"What would you like to happen this time? How would you like to approach it differently this time, Hannah?"

"I guess I need to stay away—wait for him to find me. Not be so concerned about who he's with, or what he's doing."

Annette said tentatively, "If he's like most abusive guys, he'll come around when he's in a bind, Hannah. Don't you deserve better than that?"

Hannah shrugged, and looked away—clearly uncomfortable with discussing it further. Her allies on this healing journey understood, and quietly waited for a shift in focus. The silence ended with Raydine's offer for a place to stay.

Ellen spoke haltingly at first. "Well, my boyfriend isn't...abusive—he's just...irresponsible when it comes to...responsibility! He won't take a budget seriously, and I'll be darned if I'm going to bail him out." Her voice revved up as she warmed to the topic. "I won't risk my credit rating by hooking up with his, but he doesn't seem to be doing anything about it. I don't know why I don't just walk away from him. I mean, if he hasn't got it together in three years, it's not likely he will in the next three. I've got to let him go!

"But it's my daughter that's my biggest problem—still. She—Rachel—decided to go to her boyfriend's family in Utah for Christmas. He's not even that serious of a boyfriend...I don't think, anyway, and yet I'm her mom, and she won't come here for the holidays. She wouldn't let me visit her for her birthday in September either—it's been almost a year since I've seen her."

Ellen's jaw tightened, and her voice became strained. "She's so angry, and I don't know how to reach her."

"It's got to be a really tough spot in your relationship, Ellen...but is it possibly a stage? Didn't you say she was twenty? You know, we never stay in the same place in a relationship. Don't you think it will unfold over time—as she matures and you interact with her as an adult woman instead of...your child? I'm thinking you'll learn new ways of relating that will change your relationship." Dana's gentle voice was reassuring.

"I hope so." Ellen's words began to tumble out, as if pressured to leave her mouth. "Sometimes I just want to forget I'm a mother, and get lost in New York—someplace where I can decorate houses and make other people happy. I'd even leave Mark behind."

She looked around at the others as if checking to confirm that she actually spoke out loud.

After a brief pause, Dana said gently, "It sounds like you have a dream sandwiched in there between the frustration and the fears."

"I do, Dana. I know I'm good at decorating—I'd love to be where I could do just that for a living—for other people, and not have to worry about...other things."

"What keeps you from it, Ellen? Why Juneau...so far from a more cosmopolitan atmosphere?"

Ellen was thoughtful for a moment before responding. "Fear. I'm afraid to be alone. I moved here because of Mark, but I was too afraid to marry him. And now I know I don't want to marry him, but I'm too afraid to let him go."

Hannah said quietly, "I guess that's where I'm at too."

Ellen slowly nodded at Hannah, silently communicating their common dilemma.

Dana suggested, "Ellen, have you thought about exploring your feelings about all this in a creative way, like making a collage or using some artistic medium, such as clay? Very often we find our best solutions when tapping into the creative part of our brains."

The idea struck a chord with Ellen. "I used to do that—as a kid, I didn't journal like my friends, but I would get lost in sculpting or paints. I've not done that since I was a teenager. I just might do that! Thanks. I'm going to. Hey! I just made a decision!"

After the laughter faded into silence, Raydine's eyes darted around to the other women, finally settling on Dana. "Um, I think I need to say something. There's something I've been hiding, and I just feel I need to say it out loud."

The atmosphere instantly changed, each woman looking at Raydine with anticipation.

"My little girl is doing okay—mostly. She seems more interested in school and music and stuff now, but that Buddy,

the Internet guy, hasn't gone away. I've been checking
Cyndi's e-mail—she's restricted from My Space and can only
use the computer when we're there. I'm actually learning a lot
about the Internet, with Doug's help.

"Anyway, I intercepted an e-mail from Buddy a few
weeks ago." Raydine scrunched one shoulder as she looked at
the others coyly. "I pretended I was Cyndi, and told him I had
a new account—one Cyndi doesn't know about. I thought I
could learn more about him, you know?"

Raydine looked up at the group. "I don't trust him! I'm
afraid she might contact him again—she's not totally over him
yet.

"So, I thought maybe I could get the dope on him, and
turn him over to the police. He's a scumbag! His innuendos
make my skin crawl. But I've gotta keep at it until I know who
he is, and can get some proof. It's really hard. That's all. I just
thought I should say that."

Ellen's voice was urgent, "Isn't that something for the
police to do, Raydine? Isn't that a police matter?"

"I talked to them, but they said they needed more
evidence that something illegal happened. They said I should
just block his messages. But he must know where she goes to
school, and maybe even where we live. I guess since she won't
cooperate with the police, they're not as interested as they
might be. So, for now, I'm pretending to be my little girl."

"Wow, Raydine—that's quite an undertaking." Dana
searched for the right words to express her concern. "You are
a she-bear, Raydine, determined to protect her cub! I don't
know what I'd do in your shoes.

"It sounds very risky to me, though. What if he turns out
to be underage, and the table gets turned, and you end up
being accused of inappropriate, or illegal activity?"

"Ooh. I hadn't thought of that. But I'll be careful. I
wouldn't proposition him, or anything. I just want to see who
he is, and see him in jail if he's an adult."

Hannah was nonplussed. "You'd actually see him face to
face?"

"Well, I was just hopin' I could see him without him
seeing me. That way I might be able to get information about
him. I'll be careful. I tell Doug everything, and I wouldn't do
anything without him. He knows what I'm doing."

***

Dana thought about Ellen as she drove out the road, recognizing a tinge of resentment toward her. She'd give anything to struggle with the problem that Ellen has — it would mean she at least had a child. *That would be so hard, though — to raise a child and then be rejected by her at the time an adult relationship should be unfolding. Alex would be — is — the same age as Ellen's daughter. I could be in the same place as Ellen.*

Dana's thoughts drifted off to what she might say to Alex if she was in Ellen's situation. She day-dreamed about how she would gently guide her, and deal lovingly with the tension between boyfriend and family expectations. She imagined scenes of connecting by phone and visiting on campus; their reassurances of commitment to each other, and their plans for her return at semester's end.

She shook herself mentally as she realized the tangent she had taken in her mind. *Will she ever forgive me? Will I ever find her?*

Did Ellen say her daughter's birthday was in September? Alex's birthday is in September. They really are close in age.

Chapter Eighteen
Temporary Disconnect

"LADIES, THIS WILL BE our last group this year. It'll be two weeks before we reconvene—Tuesday after New Year's Day. As we do *check-ins*, why don't you share a little bit about what you have planned these next few weeks, and what might be challenging for you. Who wants to start?"

"I will." Ellen sat straight with her hands clenched in her lap. Her voice and the set of her jaw reflected that something was different with her today. "I made a decision!" She glanced around at the others, encouraging their laughter by repeating herself. "I made a decision! I am going to Minneapolis for the holidays and spend time with my best friend. No boyfriend. No daughter. I'm not even going to worry about them. I'm just going by myself.

"I ended up getting out my water colors because I had them on-hand, and it was surprising what came out on the paper." She looked at Jodi and nodded toward her. "You inspire me. You just get on those little planes and tromp around the woods by yourself with all kinds danger—real danger, not just the kind I worry about. My fears are just in my head. I worry about what people think I look like; or if I'll pick up some rare incurable virus through the air vents; or if a terrorist will be on the same plane; if the window will explode and I'll be sucked out at thirty thousand feet.

"I know it's unreasonable, but the thoughts are constant in my head. So…the picture I painted was of me in an airplane above the clouds, and all those worries were scattered out among the clouds below, but I put mesh walls around each one.

"It's silly, I know, but it helped me to have some resolve.

And, I'm going to get on that plane Thursday morning…by myself, and spend two weeks with a dear dear friend."

There were lots of accolades from the group, each knowing what a step forward this was for Ellen.

Dana said, "That's great, Ellen. It sounds like you have a solid decision, plus a plan. Is there something else that helped you overcome your apprehension?"

Ellen paused before responding. "My daughter doesn't want to be with me; and I don't want to spend the holidays waiting hand and foot on my boyfriend—making his life easier while I do all the work. I did that for twenty-three years with Steven, and I can see it happening all over again with Mark—me slipping into that same old rut."

Dana looked at Ellen, cocking her head to the side with that searching look in her eyes. "There's something more, Ellen, isn't there? Isn't there something within you that shifted? That gave you this determination?"

Ellen looked straight ahead, clearly considering what Dana was asking. When she responded, each undulating sentence joined to the next. "I'm fifty-two years old. I've lived my life in fear…fear of not pleasing others. I constantly worry about what everybody else wants or thinks. I'm weary of that. I want to be free of that."

"And what are some of those wants, Ellen…what might be just one of those dreams you have held in the back of your mind?"

Ellen held Dana's gaze, shifting her body slightly so that she sat a little taller. "Well…I've always loved to decorate. I've mentioned that before. I've been told I have a good eye for color and design. And I have a lot of repeat customers who ask me about displaying their purchases. When I lived in Washington, several of my friends had me help them redesign rooms. I get pretty excited with a project—it takes over my whole being. And that's when I feel the most alive."

Ellen looked down, as if garnering the courage to go on. Without looking up at first, she said, "I'm probably too old. But I'd like to go to school, or take some classes. I've read everything I could get my hands on, and gone to home decorating demonstrations when I could…" Ellen's face showed her excitement as she finally shared her dream and looked up to see the encouraging faces of the others.

"But it would be such a dream to be around people who decorate professionally—to learn from the people that get to do this for a living."

Hannah was firm in asserting, "You're not too old—you're still a chick. Your boyfriend doesn't hang around for nothing."

Dana smiled as she thought, *Hannah is so quick to see the possibilities and strengths in others, yet she is so blinded to her own.*

Annette inserted, "You can come practice on my place. I'd love to have your talent."

"Mine too." Raydine sat back, then added another thought. "And Ellen, you always dress like a professional...you're so coordinated and beautiful. You could go to the White House and impress them with your abilities."

Ellen was unaccustomed to such praise, and began to discount it. "Well, at least I've managed to fool some of the people some of the time. But thank you. I don't know that I can live up to your kind words, but it feels good to think about it. If I can just get over my fears and learn to make decisions...important ones. About my personal life. I will feel like I've arrived."

When there was a pause in the discussion, Jodi said, "You know, there are a lot of universities that allow credit for non-traditional learning, and you can get through their programs a lot faster than traditional colleges. Sometimes they require testing. Sometimes they have you do a paper on how you learned what you already know. Sometimes they ask for a portfolio of your work. It seems like you already have a lot of knowledge and maybe it wouldn't be such a long time before you could get the credentials you want. And being fifty-two has a lot of advantages over being twenty-five—you have a lot of experience to draw from."

Ellen nodded, her eyes widening as if it was a lot to take in.

Dana observed, "It seems to me that you have made a big decision, Ellen—going to your friend's for Christmas, and that's a first step. And you've shared a dream that appears to be fairly well developed. You've gotten a lot of feedback here that says it's an achievable goal. Perhaps there is still some fear and unknowns, but what if you allow yourself the freedom to *explore* that dream...make some contacts; get some college brochures; talk to some professionals; talk to your friend about your dreams while you're in Minneapolis these next few weeks."

"I will. I will do that. Hey...another decision!"

"What will be challenging for you these next few weeks, Ellen?"

"Oh, I guess not stewing over what my boyfriend is doing; whether he'll forget about me while I'm *outta sight outta mind*. But really, I don't know if I'm that serious about him anyway. If I did do something far out, like going to school, I wouldn't want him tagging along."

"What is it that you normally do when you are *stewing* about him?"

"If he doesn't call me, or I don't know where he is, I call him...incessantly. I get so upset, I say things I wish I could take back. My stomach churning goes into overdrive and I can't enjoy whatever it is I'm doing. I'm a mess, huh?"

Dana's big brown eyes softened as she gently shook her head, "Ellen, you are not a mess. You are a very bright, capable, beautiful woman with wonderful dreams of using the talents God gave you.

"It's difficult for any of us to move into uncharted territory. And that's what you're doing...you're going against what is *familiar* to you; how you *know* to respond. It's very courageous of you to take these steps. And if you don't do it perfectly, that's okay. Give yourself credit.

"And remember, it's not only habit and fears you're overcoming, there's also a physical component to compulsions and anxiety. All of us need to remember to take care of ourselves—finding *calm* several times a day; being aware of our bodies; releasing the tension. Exercise. Good sleep and nutrition. And sometimes medication is helpful, at least temporarily. "

"I know. I need to get back to my workouts. I just don't like medication. I'll think about it...see how I do these few weeks."

The momentary silence signaled the invitation for the next person to share. Raydine's voice was just above a whisper. "I wish I could say something as positive as Ellen has. I'm happy for you, Ellen, but the holidays are always hard for me—Christmas especially. Lots of memories. As a kid, there was so much excitement…about the presents and decorations and stuff, but it always ended up with a lot of fighting and drinking. And other stuff. And now, I don't even want to be around my parents…my mom and her husband, that is — the creep that stole my childhood from me." Raydine's shoulders drooped, her eyes watered.

"My mom has already left a message wanting us to come for Christmas. I want my little girl to know her grandmother, but I don't think I can go out there — to be around The Creep. I can't pretend anymore that it's okay. And my sister and her family will be there — I want to see them, but she even thinks I should just *get over* it. I can't. I hate him so much."

Ever so gently, Dana probed, "Do you have any other choices to see your family without him?"

"Not really. My mom thinks it's up to me to forgive. I'm the outcast. I'm the one that always messes up. My brother is the hero Coast Guard guy; my sister is *Mrs. Homemaker*, and then there's Raydine, whose a drunk and a loser."

Hannah nearly shouted, "You're not a loser! Just because a person has some problems doesn't mean they're not important. And you're cool! I'd love to be your daughter, even though you're not old enough to be my mom. I think Cyndi is lucky to have you for a mom — you're so caring. And you pay attention to what she's doing."

Raydine's voice quivered. "Thank you. That's the nicest thing anyone has ever said to me."

Jodi said, "It sounds to me like your family might not be the best judge of your character. I'd take their opinions for what they're worth."

Dana let the comments stand for a moment. She took a closer look at Raydine's appearance. She held her coat in front of her, as if hiding behind it. Her hair was combed, but in need of attention. "Raydine, what are the chances you might relapse over the holidays? Have you had thoughts of drinking; or hurting yourself?"

Raydine looked up at Dana slowly. "Yeah. Yeah, I have. Not hurting myself so much — it helps to have Doug home. But I did get a couple six-packs after my mom called, and that's almost gone. And I want more — just to forget about them and their pressure to act like nothing's wrong. But I know I can't give in to it — I won't let it go that far."

"It sounds like you've already taken that first step down a slippery slope, Raydine. Can you think about how hard it has been to get this far? How difficult it was in those early weeks to get sober?"

"Yeah, I remember. It just feels like nothing's changed. It's just the same. I'm just the same."

"Really? Friends, can we hold up a mirror for Raydine? I see a lot of change over these last several months."

Ellen said, "You handled that scare with your daughter very wisely, Raydine. I wish I had your courage—I would have gone to pieces while Steven figured out what to do about it. And I certainly would not be masquerading as your daughter on-line. You're very brave—even if I question your wisdom at taking on such a dangerous thing."

Hannah pointed at Raydine, pounding her words with her finger, "You-have-stayed-sober for all these months! That all by itself is huge! And you didn't have a PO on your back— you did it on your own. I've got so much hanging over my head, and I still can't do it. But you are!"

Annette was more casual, but direct. "I've enjoyed getting to know you, Raydine...not just here, but when you joined us for Thanksgiving. I've been looking forward to knowing you better—I already consider you a friend. And I need a friend, Raydine.

"I think you've opened up a lot more in this group, and that takes a lot of guts. It's hard to be vulnerable to others, and I'm learning from you.

"I'm not saying this because of what you just said, Raydine...I had planned to ask you after group, but we'd like you and your family to share Christmas with us. We're going to stay here for the holidays, and we don't have any family here, so if you want to, we'd love to have you come over. Maybe you won't need to go to your mother's."

Dana questioned, "Might that be an option, Raydine? Or can you consider other options...like declining the invitation from your mother; or meeting her and your siblings on neutral grounds? Perhaps finding a time when your mother's husband is not there?"

"Maybe. I'll have to think it over."

"The important thing, Raydine, is to make a plan that will help you cope in healthy ways. Perhaps increase your AA meetings? Call someone who will hold you accountable—your sponsor maybe? Is your husband helpful in avoiding alcohol?"

"Yeah. He doesn't like it when I drink. And he's been cool."

Raydine took a deep breath before she responded, as if resigned to the truth. "You've given me some good ideas, and I will make a plan. Tonight. I'll write it in my journal. Thank you…all of you." She looked at Annette. "And thank you so much for your kindness. I'll have to see how it goes…if I can handle going out."

Dana's voice lacked conviction. "We'll all be pulling for you, Raydine. You've gone through a lot, but it didn't win—you survived because you have it within you. You're on the right track, and it does get better…easier…each time you choose the alternative.

"Jodi, would you like to go next?"

"Umm, yeah." Jodi took a deep breath, as if bracing herself for what she had to say. "Well, I'm going to go visit my sister in Nebraska for the holidays. Mrs. Barrett is going to keep Bounder for me." She chuckled—that throaty sound that was so uniquely Jodi. "It'll take me two weeks to unspoil him when I get back.

"I uh, I've had some pretty rough weeks. I've been having a lot of nightmares…more than usual—for several months now. It's been getting me down. The dreams. Actually, I've been having the same dream for many years—since I was in grade school, really.

"In the dream, I'm tied up in a barn, and there's someone—a man—who is…uh…coming to hurt me. But then I wake up."

She took another deep breath, her eyes focused in the center of the group with an occasional glance toward Dana. "Well, I'm thinking that maybe these nightmares might not be just dreams. Maybe stuff really did happen. Dana has been helping me to uh…to look at it a little bit at a time. To keep me out of the loony bin."

Jodi glanced up at the other women in the group—her voice strained and barely audible, "I guess I've got a lot more to work on than I thought."

"Jodi, what are you feeling right now? What is

happening in your body?" asked Dana.

"I want to throw up. I'm dizzy."

"Can you breathe through it, Jodi? Stay present…maybe shuffle your feet?" Dana spoke slowly as she guided Jodi. "Be aware of your body and where it connects with the chair. Notice the temperature of the room. Good. And as you breathe, listen to what we have to say to you.

"You're going to get through this, Jodi…whatever may be true, and whatever may be distortion, you survived it. It did not destroy you. You've carried this burden in silence all these years, and somehow managed to be successful in life and in a very demanding career.

"You're a loving and responsible person. You've trained a wonderful dog, Bounder. You've developed relationships with your colleagues and friends. With us. We care about you, and we're going to be here for you."

Jodi nodded, as her breathing became more relaxed, but still deep. "Thanks. I can feel that support. It helps." She chuckled, then looked around, "Sorry. I didn't mean to splash cold water on Ellen's good news."

"I'm glad you shared with us, Jodi." Raydine glanced around meekly, as if seeking approval to speak out in such a manner. "It helps me to know that someone like you…with your life…your education and all…that you have some of the same problems as us. As me, anyway."

Hannah leaned toward Jodi. "I've had that too…dreams that keep repeating over and over again. And they make sense, sort of—like it might have really happened. But it's fuzzy, or just glimpses, so I never can tell. I'm sorry you're having them, Jodi, and if I can help, I want to. You can call me any time—day or night. I'm up all the time anyway. So call me. It's no bother…really."

Ellen and Annette affirmed their support through their nods and comments. Jodi nodded her head slightly as she looked each woman directly in the eye. "Truly, I can't say how much this means to me. It helps to know I'm not facing this alone."

After a moment of silent transition, Dana asked, "Hannah, what are your plans and challenges these next few weeks?"

"Well, I'm sort of in the same boat as Raydine. It's been

hard to not go to the bars. I'm not sleeping at all. There's no fun in my life any more. All I do is think about Richard. I saw him at the Drop Inn, and he didn't even speak to me. He turned his back when I walked in the door—I know he saw me. Then he put his arm around some chick that was sitting next to him. They just laughed at me.

"I thought about slashing his tires...doing something to get back at him, but there was a police car across the street when I went out to the parking lot, and I thought about my PO and what trouble I'd be in."

Ellen asked, "Is he really worth it, honey? You're so much more than he is—you've got so much to offer a good man. Honey, don't settle."

Hannah blushed, and looked away. "I wish I could feel that way. I miss him so much—he's really a nice guy. We had something going for us. If he'd just give it another chance, I could show him, I'm sure."

Jodi cleared her throat. "Isn't this the same guy who left you with the turkey on Thanksgiving? And left you to find your own way...and place to stay...in the middle of a rainy night? Hannah, I don't claim to know what love is, but I have to wonder about this guy. Are you sure you want him back?"

"It sounds pretty cold when you put it like that. But it's not always like that. Sometimes it's really good. Well...it was. I hear what you're saying, though." Hannah gave a half-smile. "Maybe I'll get it together. Maybe I'll just join a convent."

Dana's eyebrows furrowed. "Hannah, I sure would worry less about you if you had a plan for being safe these next few weeks."

"Well, I think I'll offer to work more shifts while others are on vacation. Maybe I'll be so tired, I won't be able to worry so much."

"Are you still staying with your friend? How's that going?"

"Okay. Bonner won't use around me, and he watches out for me. I'm safe with him."

"Use around you?"

Hannah's face clearly showed she hadn't meant to disclose so much. "He doesn't use the hard stuff—just marijuana, and it's never been my thing. It doesn't bother me."

"Hannah, is there any legal risk to you? I mean, if he got caught in possession of marijuana, wouldn't you be in trouble by just being around him?"

"I guess there's always a possibility. But it'll be alright. Really. I'm going to take your suggestions."

Dana was unconvinced, but sensed it would not help to keep pursuing the issue.

"Annette, what about you? How are you doing and what are your plans and challenges for the holidays?"

"Well, I'm doing okay. Jackson has several weeks off, and has been in a pretty good mood. He's been helping me out with the boys, and it's given me some freedom. My mother is being a witch about us not coming down for Christmas, but it's not bothering me like it usually does. I keep thinking about you, Raydine, and how you've had to avoid your mom because of your stepfather. I figure if you can do it, I can too. It helps to know I'm not the only one with a psycho mom.

"And, I have something I'd like to give to each of you." Annette reached down to lift little gift bags from a satchel next to her chair. "This isn't much, but I wanted each of you to have something I made."

"Oh goodie, can we open them now?" Raydine's glee was infectious among the group.

"Yes, go ahead if you want."

There was lots of paper rustling, and oohs and ahs as the women unwrapped their gifts from Annette, and inspected them closely. Raydine let out a soft squeal as she lifted a miniature pewter frame that perfectly complemented a painting of forget-me-nots. "Oh Annette, this is beautiful! That's the State flower ...forget-me-nots."

"Uh huh. I don't want any of us to forget this group, and what we're learning together—and from each other. It's not much, but I thought you might like it."

"Not much! Annette, this is incredible. How did you make such tiny flowers, yet so detailed?" Hannah turned to Jodi, "Yours is different, isn't it?" Then turning back to the group as the women compared their gifts, "They're originals, aren't they? Each one is an original."

"They're very authentic," said Jodi.

Ellen held her miniature painting toward Annette.

"Annette, you could sell these. Have you ever thought of doing that? I could carry them in my shop and sell as many as you could make. They're so unique, and such a great Alaskan souvenir."

"Oh thank you. I haven't thought much about selling them commercially—just at church bazaars. But that's something to think about."

Raydine's enthusiasm seemed to rally her. "Oh Annette, you could do a business from home. You wouldn't have to be away from the kids…or even get out of your pajamas all day."

The laughter and small talk changed the mood of the entire group, attesting to the friendships that had developed over the last several months—the intimacy these women shared with each other.

Dana's face was smiling and nodding at the right times, but her thoughts were in a different place. She was evaluating the emotional state of each woman—how stable she was at this point in time; how much her insight and coping skills had changed within these last few months; how capably she was likely to handle the anticipated challenges over the next few weeks; what resources were available to her. *I think they'll be okay. Lord, please protect Hannah. She's so vulnerable; so precious. Why couldn't I have been her mother?*

Chapter Nineteen
The Therapist's Consultation Group

"DANA, YOU LOOK LIKE you're carrying the world on your shoulders. Anything you want to share with us?"

Dana's monthly peer consultation group had everyone present. Marla Anderson, an alcohol and drug counselor, had just shared her latest project for working with the schools on a drug prevention initiative. Amy Smith was the youngest, a Social Worker who worked mostly with teenagers. She didn't look much older than her clients, fostering spiked hair and tattoos. Lisen Velvick, a Psychiatric Nurse Practitioner, had briefed the group about the new federal regulations on controlled substances. She ended with a light note, "It'll create more cranky patients, that's for sure. If they're too belligerent, send 'em to the hospital instead of me, okay?"

The banter among the women was a great stress reliever. They understood the reality of compassion fatigue so typical of their helping professions, and these monthly meetings were important to each of them. What had begun as collaboration among professionals had quickly become intimate, supportive relationships based on deep caring and respect for each other.

Phyllis Barton was the senior therapist among the women. She had been a Clinical Social Worker with the State of Alaska for twenty years in Anchorage. She had worked tirelessly to provide mental health services to the villagers in the Interior. After her husband and son were lost in a small plane over the Aleutians, she moved to Juneau and shifted her counseling focus to bereavement. After the enormous grief she experienced herself, it was a natural fit for her to become an expert on grief and loss. She was a popular speaker at conferences in Alaska and the Lower Forty Eight.

Phyllis was a large woman, filling the roomy chair in which she sat. Her beautiful skin and thick cascading blond hair belied her age. Her humor and presence permeated the room, yet she missed nothing about her dear colleagues.

Phyllis facilitated the meeting this month, and that loving insightful expression came to focus on Dana.

Dana couldn't speak for a moment—swallowing hard to hold back the emotion. Phyllis' empathy made her feel too vulnerable. She didn't want to break down in front of her friends, yet she knew this was the place she could process what was on her heart and hear some loving objectivity.

"I uh, I don't want to burden you all with my stuff, yet I know I need to let it out. You're the sisters I never had. Phyllis, you're the mom I don't remember."

Dana's voice faltered, hinting at the depth of emotion she tried to hide. Her colleagues refrained from crowding her, but showed their support with gestures and a few encouraging words, allowing Dana to collect herself.

"Why is it so hard to take the advice I give to my clients every day? I feel like such a fake at times—I get caught up playing the same old tapes, even though I know in my head they are lies. You'd think I'd get it one of these days, and just be able to move on."

"Dana, why don't you let yourself be human like the rest of us? We all struggle with...overcoming. Let us walk with you as you sort through what's heavy on your heart?"

Phyllis' reassuring voice was so soothing, Dana took a deep breath, as she seemed to resign herself to a course of action. "I've told you all before about giving a baby up for adoption. It seems like so long ago—another life time, really. She would be twenty now...if she's alive. And I believe she is. I think I would somehow know if she wasn't.

"I hope she doesn't hate me. I put my name on the adoptive reunification registry years ago, but I've never heard anything from her. She could find me if she was interested in knowing who I am...at least for the last two years since she turned eighteen. It feels like such a rejection." Dana paused until her chin quit quivering.

"I think I'm pretty resolved about giving her up. It wasn't the right decision—I know that now. I was just so young—emotionally. So confused. Misguided. Determined to not be dependent on anyone." Dana's mind quickly replayed the chain of events in those months of graduate school that so dramatically altered the course of her life.

Mario. Charismatic. Calculating. He knew she was engaged to Hub, so at first, his flirtatious attention seemed innocent. Then his teasing became more suggestive — *why don't you tell your Eskimo boyfriend you need time to experience life...let me show you the world, Dana. There's so much I want to give you.*

Then the senseless argument with Hub over Christmas break — tossing their five-year relationship away like tattered nautical charts. His despair was so crushing, she had to escape. She returned to campus early, lost in her grief over hurting Hub and missing him desperately. Mario's attempts to comfort her seemed honorable. At first.

She looked up at the women in her peer group, wondering how long she had been replaying this history in her mind. "I didn't tell any of you this before, but my daughter was the product of a sort-of-date rape. I blamed myself for a lot of years — not seeing how I was manipulated; and how I did not invite or consent to have sex with him. But I blamed myself for not seeing it coming; for not being able to stop it. I couldn't report it — I just holed up in my room except for classes. Avoided my friends. I was so ashamed!

"I've come to realize I was pretty naïve...but I didn't invite it."

Dana continued haltingly with her narrative. "The part that still haunts me is knowing that I betrayed Hub. Even though I didn't expect to be raped, I had broken up with him. And when I am honest with myself, I did flirt with the possibility of someone else.

"When I found that I was pregnant, I nose dived into a depression. I didn't recognize it at the time, but it was clinical depression. I still don't know how I continued to function, but I kept up my classes. I told so many lies — to my father; my friends — about school being the stressor; demanding my time — the reason why I couldn't join in. And I avoided contact with Hub at all costs."

Lisen quietly inserted, "You poor kid."

After a brief glance at her, Dana continued. "Summer break — I returned to campus early so my father wouldn't suspect anything. I hid out the last few months when I couldn't hide my pregnancy any more. I determined early-on to have the baby, but to give her up."

Dana's voice had become quieter, recounting that period in her life as if she were an observer. "I was so…my thinking was so distorted. I don't remember my own mother much, and I knew nothing about babies. I didn't want to hurt her — the baby. She deserved more than I could have given her."

Dana looked up at Phyllis. "When I can think clearly about it, I still believe that—I was such an unsettled kid myself. Who knows what kind of neuroses I would have passed on to that innocent child." Her eyes were misty as she continued. "But then I think about how other women manage—maybe my daughter would have been one of the lucky ones who thrived in spite of life circumstances and an inept mother.

"I knew I couldn't return to Juneau with her…or to Hub. There's no way I could face him again with someone else's child. Without her, I could at least come home. I didn't think I could ever face Hub again anyway. I told myself he would find someone else and eventually we could simply avoid crossing paths."

"That's the part I can't get past: Hub." Dana looked around at her friends, encouraged by their quiet empathy. "We eventually did work things out—obviously, and married, but I couldn't get pregnant again. Ironic, isn't it—one wretched man's sperm attaches in a few heart-wrenching moments; yet with the most adoring man and a marriage of seventeen years, we're unable to get pregnant.

"It wasn't his fault; or mine—it just didn't happen. And here I am now…grateful for the life I have. I love my husband; my work; and yet I can't allow myself to just enjoy him…to be…real. To be vulnerable in some ways. I push him away — emotionally…because of my own guilt. And he's such a good man. He would have been such a good father."

Dana's voice faltered as she looked down at her lap, her fists pounding her thighs. "He deserves more than I can give. What I have been giving. I just keep perpetuating one bad decision after another."

Phyllis spoke gently to Dana. "I know you're feeling that way right now, Dana, but the bad decisions, as you call them, weren't ones you could judge at the time. You'd have to be

Master of the Universe to know if the few choices you truly had were the best or not. Even when you're able to look back and see how things turned out, you still don't know what might have been. Maybe it really was the best option for your child to be raised by a more mature couple. You don't know how it might have turned out, Dana, and the choice of your having another child wasn't up to you. I'm sure you and Hub did your parts, didn't you?"

Phyllis' subtle humor elicited a snort from Dana. Then her obvious embarrassment erupted into laughter. "Yes, we most definitely have enjoyed trying."

The heaviness in the room lifted as the others could see Dana's grief discharge.

"Dana," Phyllis continued, "I wonder...what is the pivotal event that has you stuck. Now is probably not the best time to pursue it — maybe we can do some individual work, or you could do some journaling on it, but I suspect there's something that is keeping you from forgiving yourself...from moving on."

Dana nodded. "Yeah...you might be right. I...I so appreciate you guys. I'm sorry to take up so much time today...you mean more to me than you could ever know. It's helped so much...just allowing me to sort some things out as I spoke. And snorted!

"I'm a mess." Dana slumped back in her chair. "And exhausted. What a reminder of how my clients feel when they leave my office."

"Dana, what can we do for you now? What will be most helpful to you, especially in these next few weeks of Christmas?"

"I think your suggestion of doing some journaling...maybe some individual work, is good. Hub goes south for a seminar next month, so I'll have lots of thinking time. And it'll be busy otherwise. I would like to do some session time with you Phyllis...after the holidays, though...okay?"

"You just call me when you're ready."

Chapter Twenty
A Fragmented Start

JUNEAU WAS BLESSED WITH colder than normal weather throughout the Christmas holiday, and enough snow to keep all the skiers at Eaglecrest happy, as well as every snow removal vehicle in town. Aside from the snow-packed roads, Juneauites seemed to slow down a bit and celebrate the beauty at their doorstep. From every view, spruce trees sagged with the weight of their adornment. The blanket of white crept to the edge of the tide line, contrasting the charcoal green water as it rippled toward the rocky beaches.

Dana shoveled the walkway, enjoying the crisp air and repetitive motion as she tried to sort things out in her mind. She kept thinking about Phyllis' suggestion that she might be stuck because of a pivotal event. Dana knew that to be true of human behavior—often her clients were unable to get over a traumatic event, or work through their grieving process because of an unacknowledged factor. It's one of the things Dana loved so much about her work—helping people find that missing link, and then to experience the freedom from the shame, self-condemnation, or other effects of trauma.

But what is it in my brain? I know the process...why can't I help myself? It can't be my mom disappearing – I've worked through all that stuff. Haven't I?

Dana thought about how it hurt Hub when she avoided eye contact, or wouldn't open up about the turmoil she was obviously going through. *I know he feels the loneliness too. If only it could be like it was when we first fell in love. Or even when we got back together...after I finally told him about the baby. And about Mario. His forgiveness and understanding made me think it was truly behind me. Why isn't it enough now? Of course...that was before I knew we wouldn't have children...before I knew he would be punished for my sin. No...no, that's not right. I know God isn't punishing us for my mistake. He forgave me a long time ago. Why can't I forgive myself? I'll be so glad when Phyllis gets back from California...she's so wise. Maybe she can help me see the missing piece.*

***

By Tuesday, the beauty of the snow had turned to frozen rivers of dirty slush, making it hard to park on the streets or find secure footing on the sidewalks. Dana was salting the steps for the third time that day as Jodi and Ellen came up the walk.

"Happy New Year, you two! Isn't this a mess?"

"I hope you've got the hot water on," said Jodi. "It's nasty out here."

Ellen's voice was brisk, "I was stuck in the Seattle airport for eighteen hours because of this mess. I'm so glad to finally be home and in my own bed."

The chitchat continued as the group hung their winter coats and scarves, and settled in with warm drinks. Annette and Raydine arrived with more boot stomping, and comments about the infamous Juneau weather.

As the women removed their coats and hats, Raydine exclaimed, "Ellen! I love your hair! That cut looks so cute on you."

Ellen almost blushed as she patted the back of her new coif. "Thank you. I...I'm still getting used to it, but it'll sure be a lot easier to take care of with this dampness. It's a big change for me."

After many complements, the group settled in, anticipating Dana's lead. "Has anyone heard from Hannah?"

Several shook their heads, and looked at each other with concern. Annette said, "I tried to call her Christmas Eve, but couldn't reach her. I left a message on her phone, but she never called back. I should have kept trying. Oh, I hope she's alright."

"Let me take a minute and call her before we get started." Dana went into her office briefly, then reported back, "No answer. I left a message for her to join us, even if she's late."

"Oh, I hope she's okay. I should have called her again—I

knew she was struggling," Annette's concern showed in her face.

Raydine added, "Me too. I thought a lot about her, but I just got caught up in other things. I don't feel good about this."

Dana could see that the group members were ready to blame themselves if anything went wrong with dear Hannah. "I'm concerned too, but Hannah is quite resourceful. She's handled a lot of situations, and survived some pretty hard stuff. And...she is free to make her own choices, isn't she? Of course your calls and concerns are important, but we need to be careful about taking too much responsibility for other's choices. Isn't that much of what challenges us—trying to figure out how to help, yet not enable? How to be connected, yet respect our individuality? Keep calling; keep caring, but honor Hannah's right to choose. And remember, she's a survivor!"

"Prayer matters, too," said Annette, getting assents from the other women.

"Hopefully she's just delayed, or had an emergency." Looking around at the group, Dana welcomed everyone back from Christmas break. "Let's do check-ins. Who would like to share what's happening? Ellen, how was your trip?"

"Good. Really good. Except for the flight—I was a little tipsy by the time I got to Minneapolis, but the wine helped me get through it." Her eyes darted toward Jodi as she continued. "I kept thinking about Jodi getting on those little planes all the time, flying out to those remote islands. I purposely wore my green slacks, and imagined them as part of a uniform, and I was just doing a job like her.

"Well, it is funny, but it worked. It took away some of the angst I have with flying. And my friend was there to meet me. She and her family treated me like royalty—I ate too much; ran around to all the sites; and got to see the Macy's holiday show—that was really something. They have professional decorators, I tell you! And the money to be creative. I even got some ideas for the shop here.

"And you'll never believe it—they have several interior design schools right there in Minneapolis! If I would have let her, Susan, my friend, would have enrolled me in school last week! She's really pushing me to sublet my apartment and the shop here and move to Minneapolis. But I'm not going to do that...yet. I have a lot of thinking to do."

It was quiet momentarily as the group sensed Ellen was not finished, but shifting her thoughts. "The only downside was not seeing my daughter. She called Christmas day, but it was...she didn't say much. I know there's something going on with her, but she evades my questions. I wish she would just be open with me."

Annette asked conspiratorially, "What about Mark? Did you miss him?"

"I guess so. I..." Ellen's eyes seemed to search for an answer from the air above her right eyebrow. "You know...I don't think I did...really. I stressed about him some — it was hard to not call a few times when I thought about what he might be doing. We did talk several times a week, but you know, it almost felt like a duty. Hmmm...that should tell me something, huh?"

Dana wrapped up Ellen's check-in. "It sounds like it. I'm so glad you had a good time, Ellen. And you're back safely. And you've got lots to think through."

Dana looked around, her eyes settling on Annette with that questioning look.

"Well, it was a rather quiet time in our home — as much as that's possible with three boys, that is. Jackson actually hung around some. We played games; he took the boys snow shoeing. We did some crafts. Had some company. It was good."

"How did it go with your mom?"

"Well, she tried to guilt me because she was stranded at my brother's. They won't kowtow to her, like I do. Used to do. They go on with their lives, even though she's there. She was incensed that they would go out in the evening and leave her there alone, or with their teenage kids. But that's just her. She complained about everything my sister-in-law did. It is so hard to not say something."

"What would you like to say to her, Annette? What would you like her to know?"

"Well, that people have their own lives to lead. That she's not the center of the universe. That their obligations and desires are important too."

"What if you started to actually say some of the things on

your mind, rather than hold them in? What if you drew some boundaries with your mom?"

Annette sighed deeply. "I know. I know I need to. It's just that she acts so hurt if we even hint that she might be wrong, or that our wants differ from hers. She has a fit. Or pouts for the next two months. One time, she didn't speak to me for four months! It was actually nice, but she talked crap about me to my siblings and everyone in the family, and I was afraid they might believe her. Yeah, you're right...everyone knows how she is; I shouldn't worry about it. But I do. Maybe one of these days..."

Raydine's gravelly voice was monotone. "My little girl loves the miniature you gave me for Christmas, Annette. I won't let her have it, but I put it in the kitchen window for awhile so she can see it too. I thank you so much for it."

Dana could see that Raydine seemed tired. Her eyes were puffy; her hair hung straight. "How about you, Raydine, how are you doing?"

"Not very good. I, uh, relapsed big time. Cyndi has been pretty hard to handle the whole Christmas break. I won't let her run around, because I'm afraid she'll hook up with that Buddy guy. She nags me a lot. Anyway, we met my mom and sister and her kids at the Prospector for lunch. My brother was snowed-in in Anchorage, and didn't get home until late, so I missed him. I didn't think I could keep Cyndi from seeing her grandmother, and her cousins. She knows what happened to me, but I don't think she really understands.

"Anyway, we got through it. And it was...tolerable. She got to exchange presents with her cousins, and my mom got her some nice things."

She took a ragged breath before continuing. "But after Christmas, Cyndi kept ragging on me to go places, and I just couldn't let her. Then New Years Day, we got in a big ole fight. She said she was going to go live with my mom—that she'd be better off with them."

There were tears in her eyes as Raydine almost snarled, "That may be right in some ways, but I will never let her be alone with that monster!"

It was a moment before she could continue. "I had to physically restrain her from leaving the apartment. We both said some things that really hurt. Then Doug came home, and took over. He handled her better than I was. Anyway, I hid out in my room and tied one on. I'm...pretty ashamed.

"We both apologized the next day, but it's still...there. She wants more freedom, and I'm terrified she'll get abused."

Annette asked tentatively, "Do you think she'll talk to a counselor?"

"She said she would. I'm hoping so. I've got to set that up yet."

"Raydine, how are you doing now...with the drinking?"

"Okay. There's still some beer in the frig, but it's almost gone. Doug said he'd leave if I get drunk again. So I need to be cool."

"Is that the only reason you need to stop?"

Raydine was quick to shake her head. With a grimace, she said, "I don't want to go back there. I can't. I've got to be here for Cyndi. And, I saw him...the monster that stole my childhood. He acted so pious...he even went to church! I wish those people knew who he really is. It makes me want to take an ad out in the Juneau Empire—tell everyone what a slime bag he is." She held up her hand to punctuate the headline, "Child Molester on the Loose: Watch Your Children."

The tick of the clock seemed to punctuate the silence as the others waited for Raydine to go on.

She looked toward the door, "I wish Hannah would come. I hope she's okay."

"Where to now, Raydine? What are your needs? How can we help you?"

"Well, I'm truly taking it a day at a time. Cyndi is back in school. And so far, she's cooperating at home. I'm taking her to a sledding party Saturday—trying to let her do some stuff.

"And I'm talking more to my sponsor. Catching a few more meetings. And I will get her set up with a counselor."

Jodi spoke hesitantly. "Raydine, what if you did write that article for the Juneau Empire. I'm sure they wouldn't print it for liability reasons, but just writing it might be cathartic—to help you sort through some things. It helps me to write things out."

"I could do that. Thanks. I think I will."

There was just enough of a pause in the conversation for Ellen to insert. "What about that guy...Buddy. Are you still pretending to be your daughter?"

Raydine turned to Ellen, her movements stiff. "Yes. I can't take a chance he'll get to my little girl again. I will do anything I can to get him. If he gives me anything to go on, I'll call the police again."

Ellen grimaced, but held her tongue.

Jodi's slender hands were restless. After taking a deep breath, her voice was hoarse. "Well, here goes. This is very hard, but I owe it to you after our last session, and to myself. So I'm going to go there."

Jodi took another deep breath. "I mentioned last week, or rather a few weeks ago, that I was going to go see my sister over the holidays. And that I was beginning to think some of my nightmares might be real. Memories, instead of just nightmares."

Jodi's voice was steady, belying the sadness that showed around her eyes and mouth. She told the group she had been worried about approaching her younger sister about her nightmares when she got to Nebraska. "She has such a busy life with her young family and performances—she's an accomplished pianist, and quite involved in playing for local events. I didn't want my problems to spill over onto her and her family.

"It seems like she was untouched by the craziness I remember growing up. My dad was pretty unpredictable. Explosive. My mom obsessed with what the neighbors had that we didn't. They're good people—Dad died some years ago, but it was pretty tough at times for me to figure out how to…how to just be me.

"Anyway, Mugs and I were pretty close growing up. I looked after her. Then she got so busy with her recitals and stuff…we seemed to drift apart. Then I left for college."

Jodi rubbed her hands together, her breath ragged as she took in extra air, as if to prepare for what was to come next.

"It was such an adjustment going from my quiet life in Juneau to…it was overwhelming to be around family twenty-four seven. My mom lives just a mile from Mugs…a name, by the way, never to be spoken in front of our mother. Her name is Marianna, I'm reminded, whenever I slip up in front of our mother.

"Any way, our mother was there constantly. Doing the same thing to my niece that she used to do to Mugs—fussing about her clothes, her looks, her manners, her every breath — constantly! And my nephew was all but ignored. It's as if he was invisible to her. I found myself drawn right back into that craziness…trying to be invisible myself, or polite when Mother would whirl us all up in her tornado to charge off to wherever she deemed important at the moment. It was exhausting.

"Finally, just a few days before I was scheduled to leave, I got an afternoon alone with Mugs when we drove to Lincoln City to pick up a costume."

Jodi became silent as her mind replayed the sequence of events that had turned her inside-out. Mugs was driving. Jodi had asked her how she got along with Mom being so prominent in her life. Mugs said she just accepted it as the way things were. "Laughter and denial help enormously," she giggled.

Jodi had been hesitant to probe further because Mugs seemed so unaffected by things of the past. It was hard to believe they grew up in the same family. Jodi had questioned herself, *How can I be so riddled with nightmares and issues, when my sister is so normal?*

Finally, the conversation got around to Jodi and how she was truly faring in the far-away-North. Mugs commented in her pronounced Midwestern accent, "I'm so proud of you, Jodi. You're so brave. But I worry about you being so far away…and out there with all those bears. Do you ever git scared? Have you ever had to draw your gun?"

Jodi chuckled at her sister's Hollywood perspective of her new home State. She took a deep breath, and decided to take the plunge. "Actually, those aren't the things that scare me, Mugs. I do have fears, but they're more of what comes to me in my dreams — nightmares, really."

Mugs glanced at Jodi before returning her attention to her driving and the road ahead.

Jodi tried to read the expression in that quick look — *was it fear?* She decided it was bad timing, and redirected the conversation, shrugging it off as nothing to worry about. The increasing traffic gave a momentary distraction.

However, when they were seated for lunch at an Italian restaurant, Mugs gave Jodi a penetrating look. "Jodi, are these the same nightmares you had when we were kids?"

Jodi was astonished. She didn't know Mugs knew about the nightmares. She looked at her little sister dumbfounded.

"I remember them, Jodi. You always tried to hide it, but I knew. You forget we slept in the same room. And I wasn't the little kid you thought I was. I heard the things you cried out; I saw the toll it took on you, Jodi. Please tell me what's goin' on? I know something has been bothering you. I'm your little sister, remember?"

Jodi's stomach was in knots as she searched her sister's face for signs of judgment or defensiveness. What she saw instead was the love and the encouragement of an adult woman—her sister all grown up. Perhaps she was capable of hearing some of Jodi's fears.

Her throat was suddenly dry, and her words came out as a whisper. "Yeah, they're the same." She used both of her shaking hands to take a drink of water before she continued. "I'd forgotten you knew about them. Not about them in detail...but that they bothered me.

"They went away for awhile—it, I should say. It's the same nightmare over and over. It went away for the most part through grad school; through most of my thirties, really. But it's back with a vengeance. And I'm beginning to wonder if maybe there's some basis to it—something that causes it to keep haunting me." Jodi's fingers tapped on the table.

"Actually, I'm seeing a counselor, and she kinda made me wonder if there was some stuff I'd blocked out. Maybe the nightmares are...real."

Mugs' voice was dry. "What are they about?"

"Oh, being somewhere like Nebraska, or Illinois. Farmin' country. I'm...helpless. In a barn, with someone coming after me."

Mugs nearly shouted, "Like Uncle Howard's barn!"

Jodi couldn't speak for a moment. The nervousness in her stomach had turned to nausea; her head felt like it would explode. She could hardly breathe, but nodded slowly at her sister. "What makes you think of Uncle Howard's barn?"

"I always had a bad feelin' about him—and you workin' with him. I always worried about you when we would go there. You were different when we'd visit them—it's like you didn't know me anymore. I wasn't important to you. Maybe it's just that you weren't looking after me."

Jodi's voice was a whisper. "I can't remember the barn — where it was on the property. The outside of it — what did it look like?"

"It was on the other side of the driveway…out the back door by the porch where we used to sleep. It was red, with a hay loft, and that big derrick to lift things to the upper floor."

Her sister watched as Jodi struggled for composure, her eyes seeing events that appeared only in her mind. Her face turned pale as she stared blankly at her sister.

Mugs' voice was firm. "Come on, we're gettin' outta here! You need some breathin' room." Mugs grabbed her sister's arm, lifting her out of the booth, and directed her through the restaurant, stopping long enough to place a five dollar bill on the counter for their drinks.

They walked the distance to the parking place, Marianna leading with Jodi's arm clamped tightly under her own. She started the engine to warm up the car, but made no move to pull out of the parking space. Instead, she pushed her seat back so she could turn and look directly at Jodi. "Okay, Big Sis, I've got all the time in the world. I am here for you this time. We can take as much time as you need to git this out."

Jodi's hands flung to her face as she wailed, her long body folding in, appearing suddenly small and vulnerable next to her shorter sister. Mugs rubbed her back and cooed to her as if she were one of her children. After a long while, the wailing turned to sobbing, and her body quit shaking. She slumped back in the seat.

"That's all right, Honey, let it out. I'm gonna take care of you."

Jodi couldn't speak, but she nodded her head and mouthed the words *thanks*. She was so exhausted she could hardly hold her head up. She gave in to the last fear of appearing insane, and let her sister take control. She leaned back in the seat, unable to think.

After awhile, she was aware that the car was in motion. She was being taken care of, but she couldn't engage in conversation. Through the fog in her head, she knew they were not headed toward home. It was all up to Mugs.

Jodi looked around the room at her therapy group friends, aware that she had been talking, but unaware of how much time had elapsed. She hoped she had been telling it coherently, unsure of exactly what she had said, so she described how her sister took her to a motel. She slept for ten hours straight. Then they carved out a full day of talking, crying, and even found themselves able to laugh at times.

"I'm still trying to get used to the idea that my little sister was the strong one—I never knew she was so capable. And that she could handle me being a basket case. She was a life saver.

"At any rate, a lot of memories have been coming back to me since then, and I'm pretty certain where the nightmares came from. A lot of it is still fuzzy, but things are making more sense to me now—why I got carsick when we went to my aunt's house, but at no other time; why I can't stand to be around farm animals and hay; why my wrists hurt when I'm nervous."

Jodi rubbed her shoulder as she looked more directly at her friends. "I guess I am a basket case, but I think I'll get through it now. Over time.

"Thanks for being here for me, ladies. Dana. I don't think I could have gotten this far without you."

Dana's voice was soft and full of empathy. "Wow, Jodi. You've traveled more than miles, these last few weeks.

"You seem to have some trust that this is part of your journey—that you've got some answers, but you expect you'll learn more."

"Yeah. That's pretty much it."

"You're very courageous, Jodi. You've survived some unthinkable abuse, and yet here you are—still the lovely capable person that you are; sharing with us; making sense of what's happened."

"Well, I don't know what more there is," Jodi chortled, "but I don't think it can destroy me now."

The group ended with Jodi's friends hugging and encouraging her.

Chapter Twenty One
Therapy for the Therapist

"THIS FEELS A LITTLE awkward, Phyllis. You're my friend, my mentor, my peer — and now I'm looking for you to be my therapist. Wouldn't the ethics board have a heyday trying to figure out what to do with this one?"

"Well, let's talk about that, Dana. What are the potential boundary issues — to us personally? Professionally? To our relationship as peers?"

"I have thought about it, Phyllis, and I really don't have any concern about ethics. We don't have any financial association — unless you'll let me pay you."

"No, we've already settled that. There won't be any fee or indebtedness between us."

"Well, hopefully I can do something for you sometime. But I accept your gift freely. If we didn't provide counsel to each other, we'd all get a little loopy in the bush!"

Phyllis shifted her considerable weight, settling into her chair. "We do provide counsel to each other, don't we, Dana? I value your perspective greatly — you've had a lot of professional experiences that I haven't. You were a Godsend to me when I moved to Juneau and started private practice. We're just taking it to a deeper level today."

"That's true. I'm not uneasy at all ethics-wise. I just worry — like any of our clients when they contemplate baring their souls to us — will you think I'm weak, or strange; crazy?"

Dana's tension eased as the friends laughed and explored the possibilities. "I just wouldn't want to lose you as a friend, Phyllis."

"You know Dana, my only concern is that somehow you would avoid me because you were embarrassed that I knew some of your secrets; or you were worried that I might have some expectations for you; or that you might worry about what I think, rather than honoring your own thoughts and feelings."

"I hear ya. And that is something I have to be disciplined about — being honest with myself. That's a big part of my problem with intimacy, I think — I worry about what Hub, and others might think. That's the crux of it — not that we're in any kind of trouble in our marriage. I love Hub deeply, and I trust that he does me. I just don't want to have this barrier between us."

Her eyes got misty; her voice nearly a whisper. "There's a spot in my heart, Phyllis, that is so hidden...when he gets too close to it, I get panicky. I don't know what it is, Phyllis, and it scares me to think there's something there that my mind has buried. That's why I thought getting you to do some EMDR therapy on me would be good. It might bring it to light."

"Then let's do it, Dana. Let's see what you can discover."

Since Dana and Phyllis were both skilled at this specialized therapy that addresses deeper issues, they were able to quickly move to a therapeutic approach.

"Dana, I want you to trust me to attend to the process. Forget that you're a therapist, and allow yourself to simply be. Allow yourself to focus within — notice what you see; what sensations you experience in your body."

Phyllis' voice was mesmerizing as she spoke more slowly. "Take some deep breaths, and allow your body to completely relax. Let the tension go with each out-breath."

Dana exhaled slowly, her shoulders and arms relaxing as she sank deeper into the chair.

"When you're ready, focus on that tender spot in your heart. What image, or memories surface with that tender spot in your heart, Dana?"

Dana closed her eyes as she began to notice what thoughts and images were coming to her mind. "When Hub gets too close. Sometimes he looks at me with such openness. Maybe it's his trust. I don't know — he's too vulnerable. It's almost like his love is too big...I can't...hold it; I can't tolerate him being so close."

"What is the feeling that goes with that, Dana?"

"Panic. It's hard to breathe." Dana's face was flushed;

her voice strained.

"Where are you experiencing it in your body now?"

"My heart. Deep down. And my arms."

"Notice how that feels, Dana. Now, float back in your mind to see if there is an earlier time when you had that feeling."

"It didn't used to be there...it only started after the baby. Later...maybe after it became obvious that we couldn't have children of our own." Dana was responding to Phyllis' questions in the present tense, but her eyes behind closed lids were searching an earlier experience.

Phyllis' cadence was almost hypnotic. "Good. You're doing fine. Notice the feeling and where it is in your body. And let your mind float back. Is there an earlier time when you had that feeling?"

Dana's eyebrows jerked and scrunched as sporadic images flashed through her mind. "Umm...maybe my dad — after my mother disappeared. We were on the boat. He looks so forlorn...so lost. It's hard to see him that way — he's my great big dad who can handle anything. He's so strong. He always knows what to do. Yet his eyes — he looks at me like...I don't know what to do — he is so helpless." A tear began to track down Dana's cheek.

"Can you stay with it, Dana?"

She nodded. "I'm about a seven though." The therapist in Dana showed as she spoke in terms of measuring her distress level on a scale of one to ten.

"About how old are you, Dana?"

"Maybe four — three and a half; four."

"Okay. And as you remember that time, Dana, what is your underlying belief about yourself? I'm...what?"

"If Daddy cries too much, I'll be totally lost. I'll die right here in this boat."

Dana griped the arms of the chair as she remembered the painful times after her mother disappeared. She spoke in a voice reminiscent of the helpless little child she was at the time. She whispered, "I'm so alone; I'll die if Daddy hurts too much."

"Take some deep breaths, Dana. That's it. Just keep breathing and return to a calm state." Phyllis watched as Dana sought to breathe evenly, her eyebrows showing the slightest tension.

After a moment, Dana collected herself, and sat back. "I'm good. I can keep going."

"Okay, Dana, while I tap, I want you to just notice what images come to mind."

Phyllis methodically tapped Dana's knees, a calming touch that served to stimulate both hemispheres of her brain, which would deepen her level of awareness.

Dana's memories flew by in her mind, covering the many times her dad looked so sad, staring into space for hours, or drinking until he was wobbly, seemingly unaware of her presence. *I'm just little – it's too much for a little girl!* Then a clear image held in Dana's mind of her father sitting in the galley looking bereft. He sat there with his arms on his knees, just staring at her. He smelled funny, and looked so scruffy. He looked directly at her, yet he didn't smile. Or frown. *What am I supposed to do? Why doesn't Daddy see me? What did I do wrong?*

She had tried at times to cheer him up, or to think of things to tell him about so he wouldn't think so much about Mommy. She colored pictures for him and sang him songs. At other times, she tried to stay out of the way, to disappear. *Maybe Daddy will be happy if I just be silent…if I'm not here.*

After a few intense moments, Dana's breathing slowed, her body relaxing, even though her eyebrows were still scrunched.

Phyllis quit tapping, and sat back. "What's surfacing for you, Dana?"

Dana's voice grew deeper as she told Phyllis about that part of her life. "I was so little. My mother's disappearance was so gradual for me – I just kept waiting for her to come home. At first, it seemed like she was in town, or away for a while. I suspect Dad must have told me that, or suggested it to keep me from worrying. Poor Dad – he was so devastated, yet he carried that burden alone.

"At some point, he finally decided she wasn't coming back. There were some credit card charges in Montana, and somehow the police determined there was no evidence of foul play. Apparently she had left before, but never for that long. I don't remember those times. It just about killed Dad.

"He tried to give me the attention I needed. He really was

a good father. But he was so broken by my mother's leaving, and...he was not my mother."

"What are you feeling right now, Dana?"

"Better. The pressure has let up in my heart. I guess I feel a sadness for the little girl that I was. I needed my mother. She wasn't there to teach me how to be a girl. How to wear makeup. She doesn't know about Alex. Maybe I could have kept her. Maybe I would have been more...grounded."

Phyllis sighed compassionately. "And what about the image of Dad on the boat, looking so helpless?"

"It's softer now. I don't have the panic with it."

Dana continued to breathe deeply, responding to Phyllis' cues. "He just needed time to grieve himself. He was hurting for me, as well as himself. I couldn't know then that we would get through it. We did get through it; and there were happy times. I wouldn't have traded my growing up for anything. And I love my dad so much—he really did do more than any man could, I think.

"I don't know why that moment in time panicked me so much. There were so many other times that were frightening. One time we were stalled for two days out in the water with an engine problem. It was just Dad and me. The waters were so rough it was hard to hold anchor. We couldn't even heat our food, because the boat was so tossed about.

"I was almost a teen by that time, so I could understand the predicament we were in, but I was so confident that Dad could handle it. I just knew he could fix it. And, of course, we did have a radio. Dad just kept working on the engine 'til he got us going. Boredom was probably the worst problem...I couldn't even read because of the motion of the boat."

"Wasn't there a big difference, Dana? As a teen, you didn't fear for your life. You weren't totally helpless. You had some understanding... logic...the ability to evaluate and communicate. You were confident that your dad could get you through the emergency. When you were a little girl...you were overwhelmed."

"I guess there was that underlying fear even then that we might die, but you're right—I had hope. I didn't feel like I was alone. I could trust Dad and his judgment."

"Dana, when you look back at the image now...the one when you were three or four...what do you believe about yourself now?"

It was a moment before Dana could gather her thoughts. "I was afraid. It terrified me to see Dad so broken. But he was the parent. It wasn't up to me to fix him. In fact, I couldn't." Dana looked up at Phyllis, not speaking for a moment as her understanding unfolded.

"I needed him! I needed to lean on *him*...to be comforted by *him*...to be reassured. But it felt like he was leaning on me."

Dana's mouth hung open as she made the connections in her mind. "That is how it is with Hub: I need him, but it scares me if he needs me. Like it's too much — I'm afraid I can't meet his needs. That I can't help him, and I should be able to."

She sat back in her chair, appearing astonished. "This is just so...simple. Yet revealing.

"Could this really be the reason I get overwhelmed if he gets too close? Why couldn't I figure this out before?"

Phyllis was silent as she watched Dana dart about in her memories, finding pieces of the puzzle that finally fit into place.

Dana spoke with more certainty. "It's different from loving him. It's like I can *love* him, but he can't *need* me. I can't...couldn't tolerate being vulnerable with him, because he might be vulnerable with me, if that makes sense. I can't bear to see him weak...emotionally.

"I *am* needy when it comes to Hub. I can't imagine life without him — it's scary to even think about, yet I know I could survive it if I lost him.

"But I want to... What? Trust that he could be weak and I could still handle it?"

Dana shook her head, as if trying to clear it. "I need some time to process this, Phyllis. It doesn't fit easily with who I am...how I perceive myself. But that's essentially the problem, isn't it? My perceptions have been getting in the way of intimacy; of being free with Hub."

Phyllis raised her eyebrows and inclined her head, affirming what Dana had said. "I think you're onto something, Dana, and hopefully it is the missing piece to the puzzle. Let's follow up in a week or so, and see how this is playing out in your life — finish this process and see if there's anything yet unresolved."

Dana's thoughts were going a mile-a-minute as she drove

out the road. *It's almost too simple. Yet, how many decisions have I made based on that fear...of being overwhelmed? How many times have I avoided closeness with Hub because he might need too much...expect more of me than I can give? Even Alex...oh God...is that the real reason I gave her up?*

Chapter Twenty Two
Dana's Confession

"I'D GIVE ANYTHING for a smoke right now. I've gotta get out of this hole." The woman's deep voice and frequent coughs attested to her years of heavy smoking. Her eyes darted around the cell, never looking directly at the other three women. She shook the bars and growled a threatening anguished sound. The sleeve of her orange jumpsuit slipped down her raised arm, revealing four hearts tattooed around the knuckles on her left hand, connecting to a tattooed band around her ring finger. There were drops of blood tattooed down to the first knuckle on each of her slim fingers.

The other women didn't acknowledge her outbursts. They acted as if they couldn't see or hear her, although there was no way to avoid her ominous presence in this cramped cell.

Hannah studied the woman's hand, wondering about the source of pain that had been captured in her flesh. She wondered how old the tattoos were, and how old the woman must have been when she experienced the pain memorialized on her hand. At first, Hannah thought she must be well into her forties with her ruddy complexion and scowling brows. But her hands told a different story — they were beautiful. Her bad haircut and rough voice were such a contrast to her lovely hands.

The woman suddenly pushed back from the bars, looking directly at Hannah as she thrust her body in her direction. She growled, "What you lookin' at? You got a problem with me?"

Her harsh voice startled Hannah, yet she didn't feel threatened. She shook her head. "Your hands. They're beautiful."

The woman turned quickly back toward the bars, crossing the room with just three steps.

Hannah drew back against the cinder blocks, trying to meld into the cold, barren wall. She wanted to ask someone what she might expect next, how long she had to wait, but she feared bringing more attention to herself. The rule seemed to be don't talk, yet it was so noisy at night, she couldn't sleep.

Maybe Monday I'll hear something...perhaps my PO will get some answers. No one even knows where I am. I could die in here, and no one would care. Oh God, why don't you just let me die.

***

Hub's parka was covered with wet snow on the shoulders just from the distance between the driveway and front door. He stomped his boots on the porch, and slapped his brown leather gloves against the corner of the house. The excited dogs charged out the door before Dana could get out of their way.

"Welcome home! Oh, Hub, I'm so glad you're back." Dana melted into his arms, kissing his face and hugging his neck. "I missed you so much"

Hub seemed to relish the uncharacteristic enthusiasm. "Mmm. I like this! I should leave town more often."

The excited dogs persisted in their nudging and playful barks until Hub and Dana included them in their laughter and reunion.

"Let's get warm by that fire. I'll fix you some hot cider while you get settled...and settle our babies. They missed you as much as I did!"

"Thanks. Actually, some of your tea sounds good. Let me get out of these jeans and remnants of the big city."

Hub and Dana conversed about his trip through the opened bedroom door as he changed clothes and she steeped tea in the kitchen. When they settled on the couch, the dogs followed suit and curled up at their feet. Lionel stretched out on the back of the couch, seemingly unaffected by the commotion of Hub's homecoming.

Hub put his stockinged feet on the old trunk that served as a coffee table, stretching out as he tucked Dana in closer to him. "You feel so good. I missed you too." He absently rubbed her arm and hand as he told her about who he'd seen at the marine diesel seminar and what they did in the evenings. She rested her head on his shoulder, drinking in his presence and the peacefulness of the moment.

The fire crackled in the wood stove as their conversation waned. Hub interrupted the quiet by leaning over to kiss Dana's forehead and hugging her closer.

Dana's voice was soft. "I've got something to tell you, Hub...that's really hard. Not bad, but something I've got to say." She could feel Hub straighten up on the seat, but she clung to his arm, holding him in place.

"Please, just stay. I don't want to look at you. Just hold me."

Hub resettled in the comfortable entanglement of arms and legs, kissing the side of her head. "Okay. I'm all ears — no eyes."

A deep sigh followed her chuckle. "I told you I had a session with Phyllis."

Hub reassured her with a squeeze, but kept silent.

"It was...it was good. Hard. Revealing." Dana glanced briefly at Hub, but hid her face again. Her fingers fidgeted around her mouth as she sought the right words.

"We talked about you...but not really. I told Phyllis how sometimes I...put the emotional walls up with you — keep you from getting too close." Dana's throat was so tight, it was difficult for her to get the words out. Her eyes blinked as she struggled for control.

"The wall wasn't about you, Hub. It was about me, and my fear of not being able to handle your pain. Or depth. I've always loved you beyond reason, yet there's this panic that over takes me at times when we're together. When we get too close."

Dana turned toward Hub, taking a ragged breath into his shoulder. "I'm so sorry, Hub. I know it's hurt you at times. You've tried so hard to be understanding. Patient. You're a saint to put up with me. But it wasn't even about you."

Hub started to speak, but Dana shook her head and her upraised fingers. "No wait. Let me get this out."

She sat up enough to look at him directly. "Phyllis did EMDR on me — targeting that panic I would get when we were too close...too intimate. And what came to mind was my dad! When I was little. After my mother left. It just seems so innocuous, but there was a point in time when Dad was beside himself...on the boat. It was when he was still drinking. Anyway, the look on his face—he was so...forlorn. And I felt so helpless. I couldn't hold his pain. He was so broken. I guess it terrified me, and I didn't know what to do.

"Somewhere in my little mind, I associated that fear and helplessness with intimacy. And so if you needed me...or you were less than super human, I panicked inside. I put up the emotional walls and withdrew—like a...a little hermit crab.

"I never put the pieces together...connecting my childhood fears and thinking...to our relationship. I just reacted to that feeling of being overwhelmed."

Dana took a deep breath, looking down, although she stayed in front of Hub. "I know it hurt you when I pushed you away, or pretended there was nothing wrong, even when everything in me was wrong."

Her chin trembled as she continued. "And then when I betrayed you with Mario, I just couldn't let you forgive me. Somehow that would require me to be too vulnerable. I know it's crazy-thinking, but somehow there was a distorted connection in my brain that would not let myself be forgiven by you—God yes, but not you."

Dana couldn't hold the tears back any longer, but she held her hands up, refusing to let Hub comfort her yet. "There's more. And then when I came to realize that we would never have children—that I have denied you the opportunity to be a father—that's still a big one, Hub. I don't know that I'll ever get past that. You would have been such a great dad—you are so wise. You have so much to give. But you got stuck with me."

No longer able to resist his comfort, she yielded to his arms. Sobbing into his shoulder, she mumbled apologies of, "I'm so sorry...I don't deserve you...you got stuck with me...can you forgive me?"

With Hub's muscular body enfolding her, and his familiar hands petting her back and shoulders—his kisses on the top of her head—her emotional storm finally ebbed. He murmured reassurance as if she were a child.

With his acceptance, Dana felt love with abandon—the emotional barriers swept away like a powerful receding tide. She sunk into his embrace, cherishing the new depth of intimacy.

Hub held her for a long time before he spoke. "I'm glad to be stuck with you, Dana. You're my soul mate. I would never have chosen a different life, even if I had known some of the heartache we would experience.

"I would rather be childless with you, than to have children without you. You're all I need — ever."

He cleared his throat, adjusting his neck before he continued. "I'm sorry this has stalled you for so long. It was so long ago — just let it go. We were kids. You couldn't see that coward for who he was. You were just trying to figure out who you were.

Hub slowly kissed a circle around Dana's face, emphasizing his words, "But you shoulda known you could never get away from me, Danella Jordan — I love you too much."

Their languorous love-making reflected a new depth to their relationship, a trust that Dana had never thought possible.

Later, as they shared a glass of wine, Dana told Hub the highlights of how things were going at the office, as well as her worry about one of her clients, who hadn't shown up for the last two group meetings. "She's so alone out there — so vulnerable. Such a precious young woman, yet she sees herself as worthless.

"You would love her, Hub. She's an encourager for everybody else, but she's blinded to her own strength and beauty. I worry so much about her. I tried to track her down, but her phone was disconnected. Her employer says she is no longer employed there. I don't know any of her friends, although she has a brother, I don't know his name. I'm just sick that something might have happened to her."

"I'm sorry, Honey. Surely something will come up. But you can't save 'em all…even if you are a miracle worker." Hub kissed Dana's nose and tucked her deeper into his arms.

"Speaking of the young and vulnerable…I sat next to a little gal all three legs from Seattle. She talked a mile a minute. About the only question she *didn't* ask me was why God gave men whiskers!

"Cute kid, really. I gave her our phone number in case she needs some help gettin' settled — I hope you don't mind."

"No, not if you think it was important. I trust you implicitly."

Dana set her wine glass on the table and repositioned herself to wrap her arms around him. She continued playfully. "You're a sweet guy, Hub. And intuitive. And loving. And so cute! Now, if you gave our number to every woman who wanted yours, that would most definitely be problematic." Dana poked his ribs, emphasizing each word as she spoke, "But I'm not worried about a …little…vulnerable…gal…from…Seattle."

Their playfulness was too much for the dogs to ignore. They all four ended up on the floor, laughing, barking, and playing together.

The weekend was long and leisurely as Dana and Hub enjoyed the rarity of being in tune with each others' energy and mood. They kept a fire in the wood stove, creating an ambiance that called for curling up with a good book under the afghan. They cooked together, spoke of plans for the new year, and enjoyed the silences in between.

Sunday evening, Hub and Dana were washing dishes. "Why was it you thought the girl on the plane was so vulnerable, Hub?"

"Oh, I don't know. She lost her dad. Doesn't have much family. Sounds like she'd gotten burned out with school. She thought she'd check Juneau out, but she didn't have a clue about how hard it is to find a winter job here.

"She must have some financial security, though, because it didn't seem to worry her that much. She wants her own apartment, even though her mother is here, so it made me wonder about that situation.

"But she's bright—she'll figure out what works for her. I thought if she called, we could have her out for dinner. Maybe suggest a few places to look for work. Could she could help you out some…with your billing, or something?"

"Oh, Honey, I don't think I've got anything. And I don't have the space. I'll keep my ears opened, though. Is she an office type?"

"Not really. She seemed pretty outdoorsy. A skier. Diver. She's interested in the fisheries. I don't know—maybe the little coffee shop at Auke Bay could use some help until she finds her sea legs. She may not even call. Who knows."

Chapter Twenty Three
A Precipitous Visitor

"I GOT A LETTER from Hannah, and she asks that I share it with you. I've also spoken with her Probation Officer. She's alright, but she is in jail." Dana paused to allow the differing emotions to undulate through the group.

"Thank God she's safe!" Annette's expression quickly changed from relief to questioning. "She is safe, isn't she? What happened?"

"I really don't know what will happen, but I believe she is safe. Essentially, she violated parole by drinking alcohol, so that is one charge hanging over her. And there was an altercation with her friend and her ex-boyfriend. There are charges pending on that—it sounds like she might have some culpability with that, but there wasn't a lot of information the PO could give me. I'm hoping to get in to see Hannah, and she may share more with us. At this point, it's all up in the air. Let me read her letter to you, and then we can discuss it."

> Dear Dana,
>
> I'm so sorry to be telling you this, but I'm in jail at Lemon Creek. I hate to drop out of group. Please let the girls know I'm sorry I let them down. You have done so much for me. I hope you'll forgive me. I'm so sorry.
>
> It isn't too bad here. I'm in a better cell now with only one other girl. My PO said I might get treatment and be able to work during the day.
>
> Thank you for all you did for me.
> Hannah

Dana looked around at the four women. She knew that

collectively, they loved Hannah and shared a sense of helplessness about her situation.

"You'd think they'd give her some slack! Why jail? What about her job?" Raydine hung her questions out to the group, not expecting answers.

"I bet that miserable boyfriend of hers had something to do with it, and he gets off Scott free!" Ellen didn't try to hide the venom behind her words. "It isn't fair. She works so hard to make it okay for everyone else, and then she slips up and gets slammed."

"Can we visit her?"

Dana nodded, "I think you can. She needs to designate you as a visitor, so if you're interested, you might drop her a note to let her know you want to see her. I sent a request to her through the Facility's front desk, so hopefully I'll hear soon that I can see her.

Dana continued slowly, allowing the women time to process what Hannah's dilemma might mean to her and to themselves. "I'm no expert on this, but I do know the Borough places a high value on rehabilitation. I would think...I hope...Hannah will benefit from some of their services. Hopefully, something good will come from this.

"I've got to work through some confidentiality issues, but I'm hoping to learn more. I think this group...our support...is important to Hannah. I'm glad we're here for her."

Raydine offered, "That outpatient treatment program they've got is a good one. My husband went through it several years ago. They let him out during the day so he could still work. Otherwise, we would have been in big trouble. It didn't help him with the pot, but at least he doesn't have the problem I do. With alcohol." Raydine ducked her head as if she regretted reminding the others of her addiction.

"Well, let's individually do what we can, and hopefully we'll have her back with us soon." Dana paused to allow group members to shift their focus from Hannah to themselves. "And how is everyone here?"

Raydine spoke quietly, nodding with each statement as if to confirm each thought. "Well, I'm thinking about divorcing my family—just writing them off. If I could be adopted by someone else legally, I would do it. Doug says I can't do that since I'm not a child, but I wish I could. Although I don't know who would want a second-hand step daughter who makes a mess of everything.

"I know it for sure now. My mom has chosen The Monster over me. That is never going to change. My sister says I'm the problem cuz I keep talking about it."

Raydine sighed loudly. "But I know that every time I try to be a part of the family, I'm the bad guy. I get depressed and then do something stupid to prove they're right."

Raydine's tears broke loose, but her face denied any shift in her proclamation. "I'm not drinking any more. I did write that article like you suggested, Jodi and it helped. In fact, I might send it to him.

"Cyndi and I are doing better. In fact, I went to the mall with her. We're going to put up some new curtains in her bedroom."

Dana waited through a silent moment, making sure Raydine was finished. "You seem pretty certain you need to separate from your family, Raydine. Do you think it needs to be as drastic as a *divorce*? What if you feel differently down the road?"

"I don't see any other way. They blame me for any stress in the family. They act like I'm being unfair to The Monster — like I should just forgive and forget." Raydine parodied her mother, "*We should just be able to be together as a family*. Frankly, I hope he burns in hell." Raydine looked up at Dana with a defiant look on her face.

"I understand, Raydine. And you don't need to apologize for how you feel. How you handle this relationship is absolutely your choice. No one knows better than you what the tradeoffs are, and I suspect all of the options are hard."

Annette squirmed in her chair. "I've sure felt like you do, Raydine. Sometimes I want to never hear from my mother again, but I don't have the guts to tell her. I think you should do what your heart tells you."

The ever-practical Ellen asked, "How would you go about divorcing them?"

"I've been writing in my journal about it. I think I'm going to write a letter to my mom; tell her she's made her choice, and to not call me again. I might change my phone number. But then I worry about my little girl—I want her to know her Grandma and cousins, but I can't allow her to be around The Monster. If my mom can't honor that...she's made her bed."

The group encouraged Raydine in a quiet way, each knowing what a drastic measure it would be for her. After some moments, Ellen spoke up.

"Well, divorcing your family is something to think about. Sometimes, I wish I had never become a mother." Ellen looked up abruptly, with panic in her eyes.

She spoke quickly. "I didn't mean that! That's not what I meant! I can't believe I said that. I wouldn't ever..." Ellen left the sentence unfinished, as she slumped back against the chair. She sighed resignedly. "My daughter showed up—totally unexpected. She ignores me for six months, then just shows up at my front door! She didn't have the courtesy to call ahead of time so I could be prepared!" Ellen looked around the group as if seeking affirmation for how bizarre it was to have a surprise visit like that.

"Don't get me wrong—I'm glad to finally see her—to know she's okay. I still can't believe she came to Juneau after all the times I asked her to visit." Ellen's voice changed, the indignation replaced by lament. "But I wanted it to be better. I would have gotten someone to work the shop for me. Rented a hide-a-bed so she could be comfortable, and stay with me. I would have had things nice for her.

"But she won't even stay with me." Ellen let out a deep breath. Her voice dropped an octave as she continued. "She said she might stay here for awhile—get a job. She dropped out of college. I don't know what that means—whether it's just a temporary withdrawal, or whether she loses everything she's done so far. All that money. I don't know if they put scholarships on hold, but I bet she'll lose them. I wish she would finish her education first—then it would be great to have her live nearby."

Ellen looked around, making eye contact with the others. She looked less frantic as she put words to some of her frustration.

Dana thought about what a change it was for Ellen to allow herself to be vulnerable in this group.

"I try not to pick at her—she gets so defensive, but I don't know what the real story is. She won't say anything about her so-called boyfriend."

Ellen closed her eyes briefly and lifted her chin as if making a promise to herself while she spoke staccato, "I'm going to take it a day at a time, and let things just be what they are. Like you said about Hannah...maybe something good will come from this."

"That sounds like a pretty good approach, Ellen — taking it a step at a time; just letting things unfold. Will you see each other soon...do you have plans to get together?"

Ellen went on, vacillating between helplessness and indignation. "We met for lunch Sunday — she's staying at a bed and breakfast out the road — and she's coming for dinner tomorrow night. I'm going to fix her favorite — stuffed manicotti and green beans sautéed in garlic. But I just don't know how to interact with her any more — she puts me on edge, and my whole body rebels. So instead of being able to have a decent conversation, I'm trying to keep my supper down. It doesn't seem to matter what I do — it'll be wrong."

"Wow. It sounds like such a mixed blessing: You finally get to have your daughter here...in your Juneau yet, but the unresolved *stuff* is hanging over your head."

"Yeah." Ellen looked pleadingly at Dana. "Could you counsel us? I mean, if she would agree to that?"

"We could look at that, Ellen. I wonder, though, if your worry is interfering with your understanding each other.

"Ellen, you're her mom. Even though you've had some differences, you have twenty years of loving each other — lots of memories and ties to each other. She's part of you. I can't speak from experience, but it seems natural to have to renegotiate aspects of a relationship over time, especially when kids become adults. That could be pretty intimidating — for both parents and young adults. It seems that if you can let things unfold, remembering that she's an adult and will make different choices than you would, maybe you'll learn to understand each other in new ways.

"And remember, Ellen, you have the opportunity to give your daughter hope. You've lived life long enough to know that storms are temporary — we get through them. Your daughter may not have that perspective yet. Whatever is going on with her, it was your doorstep she came to — not anyone else's. I think she needs her mom."

Ellen released her breath. "You're right of course. She did

come home...wherever that is. She doesn't have a real home any more, other than with me. I sold the last house she grew up in after she left for college. All the reminders of her dad are boxed up in storage. I have very little here that would make her think this is home."

Annette asked tentatively, "Ellen, what about your plans to go to college yourself — to work with other interior decorators?"

Ellen responded with certainty. "I have to let that idea go — unless she moves away from here. There's no way she would ever forgive me if I left now. No, no — that is not an option. She has some very strong opinions about parents' obligations to their children. She is very vocal about mothers who neglect or give up on their kids. I would lose the war right there, and she would never speak to me again."

Dana's face flushed. She felt like she had been slapped by the young woman's conviction. *Yes, what about those mothers who give up on their children before they even have a chance? Mothers like me.*

She mentally shook herself, shifting her personal pain to the far corner of her mind to be dealt with later. She stumbled through what seemed like a cliché, "Umm...that is a dilemma. Well, don't close the doors too soon. I'm sure there are answers waiting for questions."

"Thank you. That helps — that reminder. I'm going to hope for the best...and take an extra happy pill!" Ellen's humor suggested she was through being the center of attention.

Annette took a deep breath. "I'll go next. Actually, I'm in a pretty good spot...except for my worry over Hannah. That girl has a hold on my heart. I guess I see myself in her so much, and it tortures me that she is so alone. Growing up, there were people *around* me...family and neighbors...but no one *saw* me. No one knew what I was going through — that I was so lost and alone; or that things were happening to me that shouldn't happen to any child. It's like I was invisible — I couldn't even hint that something was wrong, or that I needed help. Everyone would be too angry. And my mother would have blamed me. So, I just tried to please everyone — whoever was bigger than me.

"And I fear that Hannah is living like that."   Annette

pointed her finger at the ceiling for emphasis, "I *am* going to see her. That girl is going to know that someone sees her…cares about her. She is not alone."

Annette's words spoke of a conviction that was new to the group, yet was not out of character. She was quieter than the other women, but they respected her. She spoke with such common sense.

The discussion side-tracked for a moment as the women expressed their concern about what troubles Hannah might be facing with no job and no place to call her own.

Jodi finally spoke. "I wish I could offer her a place to stay, but my apartment is so small, it's hard to not crowd Bounder. He doesn't have a problem with crowdin' me, but I try not to reciprocate."

Laughter eased the worry that had settled on the group.

Dana summed up the topic of Hannah. "Each of you has a wonderful heart. Hannah is blessed to have you for friends. And I am blessed to be associated with each of you."

Dana looked at Jodi. "Jodi, we've not heard how you are doing tonight. Is there something you'd like to share?"

"Not really. I'm still sorting through memories that seem to come in snatches. They come from out of nowhere. They're…startling. Terrible. My first reaction is to deny they're real, but I'm realizing they are true. They're real. They're hard. But no longer debilitating. I know I'm not crazy. I don't know why he picked me, but my uncle singled me out for torture." Her voice was now no more than a whisper. "And torture me he did."

Jodi's sad face was still, her eyes tracking images in her brain, momentarily losing awareness of the present and the people around her. She shook her head, and looked around at her concerned friends. "I'm sorry. I seem to be doing that a lot lately…zoning out at the most inopportune times. They're going to start calling me the crazy white lady."

"Is it affecting your work, Jodi? Is it too much?"

"No. No. It's actually getting better, if you can believe that. Somehow, knowing that it's not my imagination makes it easier to handle. The scientist in me deals better with facts. I can handle just about anything if I can understand it. But I am very thankful for the happy pills, as Ellen puts it."

***

Dana sat alone in the dark after the group left. She was vaguely aware of the wind blowing in from the channel, the rain pelting the south window. Emotionally drained, she wanted nothing more than to crawl into a closet and hide among the coats hanging on the hooks.

She suddenly remembered... *that's what I did as a child — hid away in the closet among Mom's coats and long dresses. If only I could do that now, and wait for this to pass.* She felt numb even as she studied the images in her mind that had been lost for so many years. She could smell her mother's lavender scent on the clothes and remember how she loved the softness, such a contrast from her usual attire of wool jackets or rain gear.

Her thoughts shifted to Ellen's comment, and the intolerance her daughter had for mothers who give up on their kids. Dana spoke quietly, "Give up on their kids — that's what I did. What if my daughter thinks like Ellen's daughter. Maybe that's why she hasn't searched for me"

Grief took control as she let the gut-wrenching sobs escape. She cried for the child she would never know. The mother she couldn't remember. The pain she caused Hub. She cried out loud, wet tears and mucus forming bubbles as she spoke out loud to the darkness, "He would have been such a good dad. He deserves so much more than I can give."

Mario's smug expression as he forced himself upon her loomed in her mind. *Why did I ever think I could possibly be interested in him, or that he could even compare to Hub. Why did I let him get close to me? I should have seen it coming. I should have screamed — clawed his eyes out.*

Dana cried until there were no more tears. She felt spent — hollowed out. Aware that it was getting late, she knew she would have to call Hub. *Thank God he's in Ketchikan tonight. At least he won't see the mess I am.* They had been so sweet together since he got back from Seattle, she didn't want to spoil it with her grief.

She finally forced herself to move toward the bathroom for a wet cloth. The mirror reflected her red, puffy, black-smeared eyes, and straggly hair clinging to her wet cheeks. "You're a train wreck," she spoke to the mirror. Hearing the words helped somehow, and her mind shifted to problem-solving mode. *What do I tell Hub? How do I contain it? How do I keep my grief from spilling over onto him?*

As she spoke out loud, Dana was surprised to hear her counselor voice. "Dana, he knows you better than you know yourself. Why not tell him truth?"

She laughed at her image. "That's a novel idea— unguarded truth." As she watched her shoulders square up, she thought, *That's what I'll do. I'll tell him I'm hurting over something said in group, but I don't want to talk about it over the phone. But when he gets home, I will tell him – all of it.*

Chapter Twenty Four
Drift to the Edge

"HANNAH, WOULD YOU STAY after class please? I want to talk to you." The addictions counselor turned to another woman to clarify their assignment, leaving Hannah waiting.

What now, she thought. She had been at Lemon Creek for three weeks, and was just starting to get used to the routine. She had almost slept a full night for the first time. It was so hard — she never had any privacy. Even the bathroom was open to others' prying eyes. The television blared all the time; the lights were always on, even during sleep time, and she couldn't have her own music. Her hands were raw from the soaps they used to clean the kitchen, which was her primary duty. The other women gladly left her that chore, and she favored it because she could have some time to think.

Hannah knew her life was over. *I swore I wouldn't be like my dad or mom; that I would make something of myself. And here I am — in jail and facing prison.*

Richard was lost to her forever. *If only I would have left it alone*

She knew she would have been fired from her job by now because she was AWOL. And with a felony, she would never be able to work in health care again. She couldn't let herself think about the clients she cared so much about. *Oh I hope Mr. Owen doesn't think I just deserted him. I hope someone is taking good care of him.*

Most of all, she worried about Bonner. Hannah fought back tears as she thought about him in the men's section, waiting for trial. *It was all my fault! He would have done anything I said — he just wanted to protect me. I alone am responsible for his going to prison.*

Hannah thought back to the day before her arrest. She had heard that Richard had moved Rena, her second cousin, into their apartment. That had been the final straw. When Hannah heard that Rena was using her things, she lost it. She tied on a big drunk with Bonner, then insisted she go get her things from Richard's house. It was pretty late. Well actually, it was early in the morning.

Rena opened the door wearing Hannah's bath robe. Before Bonner could stop her, Hannah attacked Rena, yelled obscenities at her, and tried to take her bath robe off her cousin. Then Richard came out of the bedroom yelling and calling Hannah names. Bonner lunged past Hannah and wrestled Richard to the floor. He kept punching Richard in the face and sides—he just went crazy. Hannah and Rena quit fighting and turned their attention to the men struggling on the floor. She screamed at Bonner to stop, but it was like he couldn't hear her; he just kept pounding Richard.

Finally, Hannah was able to get Bonner to stop when Richard was unconscious. Bonner backed away like he was in a daze—not realizing what he had done.

The police came, and Hannah kept sobbing and telling them it was her fault, but both were arrested for assault and battery. Of course, Hannah had broken conditions of probation by drinking, so she was also facing a probation violation. This time she couldn't beat it—she could never get past this one. It wasn't simply being drunk and disorderly, or driving under the influence. This meant prison, the loss of her job and any future that she cared about. Hannah didn't want to live any longer. Life was too hard.

Her thoughts dwelled on suicide. *I've screwed up everyone I ever cared about—my little brother, Bonner, Richard, Mr. Owen. Please God, I can't do this anymore. Please won't you help me die?*

Death was her only option. She had to find a way. In the mean time, she would go through the motions—act like she was okay; keep from being noticed. But she would be prepared when she got an opportunity to end her life.

Hannah's' hands had formed into fists, her eyes downcast. Her normally expressive face was unreadable. *I won't let anyone get close to me again. I'll wait it out...be ready to end it when I get the chance.*

Hannah's thoughts were interrupted when the counselor

called her name the second time. She motioned for Hannah to sit in the orange plastic chair across from her.

"How are you getting along in here, Hannah?"

"Okay."

"You don't say much, but I get the idea it's pretty rough for you."

"I do all right. It's not my favorite place to be." It was hard for Hannah to be so unfriendly with Ms. Hadway. She was a nice lady, but Hannah was determined to keep everyone out of her heart.

"Hannah, I'm worried about you. You have so much to offer, but you need to let us in. We can't help you if you won't open up to us."

Hannah's response was perfunctory. "I'm okay."

Ms. Hadway's face showed her frustration and sense of helplessness. "Hannah, Dana Jordan called again, and Annette Shipley has come to the front desk three times asking to see you. Won't you at least speak to them? Sign a release so they could visit you? They must care a lot about you to keep coming."

Hannah dropped her head, and in a whisper, said, "Can I go now?"

Hannah sat for long moments after she returned to her cell. She looked over at the stack of letters, opened at one end by the facility's security staff that must have screened for drugs. Hannah's hands shook as she reached for the stack of letters. She longed to know what they said. The women from her former life—*before I destroyed everyone I touched.* She pushed the letters back under the mattress so she wouldn't see them.

***

Annette walked away from the front entrance of the Lemon Creek Facility, her jaws clenched. *Lord, what am I to do? How can I reach this girl if you don't show me? You put her on my heart, didn't you?*

Annette's steps slowed as she examined the thought that came to her mind, then briskly turned and walked back to the entrance. "Do you have a volunteer program? I mean, is there some way I could come and visit with the women in this facility—you know, to encourage them? Or teach them a skill?"

"You'd have to speak with someone in administration," the young woman in uniform responded. "There are groups who come here—churches and twelve-step groups. There might be others, but you'd have to talk to them in administration. Down the hall, then take a right."

Annette couldn't believe what she was doing, but there was no way she could stop now. She had to find a way to reach Hannah.

Later, as she drove home, Annette's spirits plummeted. *What was I thinking? Of course they won't let just anyone walk in.* She had received a discouraging reception at the administration office, an official-looking packet of information for potential volunteers, an application for a background check, and a list of approved volunteer organizations. Presumably, she would have to participate in an orientation and training with them, and then work according to their schedules and dictates. It just wouldn't be feasible.

I just want to help Hannah, Lord. With three boys, I don't need to take on the whole population of Lemon Creek!

Chapter Twenty Five
Truth Unfolding

DANA FELT WEARY AS she slung her tote and scarf across the big chair, and stared out the window, slowly unbuttoning her sweater. The Matanuska ferry was headed north from Auke Bay in a misty fog that had settled just above the water.

From this distance, the blue and white ship showed no sign of propulsion or disturbance of the water, yet it moved steadily and quickly past Shelter Island and beyond view from her window. The ferries reminded Dana of the humpback whales that frequented the channel—their heads quietly breaking the surface of the water, clearing their blow holes with a distinctive *whoosh,* their massive arched backs appearing to stall before their tails flipped up, signaling their descent to greater depths.

She stared at the fog that had swallowed the ship.

"Hi, you." Hub walked toward Dana slowly with his head cocked to the side with that questioning look.

She walked silently into his embrace and closed her eyes, sinking into his warmth and strength. They stood quietly a moment before Dana spoke into his broad shoulder, "I'm so glad you're home. You fill me up."

Hub stroked her neck and shoulders, waiting for her to go on. Ever since she discovered the source of her fears, they were different together. Slower paced. Attentive to each other's mood. Dana was reminded of their teenage years when their relationship was so sweet and uncomplicated. She found herself again blushing at his tender affection, giddy with anticipation.

It seemed he was different too—more confident as a husband these last few weeks, responding in-kind to her slower pace. He delayed going to the shop in the mornings; lingered with her over coffee. He was more attentive to her thoughts and plans for the day. Their eyes communicated as much as their words.

Dana couldn't get enough of him—his presence; his smell, his body; just looking at him with new eyes. She was noticing little things about him that made her smile, like how he reserved the last touch for Mica after he loved on both dogs, and how he pushed his cap up and scratched his forehead when he was searching for the right words.

But they hadn't had any tension or problems either. She wondered now if it had been just a honeymoon phase and she would slip back into her habit of putting up walls between them. She had been tempted to hide away...think about it in isolation the way she had done most of her life. Figure things out before she spoke about them...if she shared it at all. But she squared her shoulders, remembering the beauty that had come from baring her soul with Hub. She was determined to not go backwards.

"It was a tough one yesterday, Hub, and today was not much easier. My little gal in jail refuses to let any of us visit her. One of the women in group has taken extraordinary steps to see her, yet she refuses to allow visitors. It is so unlike her — I can't help but worry about her."

She took a deep breath. "And then a comment was made in group, Hub." Dana's lower lip trembled. "One of my clients spoke about her daughter's venom toward mothers who give up on their kids. Her daughter is about the same age as Alex.

"I know she's young—and probably privileged. I doubt she's ever had to experience those kinds of choices, but it makes me wonder what Alex believes—if she thinks I just tossed her aside. That I didn't love her. That I...gave up on her before she even had a chance.

"I just want to know that she's okay. I keep hoping that somehow she'll know I love her—that I didn't give her up thoughtlessly. It was the hardest decision I've ever made in my life. The most important. And I made the wrong choice."

Hub hugged her tighter, silent for a long moment before he said, "Don't forget, Dana. God has a plan, even if we don't know the details. We've gotta wait on Him."

That night, Dana had another nightmare about Mario. She was running out Lena Loop Road when a black car swerved next to her, forcing her to step off the pavement. The windshields were darkened, and she couldn't see who was in the car. She was running around it when the car door suddenly opened and Mario lunged toward her, grabbing her arm. She tried to pull free, but his hand was like a clamp on her arm. She tried to scream, but no sound came out. Even as she struggled to get away, she saw the scene in slow motion — noticing how attractive his lavender polo complemented his olive skin. He was still beautiful, his expensive clothes hanging perfectly from his sculpted frame.

He had a smirk on his face, just like the night he had forced himself on her. She couldn't hear his words — his mouth seemed to swallow them before they could reach her, but she could tell he was accusing her.

She tried to scream *no*, but still her voice failed. Then his appearance changed. His sophisticated facade turned into a crazed monster, his face contorted and his thick curly chestnut hair spiraled out like spiked dreadlocks. Only his extraordinary hazel eyes seemed unchanged.

Dana kept pulling back from him, trying to run, trying to scream, but she couldn't get away from him. She couldn't breathe.

Finally, she woke up to Hub holding her shoulders, repeating her name reassuringly. Her heart was racing, and she was sweating profusely. She gulped air as she repeated, "I'm okay. I'm okay," trying to convince herself more than him.

Hub held her shaking body for several minutes, murmuring comfort. Finally, she was able to tell him that it was the old dream.

The nightmare had been absent for awhile, and she had hoped it had gone away with her break-through in therapy with Phyllis. It had always been so unsettling — ending her sleep for the night and often hanging at the edge of her subconscious for days. But this time, she was able to settle back into Hub's arms and talk about it.

"It's always the same...or a variation on the same theme. He catches me unawares. He's very attractive at first...chic. Then he changes into a monster, and I can't get away. He mocks me…accuses me—blames me. I can't stop him. Or speak. I can't tell him to stop.

"But I did tell him to stop. Then. Back then. I kept saying *no*, but he wouldn't listen, Hub.

"It was a rape, Hub. He…raped me. It wasn't a date or *unintentional-crossing-of-boundaries* type of a deal—it was a rape!"

Dana slumped back against the headboard, thoughtful of what she had just said. She used the word. Rape. She couldn't take it back. Never before had she told Hub that it was a rape. She had always hedged about their one involvement that produced Alex.

For twenty-one years, Dana had owned a part of the blame for that night. She told herself she had allowed herself to be vulnerable. She had dropped her guard—didn't see it coming. She blamed herself for being so naive. For not fighting against him harder. For not screaming until someone came to her rescue. She should have been able to prevent it.

For the first time, she could clearly see it for what it was. Yes, she had been naïve—she trusted a friend who was untrustworthy. But she had not led him on, nor invited his sexual assault.

She told Hub the story of Mario—admitting to being attracted to his sophistication and worldliness. "He was entertaining and always the center of attention. I guess I was sort of flattered that someone so popular would pay so much attention to me.

"He teased me about you, calling you my *Eskimo boyfriend* who would keep me in an igloo. He knew I loved you desperately. But after…after we broke up, I told the study group…and him…that we had broken up. I can see now that his teasing changed then to something more…earnest.

"I guess that's where my shame lays, Hub. I think I wanted the freedom to explore the possibility of a relationship with this guy who seemed bigger than life to my small town experience. But after you and I broke up, I realized my mistake. I couldn't think of him or anyone else. I was miserable without you, but I couldn't bring myself to beg you to take me back." Hub's arms tightened around her.

"Mario commiserated with me, but I can see it was just an excuse to…manipulate me, really.

"I kept him at arm's length emotionally...but I did let him comfort me. It seemed...okay.

"Then. Then...that night, I didn't feel like partying until the crowd decided to call it quits, and I let him drive me back to the dorm.

"He insisted on walking me to the door — *No gentleman would allow his lady to enter a dark dorm room alone*, he said.

"But then he came in my room, and started to kiss me. At first, I didn't want to appear dorky, so I tried to politely dissuade him. But he got more aggressive, and...it was like he couldn't hear me.

"He...then we were on the bed, and he was pulling my clothes away. I couldn't believe it was happening. I pleaded with him — *Don't do this, Mario. Don't do this!*"

"Afterwards, he cried. He pleaded with me to forgive him." Dana's tears flowed freely, her words erupting from the volcano of anger finally released. "He said he loved me, and never meant to hurt me. He wanted us to be together, to return to Brazil — his family would love me.

"I told him to leave; that I never wanted to see him again."

The muscles in Hub's jaws bulged as his teeth clenched, but he remained quiet as she collected her thoughts. She was calmer when she went on. "For a while, he kept calling, but I wouldn't answer the phone. Then he disappeared from campus. Later, I got a number of letters from Brazil, but I threw them away."

Dana's voice got husky as the tears began to spill over. "I'm so sorry, Hub. If there was any way I could rewrite that night...that month...I would. I would give anything to take away the hurt that you experienced because of my idiocy. I wanted to have a baby with you...to raise children with you. You would be such a wonderful dad."

It was awhile before he could speak, his jaws continuing to work. When he spoke, his gentle words came slowly; his voice hesitant at first. "Thank you...for telling me.

"I wish I could have protected you. It wasn't your fault. He's the kind of guy who preys on innocence. And that's who you are, Dana. You were...and are...innocent. You couldn't have seen it coming.

"I hate that it happened to you, but it in no way effects

my feelings for you. Yes, I wanted to raise children with you too, but God had a different plan, and I accept that. I couldn't have accepted living without you, though. You are my life. Always will be."

Eventually, Dana and Hub drifted off to a sound sleep encircled in each other's arms.

Chapter Twenty Six
Counsel From Uncle Hub

"DO YOU THINK I could talk to you sometime...about something personal? I mean, I don't want to bother you, but I just need to talk to someone older."

Hub's grin seemed to fluster Rachel even more as she sought the right words. "I don't mean that you're old...I mean an adult. An older adult. Like someone whose lived long enough to have some understanding of crazy-making parents, and yet can relate to what it's like to want your own life." Rachel exhaled, as if that was the tail end of the words bottled up inside.

"Sure Rachel. Do you mean right now?"

"Well, no, I've gotta finish my shift, but afterwards, or any time that works for you. I promise I won't take a lot of your time. And I hate to impose – I just don't have anyone to talk to yet – you're the only old person I sorta know here...I mean...you know what I mean."

Hub smiled at Rachel, enjoying her transparency. She was such a delightful, wholesome kid, and he wanted to help if he could. He grinned as he said, "I do know what you mean...I think – younger than an old geezer, but old enough to shave." Rachel's smirk showed Hub that he was somewhere in the ball park.

"Well, let's figure out when and where. I could check with my wife to see when it might be okay for you to come out to our place when she's home. Or we could visit over a cup of coffee here...or at a restaurant."

Rachel's expressive eyebrows furrowed as she shook her head. "Not here...too many of my customers coming and going. Would it be okay to meet at the Mexican place over by the airport? Any time it works for you. I get off at three o'clock generally."

"Well, that would work for me. If you want to meet me at Mi Casa's at three-thirty, that would be okay. Today?"

"Yes! That would be so awesome. Thank you so much, Hub. I hope your wife will be okay with sharing you for an hour or so. Would you please tell her how much I appreciate it?"

Hub left a voice mail on Dana's phone saying, "I don't think I'll be late, but you remember that little gal I met on the plane? The one who wanted to get a job here and an apartment? Do you remember my telling you that she's working at that coffee house in Auke Bay? Well, she asked if she could talk to me about *something personal*, insinuating that my advanced age might be of help. Anyway, I said I'd meet her at Mi Casa's at three-thirty and see if I can help. Stop by if you can—I would love for her to meet you. Otherwise, I'll see you when you get home. I love you. Oh…she said to tell you she appreciates your sharing me for a bit."

As he drove to the restaurant, Hub thought about the girl with the wild hair he'd been getting to know over the last several weeks. Her enthusiasm for life was contagious. He had watched her interact with her customers at the coffee house, and could see she was developing a network of friends in Juneau. People were drawn to her friendly personality and demeanor. She was also very attractive, with dark eyebrows and thick coffee colored hair that tensed against the hair band trying to hold it captive. Hub noticed that several local young men, including his best mechanic, had suddenly become coffee connoisseurs.

Rachel's face was so animated you could guess what she was thinking before she got her words together. Those expressive eyes danced as she questioned every detail about Juneau and Southeast Alaska, showing an excitement that reminded him of what an incredible area they lived in. She had told him of her dreams to work in the fisheries somehow—perhaps going to University of Alaska-Southeast and getting a degree in Fisheries Biology.

Hmm. She makes me feel kinda like an old uncle. Hub thought about how wonderful it would have been to have such a vivacious young woman in his family, perhaps even for a daughter. *She reminds me of Dana when we were just kids. In fact, she's kinda built like Dana — her long legs and slim hands that are always in motion. The poor kid…she doesn't have much family here.*

As Hub pulled in to the parking lot, he could see that Rachel's yellow Jeep was already there. *She must already be inside. Lord, please give me wisdom. Help me to serve You.*

Rachel waved vigorously when Hub walked in the door, greeting him with her usual enthusiasm. "Thanks for meeting with me, Hub. You don't know how awesome this is. I don't want to impose…I just needed to talk to someone older…oh, I don't want to go there again! Someone more mature. Here, have some chips and salsa; and a drink on me, okay?"

After the server had left their order on the table, Rachel suddenly seemed hesitant to speak. Hub allowed the silence, looking at Rachel with gentle encouragement. She finally let out her breath, and said, "Okay. This is harder than I thought. You don't know me well, and I hope I'm not crossing some invisible line. It's just that I trusted you from the first minute we started talking on the plane from Seattle. And…well…I don't have anyone else to go to."

Rachel focused on getting the salsa to spread evenly on her chip, while she searched for a way to start. She spoke slowly, presenting a quieter side that Hub had not seen before. "I moved up here to get away, mostly from the chaos with school and my old boyfriend. I didn't know I would love it here so much, but I do. I don't ever want to leave. I think I was destined to live here, ya know? It's the first time I ever cared about a *place*. I grew up in California, then Washington, but they were just places where I lived. *Here* is different. It's like my soul found *home*. I've never felt like I had a home before, even though I don't really have a *home* home — just an apartment.

"I'm talking in circles, I know. Sorry. I moved here at first because my mom was here. I thought I could at least see her for a bit while I was sorting things out. See, she and I haven't been on the best of terms for a long time. She's kind of…high strung. We're just not good together — I'm always angry and she's always super critical.

"Anyway, coming up here, I thought I was caving in to her constant nagging, but when I got here, she blew a gasket cuz I didn't do it *properly*." Rachel's eyebrows danced as she playfully mimicked her mother's expression. "That would mean thirty days advanced notice; negotiations about everything from what I planned to bring, where I would park my belongings, how I would prepare for Juneau climate, and did I have my mail forwarded!"

Rachel laughed, her eyes and hands exclaiming her frustration with such details. "We've always been oil and water together. Dad used to intercede for us a lot—sort of calming the storms. But I lost him seven years ago. Since then, it's been even harder to get along with her.

"Thankfully, I started college early and she moved up here, so our time alone and in the same house was short. It's helped to be a thousand miles apart. We were actually adjusting to each other a little better."

Hub interjected, "But now that you've moved here, it's a different story?"

"Exactly." Rachel rubbed her hands, setting her jaw before she continued. "I don't want to be angry all the time, but frankly, she-drives-me-crazy! Every time I try to interact with her, I find myself feeling like a little kid again, trying to please her, then blowing up because I can't. It's impossible to please her."

Hub set his coffee cup down. "That must have been pretty tough—losing your dad. Tough on you both."

Rachel's eyes got watery, her voice catching. "Very tough. He was my world. I was his little girl. He was the one who was fun—he made everything playful. He softened Mom's harshness somehow—made it less of a big deal. I could handle things because I knew he'd be home on the weekend and we would go skiing or rafting...hiking...or just for a walk around the lake and end up at Lakey's for a Loganberry milkshake. That was our favorite!

"When he was killed, I didn't think I could go on. I holed up in my room, wanting to simply disappear. Luckily, my best friend's mom insisted I go with them to the cabin for the summer, and I eventually came back to life.

"Mom just got busier and more...*industrious*. That actually describes her quite well—industrious." Rachel emphasized the word by lifting her eyebrows, looking down her nose, and shaking her head stiffly from side to side.

Hub couldn't help but chuckle at Rachel's pantomime.

"Do you think that might have been her way of dealing with the pain of losing her husband?"

"I guess so. I don't know. They were always fighting anyhow. Sometimes I wonder if maybe his death was even a relief to her." That thought caused Rachel to pause before continuing.

"She constantly nagged him about his drinking, or his work, or his hours, or his partying. He couldn't be good enough—like me."

Hub could see the hurt that Rachel kept trapped beneath the surface. "I'm sorry you had to experience that, Rachel. You're a pretty special gal in spite of the hardships. What kept you from rebellion, or drugs?"

"My mother would say I rebelled, and I guess I did some. My rebellion has been to avoid *her*. Dad left me a trust that has allowed me some independence.

"And drugs are for losers! I just won't go there. I don't even want to be around anyone who uses. And frankly, I'm a little afraid of alcohol or drugs. I don't know much about my biological parents, and some part of me fears there's a gene in me that would awaken if I tried them, and then I'd *really* lose control."

"Well, that seems pretty mature to me—caution at your age is not the norm, it seems. It sure wasn't for me when I was your age."

Rachel beamed, her dimple deepening. "Thanks. I do take some hassle over it at times—I think some guys see it as a challenge to test my resolve. But I don't care—that's who I am."

She scrunched her eyebrows, nervously tapping her front teeth with her thumb nail. "I guess what I wanted to talk to you about is... I want to know if you think I'm way off base. See, I'm thinking about writing my mom a letter, saying I'm taking a sabbatical from her, and that I'll call her after I've worked some things out. It's not like it would be that different from what it's been the last several years—we've been apart since I was seventeen. But since we're now in the same town, I need to make a statement about my independence. I don't want her hovering or getting into my space. I don't want her to call me or come to my apartment. I just don't want her constant ...nagging!" This last word spewed forth from

Rachel as if she had swallowed salt water. "I want to have a breather from this resentment I have every time I talk to her."

"That seems pretty drastic, Rachel. I'm no expert on parenting—I never got to have kids of my own, but it would seem pretty harsh to be banned from seeing my own daughter. I imagine that would hurt a lot. Have you tried talking to someone like a pastor or counselor about this?"

Rachel's face showed her rejection of that idea before she said a word. "I know what a pastor would say." Rachel's head bobbled on her neck as she mimicked a graceless erudite. "Honor thy father and thy mother; think about all she's done for you; what you are doing to her; you're very young yet; yada yada yada. I'm sorry, that is not an option."

Hub couldn't help but smile.

"I don't know about the shrink option. Maybe. I think it would take too much. They'd have to work miracles on my mom. She'll never change. And I don't want to go there...to drag it all out and bleed all over it."

Rachel put her elbows on the table, palms on her eyes. "I just want to be left alone. But I love my mom too; I don't want her to be too deeply hurt. I just want to have some time to establish myself here, make my own decisions, and not be angry all the time. I don't want to leave here. But I have this constant gut-churning.

"See, that's the thing. I'm either worried she's going to call; feeling guilty because I haven't called; or bummed because we did talk. There's always so much drama—I hate that!"

Hub chuckled, truly enjoying Rachel's sincerity. "You've got a good heart, Rachel. I'd listen to it. And if you want to talk to a pro, Dana, my wife, is a counselor. And she knows all the counselors in town, so she could either see you or refer you to someone if you want."

"I remember you saying your wife was a counselor. Cool. Does she psychoanalyze you?"

Hub's robust laughter was instant. "As a matter of fact, she does at times. Or rather tries to. But that's the beauty of marriage, Rachel—we're always trying to figure each other out. I'd like to say it was always in an effort to support and encourage each other, but we get pretty selfish at times too, and have to make apologies."

"That's something my mother would *never* do for my dad. He was always saying he was sorry about something, but I never heard her reciprocate."

"And then it was too late." Rachel's eyes watered again, and her voice softened. "He died in a one-car accident. Mom normally would have been with him, but she was mad at him and didn't go that night. He shouldn't have been driving — he'd had too much to drink."

"And you think if she would have gone with him, it would have been different?"

"I would still have my dad. I miss him so much, sometimes I think I'll go crazy."

"That's a tough one.

"Aren't you assuming a lot, though, Rachel? If she had gone, the accident wouldn't have happened? What about other possibilities?"

Rachel nodded. "I know. I could have lost them both. I know that logically, but...they just fought all the time, and I think the more she nagged, the more he...stayed away. And drank."

"Well, that's a lot to work through, Rachel. I'm no expert, but I'd sure hate to see you give up on your mother."

"That's what I was afraid you'd say. But thanks, Hub. At least you didn't do that *honor your mother crap*."

He chuckled at her youthful perspective. "What advice would your father give if he was still here?"

"Don't let it bother me. She means well." Rachel slumped back in her seat.

"Sounds like some good advice, Rachel. I'm humbled that you shared this with me. I don't know if I'm much help, but I'll be glad to lend an ear any time."

Hub gave Dana's card to Rachel, and encouraged her to seek counsel from someone who would know how to help. "Maybe Dana could help you *and* your mom talk things over."

As they left the restaurant, he gave her shoulder a squeeze, and said, "You'll figure this out, Kiddo. Don't get stuck thinking this season represents the whole year."

Chapter Twenty Seven
Tentative Return

DANA AND HUB WERE bundled up in their parkas, hoods pulled snuggly around their faces, red rubber boots gripping the rocks as they walked the dogs along the beach. Their breaths created little clouds when they spoke, although they didn't say much.

Dana thought the night seemed magical—it felt so private, she didn't want to interrupt the moment. The moon was so bright she turned off her flashlight, as they both paused to watch the dogs explore every nuance of the beach. They could hear a raven in the trees above them; its loud warble toggled through the slight mist.

Hub pulled her close, his arm around her shoulder, as they looked over the scene before them. "It feels almost holy. It has my whole life, yet I'm still astounded by its splendor. You'd think a person would become accustomed to it, but I'm not. The beauty surprises me every time. I hope I never lose that sense of awe at His creation."

"Me too." Dana couldn't think of when she'd felt more content than this very moment. The night's beauty surrounded them, hiding any blemish of the world or worries she sometimes carried. Southeast Alaska did that to her. It was like she couldn't hold the magnificence of this small part of creation and a distressing thought at the same time. "It fills me like no other place I've ever been. And you fill me, Hub, in ways that's scary at times. It's scary to love someone as much as I love you."

Before long, the cold drove the lovers back to the house, followed by two excited dogs. As they removed their coats and boots in the mud room, Hub said, "Oh, I forgot to tell you. I gave your card out today. To Rachel... at Mi Casa's. Too bad you couldn't have joined us. She needs to talk to you, but for some reason I'm the trusted uncle. Anyway, she's got problems with her mom, and probably could use some professional perspective, so I suggested you might talk to her or give her a reference. I hope that's okay."

"Sure. She seems to be taken with you, my handsome husband. Could there be a little infatuation going on there? Maybe a little hero worship?"

Hub chuckled. "Not likely. She said she needed the perspective of an *old* person. I think she just hasn't found her sea legs yet—still getting to know people. I'm probably the only geezer among her acquaintances so far. Although, it seems she's become a favorite." He chuckled again, "Even the boys at the shop have come to prefer the coffee drinks over the mud in the shop pot!"

Dana was thoughtful before responding, so content with the moments with Hub. "I'm sure your wisdom is just what she needed. But if she calls, I'll do what I can. It might be best to give her Amy's number—she works so well with teens. How old is she?"

"She's got some college. Must be twenty...nineteen. She's got a year and a half of college."

"Hmm. I wonder if she could be related to one of my clients. *That* would be a trip. Yeah, if she calls, I think I'll refer her out just in case."

***

Dana refilled the teapot in preparation for her Tuesday group. *I wonder if there is any connection between Hub's Rachel and Ellen's daughter. I don't know that Ellen has ever mentioned her daughter's name. Aha...I can check that out! She probably listed her on the in-take documents.*

Dana pulled Ellen's chart and thumbed through it, hoping she included her daughter's name and that it wasn't Rachel. *Rachel Patton. Crap!*

I wonder if Hub knows his Rachel's last name. What then? I need to protect Ellen's identity. Yet I need to avoid any conflict of interest. This could be a problem if she keeps close to "Uncle Hub."

***

The front door opened — a little too early for the group to start arriving. Dana walked out to the group room, and was surprised to see Hannah standing there, still in her parka. Her nose was red and eyes watery from the cold.

"Hannah! Oh my darling girl, you're here! I'm so glad to see you. Take your coat off — come get warmed by the phony fire."

Hannah's expression was hard to read. Her shoulders drooped as if in relief, but only for an instant. Then she began to fidget, stepping away from Dana and looking at the wall as if studying some unseen object.

She spoke without expression, "Is it all right if I come back? I'm out of jail, for now anyhow. I'm required to be in counseling."

"Of course you can come back, Hannah. I'm so glad you're here. I'm certain the gals will be thrilled too. We've all missed you so much." *Calm down, Dana...give her some breathing room. There's something else going on here.* "How about some tea or hot chocolate?"

"Thanks." Hannah quickly shifted her attention to the fixings on the counter.

"I'll let you catch your breath, Hannah. This must be uncomfortable for you after being gone for so long. I hope you'll forgive my exuberance. Just know that you are loved here, and we welcome you back."

Hannah spoke quietly without looking at Dana. "My ride needed to drop me off early tonight. I'm sorry. Could I just sit here until the others come?"

"Of course. Yes." Dana turned back to her office. "I'll just give you some quiet time and see you in a little bit."

Hannah settled in a chair by the fake fireplace, letting the steam from her hot chocolate warm her hands and face. Her mind was racing; her gut shaking. She feared she would explode from the tension inside her chest. She wanted to reach for Dana and cry into her shoulder. She wanted to run, to get out of here before Dana could see her turmoil...her plan. *Go before the ladies get here!* But if she ran, she would simply be arrested again and go back to Lemon Creek. If that happened she'd never be able to carry out her plan. *Yet how can I stay and not let the ladies know what I'm feeling. I can't look at them. I've got to be strong. Otherwise, I will hurt them like I've hurt everyone else in my life.*

Her sad eyes stared at the floor; her body still. She thought about Emma, who had dropped her off, and would be waiting for her after group ended. Emma, the sweet sweet lady who had taken Hannah in, prepared a cozy bedroom for her, and said she would be there for Hannah as she did outpatient treatment. She wouldn't let Hannah lift a finger those first two days, saying she just wanted to spoil her for awhile; that Hannah could *earn her keep* later.

Hannah was so angry at God—how could He do this to her? It was hard enough already to stay away from people—to keep from ruining anyone else's life. And then she ended up in Emma's home. It was so safe and comfortable there. It seemed that every inch of the walls were filled with pictures of people—grandkids, Native dancers in their native dress; salmon and halibut held up by excited fishermen; Emma as a young woman accepting an award of some sort. There were old pictures of cabins along the beach with fish drying in the traditional way.

The walls told Emma's history, and displayed such lovely emblems of Alaskan culture: A Chilkat blanket; beautifully woven baskets; dance fans; and several intricately carved ivory pieces. Hannah had almost cried out when she saw a hide drum with the Tlingit-Haida raven painted on it. Her grandmother had one very similar to this when Hannah was a little girl. *I wonder whatever became of it.*

Hannah thought about the sequence of events leading up to her release to Emma's care. Ms. Hadway, the addictions counselor back at Lemon Creek, had approached her again after class one day. She'd said, "I wonder if you would be willing to consider being part of an experimental program we are just implementing here at Lemon Creek. I don't expect you to make a decision right away, and I don't have the authority to say *yes* or *no* to the proposal—there's a lot of hoops to jump through with the charges hanging over your head, but here's the deal: Rather than living here in the facility, you would be placed with a family. A Tlingit family. The idea is that you would be able to learn some things about your culture and have good support while you're working your recovery program.

"You'd come here for classes, but stay with the family in

their home. Eventually you'd be able to get a job, and have more freedom, but the idea is that the family, the program, and your Probation Officer would all be working together to make sure you have the best support to be successful. Would you think about it?"

Hannah started to reject the idea immediately, but then thought it might be the opportunity she'd been looking for to carry out her plan. Maybe this would be the avenue to get a hold of some drugs or a rope so that she could end the suffering. *I can't seem to find a way in here.*

"Okay. I'll think about it. Who would I be living with?

"I don't know that yet. Like I said, it's a new program. But there are some volunteer families who have been taking classes so they can learn how to help people with addictions effectively—avoid enabling."

"What would I have to do?"

"You'd be part of the family, so you would need to participate—help around the house; join in family activities. You'd have to always be with someone initially. The family would transport you to your classes, and eventually your job. Over time, you would earn more independence. I'd like to see you return to your therapy group with Jordan Counseling."

Hannah's head came up sharply, looking at Ms. Hadway. For just an instant, there was hope showing in her face, but Hannah quickly closed off all expression. "I'm no longer interested in that group. I would rather just come here for the addictions stuff."

"Well, we'd have to see what would be required. Just think about it, will you? It's a rare opportunity, Hannah, and I think it might be life-changing for you."

Hannah's attention returned to the present with the hot chocolate. She looked around, wondering how long she'd been thinking of the past, holding the steaming cup close to her face.

Dana came back in the room, setting her papers on her chair. She smiled briefly when Hannah glanced up at her. As Dana stirred her tea, Hannah spoke softly. "I don't know if this is such a good idea. I've been gone a long time, and things are different for me now. But my Probation Officer required me to come back. Well, she's not really a PO in this program—more like a case manager. I just don't want to hurt anyone, and I seem to be doing a lot of that. I don't blame the girls if they don't want to see me — I deserve it."

"Why don't you give them a chance to tell you what they think, Hannah? They'll be here in a few minutes. I, for one, care deeply about you, and I hope you'll stay."

Ellen was the first to come through the door, bringing the crisp night air in with her. She was obviously cold from the walk. Her teeth chattered as she shed her coat and scarf, "Oh, it is so cold tonight, I almost wish I...well, hello, Hannah! This is a surprise."

Hannah gave her a fleeting glance and turned away to avoid seeing the condemnation in Ellen's face. "Yeah, I'm just like a bad penny."

"Well, are you back with us? Does this mean you're out of jail? Sorry, I shouldn't rush you — you'll have to repeat yourself five times! Well, welcome back anyway." Ellen turned her back as she fixed some tea.

Raydine and Annette soon came in, absorbed in a conversation about on-line college classes. When they noticed Hannah, they both exclaimed their surprise and welcome.

Annette spoke excitedly as she hugged Hannah to her. "I've missed you so much. I was afraid I wouldn't get to see you for a long time. You're so special to me, Hannah."

Jody slipped in the door unnoticed in all the excitement. "Well, I'll be darned! We're a full house again. Glad to see you back, Hannah."

The session turned into quite a reunion, with lots of tears and laughter. Hannah fought to stay aloof, but she couldn't be rude in the face of their interest and love. Her natural tendency to love them was at war with her determination to protect them from being hurt by her doom.

She avoided talking about herself for most of the session by asking for updates on the others. Ultimately, though, the talk settled down and five sets of eyes looked at her expectantly. Dana had told Hannah she could share as much or as little as she wanted to.

"Well, I'm here...and still can't quite take it all in. I'm still getting used to civilian clothes and a quiet bedroom. A really nice lady, Emma Newhart, is letting me stay with her. She did some training as a volunteer to do this — to do this program to help people like me do out-patient treatment."

Hannah's voice was soft, her words spurting out in pieces. "I don't know though...it might be too late. I made a terrible mistake that hurt a lot of people. Bonner, my friend, is in jail because of me, and he might go to prison. It wasn't his fault—he was just protecting me. I guess Richard was hurt pretty bad—Bonner beat him up. He called me some names, and Bonner just lost it. And I still have felony charges hanging over my head, but the case manager lady said it might be dropped if I complete this program. So...here I am.

"It was really hard coming back here. I was afraid you...I'm embarrassed. I let everybody down."

Jodi broke the short silence that followed Hannah's speech. "Well, I'm glad you're here. It's like we're a five-piece orchestra, but the cello has been missing. We sound tinny without you."

Ellen said, "You're as important as the rest of us. You need to be here."

Annette looked at Hannah, willing her to make eye contact. "I don't know if I can say this right, Hannah, but I've not had a good night's sleep since you've been missing in action. You've taught me a lot about myself, and I felt like a part of me was missing. You're so important to me. It's not like you're one of my kids, it's like you're a part of me. I don't know how to explain it cuz I don't even understand it myself. I just need you to be part of this group and my healing, and I want to be part of your healing. You matter—I want you to know that."

Hannah's chin trembled, but she didn't speak.

"I feel that way too." Raydine looked at Annette, then Hannah. "I'm older, but I feel the same way as Annette. You're really important to me. You have to be here...part of us.

"Dana, can we schedule another meeting? We just didn't have enough time tonight."

"It's hard to end this evening, isn't it? We're finally a *full house* as Jodi says. I'm afraid we will have to wait until next Tuesday, though. Hannah, can you make phone calls during the week? Or even write to keep in touch?

"I think so. It's just that someone has to be with me all the time...someone who has had the volunteer training, so it's kinda hard. I'm going to try to get in touch with my little brother, so I need to figure that out first thing. I'll call if I can."

"Well, could you do an individual session with me? Would you like to do that?"

"Umm...I'll have to see."

The women left reluctantly, with lots of assurances and attention to Hannah. They stood out front watching her drive away with Emma.

***

Juneau's weather changed for the next several days with a warm Chinook wind coming from the west. The snow melted fast, inviting Juneauites to get outside during the day. But as the temperatures dropped in the evening, the streets became treacherous with black ice.

Dana cancelled Friday afternoon appointments, wanting to avoid unnecessary travel when the roads were dangerous. She welcomed the extra time to be with Hub in the evening. It wouldn't be long before his business would demand longer days.

The shop door was opened when she arrived home early. Hub walked out to greet Dana with a coffee in hand. "Dang, if I'da known you were coming home so early, I would have waited — even bought you a mocha latte."

Dana walked to the shop, grinning at Hub. "Are you thinking that might count as a date? One *grandé* mocha latte, and my sweetie will think I'm marvelous?"

Hub hugged Dana to him as he chuckled deep in his throat. "Well, it used to work — even before we had fancy coffee. Only it seemed like it was a Diet Pepsi in those days. What would it take now to make you think I'm marvelous?"

"Hmm...not much, I think. You're already Mr. Wonderful to half the Borough. And I'm president of the fan club.

"By the way, Uncle Hub...how's it going with Rachel? Have you talked to her any more since your afternoon counseling session?"

"Not really — just pleasantries with the coffee. I'd like her to meet you."

"Honey, I'm not sure, but I might have a conflict of interest there. Do you know her last name?"

"Let's see...I think it's Patterson...Peterson...Patton.

That's it—Patton."

Dana looked chagrined, "I was afraid of that. Yeah, I'm going to need to avoid associating with her, I'm afraid. I hope that's okay with you—you do seem to be smitten with her."

Hub rubbed his unshaven jaw, his eyes adrift as he quickly processed several unspoken scenarios. They had spoken before about the tight rope Dana walked in this small town, trying to avoid relationships with clients and their families. Finally, he said, "Dang. I didn't want to hear that."

Dana watched as Hub's scrunched eyebrows and mouth reflected his internal debate. "Dang, Dana. Are you sure? I mean, I know you can't say much, and I don't want you to, but this little gal really tugs at my heart. It's not that she's needy...she's just...sweet.

"Reminds me of you in high school...although my thoughts are more fatherly—unlike my thoughts of you twenty years ago...and now." Hub looked directly at Dana, holding her shoulders affectionately.

"We've joked about me being *Uncle Hub*, but that really does fit how I feel about her. She's sorta like a niece. I find myself thinking about her future, and wanting to help her along the way. I wanted you to meet her."

Dana studied Hub's face, aware that his connection to this young woman was more than casual. "Honey, I won't ask you to give up a friendship...or whatever this is. I suspect you're important to her too. I'll just need to be cautious—avoid social situations that might be intimate."

"I guess that means a fishing trip would be out, huh? Even if we took a number of people?"

"I'm afraid I couldn't be a part of it. But you could take a buddy—or Dad—and show her the waters. Or maybe one of her friends. Maybe her boyfriend?"

"Yeah, maybe. I guess we'll figure it out. It's just...a bummer. But that's what I get for marrying such a beautiful, successful, woman of integrity."

As they walked to the house arm in arm, Dana made a mental note that she needed to speak with Ellen about the connection between her daughter and Hub so they could alleviate any possible conflict of interest.

Chapter Twenty Eight
Intercession Offered

JODI SPOUTED OFF BEFORE the group started. "I saw my first skunk cabbage this week! Spring is definitely on its way. It's my own personal reminder that these long dark nights come to an end, and I can make it. The sun will shine again...I'll be able to get back out in the woods soon!"

Jodi's enthusiasm garnered some kudos.

"How is the depression, Jodi? It seems different for you now." Dana had that inquisitive look on her face that suggested some exploration.

Jodi's laughter was stuck in her throat, but rolled out with her smile. "You know...it is different. Lots different. I hadn't realized it until just this moment, but it was a lot different for me this whole winter. It was hard to drag myself out of bed last year and hard to go to sleep. I dreaded the nightmares. But they're almost gone...maybe once a week they wake me up.

"That's a big difference. Before, I was having a couple a night. I think Bounder especially likes the change."

The group waited, seeming to anticipate there was more to this discovery.

"When I stop to think about it, just about every aspect of my life has changed since I discovered that the dreams were memories — recovered memories, is that what it's called? Anyway, I can stay focused during the most grueling budget meetings now. I'm not zoning out as much — I can catch myself starting to numb out and make a conscious choice to stay present. And I'm lovin' it here in Juneau!"

"Great. And how are things going with your family?"

"Much better. My sister and I are like friends now. I used

to feel like I needed to take care of her...be an additional parent to her — Lord knows she needed more than we had. But talking about personal stuff with her — like what happened to me as a kid — has allowed her to grow up. I mean, grow up in my eyes. She's a wonderful, responsible, insightful person, but I was kinda blinded to that before.

"In fact, she's pushing me to *blow the whistle* on my uncle. He's an old man now, and I don't really see the point, but Mugs, my sis, is pushing me pretty hard to do something — do a police report, or something."

Dana asked, "How do you feel about *blowing the whistle?*"

"I don't know that I'm ready for that yet. I do worry about his access to other children, but he's so old, that's not likely a problem anymore. We haven't had any contact with them for a lot of years."

Dana paused as she looked around the group. "That is a question some of you may be grappling with, isn't it: Whether or not to reveal the ghosts in the closet — to expose your perpetrators? To take the chance of alienating yourselves from those who side with them, or simply don't know what to do with the fact of it. To expose your own pain with the truth of victimization."

Raydine said, "I'd like to say something. You remember that I divorced my family awhile back? They already knew to some extent what had happened to me as a little girl. They knew that The Monster was inappropriate with me...sexually, but they didn't know the details. I used to think they didn't need to know the ugly details, but they didn't seem concerned about him being around other kids. I wanted them to know enough so they would keep my nieces from him.

"So, I wrote a letter. I copied parts of my journal, and wrote a letter to my mom telling her why I could no longer be part of the family. I copied that letter, and sent it to my sister and to my brother, in case he ever has a family. I don't know if they read it...or ever will...but they have it. They know now. They have no excuse. It's on them if another little kid gets hurt by him. But I hope not."

"Wow, Raydine...that's a big step. When did you send the letters?"

"A week or so ago. And I'm still glad I did. I know I made the right decision to divorce them." Raydine's eyes filled with tears. "It's okay. I'm making a new life, and new friends." She glanced at Annette. "And this group. This is family now.

"I'm not saying that's what you need to do, Jodi...it just seemed like a good time to tell what I did."

"Well, that's something for me to consider. Thanks, Raydine. I've got my sister solidly behind me, so it's better for me in some ways. And my mom doesn't know about it—she's just...a bit clueless about life, I guess. It's the Midwest relatives—the ones who are in his circle in Nebraska who maybe should know. Actually, I'm going to do some prayin' about it before I do anything—one way or the other."

Dana shifted in her chair, taking a moment before asking, "Raydine, how is it going with Cyndi?"

Raydine tipped her head side to side. "Good in some ways, and...tough in other ways. I think she understands a little better why I won't let her be around my parents. She seems to accept it a little more. But she doesn't believe it could happen to her—she's older than I was, and she thinks she could speak out. But when I bring up her emails with Buddy and how inappropriate he was, she shuts down."

Her shoulders scrunched as she summed up her position, "So, I'm trying to keep the doors of communication open and take it a day at a time."

Dana nodded. "It sounds like you've got a good handle on it." Turning to her left, she asked, "Hannah, how is it going for you?"

Hannah glanced at Dana, but avoided holding eye contact with anyone in the group. "Okay. I'm doin' what I'm supposed to do. It's all right."

"You don't sound very convincing, Hannah. It's been a rough year for you so far. How can we be there for you?"

"I'm fine. I want to pass."

The silence in the room hung heavy as the women must have thought about the agreement made at the beginning of group—*you don't have to share in group; you can pass.* But it was obvious that things were not okay with Hannah. She was troubled, but secretive about it. Tonight she wasn't offering encouragement or attention to the other women like she normally did.

"I'm worried about you, Hannah." Dana spoke gently.

"You seem pretty depressed. We'd really like to hold some of that burden you're carrying."

Hannah didn't speak for a moment, staring at the floor in the center of the group. She gave a perfunctory smile, her eyes only glancing toward Dana. "Really, I am okay. I'm just doing a lot of thinking. Maybe I can share it next time."

Dana decided to not push the issue further in group, but to contact Hannah's program manager and discuss her concerns. Something was going on with Hannah, and Dana worried about the potential for suicide. It could be the adjustments of being out of jail, participating in a new program, living with a host family, or a myriad of other issues. It could also be that she was overwhelmed, and feeling hopeless. Dana decided she would have to catch up with Ellen later regarding her daughter and Hub.

***

"Emma, I feel terrible that you have to come out in this cold and darkness to pick me up at group. I'm so sorry to have put you in this position."

Emma showed no response to Hannah's comment, her eyes holding steady to the dark road ahead. She was a small square woman, with short black hair that framed her round face. Her high cheek bones and heavy eyelids spoke of her Native heritage. Although she was quiet by nature, there was something about her that made Hannah believe she held the wisdom of their people.

After a moment, Emma said, "I am happy to be the vehicle, Hannah. It is honoring."

Hannah glanced at Emma in the dark, but decided to say no more. *Honoring. I don't want to know what she means – I cannot love her. I am not deserving. My plan is not honorable. I have no business being around such an honorable woman. I've got to leave before I hurt anymore people. Tonight. It's got to be tonight. I'll slip out after she goes to bed.*

Hannah stared out the window as they crossed yet another intersection. She focused on the contest between the car's defrost system and the ice that quickly chased each swipe of the windshield wipers. Emma's soft voice startled Hannah back to the present.

"Hannah, the struggles within you might seem like a

boulder to you at this time. It weighs heavy in your heart. Maybe it hides all the pathways.

"Did you ever play on the rocks when you were a little girl? Do you recall being behind a big stone where your whole view was blocked—you couldn't see the road...or trail?"

Hannah was aware that Emma glanced at her. She muttered, "Yes," but continued to stare out the front windshield.

"Perhaps you couldn't even see the trees or the water, but you knew they were there. Even though you might have been playing, or even gotten scared when you couldn't see your grandmother, you knew the paths were there. The trees. The water. You knew that if you would just walk a few steps to the side, you would find them again.

"Try to remember, Hannah. The paths are still there.

"Our people have lived through war and famine. Death and injustice. Separation from loved ones. And our own weakness with the white man's liquor. But it has not always been this way. Even that is changing. Our young people are starting to return to the old ways. Our values."

When Emma stopped at the stop sign, she waited, even though there was no cross traffic.

"We are a strong and wise people, Hannah. We have endured many hardships, and yet we remain whole. We have adjusted to the white man's world, but not lost our culture. Our identity. Our history. Our ancestors continue to give us wisdom.

"You may not see the path before you right now, Hannah, but it is there. A good path that holds happiness for you. And purpose. Your people are a part of you. And you are a part your people."

Hannah fought the urge to jump from the car—to escape from the overpowering emotions welling up inside her. *She doesn't know what I've done. She's too good to me. If I stay, I will just hurt her too.*

***

"Jackson, I'm not coming home tonight—at least for awhile. I'm asking for your support, even though this may sound kinda crazy to you."

Annette took a deep breath before she went on. "I'm very worried about Hannah—the girl in my group. Jackson, it's important that I be here right now. I'm sitting across the street from where she lives.

"I don't know what I can do, but it just feels right to be here...and pray for her. I don't know what else I can do, but I feel it's important. I followed her home—I just had to."

"All right. I don't like it...but... It's pretty cold out there, Annie...will you be okay?"

"Yeah. I'll burn some gas, but the car is warm. Thank you for understanding, Sweetie. I'll call you if anything changes."

"Well, just check in with me, will ya? I want to know you're okay. You won't get into something dangerous, will you?"

"No...no. I'll be careful. Thanks. You're the best!"

Annette began praying earnestly for Hannah. *God, I believe it is You that put this idea on my heart. I'm counting on You. You know how Hannah is hurting, and what's on her mind; You know what she needs. I pray Dear Lord that you bring that to her. Keep her safe. Help her to see you. Please guide me...tell me what I can do or say.*

Annette found herself repeating her words, pleading for Hannah's life and future. Her tears flowed; her heart squeezed so tight she could hardly breathe. *Please God. Please God. She's so special. Please let her see You. You created her—fearfully and wonderfully. Wonderful are your works.*

Annette's prayers slipped into Bible verses that she had memorized years ago, verses that reassured her of God's unfailing love. *Nothing can snatch you from the palm of His hand...you are my child...if God is for me, who can be against me...ask and you shall receive...*

After awhile, the intensity of Annette's prayers changed to gratitude. She felt such a wonderful peace, she was giddy — filled with joy. She knew that it was God's peace filling her — that super natural peace that comes only from Him. It was like she could feel God's hand on the back of her head, reassuring her, filling her with hope and confidence. *Thank you, God. Thank you. I know You are near.*

Annette sat for awhile in her van—waiting for God's prompting; reveling in His peace. It seemed like no time had passed, but she sensed it was time to go home. She looked at the dashboard clock and was amazed that it was already eight-forty-five. She reached for her cell phone to let Jackson know she was on her way home. *Okay, Lord. I leave Hannah in your hands.*

***

On Dana's drive home, Julie Halverson, Hannah's program manager, returned her call. "Thanks for calling Julie. I'm concerned about Hannah. She was in group tonight, but she seemed pretty depressed—very quiet. And I guess that's what the concern is—it's not like Hannah to *not* get involved with the other women in the group. She's usually very encouraging of the others—even when she can't apply her insight to herself. But tonight, she was withdrawn, avoided eye contact; responded to our concern with clichés—*I'm all right; I'm fine.* She slipped out before I could corner her, although the women from group said that her ride picked her up—Emma, is that her name?"

"Yes, Emma Newhart. Okay, I'll follow up with her...or Emma. We might need to bring her in for her own safety. I suspect she heard today that her friend, Bonner, is charged with Felony I. She holds herself responsible for the trouble he's in, along with the rest of her screwed up family. Her brother is flirting with some trouble too."

"Oh, I hate to see her go back to Lemon Creek. What if she's just having a hard time, but not really dangerous to herself? She's had so much grief...I don't want to add to it. I'd be glad to meet with her if you could arrange it."

"I'll keep that in mind, but you probably won't need to. There's a Social Worker on duty who could do an evaluation. Let me see what I can find out. It might be...uh oh, gotta go. Emergency."

Dana hung up the phone, realizing her gut was churning. She stopped to breathe...and pray. *Oh, Lord, watch over that girl. I hope I didn't run her off from group because I alerted the authorities.*

Dana arrived home late to the delicious smell of Halibut Parmesan sitting on the stove and Lionel watching the crackling fire. The house was quiet. She spoke aloud, "Where is my husband?"

Disappointment settled in with not finding him home.

She looked for a note or clues as to where he might be. She changed into her sweats, still puzzling about his whereabouts. Finally, she thought to check her phone for a missed voicemail. The message was brief: *Honey, I'll be back soon. I'm running out to meet the plane. Your dad flew down for a few days. Don't worry — we'll be home as soon as we can.*

Dana wondered what was up — this was a sudden trip. Usually her dad planned his trips to Juneau well in advance. He hadn't said anything about coming down Sunday when they had talked. Her dread threatened to become panic.

Just before she called Hub's cell phone again, the men arrived, shedding their rubber boots and jackets in the mud room, quieting the excited dogs vying for attention.

"Dad, are you okay?" Dana moved to help him remove his parka, looking over his face for any sign of trouble. "You don't look well, Dad...what's going on?"

"Now Danella, don't be seeing things that aren't there. I'm just fine. I'm sorry to worry you — I just decided to come at the last minute. Had to squeeze it in between Bingo night and Sunday potluck, y'see. I think I need an adjustment on my meds is all. I've got an appointment with Doc tomorrow."

"Are you sure you don't want to have them check you out at the ER, Daddy? I'd sleep so much better if I knew you were really okay."

"Now none of us would get any sleep if we hung around the ER. I prefer a good night's sleep in your Murphy bed, if you don't mind." Dan held his daughter, then kissed her forehead.

Hub asked, "Dad, would you like some of my Halibut Parmesan before you crash?"

"Thanks, Son...no. I ate hours ago. I'd just as soon get some zzz's."

After the house was quiet, everyone in their beds, Dana curled into Hub. In a whispery voice, she told Hub, "I don't know what I would do without him, Hub. He's always been there. It's hard to even see him getting older — he's always been so healthy. Impervious to nature it seems. I'm afraid something is wrong with him. His coloring isn't right."

Hub squeezed Dana tight. "We've just got to hope for the best. He's a pretty tough guy — a little slower than when I was sixteen, but I still wouldn't want to arm wrestle him. Let's wait and see what the doctor says tomorrow."

Dana and Hub both tossed and turned all night, greatly relieved in the morning when they heard the shower running, knowing that Dan was at least up and around.

Dana cancelled her appointments to take her dad to the doctor's office, insisting that she be with him to hear the doctor's report.

"Well, Dan, I think you're doing okay, but I'm glad you came in. We do need to adjust your meds some. To be on the safe side, I want to run some more tests, and have you come back in a few days. Can you find someone that'll put up with you for awhile?" He winked at Dana, knowing their close relationship.

Doc had known Dana since she was a little girl. He was there for her when her Dad lost himself to alcohol those years after her mom disappeared. He was the one to explain her menstrual cycle to her. He held her secret about the pregnancy and birth when she was in college. He and his wife were at the wedding when she and Hub married. He encouraged and comforted Dana through all the years of fertility tests and attempts to become pregnant. Now he held her father in his care.

Dana walked out of the office next to her dad, unable to make small talk — her thoughts raced. Life had suddenly become compressed. One thought chased after another — Doc's assurances that Dan was in good shape — *nothing to worry about*. Then seeing many scenes of herself as a little girl on the boat, watching Dan as he baited the lines, smiled at her catch, taught her about the waters; his pride when she graduated from high school; his smile when she and Hub told him of their engagement; his reassurance when she launched her own practice.

Dan had never chastised her — for anything really — not even when she avoided him after the birth of the granddaughter he would never know about.

Dana noticed that her breathing had become shallow as her fear escalated. *Stop it, Dana — you're headed for a panic attack, for crying out loud!* "Oh, Dad, I just don't like the idea of more tests...what that could mean."

"Danella Lynn Jordan — I don't want you hovering...or fussing over me! There's plenty ladies who try their hand at that in Haines. Let's take this a day at a time. I feel good, and I'm grateful to spend a few days with my favorite people. Every day is precious, and I want to enjoy this one. Let me buy you lunch."

Dana knew it was a closed subject with her dad, so she tried to hold her thoughts captive. She unconsciously lifted her right hand as she closed the imaginary door in her mind. She took his hand as they walked toward the restaurant, and soon found herself slipping into that comfortable spot where she was a daughter in love with her daddy. *I can't let my fears ruin what precious time we have together.*

Dana reduced her schedule through the week so she could spend more time with her dad and take him to his appointments. The doctor said the test results were reassuring, but Dana talked her dad into staying over a few more weeks. She said she needed him — she was feeling lonely for him. Hub's pronouncement that the king salmon were running and he needed Dan's help to get the boat ready for the fishing season was the clincher — Dan said he would stay for awhile.

Chapter Twenty Nine
A Merging Heritage

HANNAH LEANED INTO THE wind, keeping her head down to brace against the rain. It had been just a mist when she left Emma's home, but it was now a steady wet cold rain. Her hair was soaked, and the dampness penetrated beneath the coat collar she held tightly under her chin.

She walked along the dark street, trying to avoid the occasional vehicle that passed, fearing she would be accosted. She knew she wouldn't be able to hide her silhouette once she got on the bridge, so she held back, waiting for a long stretch between the late night travelers.

As she leaned against a utility box on Egan Express, she rehearsed the steps once again as she stared at the Juneau-Douglas Bridge: *Walk steady to the center of the bridge as if you're returning from a late night shift. Don't look up if any cars do pass. When you get to the center, quickly put the duct tape on your wrists behind your back, swing your leg up and roll over the railing and drop. Don't stop to think; just move quickly before someone can spot you.*

Another car passed. Hannah leaned back into the bushes that framed the utility box. *Dang it! A cop. Don't stop...don't stop. Please don't stop.*

Her heart was beating so fast she could feel her temples pulsing. It was a few minutes after the cruiser passed by before her heart beat slowed down. Hannah repeated the steps in her mind. *Walk to the center of the bridge...look normal; don't look up if anyone drives by.* It helped to keep from thinking. She didn't want to think. Or feel.

As the minutes passed, Hannah began to tremble from the cold. Subconsciously, she began to rock from side to side, trying to keep warm as she watched the sporadic traffic. She was so tired. Her head ached. *I just don't want to feel anything anymore.*

As she watched a delivery truck pass, her steady rocking shifted, favoring her right foot, which was a step ahead of her left. After a minute, she began to hum, the cadence corresponding to the rocking motion of her body.

The melody was haunting. Familiar. Hannah's thoughts turned inward, searching for the words. It was an old Tlingit lullaby. It's what Emma had been singing the first time Hannah tried to sneak out of the house this evening. Hannah had quickly retreated to the bathroom. As she returned to her bedroom to wait for a later hour to escape, she heard Emma more clearly. Hannah couldn't see her, but imagined she was in her rocking chair by the window, watching the street below. Many times she'd seen Emma sit there, so quietly intent. She said so little, but she seemed to know what Hannah was feeling. Thinking. It was hard to look directly into her eyes. Hannah feared she could read all the secrets. Her shame. Yet Emma was so kind—never criticizing her or questioning her actions. She was the epitome of The Wise Woman—the ideal Hannah held in her mind of an aging woman, content in her life, surrounded by people who admired and loved her. A woman who was not tormented by choices and past mistakes, but was confident of the directions she had chosen in life. *I've got to get away before I destroy her too*

The tune continued to play in Hannah's mind as she watched two more cars go by—some teenagers testing their brawn behind their engines. As she drew back in the bushes, Emma's words came back to her mind...*behind the rocks...couldn't see, but you knew the paths were there...our people are a part of you.*

The melody became more definite as she hummed it, reminding Hannah of another life time. Yes—when she had lived with Grandmother.

The Tlingit words came vaguely to her memory—*I-sik, i-sik, i-sik yéil...* Hannah remembered lying on the couch next to Grandmother, with her head in her lap. It was so warm in their little house. So safe. She could almost feel her Grandmother's hand petting her hair.

Life was simple then. She was safe. She believed

Grandmother would always be around. Protect her. Even when Mother came to stay, and Hannah began to worry about when she would leave, Grandmother was there—quieter, but present. Steady.

Hannah closed her eyes as she tried to piece the words together, hearing Grandmother's voice in her mind. *Oh Grandmother, how I miss you. I'm so alone. If I could have just stayed with you. If you could have kept Shane and me—it would have been different. Her tears merged with the rain dripping from her chin.*

I-sik', i-sik', i-sik' yéil ak' axaaheen i-sik áyá xát. The words…what did they mean?

Hannah was no longer aware of the cold, or that her face had scrunched up as she tried to recall the meaning of the words of the song. Emma's humming now seemed to blend in Hannah's mind with her grandmother's voice, the cadence steady. The raspy Tlingit words began to connect in the right order as Hannah began to recall the meaning. *Your daughter, your daughter, your daughter O Raven. I believe I am your daughter—your wee girl, your baby girl.*

Without her realizing it, Hannah's trembling stopped. *I am your daughter. I am…I am me. I'm my Creator's daughter. I am part of the Killer Whale Clan.* She became aware of how damp her coat was across her shoulders. Her arms felt heavy. Her fingers were numb. Her legs ached, and she just wanted to lie down.

What am I doing? I don't want to die. I can't give up. I want to go home. Home to Emma.

Hannah stepped from the shadows and began to walk back toward the home, her urgency increasing with each step. *If only I can get there before she knows I've left. Oh God, please help me make it right.* Hannah's mind raced as she re-thought her reasons to block everyone from getting too close. *Annette…Annette came three times, Mrs. Hadley said. It all seemed pointless now. Why didn't I see it before? I'm a daughter. I'm a friend. I'm a Tlingit woman. This isn't the end of the world. I can work through this—it was harder than this when I was a kid, but now I've got people to turn to. And Emma really cares—she's been trying to teach me. Annette cares about me. The ladies do. Dana does.*

Her quickened steps belied Hannah's weariness as she

rushed toward Ninth Street. Her mind was racing — *how will I get back into the house without my key? What should I say if I have to wake Emma up.*

She was within two blocks of home, when she saw out of the corner of her eye, a dark sedan creeping up alongside of her. She refused to look at it. The muscles in her body instantly tightened, ready to run. Her eyes darted, searching for an escape route. She was next to the Federal Building — no alleyway in sight. *God, help! Please don't let them get me.*

The sedan inched forward, as if demanding her attention. Hannah steeled herself against the unknown danger, knowing she was alone to face whatever malice this might be.

***

"Ellen, thanks for coming in early. I've discovered something that has the potential to be a conflict of interest, so I wanted to discuss it with you.

"My husband befriended a young woman he met on the plane from Seattle several months ago, and has since had some discussions with her — very appropriate, I'm certain. But they seem to be developing sort of an *uncle-niece* relationship, and...I think the young woman might be your daughter."

"Really!" Ellen sat still, staring at Dana. "Your husband."

"Yes. His name is Robert Cordell — Hub is his nickname. Has she ever mentioned him?"

Ellen laughed sardonically. "Dana, I wish I knew who she was friends with...she tells me as little as she can. She could be having dinner with the governor, and I wouldn't know the difference.

"I went to her coffee shop once, thinking it might be a way of bridging the gap. She all-but-ignored me. I won't do that again.

"What has your husband said about her?"

"Well, I'd have to search my memory a bit. You see, I never knew her name at first — Hub mentioned meeting a nice young woman who was moving to Juneau, and seemed interested in everything about the area. And I think Hub was glad to interact with her — he said she is delightful. Recently, he mentioned her first name — Rachel, but it was only this last week that I thought to ask her last name: Patton. That's your daughter?"

Ellen nodded, her eyes opening wide, yet she remained quiet.

"This is a predicament, Ellen. I think their acquaintance is more than just a...*customer-patron*...*I'll-take-my-coffee-black* kind of a relationship. He's taken a lot of interest in her in the last several months. He helped her move into her apartment when her things arrived.

"He's a good man, and I trust him implicitly—he is a *sweet uncle-kind-of-*a guy. And Rachel seems to have seen that quality in him. She's confided in Hub to some extent—like he was a lost uncle. That's what alerted me that Rachel was perhaps your daughter. Hub said she might be interested in a counselor or mediator to help her and her mom deal with some relationship issues."

Ellen looked hopeful. "Oh Dana, that's what I've been wanting—would you help us? I think this is an opportunity, not a predicament. I'm so surprised that she's even interested. With me, she acts like I'm the enemy."

Dana lifted her hair off her shoulders. "I don't think it would be a good idea, Ellen. I can recommend someone for you both to see—Amy Smith is excellent with young people, and I would think the two of you. Or Phyllis Barton. She's also very good. But see, I'm *your* therapist. And Hub's wife. And then the two of you have a connection with Rachel.

"It would be unethical for me to tell Hub that Rachel's mother is my client. And it would be inappropriate for me to share with you anything that he might say about Rachel. Do you see the predicament? And it could be hard for me to remain unbiased since I know you fairly well, and my first commitment is to you."

Ellen was silent for a moment while she thought about what Dana said. "I've not told Rachel I'm seeing a therapist. It would be just one more thing that speaks to why I'm a failure in her mind. Yet I would love for her to know you—I think you could help her."

"Well, let's do some thinking about it. I don't feel like I can tell my husband he can't see Rachel. It sounds like she has sought him out—he's a good listener, and young people do relate well to him. If he's helpful to her, I don't want to interfere with that. Yet I won't disclose our relationship—yours and mine—unless it's absolutely necessary, or you give me your permission.

"It may correct itself over time. As she gets more established here, I'm sure people her own age will become more important to her."

Ellen grasped the arms of her chair as if she reached a resolution. "Well, I am glad she's got your husband, and that you're so considerate of the situation. I doubt she's had a father figure to talk to since her dad was killed. I hope it's not an imposition on him...or you. It seems like your whole family is helping my whole family. Thank you, Dana."

Dana and Ellen agreed to think about the situation and potential problems and talk again soon. After Ellen left her office, Dana's thoughts continued to chase around in her mind. *What if some misunderstanding came between Hub and Rachel, or Rachel and Ellen? What if Hub's advice to Rachel is contrary to Ellen's values, or preferences for her daughter? But Rachel's an adult, really. Could they resolve conflicts and not involve me, or know about Ellen's relationship with me? What if Hub seeks my advice about something involving Rachel, and I have a bias because of knowing Ellen?*

I just can't let that happen. Yet I don't want to bias Hub by telling him Rachel's mom is my client. This friendship seems to be important to Rachel...and to him. He's so good with teenagers — she's not far from that uncertain stage when a father figure can mean so much. Maybe I should just tell Hub that I have a conflict of interest, and leave it up to him what he does with it. He'll honor Ellen's privacy. It'll work out somehow.

Chapter Thirty
Jodi's Exposé

DANA JOINED THE GROUP, disappointed that she didn't see Hannah among them. She watched briefly as the four women wrapped up their animated conversation.

"You girls are so chatty tonight, I hate to interrupt...is it the promise of spring, or is there something else going on?"

Raydine was the first to respond to Dana. "Oh, I can hardly keep myself from floating off, I've had such a good week."

Raydine moved toward the circle of chairs, followed by the other women.

"Have you heard from Hannah?" Annette directed her question to Dana.

"No. Has anyone else?" She looked around the room to concerned faces shaking their heads. "Well, we'll hope she's alright and back soon.

"Raydine, why don't you tell us about your week."

"The cops are looking for Buddy!" She nodded toward Ellen, "You'll be glad to know I am no longer posing as a teenager! Hoo-boy, where do I start?

"Cyndi and I got into another argument...same ole thing about wanting to hang out with no adults around. I ended up... I spouted off about Buddy, and ended up telling her what I was doing — posing as her, and some of the things he had suggested. She threw a big ole fit, but I stood up to her." Raydine held her head to one side, "I'm pretty proud of myself for that. Anyway, she spent some hours in her room, then came out and wanted to talk. We spent a long time talking about hard stuff — what happened to me; why I am so afraid for her. And why I am so against Buddy. She did a lot of thinking over the weekend, and I answered all her questions right up front. Finally, on Sunday, she said she would cooperate with the police. So she gave the detective her statement. They took mine too. Then they took our computer...for evidence, but we should get it back.

"So! I feel very relieved. I think they'll get him. And better yet, Cyndi seems to see what a slime bag he is, so I'm not as worried as I was. Things will work out. I'm real hopeful.

"Oh, and guess what! I got a job! I'll be starting in a month." Raydine's excitement bubbled over, bringing smiles to the faces of the other women as they offered high-fives and congratulations. "It's not my old job...yet. He said...my boss...said he needed me to be a dispatcher—coordinating the shuttles with the ships and charters. Plus I'll handle all the last minute changes and problems that come up with customers and reservations. I've got to get some training beforehand, so I'm gonna be a busy little girl. I'm so thankful." Raydine clapped her hands and beamed.

Ellen asked, "That isn't what you used to do, is it?"

"No, I used to drive. A shuttle bus. I drove people from the cruise ships and ferries out to the docks to meet up with their fishing charters. Or sometimes to the lodge or hotels. And I was a sort of guide to Juneau. I had a microphone, and would tell people about Juneau. I'm hopin' I'll get to do that again. The pay is a lot better.

"I don't get anxious talking to people about Juneau. Somehow it's different. It's my job—not about me. You get to meet a lot of people...from all over the world. I didn't get to work last year because of my bi-polar, but I'm sure I can handle it now."

Annette said, "I bet you're good at it too, Raydine. You're so sweet—you'd be a great ambassador for Juneau. Unlike me...I'd treat 'em all like my children—sit down NOW and don't say a word until we get there! No, you can't have an ice cream. You'll just have to hold it 'til we get there!" Annette's pantomime of a hectic mother was hilarious.

While the exuberant laughter and discussion about Raydine's job continued, Dana noted the change in Raydine since she started group. *Her progress has been dramatic. Thank you, Lord—getting to witness her recovery is such a gift.*

When there was a pause in the discussion, Dana added, "Raydine, I can't imagine driving one of those fat shuttle buses through the narrow streets of Juneau with a gazillion tourists flooding downtown. How in the world did you do it? How did you learn it?"

Raydine blushed with the complement, twisting her shoulders in a shrug. "I don't know. I guess I just did it...started out in an old Dodge van, helping out Doug's friend when he started in the charter business eight years ago. It just kept growing. Then he suggested I get my CDL...Commercial Driver's License...so he could contract with some of his friends. Then some charter boats got together and formed a company and bought the shuttle bus. They've got four now. I just grew with their business, I guess."

Dana's look was intent. Sincere. "I'm so happy for you, Raydine. I think I would love to get off a boat and have you tell me all about Juneau. You're expressive and enthusiastic...a real bonus for visitors to our great state.

"And Raydine, what's different with the depression and bi-polar?"

"I'm still scared it might come back—the depression. I'm just on two meds now, and my doc thinks I can handle it as long as I keep doing what I'm doing. I don't know what I'll do when this group ends—go to more AA meetings, I guess. And hopefully I can keep seeing you, Dana."

"Absolutely. And it sounds like the AA meetings will be a good transition. I'm happy for you.

"Who would like to go next?"

Jodi moved in her chair as if searching for the right words. "Well, you inspired me, Raydine. I've been struggling for some weeks about blowing my uncle's cover... *speaking truth*, as Dana says."

Jodi pursed her lips, glancing at Dana then around the group. In a softer deeper voice, she said "He's an old man now, and it was a long time ago, so on one hand, I thought I should just move on and not create havoc in the family—by bringing it up for speculation. To the Nebraska family, anyways.

"On the other hand, I wonder if some of my cousins...or others...were in the same boat as me—doubting themselves. Their sanity. As I think about it now, I doubt he would have confined his evil to just me—there are probably other girls who suffered at his hands.

"So, I decided to take the first step, and just write a letter. Dana said I could decide later whether to send it or not. Or who to send it to. So, I just wrote it.

"I'm thinking about sending it to him. And, I'm thinking about sending a copy of it to my aunt, who would be his sister-in-law. She has kids my age, and I've been wondering if at least one of my cousins fell prey to him...she's really struggled with alcohol and drugs. I figured my aunt could share it with her daughter if she thought it would be of value. I don't know. It's a big step."

Jodi held out some folded yellow sheets of lined paper. It shook as she questioned the others. "I'd like to read this if it'd be okay with y'all."

Dana looked at each woman around the circle, raising her eyebrows in question. "It looks like you've got the go ahead, Jodi. What would you like from us as listeners and supporters?"

"Umm...I guess if you have any ideas about what I've said...or haven't said, I'd appreciate your telling me. Actually, any kind of feedback you have would be good." Jodi looked around the group, then took a deep breath before she began to read from the papers in her hand.

To Uncle Howard,

   I am writing to you to tell you that I remember what you did to me when I was just a little girl, and continued to do to me until I was a teenager. I blocked out these memories for many years, but they haunted me in my dreams. Then one day, the memories started to break through, and I began to remember clearly what you did to me out in the barn.

Jodi looked up from her paper at Dana. "I started to put here that I had started therapy and it gradually became clear to me then, but I decided to not give that information. It would be like him to claim that some evil witch doctor planted that idea in my head, but I know differently."

Dana simply nodded at Jodi, who continued.

   You tortured me. You tied my wrists behind my back and tethered me to the barn wall like an animal, and left me there for what seemed like hours. You invaded my body—my most private and delicate parts.

You caused me great physical pain—pain that I still feel, even when I try to deny it.

I can still hear your footsteps outside the barn, returning to harm me further. I can still smell your evil scent. I still hear your words, saying 'Look what you made me do! What have you done? This is your fault, you demon of the devil.' And then you would beat me.

Jodi's voice failed her momentarily. She stared straight at the shaking papers as she fought to control her emotions.

I believed you then, and feared I had done some horrible thing to deserve such treatment. Your threats kept me silent. And for many years, I blocked the memories, probably because of the guilt I felt for your actions. But I know now that your words were meant to justify your own evil. And to silence me.

I am free of you today. I neither hate you nor care about you, other than pity.

I don't know how many others you abused—sexually, mentally, physically, emotionally, spiritually. If there are others out there, I hope they hear about this letter. I will gladly speak with them about what you did to me. And I will do everything in my power to help them be free of you also.

It is only because of my love for Christ that I am able to heal and forgive you. I release you to God's wrath and hope that you will seek His truth and forgiveness.

In His truth,
Jodi

Jodi slowly folded the papers, hesitant to look up at the group. The room was so silent, the ticking of the clock seemed intrusive. Dana noticed that several of the women had tears slipping down their cheeks. She knew they all hurt for their friend, and were perhaps reminded of abuse they each had experienced.

Finally, Annette broke the silence, her voice cracking. "You're very courageous, Jodi. I am a Christian, but I still struggle with forgiving those who abused me. I don't think that I could do what you're doing. But then I think about the others who may have suffered at his hands, and what your letter might do for them—if they hear of it. They may be suffering all alone like you said—doubting their own sanity."

Annette looked around the group before she continued. "I doubt very many people have the benefit of a group like ours. I don't know what I'd do without all of you. But I think what you've said would be very helpful to me if I was holding that kind of secret."

Raydine's voice was deep and menacing. "He doesn't deserve your forgiveness, Jodi. He deserves to be chained up and left to die! Or maybe hung so that you and anyone else he harmed can give him a taste of his own medicine." She sat back in her chair, looking surprised at the intensity of her own words.

"I'm sorry for being so unforgiving...but, Jodi, you're so good—you didn't deserve that."

Jodi smiled her thanks to Raydine.

Raydine continued. "How will the others hear about it, Jodi—if there are other kids who were abused? I couldn't figure out how to spread my letter past my immediate family."

"I think just giving a copy of it to my aunt will result in it getting around. I don't think there's ever been any love loss between them—she seems to avoid being at the same gatherings he's at. I never knew why, but now I wonder if she suspected something. Or maybe she knows something."

Dana scrutinized Jodi, clearly looking for the right words. "Jodi, you've written a wonderful letter—straight forward; clear; placing responsibility where it lies. With him! You were an innocent child. Your forgiveness is very generous, and regardless of what he does with it, you can be truly free from him.

"I'm wondering, Jodi, what about those in your family system who may hear about your trauma second-hand? I'm thinking especially of your mother."

Jodi took a deep breath, obviously still struggling with the idea. "I've been thinking about that—a lot. I've not told my mom about what he did to me. She's just so...so...oblivious to anything that's contrary to her fantasy world. I don't think she could deal with the idea that one of her daughters was abused—it might reflect badly on her as a mother. It's possible she'll blame me for what happened. Or deny that it could have happened.

"I can still recall how she ranted and raved any time my dad tried to say anything that was contrary to what she believed. She'd get on a tangent...raise such a fuss that the whole family would try to avoid the house." Jodi chuckled, "That's when the yard would become urgently in need of my and Dad's attention — often 'til way past dark.

"I don't know. She'll have a fit if she hears it from a distant relative. Yet I know she'll have a hissy fit anyway. Blame me. Try to convince me to bury it. If I tell her, it won't be until after I've already mailed the letter off to him and to my aunt. That way, there's no question of keeping it quiet...denying the truth any longer."

Ellen had been quiet the whole evening, picking at her fingers while Jodi spoke. Raydine nudged her arm, and asked, "Are you all right? You look like you've got something on your mind."

Ellen's face flushed, and she swallowed hard, as if holding back the intensity of her emotions. "I'm okay. I'm just thinking. You've all had it so much worse than I, and yet you're all so decisive. Jodi, you're so strong to stand up to that fiend. You're telling the world, really...you're not hiding behind a door, like I am.

"I feel so weak. I can't even stand up to my daughter, much less make a decision that could have such huge repercussions. Just the thought of making a decision when I don't know what the outcome will be is...is enough to make me sick for a week. I wish I could be more like you. You're just a wonder, Jodi."

Jodi chuckled. "Well, I sure don't feel like a wonder. But thanks, Ellen. Although it seems to me that you've made some pretty big decisions since I've known you — you broke up with your boyfriend after some years with him. You couldn't have known all the ramifications of that. And you had decided to go to college until your daughter put a crimp in that plan. And being a single mom must require a lot of decisions that are guess work."

Ellen remained thoughtful, pausing before she replied. "Maybe. But most of the time, I've been enslaved to my own body. My gut churns whenever I worry, so if I'm stewing over something, I can't keep any food down. I call it The Dread. I'm so sick of being tethered to the porcelain throne — I just want to be confident; to live by my own direction; to make choices in a reasonable amount of time, and be able to say what I think, regardless of what others might think! Especially my own daughter. I'd like to be able to give my opinion without being afraid she'll hate me forever."

Annette's voice was soft as she leaned toward Ellen. "You're-her-mom, Ellen! She's always going to need you. My mom really was negligent when I was a kid—I would never allow one of my children to roam the neighborhood unsupervised all day; or allow men I hardly knew to have access to my children in my own home. And yet, I still need and love her. She's my mom."

Annette's eyes swept around the room. "I can't believe I just said that, but it is true: That's the crux of it, isn't it—she drives me crazy, but I really need her in my life.

"I'm not saying you're like my mom, Ellen. I'm just trying to say that you have a special bond as mother and daughter that will withstand your differences. I think you're being way too hard on yourself. Don't give up on yourself. Or her!"

As she looked up at the group, Ellen's tears fell—the first time she had shown such vulnerability in this setting. It took a minute before she could speak. "I hope you're right, Annette. How did you get to be so wise at such a young age? Does it come with more kids? Maybe I should have planned for a lot more...adopted a whole soccer team."

Chapter Thirty One
Rescue Trumps Caution

THE DAYS WERE GETTING blessedly longer, and the energy among the Juneauites reflected the changing weather. The mood was jovial as the locals stopped to talk on the sidewalks downtown. Walkers and runners were out by the dozens once more, joyously freed from their rubber boots. Street vendor carts began to show up around the capital building, catering to the locals' passions for halibut chips and gourmet hotdogs.

There was excitement around the valley, especially the harbors. Small boats had been uncovered and launched. Larger boats were lined up for their turn to be lowered by the dock master when the tide was in. The king salmon were running, and conversations were endless about where the fish were biting, the size of the catch, and what was the perfect way to tie a herring.

It was always Dana's favorite time of year. As long as she could remember, she and her dad anticipated opening day for the commercial season, a valid reason to skip school if it interfered. The boat would be orderly with all the fishing gear stored in its rightful place, newly repaired, oiled, cleaned and readied for the season.

She recalled how frenetic her dad would get the few days before opening day, always hopeful for a big enough catch to justify and maintain their cherished way of life. Dana would get so caught up in her dad's anticipation that it was difficult to focus on school for the remaining weeks.

Even though she no longer fished commercially, she was still attuned to the industry's quickened pulse, and was anxious to get on the water. *Who would catch that first and biggest salmon* had become a friendly competition over the years with Hub. He had an advantage, she accused, since he worked in the industry and had the opportunity to talk shop with the fishermen coming off the water. He accused her of having the unfair advantage of growing up on the water and learning the ropes from her father, who seemed to effortlessly out-fish them both.

Dana stood on the back deck of their home watching Hub as he walked up the beach after bringing the big boat around from the harbor and anchoring it behind their house. The air was fresh and still. Even the seagulls had quieted with the high tide.

Hub waved and cocked his head to the side as he squinted against the sunlight. He thumbed toward the boat, his head jerking the same direction to suggest that Dana take a spin with him on the water. She laughed at his boyish good looks, noticing the spring in his step. She cupped her hands around her mouth to project her voice. "You'll have to wait for Saturday — *then* I'll give you a fishing lesson!"

They both laughed as he quickened his step up the beach to the metal steps and climbed them two at a time. He and Dana greeted each other enthusiastically, then stood arm-in-arm as they looked back over the wonders at their doorstep. They both cherished this small corner of the world — the vast blue water reaching within thirty yards of their house with the high tide today. The Sitka spruce trees shielded their view of the few neighbors on this stretch of beach, adding to the feel of a private haven.

"The weather and tides are perfect for next Monday — any chance you can close up shop and go fishing with us? Your dad is raring to go."

"That is so tempting, but I'm booked until three o'clock. You'll just have to get a head start on me. You'll need it, actually, cuz I'm gonna embarrass you with the size of the king I plan to bring in." Dana's face was close to Hub's as she playfully taunted him. "If you do catch anything, you may want to just cut it up and put it in the freezer before it can be measured against mine."

"Ya think so? What would you like to wager on that bet, my little fisher woman?"

Dana snuggled into him suggestively, kissing around his face. Speaking with their lips together, "Oh, I bet I could think of something that might interest you."

Hub chuckled as he nibbled her ear, taking in her scent. "I don't think I could lose either way."

After some laughter and their fill of the scene before them, Dana and Hub headed back in the house. Hub asked, "Honey, would you mind if Rachel came along with your dad and I when we go out? She's been wanting a chance to go out on the water—she's pretty enthused about fishing. I thought it might be a good opportunity with your dad here. I wouldn't want to take her out alone.

"By the way, I think she won your dad's heart yesterday. We were at the coffee shop, and she had him telling stories about himself and his *little fisher girl*. I think I heard a few new ones about you myself!"

"Oh that father of mine. What he doesn't remember, he'll make up. I don't know about you two telling her stories about me. She has captured the hearts of both my men!

"Seriously though, I'd just as soon you keep me out of it, as much as you can."

"Well, it is hard to not talk about you—you give us such fodder."

Dana playfully punched him in the stomach, and Hub exaggerated his recoil from her, laughing, "Okay, okay. If you'd rather us not, I'm okay with that. I just thought it would be a nice thing to do."

"No, no...take her out. I really don't have a problem with you guys doing that. You're very sweet to do so. It's not every Cheechako who gets to learn from the best. Well, almost the best...next to me, that is. I'm just a little jealous, I guess, cuz she gets to spend time with my favorite men. But I can wait 'til Saturday. I know where the fish are lying. Waiting. Just for me."

Dana laughed as she spun away from Hub, joining her dad in the living room.

Her cell phone interrupted the frolic. "Dana, this is Julie Halverson. I'm sorry it's taken me so long to get back to you, but I do have some information for you. Hannah is in custody."

Dana's stomach contracted, dreading what Julie might have to say. *Please, Dear God, don't let it be too bad. That girl has gone through so much!* "Is she all right?"

"I think so. I didn't talk to her very long—I'm really swamped, but she seemed fairly settled. She was quiet, but didn't avoid eye contact, which is always a good sign. She said she was okay. But she is facing a PV. She was picked up after curfew. Unsupervised. I need to investigate a bit more, but I don't think it's as bad as it could have been. I'll know more in a day or two."

"Could I visit her? I assume she's at Lemon Creek?"

"Yeah, she's at the facility. I would think you could visit if she'll give permission. You'll just have to go during visiting hours, which is a pain considering your professional status, but unless you're the lawyer, they don't cut much slack."

"Thanks so much for getting back to me, Julie. She is such a neat little gal, I would hate to see her get caught up in the system. She's a winner! She's survived in ways that would bring most of us to our knees, and I really do believe that if she can get through this, she'll make it."

"I agree. Well, let's keep working on it. I'll call you when I learn anything else."

Dana's playful mood was dampened, but not drowned. *Thank you, Lord, that she's okay. Please unravel this mess and help her to overcome. She is your delightful child, and I care so much for her. I know your love is beyond my understanding.*

The next day, Dana planned to visit Hannah before heading home if she could get through the red tape. She was glad her men were on the water, and she didn't have to worry about taking time from them.

Just as she had finished her bookwork and locked the office door, her cell phone rang. It was Hub.

"Honey, I hate to bother you for this, but I couldn't get a hold of anyone from the shop. We're anchored up here at North Pass with engine trouble. I blew a circulating hose, and there's no way to Jerry-rig it. I'm wondering if you might want to make an afternoon run and bring us a hose."

Dana could picture Hub turning away from Dan and Rachel as his voice dropped to say, "I can come in with the little Johnson, but I'm thinking your dad might appreciate getting home earlier than that. And…it would be wonderful to have you with us. It's beautiful out here."

Again, his voice changed as he obviously could be heard by the others. "Besides, God is putting on a show for us.

There's a couple sea lions out here teaching their youngsters to hunt. They've tossed a baby seal between them for ten minutes."

"No kidding! I hope you're getting that on camera."

"Rachel's doing her best. What a sight! I've not seen anything like it."

Dana could hear some tiredness in Hub's voice. She assumed he was minimizing the situation for her dad and Rachel. She quickly rearranged plans in her head. The trip to see Hannah would have to wait.

"Of course. Is Dad okay, Hub?"

"Oh yeah. Fine, fine."

"It'll be good to be on the water with you. What do you need?"

"A fourteen inch circulating hose — two inch diameter. If I can get hold of Woody, I'll have it waiting for you. You're all gassed up in the skiff. You should be ready to go."

Hub paused before he bantered, "By the way, I've got an extra pole here when the sea lions leave if you want to drown a herring...that is if you think you want to compete with the best."

Dana felt that familiar excitement about being on the water, especially with Hub and her dad. Her first time out this spring. She thought about her determination to avoid being involved with Rachel. *I guess this is justified...I'm rescuing them...even though I am curious. Surely I can maintain a professional distance from her for the few hours we'll be together.*

Within the hour, Dana pulled away from the dock behind their house, engine part in hand. Her reliable Johnson started right up, and her skiff quickly planed on the smooth waters of the Lynn Canal. Being at the helm of her little boat, scooting around the shallows and rock outcroppings, was as familiar to Dana as putting her boots on in the morning. *Lord, thank you for this incredible part of your creation — it shouts of your glory.*

As Dana skimmed along the water, she began to second-guess her quick decision to be meeting Ellen's daughter in this setting. *How could it not be a personal setting? But there was already an unavoidable boundary issue when Hub befriended Rachel.* It was not a conflict of interest for Dana per se, but there was always the possibility of expectations and misunderstandings. The standard test for these murky situations is, *What is in the best interests of the client?* It was impossible to completely avoid secondary contact with clients and their families in a community the size of Juneau. For seventeen years Dana had navigated those run-ins well, maintaining the client's privacy and keeping the social contacts at arm's length. *Surely I can.*

Hub sounded tired. He must have been upside down in that engine for some time trying to get it going before he called me. I know I was a last resort for him – he knows I wanted to keep a distance from Rachel.

Dana's thoughts shifted to curiosity. *She must be a pretty special person to have impressed Hub and Dad so much.* Dana tried to recall what Hub and Ellen had said about Rachel before she realized they were talking about the same person.

She wondered if the tension between Ellen and her daughter was simply differences in personalities, combined with the transitions in both their lives, or if it ran deep. Where Ellen was controlling and fearful, Rachel seemed pretty bold and decisive. Moving to Juneau on what seemed like the spur of the moment, dropping out of school, getting her own apartment... *I wonder if she's sort of wild. Or has experienced some trauma. Maybe their differences are more than superficial.*

Then there were the impressions she got from Hub – he had spoken of how personable she was at the coffee shop. She sounded like the darling of the coffee crowd at Auke Bay. Yet Ellen made her sound strong-willed – intolerant in some ways too. Certainly she had clear opinions about how mothers should behave. Ellen had feared her daughter's disapproval if she were to leave Juneau to follow her dream, even though Rachel seems to avoid closeness with her mom.

Strong opinions about a mother's responsibilities. *She's right, of course. Mothers should care for and protect their children. I wonder what made it such an issue for Rachel, and how her insight will change now that she's a grown woman*

Dana shuddered even though the afternoon sun was beating down on her as she planed across the water. Her spirits dampened as the ever-present angst came to the surface of her mind. *Will I ever see Alex? Will she ever be able to forgive me? How is she, Lord? Does her family cherish her? Does she have siblings? Why hasn't she looked for me?*

Chapter Thirty Two
Disturbing Encounter

DANA COULD SEE THE *Annabella* ahead, trolling against the tide with the little outboard motor. *The sea lions must have left and they're fishing again. It's so beautiful...I'm glad Dad got to come out with Hub.*

By the time Dana pulled up alongside, the fishing poles were back in the boat and Hub was dropping the anchor. Dan's smile was brilliant as he reached out to retrieve the line to Dana's skiff and pull her up tight against the bumpers of the bigger boat.

"There's my girl—come to the rescue. Does this put you in mind of some previous runs, Dana?   I've been reliving memories out here all day." Dan grasped Dana's forearm to help her swing up onto the *Annabella's* deck.

Dana hugged her dad, exulting in the familiarity of being on the water with him. The fresh salt air, silver green water, and closeness of the Chilkat Mountains flooded her senses. She could almost close her eyes and believe she was a twelve year old totally secure in her daddy's arms, knowing that she was loved unconditionally.

"Oh, Dad, it's good to see you out here...I'm glad I got to join you all. I had to come out to defend myself with all those stories you've been telling about me."

Dana's eyes had swept across the other two smiling faces—Hub right behind her dad, ready to lend a hand, and certainly waiting for her embrace. Rachel stood on the other side of the boat, making room for the three of them to move around on deck.

As he embraced her, Hub whispered, "Thanks for coming. I'm glad you're here." He turned toward Rachel and said, "This, of course, is Dana...the subject of all the stories you've been hearing. Dana, this is Rachel, the future derby winner. She's already caught a twenty-five pounder."

As the greetings were exchanged between the two women, Dana still catching her breath, her mind was quickly readjusting her impressions of Rachel. She was surprised at how tall Rachel was—a little taller than herself. Her lovely face was more square than oval, with a defined jaw line that set perfectly on her long neck. Her flawless olive skin needed no makeup—she was lovely. Dana was reminded of herself at that age—tall, slim with curvy hips; outdoorsy.

It looked like Rachel had easily adapted to the functional Juneau attire—red rubber boots, rugged worn Levis, layers of shirts. Her wrap-around sunglasses and cap were essential to sunny days on the water.

Dana could see that her thick hair was dark, held by a number of hair bands to contain a thick pony tail through the back of her cap. *I would never have guessed that Ellen's daughter would be so tall and muscular – so unlike her mother. She must have taken after her father's side completely.*

As they shook hands, Dana saw no hesitation or affectation in Rachel—she seemed fresh, confident and genuine. Dana thought, *this is a person I would like to know better under different circumstances.*

Dan, Rachel and Dana settled into the cabin, allowing space for Hub to access the engine. Dan was in high spirits, and took the lead in pouring coffee all around. "That Hub can fix anything—I'll do best to stay out of his way.

"Dana, do you remember the time we were stuck off Baranof Island at Port Alexander for two days?" He turned to Rachel, "She was just a little squirt, but there couldn't have been a better first mate. Not one complaint!" Dan chuckled, almost to himself, then looked up at Rachel. "We lived on beans for two days—couldn't even heat 'em up, the water was so bad. That was the worst time I ever had on the water. And can this girl fish! I'd put her up against anyone I know."

"Now Dad—your biases are showing. You'd better not let Hub hear you saying that."

While her dad continued with stories of Southeast Alaska, Dana was aware of Rachel's scrutiny. She was glad her father had diverted their attention.

When the conversation paused, Dana said, "I think I'll see how I can help Hub—you two see if you can find truth somewhere in his stories!"

Dana got a whiff of the diesel from the opened hatch as she stepped up on the deck. It immediately brought to mind memories of her dad's commercial fishing boat, and her identity that was so closely tied to all that it represented. Out here, she didn't have doubts about who she was, what was important, choices she had made throughout her life. It was clear...solid. Even the secret about Alex was less haunting. She could be more objective about it. Although she had wanted children, it was okay that her life had taken the direction it had. *If only I hadn't taken Hub's choices away from him.*

Hub quickly wrapped up the repairs and had the engine running smoothly. They decided to fish from where they were, so the skiff was secured and the lines were soon in the water. Each person settled comfortably into their own space. Dana found herself relaxing into the banter and friendly competition.

Dan got a solid strike. The others brought in their lines, and Dana readied the net. The excitement was palpable as they all watched his beautiful salmon jump, dive, and make several runs.

Hub said, "He's a beaut, Dan. I'm betting he'll reach forty pounds."

After twenty minutes, the King was getting closer to the boat when Dan's line suddenly went slack. Dan let out a soft expletive as they caught a glimpse of a sea lion diving away from his line.

He finished reeling in, pulling up only the head of the salmon. Rachel was astounded with the turn of events, expressing her sense of injustice after all of Dan's work to coax that salmon so close.

"Well, I guess that sea lion got his turn at a feast this afternoon." Dan allowed Rachel to study the head before he removed it from the hooks and threw it overboard.

Hub suggested they pick up and run over by Aaron Island. "There's no reason to continue here and feed the sea lions. We can troll on back home from there."

Again in the cabin as they made the run to their new

fishing spot, the four were in closer proximity. The bantering had quieted — everyone celebrating Rachel's catch as being in the lead — quite fitting for her first time on the water. She was curious about everything, peppering Dan and Hub with questions about the islands, habits of sea life, and fishing techniques. She obviously loved the opportunity to experience Alaska from this perspective.

Rachel swept her sunglasses off, placing them above the bill of her cap. Hardly containing her excitement, she shook her forearms and torso reminiscent of a child trying to contain herself. "This is so awesome — I can't thank you all enough for letting me come out with you. I love this place. I don't ever want to leave Juneau. This is home to me now...I'm going to sink my roots here."

Turning toward Dana, she said, "Dana, I want a little boat just like yours. That's so cool that you drive your own boat. Maybe you could give me a lesson on being my own captain some time."

The blood drained from Dana's face and her stomach lurched as she looked directly at Rachel. She was stunned. It seemed like moments before she could manage a weak smile and nod. Her mind instantly connected Rachel's unusual dark hazel eyes with the ones Dana often saw in her nightmares. They had wide dark circles around the brown and green irises, highlighted by dark eyelashes and brows. They were Mario's eyes. They were the dancing eyes as he flirted with Dana, trying to entice her — always watching her. Teasing her. Pleading with her. They were the eyes that were so penetrating that she had to look away. The eyes that changed from urgently pleading to cold determination as he forced himself upon her. They were the eyes that tried to comfort her as she sobbed after the unwanted taking of her body.

Dana lurched to the back of the boat, holding her stomach and waving away her dad. She drank in ragged gulps of air as she leaned against the gunwale. She couldn't stop the shaking as her mind raced — *I've got to get away!*

Hub had slowed the boat and gone to Dana after Dan took the wheel. "What's the matter?"

Dana brushed his concern away with her hand, shaking her head as if it were unimportant. "I'm okay. I must have eaten something bad. I'll be fine. I think I'd better just go home. Why don't you free my skiff at Aaron Island and I'll run on home while you guys keep fishing."

"No way. I don't want to leave you alone."

"Really, Hub…it's what I want. I'm not sick-sick…just queasy. Please…I want to stay here in the fresh air — by myself. I don't want to socialize. Will you make it okay with Dad and Rachel?"

Dana collected herself by staring at the wake behind the boat as they got underway again. *What's wrong with me? How can this poor girl's eye color throw me for such a loop? Pull yourself together, girl!*

Dana tried to analyze why she reacted as she had — what had triggered such a response? Were the dreams about Mario more frequent lately? Had she been especially vulnerable — overly tired? She had been thinking about Alex more lately — her worry about Hannah had probably triggered that. *I need some space…time to think. I shouldn't have come. I knew I should have kept away from Ellen's daughter! This is what I get for not listening to my gut!*

Dana was more settled as they got closer to Aaron Island. She was able to reassure the others as Hub and Dan unfastened her skiff from the *Annabella*. She apologized to Rachel several times while avoiding eye contact, assuring her that she was fine — she just needed to curl up at home. Dana encouraged her to show the men up with her beginner's luck.

As her skiff pointed toward home, Dana's tears formed rivulets from the corners of her eyes to her hair. Her scattered thoughts bounced from Mario to Rachel to Hannah to Hub. *It's not fair. How can Ellen have such a lovely daughter and not appreciate her more? How is it that her daughter could look so much like the one person in this world I hate? I do hate him, Lord. I'm sorry, but I do.*

Dana found her way to the couch after beaching the skiff behind her house. Wrapped in a blanket, she curled up in front of the window, giving in to the grief she had held back for the last hour. Nikki laid her head on Dana's knee, while Mica and Lionel snuggled against her legs. Her sobbing ebbed as she comforted her pets, saying aloud, "It's okay babies. Mommy's just having a bad day." The irony was not lost on Dana — mommy to her dogs, yet not her own daughter.

Her men would soon return, surely with appetites

stimulated by a day on the water. She searched the freezer for something easy yet hardy. *Perfect – beef stew*! She set out some sourdough rolls from the freezer.

What am I to tell Hub, Lord? Surely he doesn't need to be burdened with the knowledge that his friend reminds me of my nemesis. There's no way he could have known what Mario looks like – he's never even seen a picture of him.

Dana feigned a headache after setting the stew and rolls out for Hub and her dad and hid away in their bedroom.

Chapter Thirty Three
Prodigal Daughter

DANA HAD SLEPT FITFULLY, waking with a headache that promised to nag her all morning. She thought briefly about cancelling appointments for the day, but decided it would be better to be away from the house. She didn't want to face Hub or her dad yet—she had to sort through what was real and what were old memories.

She started the group, searching the faces of the four women who had bared their souls over the last eight months. Hannah was still missing.

"We are coming to the end of our group, and I'd like us to spend some time tonight preparing for that."

Dana had suggested before that the group was nearing closure, so the topic was not a complete surprise to anyone. Still there was a collective moan among the four women. Raydine was the first to comment. "I hate the idea of not having this group every week. I don't know how I can live without you all in my life—every week! But I know that my boss won't let me off this early. And within a month, I'll be working twelve-hour shifts. I've been trying to think of a way to keep coming, but it's not looking good."

Jodi's long face reflected the sadness on the other women's faces. "I'll be missing the next two weeks just for meetings and travel, so I've been worrying about telling the group. My field work during the summer is unavoidable, so I know my participation with the group is going to be very limited from here out. Can we just pause for the summer maybe...start back up in the fall?"

Dana responded hesitantly, "It's...it's very hard to maintain a group on an intermittent basis."

Ellen added, "I need to start keeping my shop open until nine o'clock within a few weeks, so if I decide to stay in Juneau, it will be hard for me to get away too."

Annette was slow to speak up, even though four sets of eyes were looking her way. "It's really hard for me to think about not having this group in my life. Yet I know life goes on, and we must go with it.

"I am a different person today because of you, and I will be forever grateful for having this time in my life. But I too have to make some choices. My children will be out of school soon, and when my volunteer work out at Lemon Creek begins, it will be even harder. I have to let something go, although I hate the thought of losing this group. Can we just meet monthly or something?"

Dana was as somber as the others, her throat constricting as she spoke softly. "I can't tell you how much I've come to cherish each of you. You're very dear to me. It's hard to think about not seeing you every week, and yet each of you are moving on in different ways.

"As much as I'd like to continue on in some fashion, my sense is we need to plan for closure. Let's focus on what healthy closure looks like, and what options you have to develop or maintain close healthy relationships. Hasn't that been an important part of our journey these last eight months...learning how to develop close relationships? Learning how to trust another person with our stories?

"What if we spend this evening exploring how your lives have changed in the last eight months — what is different about you? Also, what are your plans for the summer, and perhaps the future if you have some goals in mind?

"Then, let's schedule another group session in three weeks. We'll celebrate closure then."

There were lots of nods and agreement indicated among the group members. "Okay, who would like to go first — what changes have you noticed in you since the inception of this group?"

Jodi began slowly. "I never, in a million years, could have anticipated the friendship I now have with my sister. We talk once or twice a week now, and have really settled into a...ah...an intimacy that I never thought possible. We share from the heart, and neither of us judges the other for our failings. I know she would never discount my struggles, or think less of me for knowing my flaws.

"We have a whole new perspective on our common history because we talk about the secrets now. That has given me a whole new insight. I can understand my mother better — looking through Mug's glasses, and that helps to have more empathy for her. My mother. She still drives me nuts, but I can love her in spite of that.

"Up until several months ago, I thought the nightmares I have had all my life were just that—nightmares. And that I was a fruitcake for letting them control me. Now I know for certain that they are real memories. I'm not crazy. But I did have a sicko evil uncle who used an innocent little girl for his perverse sexual interests.

"I've not gotten any response from the letter I wrote to him, and I may never get anything; but I'm confident that whatever happens, I'll be able to handle it just fine.

"Oh…and there's a big difference in my brain: No more migraine headaches, or fogginess in my thinking. I'm not so distracted."

Jodi's throaty laugh hinted of the coming humor. "I think my boss would send Smokey Bear to deliver roses to Dana if he knew the reason for the change."

Dana's grin engaged her eyes. "Now that would be a shocker!

"Any special goals you have for yourself in the months to come, Jodi?"

Jodi seemed to contemplate the answer. "Yes…to truly enjoy this summer. Each moment. To stay in the moment, and to cherish doing the work I love to do."

Raydine sat up a little straighter. "Well, I'm certainly going to enjoy my work completely. After being unemployed for over a year, and going through a year of ups and downs, I want to show how grateful I am to be somewhat normal. Not just with my work, but with my family too.

"You know, Doug has been through a lot. He's had his own issues, but I'm really grateful that he stood by me through all of mine. I want to be a better wife. I want to make him feel like he's important—that he knows he's important to me, and to Cyndi.

"And Cyndi. I'm so excited about her. Since that scare

with that Buddy guy, she has done a one-eighty. Her grades are much better. She talks to me a lot more—and is serious about being a teacher.

"I have a lot to make up to that little girl. She was the mom when I was so depressed I couldn't get out of bed. She was the one that prodded me to go through the motions of life. If it weren't for her, I don't think I would've made it.

"Now, we talk about stuff—*her* stuff. Things that are important to her—boys and clothes, and dreams. It isn't about taking care of me anymore. That's a lot. I have my life back."

Dana asked, "Raydine, have you noticed changes in cravings or sleep patterns?"

"Oh yes! I don't need to drink. I don't even think about it much anymore. I still have to take a sleeping pill, but I'm sleeping better now. I can get up in the mornings, and take care of my own house. I went to Fred Meyers all by myself, and didn't get panicky. Of course, it was early before the crowds hit, but still...I did it. And I think less about what others might be thinking about me."

Raydine jiggled her shoulders and smirked. "In fact, I want to take a class in the fall, after the tourist traffic quiets down. Something just for fun...maybe Alaskan History. Maybe at the college."

"Wow, Raydine. Your life is very different now, isn't it?"

Raydine affirmed Dana's observation by nodding, her mouth set with determination.

Dana's attention shifted to the next chair. "Annette, you look like you're ready to go next."

Annette took a deep breath, then began to speak slowly. Thoughtfully. "I feel like you've handed me a great big box—one that a complete set of wood carving tools might come in. Inside there are all kinds of sections that reveal different kinds of tools, and boxes inside of boxes. I've only opened up the first few sections in these eight months, and I'm learning to use those first few tools.

"I know there are even better things inside those other sections and boxes, but I want to get comfortable with the first few before I take on any more. It's like I need to go about it methodically, but I'm no longer afraid of what I might find or what might be expected of me. I almost look forward to opening the other boxes to see what things I might discover.

"This group has taught me to be me. To listen to my gut. To trust my instincts. And even though it's hard for me to speak out about what I'm feeling inside, I'm learning. That's something that has changed in the last eight months—I have been able to tell Jackson that I need him. I need his attention. I need him to hold me, not just when he wants sex, but when I need affection.

"Before, I had to be mad and yelling before I could say anything to him. Now, I plan it out and speak to him calmly. I write out ahead of time what I want to say, then I pick the right time to calmly explain to him what I want or need.

"And to my astonishment, he is responding really well. He's not perfect, but he's working at it. And I'm finding that I love him so much more. That, of course, pleases him because that plays out in ways that he likes." Annette gave a conspiratorial grin to the women, assuming they would get the connection to their private life.

"And it's not just with Jackson. I'm firmer with my rambunctious boys—they're listening to me more since I'm not yelling all the time. Even with my mother, when I talked to her last week, I wasn't so…needy. I'm learning to catch myself—to not have a lot of expectations. She is quite self-centered. She was self centered before I was born, and will probably die dictating how we should make her look good." Annette smiled as the humor was acknowledged by the other women.

"It's taking some practice, but I'm learning to consider *my* wants and needs along *with* hers and everyone else's. It'll take some time with that one…and a lot of practice.

"I'm not as depressed as I was eight months ago, even without the medication. I quit that a few months ago, and I've been doing fine. I'm back in my church, and that's really important to me. And I've lost twelve pounds! I don't need to binge to deal with my feelings—I journal, or talk to you guys. I'm going to have to buy a few more journals if we don't meet every week!"

"That's so wonderful to hear, Annette. My guess is that you'll be opening the rest of those boxes much faster than you did the first few." Dana went on, "Annette, you mentioned volunteering at Lemon Creek…do you want to share more with us about that?"

"Oh yeah. I'm scheduled to teach an art class out at Lemon Creek starting in two weeks. I've been writing plans and listing supplies that they'll need. It's sort of a challenge to work around their security rules. I have to improvise for any tools that could be made into a weapon, so for now, I'm focusing on paints and paper and Sculpey clay. I'm really looking forward to starting."

"What a blessing for those women."

Raydine said, "I wish I could go to your classes!"

"And how about you, Ellen…what have you noticed that is different in your life since this group began?"

The door suddenly opened, diverting the group's attention. Hannah removed her knit cap as she stepped in, out of breath. She looked around at the women who had shared so much of her trouble, aware that all eyes were on her.

"I'm so sorry. I've interrupted the group. And it's almost time to break up—I'm sorry. I just had to come." Hannah couldn't contain her tears any longer. As she hung her head and gave in to deep sobs, Annette and Raydine rushed to her side, comforting her as they would a child. They ushered her to the vacant chair next to Dana.

Words of encouragement and reassurance flowed from all the women as Hannah collected herself. Ellen reached for the tissues for Hannah; Dana squeezed her forearm.

After a few moments, Hannah's sobbing quieted, but her voice was still constricted with emotion as she spoke. "I love you all so much…I'm sorry I couldn't get here earlier. I've missed so many meetings. And I was so rude when you reached out to me last time."

Hannah's tears started anew as she turned to Annette, mouthing, *I'm so sorry.*

Dana reached over and touched Hannah's forearm, speaking softly, "It's all right. You're here—that's what matters."

Hannah became more settled as she spoke, telling the group over and over again how much they have meant to her; what a difference they made in her life; how she'd never known what love was really about until she experienced their acceptance and encouragement.

Dana found a pause to gently insert herself. "Ladies, we're nearing the end of our time—I'm wondering if we can extend this evening or agree to regroup tomorrow. What are your thoughts?"

Annette said, "I just need to make a quick call to Jackson about the boys, but I'll be here all night if need be."

Jodi looked at Ellen as she suggested, "There are advantages to being single, huh? I'm here for the duration."

Ellen's hands settled firmly on her knees as she nodded at Hannah. "There's no place I'd rather be right now than with you, Hannah. I'm so glad you're back."

Raydine shook her jacket to release her phone from its pocket. "I wouldn't step out that door now for first prize in the derby."

Dana's awareness of how close these women had become filled her heart. She spoke quietly. "Wonderful. Let's take ten minutes to allow necessary phone calls and potty breaks; refills on the beverages, and then, Hannah, you can share with us what's on your heart."

As the group reconvened, Hannah was settled and began to recount the events that had consumed her these past months. "I don't even know where to start. The last time I saw you all, I had just been given the chance of a life time, but I couldn't see it for what it was.

"Instead of jail, I got handed over to Emma Newhart, who has become my Tlingit grandmother. She is so patient. She didn't nag me or put me down—she was just always there. She drove me to my appointments. She fixed my meals. She washed my clothes. She has loved me like my grandmother used to love me. My grandmother was Tlingit too."

Hannah told of her depression and how she felt like such a failure. She believed it was her fault that Bonner lost his temper and beat up her ex-boyfriend. She had lost her job and let everyone down. She worried about her patients, and how they were managing without her; what they must think about her. Her little brother was following in her footsteps, and now having trouble with the law.

"It just seemed to be more of the same—*I* caused all this heartache. Just like I did when my father took us from Grandmother. While I've learned from you all that I didn't cause my dad to do what he did, it still felt like it was happening *because* of me, if that makes any sense. Because I'm not good enough.

"It got so bad that I decided to…kill myself." Hannah's voice had become very soft. She paused, pushing herself to tell these dear women of her shame. She sensed they were attentive, but she avoided eye contact so she could continue with her story.

"That's why I avoided you all—I couldn't face you and stick to my plan. You all were too kind and loving, and I didn't want to hurt you.

"I know now that I did hurt you…and others. But that is where I was. My whole focus became The Plan—how could I do it, and do it completely. I didn't want to just *attempt* suicide—I wanted to be *dead* dead. The more I thought about it, the more determined I became. But I couldn't find a way to do it while I was in Lemon Creek. So I started faking life so no one would be suspicious.

"When Ms. Hadway gave me the opportunity to live with a family on the outside, I took it, thinking I could find a way to end the pain. And then Emma turned out to be so kind and so much like my grandmother, it got harder to keep my resolve.

"And then I had to come here as part of my probation. That just about did me in—you were all so welcoming. You acted like you really cared about me. I couldn't get out of here fast enough."

Hannah continued on, stumbling through her confession. "It was that same night that I finally decided to do it—the last time I was here. I waited until Emma was settled in her room—I thought she was asleep. I had taken a roll of duct tape from her garage, and I was going to use it to help me drown after jumping from the bridge." Hannah dropped her head, tears rolling down her face as she paused, remembering the depth of her desperation.

"I started to leave the house once, but when I got down the hall, I heard her singing a song. She had come out into the living room, so I couldn't sneak past her. She was singing the same song my grandmother used to sing when I was little— *I-sik', i-sik', i-sik' yéil ak' axaaheen i-sik áyá xát*. It means, *your daughter, your daughter, your daughter, O Raven. I believe I am your daughter.*

"I was determined to block it out of my mind—I couldn't

let my heart be opened or I would never be able to follow through. I couldn't think what I would do otherwise—the pain was just too great."

Hannah described her cold walk to the bridge, her plan clearly laid out to end her life. "As I've thought of this over the last few weeks, I can see I wasn't really alone out there. Too many things happened together to keep me from getting to the top of that bridge: Emma came out of her room that night. She never did that before...once she was settled in for the night. And I had never heard her sing before—she would just hum—and not that song. I know I was meant to hear her singing that particular song.

"The traffic by the bridge was just enough to stall me—to keep me from getting on the bridge. The policeman who picked me up for curfew said he had been headed out to the valley, but the call had just been cancelled, otherwise he wouldn't have seen me.

"And the words to the lullaby...I hadn't thought of them since I was a little girl. They told me I am more than just me—I am part of my grandmother. And my Creator. I am not alone. And it would be so wrong for me to give up."

Hannah stopped to drink some of her tea, glancing around at the women who were so attentive to her story. She knew the misty eyes and flowing tears were part of their love for her. For the first time in her life, she was able to accept that tenderness. Even though her eyes got misty, she continued.

"The policeman—I was terrified at first. He could have been anybody. And we were alone in the middle of the night. I prayed he would be a good man. At the same time, I thought, *Why now, God—now that you've finally gotten my attention, why couldn't I have just slipped back into Emma's house and gotten my life turned around.*

"But the cop, Officer Duncan, took me straight to Lemon Creek. He didn't say much until we got inside the door. Then he put his hands on my shoulders so that I couldn't help but look him in the face. He said, "Young lady, I don't know what you were doing out there, or what you had in mind to do. I don't know what lies ahead of you in here. But I do know you had no business being out there all alone at this hour. I'm just glad I found you and not your cold body, ravaged by the evil that lurks in the darkness. Please don't do that again."

"With that, he turned to the desk people, filled out some paper work, and left without talking to me again.

"It was another one of those *coincidences*." Hannah gestured with her fingers to highlight her choice of words. "His lecture jolted me. It was like he shook me mentally, *What are you, stupid?* I realized how I could have been attacked or killed...or dead. And it was suddenly so important that I live—that I would be able to thank Emma...and all of you for not giving up on me. And just maybe, I have some value in this world."

Hannah paused, and the group couldn't hold back their questions that came one on top of the other.

"How did you get out?"

"Are you at Emma's now?"

"What will happen now?"

Hannah shook her head. "I'm going to be okay—I know that now. But let me tell you the best part. They put me back in the cell block, and my roommate was a girl I met the first time I was arrested. She's a woman, really—very tough. Her face shows a very hard life. Only her hands gave a clue that she wasn't much older than me. I noticed them when I met her the first time. I was sort of afraid of her then. She's been a drug addict since she was just a kid.

"Well, this time I wasn't afraid. I told her I had been clean for two years, except that one relapse with alcohol. And I told her she could do it too—that she was important; that she could get help too—that she wasn't alone. All those things you all have been telling me this last year, I was able to tell her.

"She started crying, and I just held her and let her get it all out—like you've done for me. I told her about this group, and all the caring people there are out here. And she said she will let me help her. That she will go to NA meetings with me as soon as she gets out.

"I know now, I have something to offer others. I don't know why I couldn't see that before. I have you all to thank for that...for not giving up on me.

"Oh! Oh! And one last thing...when I went before the judge, the prosecuting attorney said he only had me for curfew—that nothing else was brought to him. He thought I could go back to Emma's and the transition program if I would promise to finish it."

The room was filled with excitement and a collective relief knowing that Hannah was going to be okay. The women left only after they had assurances from Hannah that she would call a few of them during the week, and that she would be back in three weeks for group. She would see Dana individually later in the week.

Chapter Thirty Four
Uncommon Perspective

"PHYLLIS, THANKS FOR GETTING me in so soon. There's still some residual stuff...from the rape...that's disturbing me. And my sleep."

Dana quickly settled into a comfortable place with her friend and therapist, aware that as she spoke, she gained more insight—just by saying it out loud.

"I never have totally resolved the trauma with Mario, the man who assaulted me in grad school. I know it wasn't my fault—I was young and naïve. I was so infatuated with his worldliness and charisma that I didn't see that aggressive side of him."

Dana told Phyllis about the nightmare she had after telling Hub about the rape, and what freedom she had experienced from telling him the whole sordid story. She thought the nightmare might have been triggered in part by the longing to know about her daughter. "I always hoped she would look for me when she turned eighteen. I kept my maiden name to make it easier for her to find me. The adoption registry people probably think I'm a nag from the many times I have called them. And of course...I have prayed constantly.

"And then, there's a young woman who's come into our lives—Hub's really. She's sort of adopted him as a surrogate father/uncle figure. Well, she happens to be the daughter of one of my clients, I learned, so I have avoided meeting her. But last week, I had occasion to meet her—Hub needed me to run a part out to him on the water so he could repair the boat, and she was fishing with him and my dad.

"She's a lovely girl and has captured the hearts of both

my husband and my father. But...she's about the same age as my daughter. And Phyllis...she has Mario's eyes—the man who raped me. My daughter's father.

Dana's expressive hands emphasized her emotion. "I couldn't believe what an effect it had on me — when I saw her eyes, I got physically ill. I had to get away from her. And I've had trouble sleeping all week.

"I know the underlying thing is Mario." Dana closed her eyes as she pushed on either side of her head. "I've just got to get him out of my head!"

"Dana, what was the worst part of the nightmare, or memory?"

Dana's eyes traced a curve as if sorting through a cauldron of images. "His face. He was so scary...and so beautiful at the same time. His eyes were crazed...liquid."

"And what is the feeling that goes with that image...that point in time?"

"Fear. Confusion." She winced, "excitement? No...fear. Right here." Dana pointed to her core.

"What's your level of distress right now...zero to ten?"

"It's about a six."

"And what is your belief about yourself as you look at that memory?"

"I'm...I've lost control. I can't control him."

Phyllis' quiet voice probed further. "And if you can't control him, what does that say about you?"

"I...there's nothing to keep me from disappearing. I might dissolve...be lost."

"Wow. Dissolve. Okay, hold all those together: The image; notice where the fear is in your body; and that negative cognition, *If I can't control him, I might dissolve*. And let your mind process as I tap. Just notice."

Dana closed her eyes as images flashed across her mind. Her first encounter with Mario, and his fluid movements as he interacted with the students at his table; his gentle touch at the small of her back, guiding her through the crowd at the barista where they hung out. Then his grip on her wrists as he took her; the beads of perspiration that formed around his nose. His gasps with his urgency.

She felt his weight on her body, the invasion of his thrusting. Then her nakedness when he lifted himself from her. She remembered his attempt to make it mutual...searching her face for approval. Trying to justify his actions. *Tell me you love me, Dana. You're so beautiful. You make me crazy. Tell me you love me, Dana!*

"Take a deep breath, Dana. That's it." Phyllis' reassuring voice reminded Dana of the present. "What's coming up for you, Dana?"

Dana's voice belied the explosion of sensation she felt. She was aware of every part of her body that had been touched by his hands; his body. Her skin and muscle could barely contain the tumult that was ignited inside her very cells. "Just pieces of it. And the rape. My wrists hurt."

"Focus on that while I tap." Phyllis monitored Dana's breathing and tension as her mind resolved the latent trauma. After a few moments, Phyllis stopped tapping, and inhaled deeply, emphasizing the slow exhale...signaling for Dana to focus on her breathing. "How about now?"

"Good. It's better. Much better."

Phyllis watched quietly as Dana regained composure after the storm of reliving the memories. She was acutely aware of the changes in her body as she sank deeper into the couch. The tension had completely resolved, and she became aware of how tired she was.

"I did do what I could, Phyllis. I feel that now. It wasn't my strength or my lack of sophistication that was at issue...it was him. He was quite manipulative, really. I was a seal pup in the face of a sea lion.

"Afterwards, his face was so changed. It was as if he came to his senses, and was aware of what he did. He kept saying, *I'm sorry, I'm sorry...over and over again.* He was crying too, calling himself a monster. I'd forgotten that. He knew what he'd done.

"I screamed at him. Called him every vile name I could think of.

"After that night, he kept trying to see me. I wouldn't answer his calls. I tore up his letters.

"For awhile, our mutual friends tried to convince me to talk to him. Of course, they didn't know what had happened. Finally he dropped out of school and disappeared. I heard he went back to Brazil.

Dana's face became more expressive, looking at Phyllis

directly. "As I look back on it now, I can see that he was a young man far away from home and things familiar to him. He had way too much privilege and good looks, and way too little self control. Hmm.

"He was young too...early twenties."

Dana took a deep breath. "He's always seemed so large and powerful...worldly, but really he wasn't much more than a kid himself. Interesting. I never thought I'd be able to think that of him."

Dana mulled over this new insight. "Wow. I'd never thought of him in that way before. I think he cared for me — in his self-centered way." Her eyes teared up, remembering how she had flirted with the *idea* of him, but always held back because she couldn't love anyone but Hub.

"Phyllis, on some level I knew he wasn't trustworthy, but I didn't listen to my gut that night. I let him drive me back to the dorm — just the two of us. There must have been something before that had suggested he was capable of force; otherwise I wouldn't have been so cautious, would I? Maybe he misread some of my cues...perhaps there's a cultural aspect to it, do you think?"

"You were both immature, Dana, and perhaps he did care for you. But he was old enough to realize what he was doing." Phyllis spoke firmly, talking to Dana as a mother would. "He was far stronger than you. He chose to not hear your words. He let himself cross that line. He might not have known how he would devastate your life, but the fact remains — he was the *only* one who could have controlled himself and his urges. He is the *only* one who knew of his intent. Are you clear on that?"

Dana bobbled her head, her eyes tracking the thoughts going through her mind.

"Phyllis, I think I'm done with him. I truly realize I was innocent and naive. He may or may not be evil, but his actions have caused me and my husband enough grief. I'm ready to let it go. I think I might even be able to forgive him....some day.

"Thank you. Let me process this a bit, and I'll follow up with you soon to reprocess any residual memories."

Dana drove home on *auto pilot*. She was exhausted from the intensity of the therapy session, but she could not contain her churning thoughts. This feeling of empathy toward Mario was totally new, and she wasn't sure what to do with it. She could remember him now — before the assault, and she kept testing her memory. *Was he devious? Was he vulnerable? Did I mislead him? Was there a cultural factor that created misunderstanding?*

But I clearly told him no several times. I pleaded with him to not do this. I tried to get him to leave. I tried to prevent him from coming through my door. No, it was not a misunderstanding. He was very intentional. While I was trying to be polite and reasonable, I was naïve to his dark side.

There was a settling in Dana's stomach, and the muscles in her shoulders relaxed. Even though exhausted, she felt lighter — as if a burden had been lifted from her shoulders. She found herself smiling as she pulled in her drive. *Oh good, Hub is home. I can't wait to tell him.*

Dana rushed through the door, stopping to give Nikki and Mica the briefest of rubs. "Hub! I'm so glad you're home." She melded into his arms, crying and laughing at the same time.

Hub held Dana, kissing her hair, and murmuring reassurances to her. "Do you want to curl up in the big chair? I'll fix you a hot tea."

Dana nodded into his chest, but kept her arms tight around his waist. He smelled like ivory soap. "I have so much I want to tell you. I haven't figured it all out yet, but I feel so much better. I remembered some things differently...and some new things. Hub...I think I'm done with the nightmares."

He squeezed her tighter. "That would be such a blessing."

"Let me go get comfortable — I'll be right back."

Dana changed into designer sweats, and released her hair from the alligator clip that held it off her neck. She returned to the great room as Hub was setting her tea beside the chair. His soft gabardine work shirt hung loosely from his broad shoulders; his muscular forearms reaching out from the neatly rolled cuffs. She was aware of how perfectly he filled out his faded blue jeans.

He was still the sexiest man she had ever seen, and she couldn't love him more than she did right now. *And he loves me – with all my flaws; the hurt I've caused him...he still loves me.*

Her body was tingling all over as she stood there a moment, their eyes intent on each other. It felt like the most natural and wonderful thing in the world to be with him – completely, freely, with no thought or image of things of the past. For the first time in seventeen years of marriage, she no longer had that hint of fear nagging in her core.

Chapter Thirty Five
A Shared Reproach

"DANA, COULD I COME in for an individual session?"

"Sure, Ellen. What's going on?"

"I want to run something by you. I'm meeting with my daughter tomorrow night, and I want to get your thoughts on what I'm planning to do."

"I've got a three o'clock opening this afternoon if you'd like to come in then."

"I'll take it. I'm pretty sure I can get someone to cover the shop for me."

Dana thought about the intriguing young woman she had met on the boat—Ellen's daughter. *Hub's...what? His project? No. His friend? That doesn't quite describe it either. But she's important to him.*

She is so lovely—even if she has eyes like Mario's. Dana noticed the absence of tension in her body when she recalled Mario now, and amazement lit up her face. *Interesting. As I think of him now, there's no anxiousness; no fear. I know I could see her now, and there would be no flashbacks to him. Thank you, Dear Lord, for that freedom.*

As Ellen settled into the comfortable chair in Dana's private office, Dana thought it best to first tell Ellen of her encounter with Rachel. "I got to meet your daughter, Ellen. Did she mention that she went fishing with Hub and my father?"

"She did. She was very excited about being on the water and catching her first salmon. Actually, she was ecstatic. That girl loves your husband, Dana. I can't thank you enough for befriending her. She says Juneau is her home now, and she's not leaving it. She's planning to start at the University in the fall."

"Great. Although, I can't say I *befriended* her, Ellen. I only met her briefly. But there does seem to be a special connection between her and Hub. Even my dad thinks she's enchanting."

Dana shifted the focus of attention back to Ellen. "You and she must be talking a great deal more—it sounds like she's telling you about her life and her plans."

"Some. And that's what I want to talk to you about." Ellen's closed fists showed her anxiousness, but as she spoke, she pressed them toward her shoulders for emphasis. "I'm going to have it out with her tomorrow night, Dana. I've decided I have pussy-footed around for too many years. I've spoiled her. I've accepted blame when it wasn't mine. I've been afraid to speak truth...as you put it.

"What Annette said—I'm hoping she is right—we've got twenty years of love and memories, and hopefully that will hold us together through this battle."

Dana emphasized Ellen's choice of words: "This battle."

Ellen was thoughtful a moment. "I guess I do approach it as a battle, don't I? Maybe that's why she always reacts like she does. Hmm. That's good to think about. Well, I'll see if I can't be more...gracious. Calmer. Let her have time to think before I get all riled up."

"What is it that you want her to understand, Ellen?"

Ellen's eyes teared up, and her voice became a whisper. "I want her to know that I love her more than anything. I want us to love each other—to enjoy the times when we are together. I want her to know I'm sorry her dad died, but it was not my fault. I didn't know he was going to drink too much and drive into a stupid bridge abutment. It hurt me too. I lost my husband—even if there were troubled times, I did love him.

"If I could remake that decision to not go with him that night, I would have. I would do anything to keep her from the pain she has had from losing her dad, but I-can't-un-do-it!" Ellen seemed to realize she was almost yelling, and stopped for a moment to collect herself.

"She doesn't understand what it was like for me—going to all his social commitments and sitting there like a mannequin, waiting for his barbs about how he had to make enough money to support my spending habits. I wasn't the one spending the big bucks—and I would have been just as happy with a simpler life; a smaller house. Happier!

"And then the predictable argument over who would drive when he got soused. I hated it! Either he would drive...drunk...and I would be sick with fear that he was going to kill us both. Or he would relent and let me drive, but badger me the whole way. More often than not, he'd pass out in the back and I'd have to deal with that. I finally got to where I would leave him in the car in the garage, but I could never sleep. I worried about him freezing, or dying. Or Rachel discovering him.

"She didn't know how bad it was. Or that I was planning to leave him. We didn't fight in front of her, and she didn't see him drunk very often. He didn't drink at home much. He didn't need to—he was always gone, mainly with his work.

"He was the *good* parent—he'd swoop in with presents that would delight her. Or when I'd hound him enough, he'd take off a few days and lavish her with attention, or take her on exciting trips—skiing, boating, parasailing. Always something with an element of risk. It was exciting for them, but for me, it was terrifying.

"He could never find time for the things that interested me. He didn't need to impress me, I guess."

Ellen paused, letting the anger subside. Her voice was steadier as she continued. "I'm glad she had those experiences, and that she's not fearful like me. I'm glad she had such a good relationship with Steven. It's just that I want her to accept me for who I am too...to be glad for me.

"I feel like, for the first time in my life, I finally have the nerve to step out on my own. I'm ready to make some choices for me—just me. Not because of what someone else expects. Not in hopes they will accept me or love me if I do it. I'm no longer going to bury my dreams, or hide behind my fears. I want Rachel to support *my* dream—to be happy for *me*. To understand that I still love her—I just want to focus on myself for a short time. It might not even work out, but I want to give it a try."

Ellen squared herself in the chair, as if garnering power. "I've decided that I am going to move to Minneapolis and go to interior design school. I've already sublet the shop here— it's all arranged. I'm leaving next month. I'll live with my girlfriend for a few months until I get the lay of the land, then get my own place. School starts in August." Ellen's smile could not be contained.

"That's wonderful Ellen—I am so happy for you. It sounds like you've thought it all through, and you're following your dream. Where is the resistance?"

Ellen expelled her breath. "Rachel. I'm afraid she...I'm just afraid. Dana, ever since she was little, she was...demanding. She was like Steven—she expected I should do for her because that was my job. She didn't seem to understand that I did for her because I love her—not that she expected it of me.

"Steven tended to treat me like the servant—*he* made the money; *he* provided the beautiful house; *he* made the big decisions: He he he—it was always about him and what he wanted. I was just supposed to be content with all that, and not have my own dreams. And maybe for awhile I was. Content. I guess my daughter learned well from her dad."

Ellen sighed, her voice deeper and showing her regret. "She learned from me too—I didn't stick up for myself. I just went along—whatever they wanted. It was just assumed that I didn't have my own thoughts or wants. Even my own *self*...my identity. I didn't have one.

"Dana, I never talk about this, but...I couldn't have children. I had endometriosis so bad that I couldn't get pregnant—another thing that Steven held against me. He never said it, but I know it was just one more thing he found lacking in me."

Ellen took a deep breath and shook her head; her eyes fluttering. "I don't know...maybe that was in my head. Anyway, when we got Rachel, I thought I could make up for it by being the perfect mother and wife." Ellen paused as her eyes wandered around a distant memory as if she was watching the characters play out a painful scene.

It was all Dana could do to keep her emotions in check while Ellen exposed her own vulnerability. *This is Ellen's hour, Dana. Keep the focus on her. This isn't about your own infertility.*

Ellen seemed unaware of the brief shift in Dana's attention. "Rachel didn't know she was adopted for a long time—we got her the day she was born—she was so tiny and perfect. Steven and I were both ecstatic. Maybe the only time we were truly happy — when she was so little. I loved her instantly, and it was easy to devote my life to her. We had waited a long time, and were afraid we would never get a baby. Steven was adamant that our child be a healthy Caucasian infant, so that narrowed our options.

"We told her she was adopted when she was eight. It never seemed to make a difference to her. She was always closer to Steven anyway — she favored him. Not that she didn't love me...she did. It's just that...

"As I look back on it now, I think she didn't respect me. Truthfully, I was a wimp. I dropped everything when he appeared. I catered to his every whim. If there was any difference of opinion, in those early years, I just caved in to Steven. And then to her.

"She won't talk about her feelings about being adopted — she says it's a non-issue. I've asked her several times over the years if she would like to know more about her birth mother, but she has been adamant that I am her mother — end of discussion. But I know different. There's an edge to her when the topic of adoption comes up. Or death. Or seeing children neglected. She doesn't say anything, but she somehow avoids those topics. Those TV shows that show families being reunited, or adoptees meeting their birth families? She always found something else to do — she would never watch them.

"I don't know...maybe it's her age. But one of her friends got pregnant her senior year, and gave the baby to relatives to raise. Rachel wouldn't talk about it, but she and her friend drifted apart. There's a hurt in her — like she's angry, but won't admit it or talk about it. Maybe it's because of the example I showed her — no spine.

"So, that's what's scaring me. If I leave, now that's she's moved here and we're finally beginning to talk to each other, she'll take it that I'm deserting her...being selfish. But if I don't go now, I know I never will. It's taken everything in me to make this decision."

Ellen slumped back in the chair. "Am I wrong, Dana? Am I being selfish?"

Dana didn't speak for a moment, trying to imagine what it must be like for Ellen, and what she stood to lose. She thought about Ellen just eight months ago, controlled by indecision; in a relationship with no future; trying to control her world by prescribing rules and counting steps. It seemed that this was a decisive moment for her.

"Ellen, I don't know what it's like to have an adult daughter — and one who is so resistant to talking about really important events that have so deeply affected your family. I don't know what the true risk is — how Rachel will respond to you claiming your own dream. Maybe her own wounds will interfere with her judgment. Maybe she will reject you...at least for awhile. Maybe it's a turning point for the two of you to establish a new adult relationship. I don't know.

"But I do know that you're a good person. You have a good mind. You're thoughtful and caring. You're a loving person. You're asking the important questions of yourself. You are not making this decision out of haste or avoidance, but from a new awareness of your identity and your dreams. And with a sensitivity to Rachel.

"You may want to share your dreams with Rachel. Give her a chance to know who you are now. Perhaps she'll be more understanding than you think.

"You could start by telling her you're struggling with an important decision, and that her opinion means a lot to you. Sometimes that sets the stage — invites camaraderie rather than defensiveness. Then listen to her... *really* listen. To her and to yourself. Then follow your heart."

Ellen sat for a moment before responding. "I'd like to believe that, Dana. And I won't say that I'm disappointed you won't tell me what to do...what would be the right way. But you're right, of course — I have to *man up*. Why is it there's always male credit for doing the right thing?"

While the women laughed at Ellen's humor, it was clear that she had more resolve. She sat taller in the chair, her chin up; her fidgety hands were quiet in her lap.

As Dana drove out the road that afternoon, she couldn't get Ellen and Rachel off her mind. *She's adopted! That's why she doesn't look anything like Ellen. I wonder why Ellen never mentioned that in group. It's such an important part of her history and identity. Well, that's probably been part of the difficulty of asserting herself — especially if Steven held it against her.*

Dana became aware that her heart was beating fast. She's the same age as Alex.

She thought back to the day she chose the birth parents.

She could only remember glimpses now — the sweet woman at the adoption agency. The small room with mauve and gray walls — rather elegant décor compared to the outer office of the non-profit organization. The woman had tried so hard to break through Dana's defenses, to understand Dana's situation and her thinking. She had assured Dana of anonymity if that was her desire, but believed the more information she could provide to the adoptive parents, the better it would be for the child. Her intentions were good, but Dana would not let her get too close.

She answered all the questions about her health, alcohol and drug use; what she knew of her genetic history, which was very little. She knew nothing of Mario's history and decided to say the father was *Unknown*. That had been the most humiliating part of the questionnaire — giving the impression that she had casual sex, or worse. But she knew it would be more complicated if a father was identified, so she lied. They might try to get a hold of Mario, even though he didn't know about her pregnancy. *He didn't deserve to know or have any say in the matter.*

The lady was careful to not challenge her response, but Dana felt ashamed anyway. Cheap. She went through the motions of listening to the options of open adoption, but she was determined that this door needed to close for the benefit of the child. She never wanted to explain about Mario. She didn't want to complicate the child's life. Nor did she want to bring her dad more pain than he already had. She couldn't hurt Hub any more...*if* she ever saw him again. It would kill him to see her with someone else's child, even if they never spoke again.

She had wanted this child to have a *Normal Family* — to know what it was like to have a mom who stayed; who knew how to apply makeup, and how to treat zits; who would be excited about the high school prom; who would take her to the theater and dance classes.

She wanted a father for her daughter who would be steady and had a good income — not worried about surviving through the winter with no revenue. Dana had thought if they were passionate about becoming parents, surely they would be good ones. Certainly better than she could be.

Even when her mind had been made up, Dana's heart

had been in conflict. From the time the child moved in her womb, she felt a love for it that was as natural as life itself. She had thought, *Surely there will be tough times, but couldn't I learn? Maybe I should drop out of school, get a job, live...where? Where could I go except back to Juneau?* Her soul was so connected to Alaska, there was no way she could live elsewhere. Her dad had no one else.

What of my shame? If I keep the child, how could it not be impacted by my shame? And being poor? A major theme in her college classes was the plight of the single mom. Statistically, single moms had limited educational opportunities. The children were more likely to grow up in poverty with the predilection of drug and alcohol addictions, teen pregnancy, and more poverty. *How could my child thrive with an inept mother and no father? I could never tell her about Mario, and surely there would be curiosity – a longing to know him.*

And how could I function with Hub in the same community, knowing that my child was not his? Dana had imagined awkward moments seeing him. He would wonder what happened – probably try to approach her. *But surely she could find ways to avoid him, and eventually he would find someone else.*

Dana made the decision twenty years ago, not knowing that things with her and Hub would work out eventually, but she was convinced then that it would be best for her child to go to a *Normal Family*. The child would at least have a chance at normalcy. Many thousands of times she had rehashed that decision since, wishing she knew if in fact it was the right one for her daughter.

As Dana passed Mendenhall Loop Road, she thought, *Alex went to a mature couple with no other children. They were well off financially. They claimed Christianity as their religion. She never knew their name, but thought they looked like a good family – a Normal Family, at least on the surface. Lord, is it possible? Could Rachel be Alex? She's got Mario's eyes, and maybe his hair – I couldn't really tell under that cap.*

No, that's ludicrous – there's no way that could happen: The mother of my child just happens to be in my therapy group? Hub just happens to befriend her on the airplane? No...that's just not possible. God, you wouldn't do something like that, would you?

Dana turned in to the Chapel's parking lot overlooking Auke Lake. She was trembling, and it was hard to see the road through her tears. She shouted out to God, the sound filling her little Subaru. "Tell me this is not possible! Tell me you wouldn't do this to me! How could you let me finally know how she is and then put her out of my reach? Her mother is my client! How could I..."

Dana gave in to deep sobs rending up from her soul. *What if she is Alex? She's built like me – wider hips; a bit taller; clear olive complexion. No, it can't be – it couldn't happen in a million years. The couple lived in California. Millions of people live in California! No way. She couldn't end up in Juneau, two thousand miles away, and just happen to capture my husband's heart.*

Dana's thoughts swirled and bounced. *That's where Rachel's venom about mothers comes from – she was abandoned by her birth mother. What if I am her birth mother – she would hate me!* Dana found she could hardly breathe. *If she finds out I'm the one who created the blank in her history, she would have a clear target. Oh Lord, what am I going to do? Hub really cares for her.*

Dana sat there hardly breathing as her mind danced around possible scenarios if the impossible was true—that Rachel was her daughter. *Would Hub ever have to make a choice between Rachel and me at some point? Would I have to tell him, Lord, that she is the child I gave up? What if I didn't tell him, and I just stayed in the background? I could at least see her, and know her a bit through Hub.*

How will Hub feel if he learns that she is the daughter I denied him? Oh, God, how could I ever tell him that? How could I NOT tell him that?

This is absurd. It's statistically impossible. But what if she is?

What if she isn't Alex? Lord...I don't think I could handle that now. Please please make it be so.

My dad! I would have to tell him. No – never! I couldn't. Oh, but he'd love it. He would love to know that Rachel was his own granddaughter. But what about Ellen and their extended family? Who are they, even? Oh, Lord, what would this do to Ellen? What if I just kept the secret, and let my relationship with Rachel develop as Hub's wife? But then, if she ever did seek out her birth mother and learned the truth, she would never forgive the betrayal. Oh God, what am I going to do?

Dana sat in a daze for almost an hour before she became aware of how cool the night air had become. She was emotionally and physically spent. Shivering, she thought about Hub and how he would begin to worry about her soon.

Lord, what am I going to do? I don't even know what to do at this moment. I can't hide anything from him — he knows me so well. He'll see my torment the minute I walk in the door. But if I tell him what I suspect, there will be no going back. Whatever happens, he will be part of it. It won't be just my grief.

Dana hung her head and winced — there were no more tears to fall. She thought about the pain he was sure to feel. The excitement about the possibilities. The dread of the potential conflict. The potential of more loss if he loses Rachel. Dana knew Hub well enough to know that he would stand by her, regardless of the outcome, but the thought of him re-experiencing the pain of hope that would likely turn to loss was more than she could bear. *Lord, please protect him from this. Please hold him up. I can't bear to hurt him again — all he wants is goodness. He's so good.*

Dana's chest constricted again, and more tears followed the streaks down her face. She felt incapable of driving the last few miles home. Her cell phone beeped, but she didn't remember it ringing. *That must be Hub. God, what am I to do?*

Dana became aware of a *lifting* in her body — a lightness. It was as if a heavy gray fog was moving from her core, dissipating from her body. She sat up taller in the seat, and began to notice her surroundings. Her breathing slowed. She nodded her head slightly. There were no words — no image — no answers. But Dana was aware of a calmness that was moving, expanding in her body, and becoming strength.

The therapist in her searched for a description of what she was experiencing. She closed her eyes, bowing her head slightly. She knew that this was peace — she was experiencing peace that passes all understanding. *Thank you, Lord. I don't know the answers, but I know...that You do. And that is sufficient for me.*

Dana started the engine and backed out of the parking place. She couldn't wait to get home to Hub.

Chapter Thirty Six
Group Ends

THE OPEN WINDOW HAD filled the group room with fresh sea air when the women gathered for their last session. The familiar room was uncharacteristically light with the summer sun still high over the Gastineau Channel. It had been nearly a month since the women had been together, and their excitement at seeing each other again filled every corner of the room.

Dana hesitated to interrupt the animated conversations that were being shuffled together, somehow still comprehensible. She paused to study each of these beautiful women. Jodi's face was radiant, sporting a tan that faded just above her cheeks. *She obviously wears a cap.* Dana suspected she would smell like the forest if she drew close enough to her. It was easy to imagine her tromping through the woods with a shovel or whatever tools Archeologists must carry.

Raydine wore a white windbreaker that sported her company's logo over the breast pocket. Dana thought she looked quite professional in her uniform, still crisp and creased this late in the day. Hannah's face reflected Ellen's excitement as Ellen talked about interviewing some women who might sublet her apartment. Annette's quiet expression was directed at Ellen, but her eyes kept flitting to the other conversation. She motioned toward the circle of chairs, hinting that the group should gather together. *She is such a nurturer,* Dana thought, *she won't be content until the whole team is together.*

She couldn't help but grin at their obvious enjoyment of each other. *This is what it's all about – learning to trust someone else; to discover who they truly are – to be vulnerable; learning to love themselves. Thank you, Lord, for the privilege of being a part of it.*

Dana entered the big room, smiling to the women as she settled her giant cup of tea and note pad on the side table next to her chair. The chatter diminished and finally quieted as all eyes looked toward her with anticipation.

"I can't tell you how good it is to see you all, and to hear your voices as you reconnect. I hate to interrupt! This could be a reunion of sisters, or dear friends, from the sound of it."

The women expressed their agreement, and commented on how they had become friends over the months — her included. Dana smiled at their observations, appreciating her inclusion in the endearments, even though she and they knew there was a difference. Dana was the therapist, and she had kept the focus on them and their needs, disclosing very little about her private life. Even Ellen knew her only as a therapist. *As it should be.*

"Jodi, why don't you start this evening...afternoon, really. It is summer, isn't it? You look to be in the midst of it with your lovely tan. Why don't we catch up with each other, and then I have a plan for us to close."

Jodi's throaty chuckle was so characteristic of her that it made the others smile, and Raydine 's laugh instinctively echoed it. "I don't know quite what I'm in the midst of, but I am getting a lot of days in the woods, and I'm loving it. It makes the winter budget meetings a distant memory.

"Actually, I've been looking forward to tonight...today. I've had some good news, and I want to share it." Jodi reached into her breast pocket and retrieved a folded lavender envelope.

"I think you were all here when I read the letter I wrote to my uncle a few months ago. You might remember I sent a copy of it to my aunt, who would be his wife's sister. I always suspected some kind of a rift between her and my...uh...nemesis, but never knew what it was all about.

"Anyway, she wrote to me after she read my letter. I don't think she'd mind if I shared it with you, since you're not likely to ever meet her. Would that be okay?" The nods from everyone clearly showed their anticipation.

Jodi took a deep breath and began, her voice taking on the Midwest cadence and accent of the aunt she knew as a child.

> *Dear Jodi,*
>
> *I received your letter a week ago, and have thought of little else since. I'm sorry it's taken me so long to respond, but I needed time to think it through. I've had to clear the cobwebs away, and allow myself to dwell on quite disagreeable memories. I'm ashamed to say, I buried them so deeply in my mind that I had almost forgot some of the events of so long ago.*
>
> *I have distanced myself from the Nebraska family for many decades—I guess since you were still quite young. I still miss my sister, but cannot abide by her husband. And your letter is finally the proof of the 'Why.'*
>
> *I am so sorry, Dear, that you had to suffer at the hands of that mad man. You are so brave to do what you did...to write him that letter and to allow me to have a copy of it. I can't imagine him doing anything with it but proclaim his innocence, but you know the truth. And God knows the truth. And I think there are others that know the truth, but aren't brave enough or able to speak it...yet. I'm glad that God is just, and I have pity for Howard, as I fear he will know God's wrath. Enough said about him.*
>
> *I feel in my heart that every word you say is true. I wish I could have had courage in those days to speak out like you are now. I suspected something—I just didn't know what it was. And I couldn't prove anything. Even if I could, I don't know that I would have known what to do, or could have gotten anyone to listen. We didn't have Oprah in those days, and we didn't know how to even talk about such things. I pity my poor sister who has stood beside him all these years. I hope you'll forgive me for not pointing a shotgun at my suspicions those many years ago and blowing him to pieces!*
>
> *I think you must suspect what I suspect: That my Nancy might have also been harmed by that man. It would make sense if that was so. I haven't seen her for near two years, but I hope one day to share your letter with her. I can't help but think that it will help her immensely if she could face her truth and know that she wasn't alone. I know she is okay through Hemit. He says she is no longer drinking, and lives about 100 miles from here. She's with a man that seems decent to her. I'm planning to write to her again and hope she will let me back in her life. I understand so much more since I read your letter. I hope and pray I can make it up to her. But I can't give her money, I know that.*
>
> *Dear Jodi, I've regretted not being in your life more. I imagine you up in all that cold country, and wonder how you withstand it. Your dear father must be pacing Heaven's floors to think of his young daughter so far from home. I do hope you are safe and can keep warm. I can tell you love the Lord, and I know He has seen you through this.*

How is your dear mother? I can't say I know her well except when we were so young. Christmas letters don't tell the whole story, but that's about all the time we correspond. I'd like to send out a Christmas letter right now to everyone in the family and say, 'See, I told you that Howard was evil!' but of course I won't. (Wouldn't that be something...a truthful Christmas letter in July!)

Well, I'd better close. I suspect your eyes are tiring of my rambling. I hope you'll write again, and come see me in Phoenix. I've got a cute little apartment, and would love to have you come for a visit.

Thank you for writing.

Love,
Aunt Clara

Jodi carefully folded the letter again, returning it to the envelope; folding the envelope, and slipping it back into her pocket. She looked up at the other women, then nodded her head once, decisively. "I couldn't have asked for anything more. She confirmed it all just by telling me of her suspicions.

"I read it to Mugs, my sister. We had a good ole sister cry, and made some assumptions about the idiot's discomfort. Then we laughed like we were little kids. It felt good."

Jodi reached the envelope out of her pocket again. She appeared to be studying the address as she gathered her thoughts and walked her thumb and fore finger along the edges. "I feel like I'm rid of some demons. Howard no longer has a place in my life. He's haunted my dreams for too many years. He's evil and sick, and it's not my business any more. I've spoken out to try to protect any other little kids he might have access to, and to let him know his secret is no longer a secret. His cover has been blown. And I'm freer of him with each day that goes by."

Jodi looked around at each woman in the group, grinning and nodding. "That's it. I'm done."

The congratulations from the other women were loud and sincere. When the din finally settled down, Annette asked, "What about your mom, Jodi? Does she know anything yet?"

"Well, I think she *will* know a little bit. My sister is pretty frustrated with her fantasies about how wonderful our upbringing was. I've asked her not to tell Mom details, but I suspect Mugs will hint at it. That'll probably shut her up, because I'm pretty sure Mom does not want to know the truth.

She's lived her whole life avoiding any reality that might conflict with her notions, so I don't expect that will change any time soon. And I'm okay with that.

"I've got Mugs now, who helps me keep my sanity, and it's all right. Mom is just who she is."

"Wow, Jodi. I am so happy for you. Your aunt is right...you are very courageous. You could have remained silent—just gone about your business. You didn't have to reveal the family secret, and take the risk of being ostracized, or be blamed for something that was not your fault. And you made it easier for others who were harmed by him to make sense of their history. That takes a lot of courage."

After a few affirmations of what Dana had said, the room became quiet again, the clock keeping cadence of their communal experience. Each of these women had confronted their own demons, and had soldiered for the other.

There was that comfortable pause as Dana looked around at each face, questioning who might want to speak. "Annette, would you like to go next?"

Annette took a deep breath. "That's my hope—that I can be like Jodi some day, and realize my mom is just who she is. But that'll take another eight months. Nine months. Man, I'm gonna miss this group!"

She grinned at the others, tilting her head, her singsong voice changing the tempo of the group. "I had my first class at Lemon Creek."

After the *oohs* and *ahhs* quieted down, Annette excitedly told the others about how nervous she was; the Security she had to clear with her giant-sized art bag, explaining how she had forgotten about the scissors; and how the package of paint brushes had fallen out unnoticed in her car. "By the time I discovered it, it was too late to go back through Security to get the brushes, and then try to make a new entrance. I already looked clueless to these people, and I couldn't do it twice in one day. So...we finger painted! And it turned out perfect! At first, the women were cautious, but after they got their fingers wet, they got as playful as little girls, and really delved into the experience. I wish I could say I planned it that way, because it was better than what I was going to do. It was a good ice-breaker."

Hannah asked excitedly, "How many were there? Was

there a big blonde girl with real short hair on just one side of her head?"

Annette nodded. "I don't think I'm supposed to talk about people in there—I know I'm not supposed to identify anyone, but there were six girls. And one particular large-girl-with-short-hair-on-one-side was extremely nice. I really liked her. Actually, I liked them all. They were all quite fun once we broke the ice, and I can't wait for tomorrow night.

"I know this is what I'm supposed to be doing. Painting, and using my art interest, it's something I can do—and teaching it feels as natural as being a mother. It gives these girls something to look forward to. They can learn so much about themselves while they're learning about the different projects. I want them to feel proud of themselves...like we've learned in here."

Raydine spoke when Annette paused. "You look so good. You're still losing weight, aren't you?"

"I am. Seventeen pounds. I'm not really working at it—food is just not that important to me anymore. My life is so full—I love what I am doing. Jackson tells me he loves me at any size, and that means a lot."

"Wonderful. You glow, Annette. Your happiness spills over, and it's lovely."

Hannah's eyes zeroed in on Dana's until she got the nod. "I can't believe how wonderful this last month has been. Best of all—Bonner got out of jail! We can't see each other because we're both on probation, but I saw a girl at NA that knows him. She said he got probation with a chance to clear his record if he completes it. Apparently Richard lied in his statement, and the judge threw it out, so there wasn't much left to charge him with. Charge Bonner with.

"I'm so happy. I just hope he gets to have a good mentor like I have. I'll see him sometime—there aren't too many NA meetings in town, and he'll have to go to them too."

"You be careful, Hannah. Don't get yourself in more trouble!" Ellen caught herself. "Oh boy...there I go again, ever the dooms-dayer. Please forgive me—I know you'll use your own good judgment."

Hannah laughed. "That's okay, Ellen. I don't mind a reminder one bit. I wish I would have had a mother who would guide me like you do."

Ellen grabbed a tissue. "Now you're going to make me cry. Go on before I get all soppy."

"I don't have any more to say. Things are goin' good. My NA meetings mean a lot to me. I couldn't give up this group without them. I've got a sponsor now — a nice lady who has been clean for seven years. And she's sponsoring that girl I told you about that I met in jail. She's doing real good, too. I think we help each other, really. She's had it rougher than me."

Dana's lips moved, as if trying out her words before she spoke. "Hannah, don't under-estimate the turmoil you've lived through. The trauma that no one should have to endure. Equally, don't under-value the stamina and courage you have in overcoming it.

"You are amazing. You are such a young person to have survived so much; to have overcome so much, and to still have such a beautiful spirit. I would have loved to have been your mom. I suspect all of us would have been proud to call you Daughter. And I think that if your mother was in a different spot in her life — if she could have overcome her own wounds, she would have been able to show you how precious you are. I hope you can remember that you were created for goodness, not the harm that came to you in your early life."

"I would adopt you in a heartbeat!" Others echoed Annette's statement.

"Thank you. I...it's hard to take it all in. You ladies mean so much to me. And I'm in a good place. Emma is teaching me...to be me. She's teaching me a lot about being Tlingit. I'm learning to be proud of my heritage. And she's helping me make a button blanket!

"By the way, Dana...I remember the first time I was in your other office. There's a picture of a woman showing her button blanket? I think that picture is of Emma. Did you know that?"

Dana was surprised. "No, I didn't know that! I treasure that picture because it says so much to me — about culture and customs, and especially the beauty of the woman, who I think of as a matriarch. I have the impression she is very active in teaching young people about her history and culture. I love that picture. After session, let's check it out. I would love to know more. That's exciting."

After a long moment, Ellen said, "I'll go next. I need to tell you what's going on before I lose my courage. It'll help to say it out loud—to convince myself more." Ellen gathered strength as she looked around at the faces of the women who had been such a big part of her journey these last months, and who now looked at her with encouragement.

"I'm leaving Juneau in ten days." After nodding at the surprised comments, she continued. "Yes, I actually made a decision. A big one. That's a real measure of what I've gotten from this group. I think you all remember how hard it is…was…for me to make decisions about my personal life.

"Well, I've made some big ones in these last few weeks." Ellen started to speak a couple times, but discarded the words. Finally, she said, "I need to go back a ways to make sense of it all. Steven, my late husband, was a good man, for the most part—he provided well for us. He wasn't mean or belligerent. Everybody loved him—he was very friendly. But he drank when he socialized. Quite a bit. And of course, he would drive when he had too much to drink.

"He seemed larger than life when I first fell in love with him. He was fun, and funny; energetic. Very handsome. It was easy to love him. I *wanted* to please him—to do the things that he enjoyed. Do *for* him—make him look good. And I put my heart and soul into doing that—making him look good."

Only Ellen's furrowed brows revealed her angst at telling her story. "As he became more and more important in his company, the social expectations were greater. And he began drinking even more. At some point, I became less and less important to him. He found much wrong with me—he criticized my anxiousness; my interests; called me a controller. And early on, I feel like he held it against me that we couldn't have children.

"We adopted Rachel the same day she was born. I couldn't have loved her more if she carried my own genes, and I was determined to give her my best. And somewhere in the back of my mind, I also thought, maybe I could be a good enough mother that Steven would be pleased with me. That didn't work out, of course—he was involved in climbing the ladder. So I poured myself into Rachel's life, trying to please her. She was a lot like her father in that she took so much for granted. I don't regret that she was most important—that's how it should be—but I see now that I lost myself somewhere along the way. She and Steven only knew the Ellen that *did* for them—not who I am. *I* didn't even know who I was.

"When Rachel was fourteen, he crashed his car into a bridge abutment and was killed. I told you about that." Ellen's voice had become hoarse, and she stopped to take a drink from her water bottle. The room was silent, as the others held sacred this time that Ellen had taken to bare her soul.

Her eyes were downcast as she continued. "I blamed myself for his death—I should have gone to the party with him. Maybe he wouldn't have drunk so much; maybe I could have driven home, even though it was always an argument. I've fought with myself for six years over whose fault it was.

"More importantly, Rachel blamed me. She never said as much, but I could tell she thought it.

"She never knew the troubles between us—we didn't argue in front of her. I had already decided to leave him, although I hadn't told him, and well…his death settled that. So, then I found myself as a single mom—set up financially, but with no self confidence, *no* true idea of who I was, and an angry daughter who became even more spiteful with me."

Ellen's intake of breath was ragged as she continued. "She was always a Daddy's Girl, and she was a lot like him—so strong. Self assured. Adventurous. I love those things about her—but we just got caught in this rip tide. The angrier she felt, the more I tried to please her…and the more I catered to her, the more I lost myself. And the more she lost respect for me. And, if I'm honest with myself, I resented her.

"Finally, she went off to University, and I came here, searching for a new life—a new me. Well, I got into a relationship with Mark. Well, he was just one more domineering person, and I got lost again.

"I did it to myself—I tried everything to be perfect, trying to please them. And of course, it didn't work. I got more and more anxious; I felt more and more like a failure."

Ellen looked up into the faces of the other women. "You didn't realize it, but you were all helping me discover who I am again. You helped me find my way. I wasn't always such a wimp—I used to dance at recitals, and give oratories at Rebecca's Lodge. I managed Easter egg hunts for five hundred kids in San Luis Obispo—I have stepped out on my own. But I forgot. I lost...*me.*

Ellen took a deep breath. "I'm sorry I'm taking so long. I didn't mean to tell you my whole life story."

"No, no—go on. We want to hear it."

"You're not taking too long."

"Thank you. I will get there." Ellen's laugh was still nervous. "My daughter—Rachel—you've heard my frustrations with her. She moved here just when I thought I might leave. Well, I was so afraid of how she would react, I backed out. She's so opinionated! She only knew me as the mother who caters to her every whim. I had no life, in her mind. And I think she believes every mother should do the same. I don't know—that's how it felt to me.

"Anyway, I was afraid she would think I was abandoning her. She's been angry for so long. She hardly spoke to me the first four months she was here.

"Well, I decided I am going to Minneapolis—with or without her approval...although I would have backed out, actually, if it had gotten too nasty. So, with Dana's coaching, I met with Rachel.

"I asked her to hear me out before she responded. I actually had a script! But I needed it, I was so nervous. I told her I love her and I want things to be good between us. I want to always be a part of her life, and to do things for her, but that I really want to try my hand at being an interior designer. I don't know if I can make it as a professional, but I want to try it. I asked for her blessing. I put my script down on the table and looked her in the eyes."

Ellen paused to take a breath. Her voice dropped an octave and her words came slower. "She didn't say anything for a few minutes. I think she really had to think about it—this was a different mom than she'd ever seen before. Then she said she was glad I told her, and that she was sorry she took me for granted. She said she didn't think she was so shallow, but maybe she needed to think about that.

"She admitted that she had blamed me for her father's death, even though she knew it was dumb. I guess I was just the one who she could direct her anger at. I think that happens a lot, doesn't it? We blame our moms when our worlds are upside down? Anyway, we talked for four hours! And we laughed...together! And cried. I couldn't believe some of the things that came out of her mouth—she had never been like that with me before. She was fun funny, not sarcastic! It just...it was...it's like the dam broke—the barrier that had been between us for years! She actually asked for my forgiveness!

"And we've talked a bunch since then. It's wonderful. We're developing a friendship I never could have imagined."

Ellen's eyes sparkled with tears that slipped down her cheek as her smile finally squeezed them out. Annette patted her arm as Ellen gave in to some tears. "I'm so happy for you, Ellen."

Raydine added, "She's a good girl, isn't she?"

Hannah emphasized, "She's a lucky girl—she has you for a mom!"

As the animated conversation continued among the other women, Dana could hardly catch her breath. Her mind was racing, her hands tingling. She tried to follow the conversation in the room with an unmoving smile on her face, but it jumbled up in her mind, and she couldn't separate the noise in her head from the din in the room. *I'm glad that Ellen and her daughter made peace with each other...did I say that out loud? Ellen is going to pursue her dream. Why does my heart ache? What else did Rachel say? What did she reveal? How is she hurting? What did she misinterpret? Has she softened her views about mothers – is she open to meeting her birth mother? Does she want to know who I am – why I would ever have given her away? If I am her birth mother. Is she interested in her birth father? What does she remember about Steven's drinking – how did it impact her? Was she truly unaware of the conflict between her parents?*

Most importantly, Dana wanted to know Rachel's birthday. *What is her birthday, Ellen – say it so I will know. Is she my daughter?*

The din quieted, and Dana forced her attention back to the group. She managed to say, "Good for you, Ellen. There were some great risks, and you faced them. I'm happy for you.

"Let's take a ten minute break—get something to drink, then we'll hear from Raydine. I need to make a call too."

Dana rose up from her chair and rushed through her office door before anyone could interrupt her. She leaned against the door inside and tried to deepen her breathing. *Ellen's news is so good, why am I feeling...what? Anger? Guilt?*

Fear? No. Dana was incredulous as she realized, *it's jealousy! Why, Lord, why am I feeling jealous? I am truly happy for Ellen — for them both! Why am I a basket case?*

Dana's mind whirled as she argued with herself, denying the emotion that glared at her, sickened by the uncharitable nature of it. She knew it was true — she was jealous of Ellen and Rachel's resolve, yet she hated jealousy and did not want it to be a part of her.

I can't do this right now...I've got to pull it together. I have to be there for those women. Dana focused on her breathing, taking measured breaths, trying to clear her mind and slow her pulse. *Please, Lord, hold this in your hand, and enable me to give them my best. Hold it back until you can help me to understand what's going on with me.*

She phoned Hub, catching him on his way home from work. "I just needed to hear your voice, Honey. Tell me again that we'll get through this. I've got another forty-five minutes of group, and...it's hard. Tell me again we're doing the right thing. I need to be the therapist in that room, not a basket case."

Dana could picture Hub calmly thinking about what she said, and looking at it from different angles, deciding how to respond. She knew he would be objective, telling her truthfully, even if she was in the wrong. She could count on his steadiness and wisdom.

"Do you know any more than what we discussed?"

"No. Not really. It's just the emotion of it all — I can't think clearly because my own questions keep interfering. Apparently Ellen and Rachel's meeting was good — lots of truth and forgiveness. They're good."

"Well, it seems like we should stay the course, Dana. We *don't* know anything for certain — she may not be your daughter. Let's wait and see where the Lord leads us. I think you'll know what to do when the time is right. Can you cut the session short? Even if you have to schedule another one?"

"No, I really don't want to drag it out. It was hard enough to find this time when everyone could be here. No, I've got to finish up. I'll be okay now that you've reminded me, and you're with me. I couldn't get through this without you, Hub. You're my rock."

"Well, even the therapist is entitled to have an *off* day,

isn't she? Don't you think those ladies will understand it if you're not on top of your game every single time? Isn't that one of your themes?"

Dana could feel herself being more grounded; her heart beat returning to normal. "You're right, of course. They're very gracious...and I do talk a lot about being real, especially with yourself. Thanks, Honey...you're just what I needed. I'll see you in a few hours."

"Are you sure? Why don't I drive in to get you — we can pick up your car tomorrow."

"No...I..." Dana stopped herself mid-sentence. For twenty-one years she had *toughed it* out; carried the pain about her daughter alone, trying to protect Hub from hurting. Before that, she protected her father. She thought about the exhilaration she had experienced with Hub after she let her guard down — after the break-through therapy with Phyllis. *Dana, let your husband in! It's okay to need him. He can handle it.*

She finally spoke again, her voice quiet. "Yes. Yes, Hub, that would be nice. I really would like it if you would be here about seven. If you don't mind."

"Count on it, Skipper."

Dana realized her hand was shaking as she ended the call, yet she felt steadier. Grounded. She paused to examine the feeling of being so transparent with Hub — anticipating his comfort in another hour. She could feel her head and torso lifting, as if a heavy load had been taken from her shoulders. *Oh, that does feel good. Thank you, Lord, for Hub...and that* knowing *that somehow everything will be alright. You have it all in your hands.*

As Dana turned the door knob, her eyes caught sight of the picture of the Tlingit woman displaying the button blanket. She hesitated, then took it off the wall, and headed out to the group room.

"Are you alright, Dana?"

Dana realized she had been hiding away longer than the ten minutes — everyone had settled back into their seats, and she could feel their concern for her.

"I am so sorry...my phone call took a little longer than I anticipated — some personal stuff. Thank you for your concern." She handed the picture to Hannah.

"Oh my gosh...that is Emma! This is so cool. Did you

take this picture, Dana?"

"I did. I got to attend a performance many years ago, and I was mesmerized by her. I watched as she danced and interacted with the people, and even though I didn't understand the significance of the dances, I was drawn to her. To me she exuded gentle strength and wisdom. It flowed from her — wrapping her people with love — her family. Every time I look at this picture, it reminds me of how important we are as women. We are the strength of the family, the community.

"I only spoke briefly with Emma that day, but those few moments touched an empty place in me. I didn't have a mother growing up, and I wished that she could have been in my life when I was young. Would you like a copy of that picture, Hannah?"

"I would love it. Thank you. She is very wise, and she is filling some of the holes in my heart. Someone should write a book about her."

"I would love to read it."

Dana was quiet for a moment as she looked around the circle to connect with each woman again. She had slipped back into therapist mode, her doubts held captive. Her eyes came to rest on Raydine.

"We're nearing the end of our time together, and we've not yet heard from you, Raydine. I think we're all anxious to know what's happening with you."

Raydine rubbed her hands together in her lap, smiling like she was holding a surprise. "Well, I don't have a whole lot to say. I've told you all just about everything. I'm working a lot. It feels so good to be back in a routine. And to be catching up on our bills. In fact, Doug and I want to get a house, maybe by next year. I'd love that so much.

"And I'm pretty sure I'm going to take a college class the fall semester. The university offers an Alaskan history class just about every year. It's something I've always wanted to do, but I thought I wasn't smart enough. But I'm ready to try it now. I do know a lot about Alaska — I've read about every book I could get my hands on, and I remember details. It helps with my job — people ask a ton of questions. They want to know every detail, from tide levels to gold mining history. And they love the bear stories! So, I'm going to do it. Doug says I'm smart enough. Who knows — maybe I'll keep going and be a college student at the same time as my little girl.

"Oh…I forgot to tell you! I got an email from my sister! You know, I sent her a copy of my letter saying why I had to divorce my parents? Before, when I tried to bring it up to her or even try to explain how I felt, she would get mad at me. She thought I should just get over it—let the past stay in the past. She never would admit to anything, or even act like it was possible our dad could do something to her kids. She said I was too dramatic, and he's old now and changed.

"Well, she still isn't asking any questions, but she did say in her note that she misses me and hopes that some day we can be friends again. That's a big step for her, so it gives me hope. I'm okay with that for now—maybe I will have some family down the road."

Dana smiled at the women around the circle, noticing the shift in energy with the last story told. There was a quiet settling in the room as their attention returned to her.

"Well, we've come to the end of our nine month journey together. It's an ending in some ways—we won't be meeting regularly as a therapy group any more. And yet it's not an ending in relationship, is it? Some of you have become friends, and I suspect, some will continue to develop connections after today—if not with each other, perhaps with other women who are becoming important to you.

"Each of you has begun a new direction in your life. The ending of this group just marks that milestone. So, what I'd like to do in this last thirty minutes is to have each of you share one thing you are taking from this group—something that you've learned; or something that someone said or did that impacted you; or something you thought about—perhaps something you notice is different about you. What has been of particular value to you during these last nine months?

"Let's take a moment to mull this over—you might want to get a refill while you're thinking, but let's get right back."

Dana was the only one to get out of her chair as she got a fresh tea bag and refilled her cup with hot water. She could hear the voice of Professor Riley in her head. He had been such a mentor to her, nurturing her interest in group dynamics. *Don't neglect closing ceremonies! Endings are important. Your clients will have been abandoned, abused and rejected. Don't create one more negative experience for them!*

Dana chided herself mentally. *Now is not the time to let personal issues interfere with their therapy. This is their commencement. Give them your best!*

Dana squared her shoulders as she reclaimed her seat, intent on giving each person the opportunity to define the significance of their work together in group. As she settled back in her chair, she lifted her eyebrows in invitation for anyone to speak.

"If we're ready, I'd like to start." Hannah's eyes surveyed the circle of women before she jumped in with a release of her breath, her voice quivering as she spoke. "This group saved my life. My mother was only twenty-six years old when she died. I'm twenty-five. I was following in her footsteps. When we started this group, I didn't think I could live if Richard didn't love me. I gave so much to be with him, and it still wasn't enough.

"I now know that he was abusive. It was an abusive relationship...and I stayed around for it. It was just *normal* to me. But now I know that is not normal, and it's not what I want in my life. I still care for him, but there is no way I would go back to that place in my life. *I* didn't care about *me*. I didn't *know* me. I didn't realize that I'm important—that God has a purpose for me—that I could help someone else, like that girl from Lemon Creek.

"I wasn't grateful for my heritage as part of the Tlingit Tribe. It has become precious to me. My grandmother's teachings...I'm remembering them. Emma is helping me to find my culture again. And it is who I am.

"And something you said, Dana, helped me understand it differently. You said, *If my mother had been able to work through her stuff, she would have been able to be the mother I needed.* I can't say it like you did, but you get my meaning. Even though I knew she didn't have it easy growing up, I still blamed her. And that just helped me to think about her differently. She was very young, and wounded.

"So, that's what's helped me the most. Being able to see things differently." Hannah paused as she looked around the circle. "Each one of you has been a mom to me. I can't thank you enough. And I *am* going to see you again...you can't quit on me now! I'm your daughter."

The laughter and reassurances were sincere and full.

Dana recalled how, early in the group, Hannah had been so encouraging of the other women, yet blinded to her own value and need. The lump in her throat kept her from speaking as she looked around to see who would be next to *throw her line in the water.*

"As I mentioned earlier, there's seventeen pounds less of me from when we started." Annette pursed her lips, looking toward the window as if searching for the right words. "I think that seventeen pounds just represents the weight of the burden I carried...the oppression I felt before I started with this group.

"There was ten pounds of depression that kept me from seeing truth. The truth is—I have the most beautiful kids in the world, and a husband I wouldn't trade for anything, and yet I had no joy in them. Everything was a chore. I couldn't do more than just survive one day after another—counting the hours until they got out of the house, or before I could go to bed, or the minutes before I had to put on my *Mommy Hat* and give them minimal attention. That drudgery is all gone.

"And I was carrying seven pounds of resentment because my mom didn't do her job. She didn't protect me when I was little. I know that is true. But I also know she had a hard life— she didn't know how to be a mom. She was manipulated by others too. And the dad that should have been there for me— wasn't.

"So, what I am taking from this group is *less:* Less burden. Less defeating self talk. Less resentment. More forgiveness. More direction. More confidence in my purpose. More determination to be who God wants me to be. And when any doubt enters my mind, I have this image of Hannah in my brain."

Annette looked over at Hannah. "I have a confession to make to you. I followed you home that night—the night you were so down. I was afraid you might try to hurt yourself.

"I stayed out in front of your house...Emma's house...for a long time—maybe a few hours. I just prayed. I didn't know what you were thinking about, of course, but I just felt led to stay there and pray for you. I felt my heart would break, but I didn't know what else to do." Annette's face showed no emotion, but the tears leaking from the corner of eyes revealed the depth of her words.

"After awhile, I had this overwhelming peace come over me, and I just knew you would be okay. It shook me when you didn't show up here for awhile, and I didn't know what had happened to you. I guess I expected to see the answers more immediately, but I know He was watching out for you.

"I'll never look at the Douglas Bridge again without thinking of you, Girl. It would have killed me if anything had happened to you. I would have always felt responsible because I didn't barge in your front door."

Hannah had tilted her head and was studying Annette's face as she spoke, becoming more incredulous as she heard what was said. "You *prayed* for me that night? For hours?"

At Annette's steady gaze and slow nod, Hannah simply cried, mouthing the words, *Thank you.*

Dana knew she couldn't speak now, nor could anyone else. Tears fell freely at the impact of Annette's testimony. Quiet voices echoed *Praise God* and *Wow.*

Finally, Dana said, "Yes, wow. It's hard to top that, but we must go on. Who would like to venture next?"

"I will." Ellen's voice seemed loud after Annette's quiet disclosure. "Jodi's courage has been a huge motivator for me."

She turned directly to Jodi and continued. "At first, it was you getting in those little planes, and hiking out in the woods with the bears that fascinated me. I couldn't do that if I had two big guys with two big guns on either side of me! Then I saw you confronting the truth of your nightmares. And then you wrote that letter to your uncle to expose him, and to admit what you had gone through. You really inspired me. I thought, if Jodi can do that, surely I can tackle Alaska Airline...and my daughter!

"I've learned from you all in different ways. And I know this: Without the support of this group these last nine months, I would be like one of those rats running in those wheels and getting nowhere. I'll never forget you all for this."

Jodi chuckled. "Well, I don't know about it being courageous, but I am glad I've been able to dump a load, kind of what we're all doing, I guess."

After Ellen sat back, Jodi decided to continue. "I guess the thing that's meant the most to me is the openness and acceptance of the five of you. I've never *bared my soul* to *anyone*—ever. You just didn't talk about stuff in my family.

And then I witnessed each of you telling about very painful times in your lives. You trusted me to know that about you. And it gave me the courage to confront my truth. To acknowledge that truth. You've all seen me at my most vulnerable time, and I didn't feel judged. You walked along side of me. You called me during the worst of it. You showed me it was easier to not go it alone.

"As a result, I've got a relationship with my sister that I've never had before. I'm kind of surprised at that, and very grateful. I'm so glad I got to know you all."

Raydine flipped her arms up and then let them fall in her lap. "Why am I always last? You all have such interesting and intelligent comments to make, and then it comes to me!"

The others chastised Raydine for her self-deprecating comment, but let her continue.

"There's so many things—my mind is full of images and memories of what you each have said in this last year, but it was a pivotal time for me when Annette asked me and my family over for Thanksgiving dinner. I didn't feel good enough to be anyone's friend, and you acted like I had some value. It was real hard for me to go that day—my anxiety would generally keep me at home in my bed, but you and your family treated us like we were important."

Raydine looked away from Annette. "And then Annette was the one who saw the potential in my little girl. She saw how good she was with little kids, and said Cyndi would make a good teacher. Here I was just worrying about getting her through school without making the same stupid mistakes I made, but we didn't have the vision beyond that. Annette helped us to see Cyndi in the future—as a successful teacher.

"I don't think she'll follow in my footsteps. She's been doing really good in school this semester, and she keeps talking about her plans to be a teacher, so I think she will be. She's got a new friend—Kayla. She's pretty serious about school. And when we get a house, I hope she'll feel comfortable having friends over. I feel like I could entertain some teens and not be an embarrassment to her. I'm really grateful for that.

"I'll miss this group, but we're gonna be okay."

Like the last grains of sand dropping through an hourglass, the energy in the group room was spent. Voices had become quieter; speech slower.

Dana's voice was deep and whispery as she leaned forward in her chair, stretching out toward the circle, her elbows anchored on her knees. "I've been leading groups like this for about ten years, and *ending* never gets easier. This is hard. Even though my relationship with you is professional, I feel like you're my sisters too. We have laughed and cried together. I have worried about each of you...prayed for you, and the outcomes in your lives. I have prayed for wisdom in leading you.

"And while I did not share as a member of the group, I have been changed by your insight. As you've shared how you make sense of life, I have learned from you. Your courage in overcoming enormous obstacles has challenged me to be brave—like each of you. You have each inspired me in different ways, and I thank you for that.

"I thank you for allowing me to join you in the most private parts of your lives. I am deeply honored and humbled by that privilege. I wish you all the very best and maybe our paths will cross again.

"Now, let's say our goodbyes, and get out the door before we are all blubbering idiots!"

The noise, hugs, and promises that followed could have marked the parting of any close knit family. Dana's emotions were undulating: Delight in seeing these women navigate successfully through rough waters; gratitude for being able to use her skills in leading them; joy in thinking about their hopes and new directions; relief that closure was reached, and the objectives were met.

After they left, she turned off the overhead light and sat back in her chair. It felt right. A good ending to a very effective therapy group—the most dynamic group of women she could recall. Dana stared into the center of the circle, smiling as she reviewed each person's growth during their nine-month journey: Jodi's release from the nightmares—at least the frequency; confident that she could deal with whatever else came up; Annette's metaphor of a box of tools; Hannah's growing awareness of her heritage and identity; Raydine's enthusiasm for the future; Ellen's courage to pursue her dream. And her resolve with Rachel.

Rachel. Dana grimaced and her stomach knotted up as

the turmoil resurfaced. Just then, Hub leaned in the front door and said tentatively. "Are you alone?" At Dana's nod, he walked over and sat close to her, taking her hand in his.

"How'd it go?"

Dana responded thoughtfully, resting her chin on her hand. "Good. Really good, actually. When I can separate my professional perspective from my personal angst, I can say it was a phenomenal group. They each dealt with some deep-seated issues. Encouraged each other. Learned to count on each other for understanding and support. They each moved toward some goals; added some tools to their repertoire. It was truly a privilege to work with them.

"And then there's the other part of me. I vacillate between elation and terror. When I come to the edge of that cliff — thinking maybe I've finally found my daughter, I want to squeal and do a happy dance — shout my joy to the world. But I can't let myself step over that edge because I don't know if it's true or not. And if it is true, she may hate me. I may lose her just when I've found her.

"And if she isn't my daughter...if she just happens to have Mario's features and just happens to be about the same age as Alex...it will be devastating. I guess I have my hopes up more than I realized."

Hub and Dana sat quietly for a moment, letting the dichotomy hang between them. Finally, Hub said, "Whatever happens, we're in it together. And I believe it will be good, Dana. I don't think God will drop the ball." Hub stood and took both of Dana's hands. "Let's go home, kick off our boots, and have ice cream for dinner."

Chapter Thirty Seven
Truth Revealed

DANA SLIPPED INTO AN old pair of Hub's coveralls —
perfect for the project. She headed out the back door with her
paint brush and gallon of preservative. She wanted to take
advantage of the clear morning to treat the logs on the back
side of the house. Hub and Eddy, one of his mechanics, had
run up to Auke Bay to fill the *Annabella's* tank before they
went fishing. Eddy seemed to have a crush on Rachel, and had
convinced Hub to take them out on his boat today.

Dana was nervous, yet hoping that Rachel would come
early so she could interact with her — get to know her a little
bit. Actually, to drink in every nuance of her being. Dana
wanted to study her; to look for any clue that she might carry
Jordan genes. Or Mario's. And yet she felt uneasy at the
thought of being around Rachel alone. Face to face. Dana
didn't like to be deceitful; she wasn't any good at pretending.
She feared her muddled thoughts would show all over her
face. Yet *truth* was yet unknown. And there was so much to
lose. From all she had surmised from Ellen's comments,
Rachel was not interested in finding her birth mother, and was
certainly not empathetic of the reasons she was given up for
adoption. Dana didn't even know how to begin to explore the
possibilities of their relationship.

*Father God, you know the truth. You know what is
possible...what is best. Please give me patience and wisdom.*

Dana's quick prayer had just left her heart when the dogs
raced around the deck, headed for the front of the house.
Dana's heartbeat quickened, knowing it was likely Rachel
arriving to meet up with Hub and Eddy. Whoever it was, the
dogs were glad too, because their barking ceased immediately.

Dana's hand shook as she dipped the paintbrush in the bucket. She called out, "I'm out here on the back deck." She tried to contain her excitement, certain that it was Rachel, knowing she would finally get to see her again. She tried to focus on the brush strokes while the possibilities raced through her mind: *Just be quiet and look for proof. Should I just ask if it's possible I'm her birth mother? I could ask questions that would lead to the subject. Did she have a happy childhood? Surely she did – she's so grounded. Did she have a best friend growing up? What does she know about God? Who taught her to drive?*

Rachel's long strides and the dogs' excitement announced their arrival by way of the side deck. "Hi, Dana. I guess I'm early. I hope it's okay."

"Oh, it's fine. Fine. Hub and Eddy will be right back. They went to top off the gas tank before you all head out. The tide will be perfect in about an hour.

"It's good to see you again, Rachel."

"Same here. Are you going with us?"

"I'd love to, but I've got a commitment this afternoon that's pretty important, so I'll have to pass on this one, as hard as that is. You'll have to show those guys how to bring in the big ones."

"That is exactly what I'm going to do, even though I'm a Cheechako. You're gonna have to take me out one of these days—from what your dad says, you're the best. And I'm so in love with your little boat, and the fact that you handle it all by yourself. I want to get my own boat one of these days. I can't be begging Hub to take me out all the time...but I'd trade a week's tips to spend a day on the water with him."

Dana laughed at her fervor. "Well it's a perfect day for it, and I know Hub enjoys taking you. Have you fished much? Before you came to Juneau?"

"A few times—charter trips mainly. My dad took me out on a boat in New Zealand when I was twelve. We fished for tuna, but didn't catch any—just smaller fish—although they were pretty big. But it was great fun. And we went a few times off the Oregon coast. But it's different here. So much more...dramatic. Vast. Beautiful. It's like..." Rachel sighed. "I don't know...there's a difference between a commercial boat and going with friends. And it feels different here...*I'm* different here."

Rachel released some of her enthusiasm—her voice dropping to a more serious note. "This is home to me now. For the first time ever in my life, I feel *connected* to a place. I was meant to live in Juneau."

Rachel laughed and opened her arms to the ocean, tossing her head back. "I can't get enough of *this*. I'm so in love with Alaska!"

Dana was mesmerized by Rachel's exuberance and lack of inhibition—her graceful movements punctuating her excitement. *She's charismatic, just like...*

Rachel turned to Dana. "How about you...have you always lived here? Do you ever take it for granted?"

Rachel's intensity as she looked directly into Dana's eyes was too much. Dana took a deep breath, trying to control her excitement and slow her pulse. She briefly studied the brush that had stalled in mid air as she searched for words that would express to Rachel the depth of her connection to Southeast Alaska. "I've always lived here, except for graduate school. But no, I never take it for granted. Even before I left the State for those few years, I knew I was blessed to live here. It's magical. So I understand your excitement about feeling like this is home to you now." Dana's gaze returned to Rachel, as she put her hand on her chest, emphasizing her feelings. "I hold almost a reverence for Alaska. The whole State, but especially here. There's...I don't know...my soul is anchored to this part of the earth, if that makes sense. I couldn't leave it."

"Absolute sense! That's what I feel. It's hard to describe it. I can't drink it in fast enough...or deep enough. I want to experience it all...now. Yet not miss any piece of it. Everyone laughs at me down at the coffee shop because I'm so manic about it, but it just goes so deep. I've never felt this way before...about a place."

"Where all have you lived, Rachel?"

"Oh, through grade school I lived in Central California—San Luis Obispo, Fresno, then we moved to Edmonton when I was a teen. My dad's company relocated us. Then he died, and my mom sold that house when I left for college. I was only seventeen. It felt like I didn't really belong anywhere then. I got to see a lot of the world, though...my family traveled a lot. But nothing compares to here."

Rachel watched as Dana turned back to painting the logs.

"Have you always been so brave about it, Dana? The water and all? My mother would never venture out on her own—for anything really; certainly not the ocean. You just seem so brave."

Dana avoided eye contact, uncomfortable with Rachel's adulation. "I don't think it's bravery, really. It's just familiar. It's what I grew up with. There was just me and my dad, and I grew up in his world."

"You must be a Scorpio. Scorpios are known for their courage. When's your birthday?"

"February ninth. I guess I'm an Aquarius, but I don't put much stock in astrology."

"I'm a Libra. It fits me—I'm pretty unconventional. Mine is September. The twenty-seventh."

Dana almost cried out. Her mind seemed to be running a race with her heart. She argued with herself, *she's mine. I know she's mine. Is now the time I've been waiting for? Without Hub? Shall I say it? How can I say it? How can I not? God, please don't let her lock me out.*

Dana's voice was almost a whisper when she spoke slowly. Her paintbrush had paused as she stared at it. "I uh...I gave birth to a daughter on that date. Twenty years ago." Dana turned to look directly at Rachel, aware that she was trembling. "In Seattle. The University of Washington Medical Center."

"You're kidding! That's where I was born! In the U-Dub Hospital!

Dana watched as Rachel's face turned from astonishment to bewilderment.

"I'm twenty. I was born September twenty-seventh, 1991. How...where is your daughter?"

Dana felt like time had slowed, and her words were jumbling up. She fought for self-control, although tears leaked out the corners of eyes. "I gave her up for adoption, Rachel. A decision I've regretted every day of my life since."

"I'm adopted. My biological mother was a student at U-Dub."

Dana began to stammer as she watched Rachel's face changing, telling the story of the myriad emotions that were unfolding in her mind. Incredulity. Doubt. Questioning.

Disbelief. Betrayal. Anger.

"I...I...heard that you were adopted. I saw you on the boat. I started to wonder, Alex...Rachel...if it was possible that you could possibly be...if you...you were about the same age, and I always wonder. Any time I meet a girl who could be the same age as my daughter, I wonder if... I always wonder, but never could imagine that I would meet you this way...through Hub..."

Dana's chin trembled as she continued. "I prayed you would find me...I kept my maiden name. Jordon. I've kept my profile on the Adoption Reunification list, hoping that someday she might...you might...want to know me. And know I love her...love you."

Dana's voice had gone up in pitch, and she was visibly crying, no longer able to contain the volcano of emotions erupting from within. Her paintbrush was unmoving, dripping log preservative on her shoes. Rachel's face had become set, her furrowed eyebrows and upper lip accusing.

"Please understand, Rachel...I never meant..."

Abruptly, Dana stopped talking, her last words swallowed by a hiccup. She realized Rachel was not accepting her explanation, and she feared she was making it even worse.

Rachel's lower jaw was shaking. When she finally spoke, her voice was flat; accusing. "You gave me away! To strangers! You didn't give a damn about me! Then you lied to me."

"No, Rachel, no...I never lied to you. I didn't know it was you. When I saw you...I didn't know you were adopted. Later I heard that. Then I began to suspect that you might be...I began to hope. But you never looked for me. I've been hoping for years that you would reach out to me...allow me to explain. I was afraid you didn't want to know me."

Dana felt even more desperate as she watched Rachel's unchanging face. Her words became whispered — she couldn't catch her breath.

"I've loved you from the day you were born...before even. And I've prayed every day since that I made the right choice. That you had a good family. That they would give you the security and normalcy that I couldn't. Then.

"I was so unsettled. I didn't think I could provide for you. Be a good mom. I was wrong, but I didn't know it then! I was so afraid…and so confused myself.

"And then when we suspected you might be Alex…we didn't know how to approach you…to see if it might be true. I didn't know for sure until just this moment."

Dana's worst fears were unfolding before her eyes. She finally had confirmation that Rachel was her daughter, and instead of the joyous reunion she had always dreamed of, she was facing the condemnation that she deserved. All the things she wanted Alex—Rachel to understand were caught in her throat.

Suddenly it became clear to her—there was nothing she could say that would change the barrier reflected on Rachel's face. She lifted her chin, as if to accept the coming onslaught. She was guilty of whatever charges Rachel might spew.

The two women silently studied each other. Then Rachel's brow furrowed. "Hub?"

Dana knew she asking, *who was my father?* She shook her head *no*.

She asked, "Does he know?"

Dana nodded *yes*. "Not for sure. I didn't know for sure until this moment."

Rachel seemed to receive that facet, nodding slowly as if to confirm what she already knew. Abruptly, she turned from Dana and stomped across the deck, breaking into a jog after turning onto the side deck. Dana listened to the sound of her quickened steps, the slamming of her car door, then the crunching of the gravel as her Jeep tore out of the drive, spewing gravel like condemning truth.

Dana was unaware of when she had dropped the paintbrush back into the bucket, but she reached for it now as she heard the dogs' toenails tapping the deck as they returned to her side. She numbly stroked the paint brush back and forth, even though there was no longer any oil on it. Finally she slumped to the deck, releasing the wail that had been fermenting in the depths of her breaking heart.

***

Hub quietly held Dana on the porch glider as she recounted the events of the early morning: Rachel's fierce reaction to Dana *giving her away*. Accusing her of lying. "The look of disgust…right in my face, Hub. She got right up in my face!

She hates me! And I didn't want to hurt her — this is the last thing I wanted for her!

"Everything I've ever feared about meeting her has come true. I shouldn't have said anything. I should have just pretended. Oh, Hub, I'm so sorry. This messes you up too." Dana buried her face in his shoulder again, giving way to the sobs.

She knew how devastated he must be too — she could see it in his face when he realized what happened. Grief. Uncertainty. Rachel was just as important to Hub as she was to Dana.

Hub squeezed Dana's shoulders. "Give her time, Honey. This is a big shock for her. Give her some time to think it through. We'll be here when she's ready to talk."

"Oh, Hub, I don't think she'll ever want to talk to us. You don't know how bitter she is about me." Dana hiccupped the words, "She-feels-so-betrayed-by-me!"

After a few moments, Hub quietly asked, "Shall I go look for her, Dana? Check at her apartment and see if she's okay?"

Dana sat up and looked at Hub questioningly. "Would you? Do you think she might talk to you about it? Maybe you could tell her how I agonized over the decision to give her up...how I've loved her all these years. That I wanted more for her than what I could give." Dana broke down again as she said, "How I long for her to be in our life now."

"Shhh. Shhh. Let me go unload the boat, then I'll drive over to her apartment and see if she would like to talk, okay?"

"Okay. What happened to Eddy? Did he leave?"

"I told him we'd have to take a rain check on the fishing trip. When I saw you, and no Rachel, I figured something like this must have happened. It's fine...we'll catch up another time."

Hub drove to the Mendenhall Loop Road, recalling the time he had helped Rachel move into her apartment. She was easy to care about — playful; vivacious; eager to experience Alaska. It was hard to reconcile Dana's description of her in such an emotional state, although it's certainly understandable. *It took her by surprise. She didn't see it coming. Maybe she'll be able to look at it differently when she has some time to think about it.*

Hub pulled in to Rachel's apartment complex, but her

Jeep was not there. He wrote a short note to leave on her door,

Rachel — I hope you're OK,
I'd sure love to talk if you
would. Any time.
    Hub

He sat for a few moments, trying to think of where she might go for solace. She had developed a few friends, but Hub didn't know how to contact them. *I bet she's finding solitude somewhere, like a harbor, or out the road.*

Hub drove out to the glacier since he was so close, even though it wouldn't be a place of solitude with all the tour buses this time of year. Then he drove the thirty miles north to the end of the road. No sign of her yellow Jeep. He spoke out loud, "Juneau's small unless you're trying to find someone!"

He made a swing through Eagle Beach on his way back, but again, there was no sign of her Jeep. He decided to give up on the search and hope she would call when she saw his note.

Dana's hopeful look when he walked in the door quickly turned to defeat when she saw his grimace. He had no news. "We'll have to just wait, Dana. I left a note for her. Drove around some to see if I could find her, but didn't see her Jeep anywhere. Give her some time, Honey. It's got to be such a shock. She'll want to figure some things out.

"I'll check at the coffee shop tomorrow if she hasn't called by then. We've got to trust God on this, Dana. He didn't bring us this far to not see us through it. You know that's not His nature...or His promise. What's that verse — *He who began a good work in you will be faithful to complete it?* I'm for trusting Him."

All weekend, Hub stayed close to home, not wanting to leave Dana alone or miss the slim chance that Rachel might come by. He and Dana puttered around the house, finishing up the wood treatment on the house logs, straightening up the already tidy garage. Dana knitted on the back deck in the late afternoon. When they did speak, it was a continuation of the same topic: *Where might she be? Do you think she'll leave Juneau...just when she's come to love it so? Do you think she's talked to her mom about this yet? How could they ever have met her if it wasn't Divine Intervention?*

They avoided the question, *how can we go on without her?*

Time seemed to move at a snail's pace.

Monday morning, Dana cancelled all her appointments. She knew she couldn't be fully present for her clients, and it would not be fair to them. Then she called the Adoption Registry office to make sure they will have her information readily available should Rachel contact them.

"We will contact you immediately, Ms. Jordan, if she contacts us. We'll do our very best to facilitate your reunion."

"I know you will, and I thank you. I just think she's very upset and will want to verify the information immediately. I want you to facilitate that — don't wait on a secondary permission from me. I want you to give her your full cooperation. Her name is Rachel Patton and I'm certain she is my daughter."

Dana hung up the phone, not knowing what else to do. She and Hub had prayed constantly all weekend, seeking comfort from each other; both going through the motions of life with no enthusiasm. Dana thought about calling Phyllis, but decided she would be too distracted — Rachel might call.

Hub stopped by the coffee shop before going to his shop. He was told that Rachel was taking some time off. That was heartening — at least she hadn't quit her job and left Juneau.

Later Monday afternoon, Dana received a call from the Adoption Registry office, advising that Rachel had called requesting information about her birth parents. They had given her full disclosure.

Dana thought often of Ellen, and wondered if she should contact her. After all, there was the therapist-client relationship; and now she was certain of the... *other* relationship. She didn't even know what to call it — *we-are-both-mothers-to-the-same-daughter-relationship*? But after discussing it with Hub, she decided it needed to be Rachel's choice — it was not up to Dana to disclose what they had learned. Again, she would have to wait on Rachel.

The week dragged on. Neither Hub nor Dana slept well. They waited. And prayed.

By Wednesday, Dana knew she could no longer continue to mope around the house. She had to at least go through the motions of life. With a heavy heart, she went to the office to see a few clients, then returned home exhausted. Thursday was a repeat of Wednesday — putting on a professional face;

trying to contain the fear that churned constantly in the pit of her stomach. She longed to know where Rachel was; what she was thinking; did she have someone trustworthy to talk to; is her resentment softening; does she have any understanding of the anguish Dana felt twenty years ago?

Dana had just walked in the back door, when the telephone began to ring. She dropped her tote and purse and hurried to the telephone. She answered a little breathless, hoping it would be Rachel. "Hello, this is Dana."

"I have some questions for you. Will you give me straight answers?"

Dana recognized Rachel's voice, even though she had not identified herself. Her tone was cold; her words accusatory. "Yes, Rachel, I will always be truthful with you. I...I would love to speak with you."

"I want to meet with you alone. On neutral ground. Can you meet me at Eagle Beach?"

"Yes...anywhere."

"Could you meet me out there in an hour...say seven o'clock?"

"Yes. Yes, I'll be there."

Dana heard the click on her telephone and knew that Rachel had hung up without any courtesies. *Oh thank you, Lord...thank you. Please give me the words...the thoughts to reach her heart. Please repair this damage I've done.*

Dana's heart was beating so hard she could hear it in her ears. Her hand shook as she called Hub. When he answered, she nearly shouted. "Rachel called! She wants to meet me in an hour...at Eagle Beach. She asked if I would answer her questions truthfully."

Hub's relief was evident on the phone. "That's great. Great. Why Eagle Beach?"

"She said she wanted a neutral place. And she wants me to go alone. I don't think she means anything against you, Honey...she just wants some direct answers."

"How did she sound? Did she say how she was doing?"

"She was cryptic—no niceties. I could tell she's still very...umm...maybe not hateful, but she's clearly holding me at a distance. She asked if I would give her truthful answers. And how I long to do just that, Hub. I've waited twenty years to give her truth. I so want this to go right...for her to know that I love her. I never meant to hurt her. I meant to *protect* her. Pray for me, will you?"

"You got it, Skipper. And Dana...don't be too anxious to get it all out in one sitting. This is just the opening day — let it unfold at a pace she can receive it, okay?"

"Thank you." Dana took a deep breath. "I needed to hear that. I'm so nervous, I'd probably overwhelm her. Thank you, Hub. You're so wise. I'll call you after we meet."

Dana refreshed her makeup and checked her attire in the mirror several times, not really seeing her image. Her mind bounced between prayers and imaginary reconciliation scenes with Rachel, then realizing her mental tangent, she would remind herself to settle down. *This is just opening day, Dana...surely things will unfold in its own time. Take Hub's advice...and your own.*

The summer sun was muted by a solid blanket of low lying clouds when Dana reached the remote Eagle Beach. She could see that whispery clouds floated at the top of the trees on the islands out in the channel. Soft droplets of water touched down on her windshield.

Dana hadn't stopped here for years, but she had good memories of exploring the tidal flats as a teenager. It was a salt marsh estuary extending for a mile, teeming with sea life that drew hundreds of gulls, ravens, ducks and bald eagles. It was a place to simply sit and watch the water fowl activity; better yet, to hike the trails around the area. She wondered how Rachel got introduced to this area, and what meaning it had for her.

She spotted Rachel's lone vehicle at the end of the beach road, and her stomach knotted up. *Please help us, Lord.* She followed the road around, turning back parallel to the Glacier Highway. As she neared the concrete public restroom, she noticed an older pickup with a small trailer and skiff. The hood was up, and a man leaned into the engine.

Darn it! Of all the times when I don't want to be distracted! She scanned her rearview mirror for anyone else who might be able to help this man if he in fact needed it. *No one.* She drove around his vehicle and stopped. "Are you in trouble?"

"Yea, it looks like my battery is dead. Do you think you could give me a jump?"

Dana could see a little girl standing in the seat. She

couldn't be four years old.

"Yes...just let me go ahead and tell my...friend up ahead, and I'll be right back."

She drove ahead to where Rachel was standing next to her Jeep. She lowered her window, and shouted, "That guy's got a dead battery. I think I need to help him get started since it's so deserted out here today. Is that okay? It'll just take a few minutes."

Rachel shrugged her shoulders and nodded. "Of course."

"Would you like to ride back with me, or..."

Rachel raised her hand, blocking the idea, but her face softened. "Uh, no...I think I'd like to stretch my legs. You go ahead and I'll just...umm...be here."

Dana turned her Subaru around and headed back to the stalled pickup.

The driver, a man in his late twenties or early thirties, looked relieved to see her. He had already hooked the cables to his battery and was motioning to Dana to come closer, then stop.

As she reached down for the hood release, he walked around to her open window. "Thanks, ma'am. I'm sure glad you come along. I cudda been here a long time."

Dana worried about Rachel's potential response to this delay, and prayed she wouldn't leave. "No problem."

The man lifted her hood and quickly hooked up the cables to her battery. Dana watched as he hopped back into his pickup, gritting his teeth as he engaged the starter. The engine turned over sluggishly with the help of her battery, but it would not engage. He kept trying to coax it to life, but the sound of the engine dashed Dana's hope for a quick rescue.

Both drivers stepped out of their vehicles as Dana hollered, "Have you got a tow rope or chain so I could pull you?"

"Yeah, thanks. I'm sure beholdin' to ya. I couldn't even get my dang cell phone to work out here." As the man spoke, he unhooked the jumper cables and slammed both hoods down.

Dana turned her Subaru around, and backed up to the front of his pickup. She was relieved to see Rachel walking toward them, then sitting on the picnic table across the road.

The man knelt down to hook a chain up to his frame,

then to Dana's trailer hitch. The little girl leaned out the window, calling to her daddy.

The man stood up again and nodded to Dana, indicating he was ready. She stepped out of her door part way, hollering, "Why don't we have Rachel hold your little girl in case there's some jerking—just to be on the safe side."

"Good idea." The man lifted his little girl out through the window, handing her over to a surprised Rachel. The little girl and Rachel looked cautiously at each other as they settled on the table top.

"Her name's Abbi." Then to Abbi, he said, "It'll be aw'right, Pun'kin. Just stay with this nice lady a minute 'til Daddy gets the pickup goin.' It'll be aw'right."

Dana noticed that Rachel's beautiful eyes were rounder than normal, but she said nothing.

The man jumped back in his pickup. Dana inched forward until she could hear the chain tighten, and feel the weight of the pickup. She pulled ahead *slow and steady*, like she'd done many times before helping her dad or Hub. She trusted herself in this manner, and was greatly relieved that Rachel was waiting for her—and even a part of the effort.

As she picked up speed, the man popped the clutch and the engine coughed to life, sputtering a bit before finally proving it would run.

Dana inched her vehicle back to relieve the tension on the chain, then hopped out to disconnect it from her hitch. She could hear Rachel talking as she carried the little barefoot girl across the gravel toward them.

The man was obviously relieved as he disconnected the chain and began to check how his boat was riding on the trailer. "You girls sure saved my hide. I can't thank ya enough. Can I give you some fish as a thank you? We had a good afternoon."

Both women shook their heads, Rachel handing over the child who was reaching her little arms out for her daddy. Dana said, "We're just glad to be of some help. I've been in a spot like that before myself! Don't worry about it."

"Well, I sure thank ya." As the man spoke, he smiled at Abbi and chucked her under the chin. She bounced and threw her arms around his neck. Dana was touched by the obvious love and trust between the loving father and adoring daughter.

Looking back at Rachel and Dana, who were now standing next to each other, he once again thanked them, then cocked his head, seeming to study them both. "Are you two sisters?"

Rachel looked away, her face unreadable. Dana shook her head and glanced down at her feet, muttering, "No."

"Well, you could be. Sorry for the mistake. Thank you for looking after my little one, here. And gettin' my truck goin.' I hope I kin repay the kindness."

Dana and Rachel watched as the man and his daughter got back in the pickup, waved and drove forward. They started to walk, maintaining a few feet between them and avoiding eye contact. When they reached Dana's Subaru, they both turned toward the tidal flats. Some noisy eagles were vying for some prize behind a stump.

Dana finally broke the silence. "Thank you for your help with that little girl. I was afraid she might bump her head if there was any jerking."

Rachel nodded, her lips tight and eyebrows furrowed. After a brief moment, she said "That little girl...Abbi...there was no car seat in that pickup."

Dana simply nodded, acknowledging Rachel's observation.

"She probably doesn't even wear a seatbelt."

Dana shrugged, wondering where Rachel was going with this. *Does she think I should have stopped him from driving off without checking on that?*

"She was a pretty scruffy little girl—more than just from a day of fishing. Her little feet were as tough as moccasins."

Rachel was thoughtful, pausing a moment before continuing. "They probably really struggle, don't they—economically?"

Dana nodded, "Probably."

It was a few moments before Rachel spoke again, beginning with a deep sigh. "But she was okay, wasn't she? She didn't seem to be...she wasn't afraid. She loved her daddy. She talked about her cat. Samson. She seemed like a happy little girl."

Dana acknowledged Rachel's observation with an unknowing shrug. *What is this fascination with the little girl?*

Finally, Rachel turned directly in front of Dana, and looked intently in her eyes. "Is that what it was like for you, Dana? When you were little? Could that have been you and Dan?"

The question stunned Dana. This was a whole different topic — so huge, she didn't know where to begin. But, she had promised to speak truth to Rachel — to answer her questions.

When she spoke, her voice was hoarse. "I guess in some ways. I don't remember being so scruffy, but I suppose I was. My dad never seemed so young, or at a loss, except when my mom disappeared. I felt secure with him — probably like that little girl feels with her daddy."

Rachel gazed at the tidal flats a moment, then again looked intently at Dana. "You were twenty-two when I was born. Older than I am now. Why did you give me away?"

Even though Dana was expecting it, the question and sudden change of direction felt like a punch. Her voice came out a whisper, her eyes immediately became teary. "I was afraid, Rachel. I was afraid I couldn't give you a good home — that I'd ruin you. I was wrong, but at the time, I felt so abnormal, I couldn't see my way through it. I didn't know how to...I didn't have a mom growing up. I wasn't around babies." Dana's voice trailed off as Rachel's look of disgust returned.

"Other single mothers raise their children — even when they don't have everything perfectly lined up!"

"I couldn't imagine any kind of normalcy for you — with me struggling to survive and living under the cloud of shame I felt. I didn't want that to spill over onto you...to shape who you were. I've wished a thousand times I could undo that decision — I would have given anything to be your mom. For Hub to have become your adopted father. But I made the worst mistake of my life, Rachel. It seemed insurmountable to me then, but in the years since, I think I could have learned to be a mother. And maybe I wouldn't have been as incompetent as I feared then."

"You said my father was *unknown*. Is that true?"

"No. I lied." Dana had expected this question, and had tried to think of different ways to soften or avoid the answer. Facing the question now, she could not recall how she'd planned to respond. She continued to face Rachel as she searched for words.

"Well, I obviously don't look a lot like you or Hub. Was he someone you…who was he?"

Dana's voice was barely audible, but she returned Rachel's direct eye contact. "He was a fellow student. In one of my study groups. From Brazil. He was a friend. He wanted more, but I was in love with Hub, even though we had broken up at the time…due to my stupidity.

"Then one night, he forced himself on me. I blamed myself for a long time because I didn't see it coming. I thought it was my fault."

Rachel broke eye contact, swearing. "That's great. My father's a rapist!"

Dana was stunned at the label, and started to defend Mario. Even though she couldn't justify his assault, she wanted Rachel to have a more balanced impression of him — to understand there was more to him — good things about him, but she sensed this was not the time to explore that topic further.

Rachel turned abruptly and began walking swiftly up the road. Dana followed quickly. "Rachel, wait. Please, let's talk this through. Please don't run away from me."

Rachel kept walking, pulling her cap off and grabbing at her thick wild hair. She stomped twice and kept walking. "I need time to think!"

"Rachel, he was not a bad man. He made a terrible mistake. It doesn't change who you are—you're smart and beautiful. You couldn't be more precious."

Rachel gave Dana a disconcerting sideways glance, but kept up her pace.

"Oh, Rachel…*you're* not a mistake! I…I don't want you to think he was some crazed maniac…he wasn't."

Dana stopped short of Rachel's Jeep, tears streaming down her face as she watched Rachel climb into the driver's seat and slam the door. She started the engine, but didn't pull away. She just stared out the front windshield.

Dana's heart prayed without words. She was bewildered, but determined to not give up until there was no longer any hope. Even though she couldn't think of what to say that would help Rachel, she refused to step away. She stood there, willing Rachel to look at her. She could smell the exhaust from the idling Jeep; the new car smell from the interior. She heard the seagulls cawing overhead. Time had slowed to a crawl.

Imperceptibly, Rachel reached up and turned off the key. Without looking at Dana, she asked, "Does Dan know about me?" Then she turned quickly and gave Dana a penetrating look, as if to challenge her.

Dana shook her head almost imperceptibly.

Rachel spoke haughtily, showing no emotion. "Then you'd better tell him pretty damn quick, because I'm claiming my grandfather!"

Dana nodded, her breath catching at the first ray of hope she'd felt in twenty years. "I will. I will right away." Her head nodded like a bobble head doll, her hopes soaring at the thought of at least know her daughter through her dad. It would give her a connection even if Rachel refused to speak to her directly. Surely it would all work out.

"He'll love you, Rachel. I think he already does...just from the time you spent together on the boat." *Yes, through Dad, I'll have my daughter! Maybe someday she'll understand me...accept me. I can hope!*

"And I want to talk to Hub."

Dana nodded, even more vigorously. "Of course."

"He...he's important to me—like an uncle or something. I really care about him."

Dana couldn't speak. She stood there shaking, tears streaming down her face, a ceramic half-smile barely containing her joy. Her large brown eyes were centered in the whites of her wide eyes. She was afraid to move—even to swipe the mucous inching down her lip—afraid Rachel would say something to dash her hopes, and this glorious moment might crumble.

Rachel started the engine again and slipped it into gear. Looking straight ahead, she mumbled just loud enough for Dana to hear. "I need time."

Rachel glanced at Dana, her face revealing an almost imperceptible grin. "Maybe I'll get used to you."

Dana's heart soared; her tears flowing freely. *Thank you, God. Thank you, thank you.*

Rachel started to pull away slowly, then stopped and hollered out her open window. "I'll call you again."

Yes, it was going to work out...somehow. Dana stood

still, her insides trembling. Overwhelmed with joy, she couldn't will her body to move. The air was crisper; the colors heightened; the seagulls louder. She felt as if the air pressing against her body was the only thing holding her up, because she was too weak to stand on her own. She feared if she moved, this truth might disappear.

She stood for many moments like a sentinel. Slowly, the shrieks of the eagles out on the tidal flats broke through her awareness, and she began to shake, suddenly chilled to the bone. The tears of relief began to stream down her face, spilling over the smile that radiated from her overflowing joy.

She started walking toward the Subaru, suddenly anxious to be home — to give it all to Hub. And to call Dad! *No...I'll fly up to Haines and tell him in person. Oh, thank you, Lord! I can't wait.*

It was going to take time, she knew. It would take its own course — not one she would dictate, but one that would unfold. She would get to know and understand Rachel — her personality quirks; her fears; her needs; what had caused her pain. They would learn to love and accept each other, defining what their relationship would be. And Dana was more than willing to take it a step at a time.

LET'S STAY CONNECTED!

I would love to hear from readers! You can email me at **HudsonCounsel@aol.com**.

Check my blog, UntetheredVoice.com, for news about the next book in the Tethered series, as well as for contests and discounts.

Made in the USA
San Bernardino, CA
03 May 2017